D0297311

Lesley Horton was a teacher and is now a full-time writer and Bradford resident, currently working on her next DI Handford novel.

SNARES OF GUILT

Rukhsana Mahmood is dead, ferociously battered about the head. But who would want to kill a kindly young woman whose job as a health visitor made her loved and respected? Detective Inspector John Handford is assigned the case. It's particularly sensitive as the Asian community is still reeling from a murder case the previous year: Handford got the right man but at the cost of enormous racial divisions. Now he's investigating another death that will rake up all the tension from the past . . . Rukhsana made a mixed marriage and her husband Amajit's family make no secret of their pleasure at her death. But is this a punishment killing? Or was Rukhsana betraying more than one person?

LESLEY HORTON

◆

SNARES OF GUILT

Complete and Unabridged

CHARNWOOD
Leicester

First published in Great Britain in 2002 by
Orion Books
London

First Charnwood Edition
published 2003
by arrangement with
The Orion Publishing Group Limited
London

British Library CIP Data

Horton, Lesley
 Snares of guilt.—Large print ed.—
 Charnwood library series
 1. Police—Great Britain—Fiction
 2. Detective and mystery stories
 3. Large type books
 I. Title
 823.9′2 [F]

 ISBN 0–7089–4871–5

Published by
F. A. Thorpe (Publishing)
Anstey, Leicestershire

Set by Words & Graphics Ltd.
Anstey, Leicestershire
Printed and bound in Great Britain by
T. J. International Ltd., Padstow, Cornwall

This book is printed on acid-free paper

To my family for all their love and support:
my husband Brian, my children and their
partners: Philip, Anne, Gavin, Julie, Joanne
and Julie and especially to my grandchildren,
Lewis, Tom, Phoenix and Ella.

Acknowledgements

My sincere thanks go to Detective Chief Inspector Tony Hennigan for his explanations of police procedure and his demonstrations of interviewing techniques, to Inspector Martin Baines, Community Race Relations Officer for West Yorkshire Police, and to Station Commander John Vavies of the West Yorkshire Fire Service.

Thanks also to Dr Gerald Partridge of the Holycroft Surgery in Keighley and Anne Hill R.G.N., Dip. Ed. for their expertise in all matters medical. I would like to thank also members of the Sixth Form at Carlton Bolling College, Bradford, who discussed honestly the problems they encounter as second generation Muslims in a western society.

Special thanks go to David Glover and Maureen O'Hara who read the manuscript and spent hours discussing it with me, and members of the Airedale Writers' Circle who have supported me throughout.

Finally, my thanks go to my agent Teresa Chris, without whom none of this would have happened, my very patient editor Kirsty Fowkes, and Jane Heller who corrected my many mistakes.

1

Odd-job man Nathan Teale felt a succession of expletives well up from his gut and into his throat. He swallowed hard to prevent them escaping into the cold November air as he remembered his promise to Janice not to swear. Swearing might be as natural as breathing to him, she had said, but it was not becoming and she would rather he didn't do it. She'd used words like 'becoming' ever since she'd seen *Pride and Prejudice* on television. And although he thought it was poncy — 'becoming' and *Pride and Prejudice* — he would do anything for Janice.

Married only three months, he still found it difficult to believe she'd said yes when he'd tentatively suggested they should get hitched.

'Married, Nathan, not hitched,' she had said, but had agreed, nevertheless.

Today was Janice's day off and she'd tried to persuade him to ring in sick and stay in bed with her, but he'd fought against his libido and gone to work because he knew he wouldn't get away with another bout of flu as an excuse. So instead of cuddling up to Janice, he'd spent the morning out in the cold, sweeping the pathways of the nursing home. The manager had insisted he clear the place of wet leaves. It was obvious she'd never tried it. The sodding things wouldn't budge. And now, to cap it all, he'd nearly been

1

run over by a car using the drive as its own private race track.

'Where do yer think you are?' he yelled as the vehicle disappeared from view. 'There's old folk 'ere, yer know.' He managed not to swear, but he took his anger out on the brush and slammed it down hard on the ground. The handle snapped.

Gloomily, Nathan stared at the two halves, his dark eyebrows pinched in a frown. That was it. He was going for his break even if it wasn't due for a quarter of an hour.

The manager finally found him in the staff kitchen. The gate needed mending, she said, when he'd finished his cup of tea.

That did it.

'Jesus Christ! Not that bloody gate again!' The job he hated most.

The gate was set in the boundary wall separating the wood from the nursing home grounds. It was overhung by large oak trees which plunged the area into darkness so that he could never see what he was doing. Why they'd decided on a wooden gate was beyond him; something to do with reflecting the rustic nature of the area, they said, although Nathan held the view that it was more to do with the tight-fistedness of the owners. But whatever the reason, the stake on which the gate fitted rotted regularly and had to be replaced.

'Don't argue, Nathan. Just do it!' the manager sighed. So he did, because you couldn't argue with a woman like her.

He had removed the gate and was about to free the rotting stake, when he noticed the coping stone was missing from the wall away to his left. Pushing his long black hair out of his eyes, he tramped over to the gap and peered through, searching the ground on the other side. In the gloom he spotted the boulder lying next to a tree. 'Damn kids!' he muttered. Throwing down his spade, he stomped back along the wall, through the gateway and turned in the direction of the stone.

Then he stepped on it. It couldn't have been a fallen branch or a surface root, because it yielded under his feet and he found himself falling backwards. Arms flailing, he made a grab for the post which cracked and gave way, taking him with it. As he slithered down the banking, he flung his arm out to seize hold of anything that would prevent him from sliding still further. What he grabbed was spongy and savagely cold. His nails bit into it, clinging on as best they could as he bumped over the rough ground. The bundle stayed close to him down the banking, its weight acting as a brake. Then, as he came to a halt, it settled itself next to him.

Once he was sure he was in one piece, he extracted his fingers from the mass and eased himself into a sitting position. The bundle shifted and relocated closer to him. Cautiously, he turned towards it. An open, unseeing eye stared up at him. Where the other should have been was a confusion of mangled flesh, dirt and rotting leaves trapped in a pool of congealing blood. Nathan recoiled in horror and vomited.

When there was nothing left in him, he sat up again, head down, arms resting on his knees. His

3

stomach continued to spasm and he was drenched in sweat. For a few moments, he remained still, allowing his brain to rationalise what his eyes had seen. Then, trembling, he turned back towards the face. Morbid curiosity urged him to cast a cursory glance over the length of the corpse, confirming that he had found the body of a young woman. The descent down the banking had left the clothes streaked with dirt, and leaves and small twigs were caught up in her dishevelled black hair. One side of her face was shattered. Shards of bone pierced the mangled flesh of her cheek and her lower jaw was skewed as in a twisted scream. Dried rivulets of blood which had trickled into her open mouth in an attempt to give her back her life were stained by loam and mould gathered during her slide through the vegetation.

As he bent closer, the smell of the wet earth and leaves mingled with the dried blood and the fragrance of her perfume, and he took a deep breath to quell the nausea that rose up again. The shiny blackness of her hair told him she was not English and beneath her coat he could see what appeared to be Asian garments in a bright turquoise material.

For a moment he sat with her, until the reality of the scene jarred his senses and fear replaced curiosity. In panic, he kicked out with his feet, pushing himself away. Trembling, he turned over and began to scrabble up the banking on all fours. As the ground levelled out, he stood upright and fled through the trees, snagging himself on the low, bare branches as he ran.

4

Each scratch, each obstacle filled him with terror. Anybody could see that girl had been murdered, and the killer could still be here, hiding amongst the trees, watching, waiting for him. His breath came in gasps and his throat ached from the exertion. He could feel his heart pounding deep in his chest as he tried to force his legs to work harder, but they were sluggish and his speed degenerated into slow motion. Glancing round, he realised he had run in the opposite direction to the gate. He turned back towards the opening, his feet slipping on the leaves and mud and his body banging repeatedly against the rough wall. He was crying now, tears streaming down his face, and the sweat, which earlier had chilled him, now coddled his flesh.

Suddenly the gate was there in front of him. He propelled himself through into the nursing home grounds and sprinted and stumbled over the wet grass until finally he felt the hardness of the concrete driveway under his feet. The main entrance to the house came into view. It was normally forbidden to all but residents and visitors, but this was different, this was urgent.

One of the sisters was behind the desk as he crashed through the door. He heard her say, 'What on earth is the matter, Nathan? Are you all right?'

The sudden brightness of the reception area lights exploded in his brain, white and red like a fireball. He struggled to get his breath, tried to speak, but his voice drifted away and he wasn't sure whether he answered her. The carpet floated upwards to meet him, and as he lost consciousness, he felt the woollen pile scuff against his face.

But he must have answered, because when he next became aware of his surroundings, the glow of the rotating blue light of a police car pirouetted intermittently across the window and the dark shape of a man in a police uniform towered over him.

★   ★   ★

Detective Inspector John Handford turned up the volume of the cassette player so that the music from the Brighouse and Raistrick brass band filled the car. As he drove he tapped out the beat on the steering wheel. Nothing could dampen his spirits today, not the heavy black clouds which had settled as a thick mist on the hillside, nor the rain streaming against his windscreen. Not even the fact that he had been summoned in to work on his day off.

The call from Detective Chief Inspector Russell had come through at five minutes past three as Handford was finishing the last of a long list of chores Gill had left for him. Replacing the receiver, he had slumped into the chair next to the telephone, his head in his hands. It was over. At last, after everything that had happened, he was back in favour and could put behind him the case which had branded him a racist and almost ended his career.

Lifting his head, he caught a glimpse of himself in the mirror on the wall opposite. For months he'd looked all of his forty-four years

— and older, but today for the first time, a more assured detective inspector stared back at him. Jowls of flagging muscle were beginning to obscure the square jaw line that had given him his youthful good looks, his face was rounder than it had been, the extra flesh camouflaging his once chiselled features, and creases were forming under his eyes, but his body was still firm and there was no sign of a pot belly. Married for eighteen years, father of two daughters, aged fourteen and twelve, he supposed he wasn't doing too badly.

Picking up the receiver once again, he dialled his wife's school. Please God she isn't teaching.

She wasn't and the receptionist put him through to her office.

'It's over, Gill. An Asian woman's been found dead and the DCI's given me the investigation.'

'That's wonderful news, John. I'm so pleased for you. I told you Russell would see sense in the end.'

He heard the warmth in her voice and imagined her eyes lighting up as they always did when she was pleased. 'I'm not sure about that,' he said. 'It's more likely it came from upstairs.'

'Don't be such a cynic, darling. I've told you before, if you don't believe you're the best man for the job, no one else will, least of all Russell. And you are. So go in there and show them. And I'll see you when I see you.'

'Oh, God, Gill, I'd forgotten; we were going out for a meal tonight. I'm sorry. I'll do my best to get back.'

She laughed. 'On the first day of a new case? I

7

doubt it. No, it's fine, there'll be other nights, other meals. The girls are staying the night at Mum's, so I can pamper myself with a long bath, a pizza and a bottle of wine and then laze the evening away watching television. For once the controls will be all mine.'

In the background he heard the sound of a bell. 'Sorry, darling, that's me,' she said. 'Got a date with Hamlet. I'll talk to you soon. And John — good luck.'

The warmth of her tone stayed with him as he drove in to work. How he had ever managed to persuade a woman like Gill to fall in love with him, he would never know, but what was certain was that without her and his daughters, Nicola and Clare, he would never have got through the nightmare following his investigation into the murder of seventeen-year-old Jamilla Aziz.

Jamilla, a sixth-form student at the local comprehensive, had been dating a white boy. Her father was in Pakistan, and her brother, Mohammed, sensing there was more to the relationship than a student friendship, had taken it upon himself to discipline her. One minute they had been seen arguing fiercely, the next she was missing. It was thought at first she had run away, until, after a lengthy police search, her body had been found in a ditch. Refusing to admit that Jamilla could have been a willing party to any such mixed relationship, the family blamed the boyfriend, insisting her death was the result of a racial attack by him. At first Handford had investigated it as such, but could come up with nothing to substantiate the claim. As killings went, it had been particularly inept, and soon evidence surfaced which incriminated the brother. The corroboration Handford needed came via the Forensic Science Service and two weeks after her death, he arrested Mohammed Aziz for the murder of his sister. The arrest sparked fury amongst members of the community and for several hours the police station and the city centre were besieged by an angry mob of several hundred missile-hurling Asian youths.

Shell-shocked senior police officers and angry community leaders needed someone to blame for what had happened and the investigating officer had been their unanimous choice. Little did it matter that Mohammed Aziz had eventually confessed to killing his sister, someone had to pay and Handford became the focus of a very public disciplinary inquiry. He had emerged exonerated and almost in one piece — but not quite.

Now, as he neared the city, his earlier optimism began to slide and he turned off the cassette player. The timing was wrong for him to make a comeback. What with the July race riots, the 11 September atrocities in America and the war against the Taliban, emotions were running high in some sections of the city and although vigorous attempts were being made to improve the situation, it didn't take much imagination to work out that handing this investigation to an officer who had had accusations of racism made against him could cause problems. Allegations of that kind stick. Certainly, for the past year, both Russell and the Asian community had wanted him far away from any crime in which the latter might be involved either as victim or perpetrator. Difficult in a city where one-third of the population came at some time in their history from Pakistan, Bangladesh or India.

Handford's craggy features darkened and taking a hand off the wheel he ran his fingers through his thick, prematurely greying hair and sighed. Had they forgiven him or were they testing him? Probably neither. More than likely he was the only person available to take on such an investigation. CID was at full stretch. Ongoing inquiries into the rapes of two young girls, a ten-year-old child who had been missing for nearly a fortnight, a series of particularly nasty robberies and an ever-growing number of aggravated burglaries had depleted the senior detective strength. Russell probably had had no option but to allocate the job to him.

As reality struck, Handford wished he'd had a stiff drink before he set off. But since he'd been ordered to report to Russell before going up to the crime scene, he had accepted that breathing whisky over the DCI was probably not a good idea.

The Central Police Station was a purpose-built, five-storey building of rectangular glass boxes which gleamed with fluorescent tubing from every window. Its modernity encroached on, but did not overpower, the listed building standing proudly on the other side of the dual carriageway which stalked the city from north to south. Handford entered by the heavy glass doors at the front of the station. The soles of his

10

shoes squeaked on the tiled floor of the large open foyer as he strode across to the door next to the desk where he keyed in the code to let him into the offices. Taking the steps two at a time, he raced up the stairs to the fourth floor and CID. At the top he walked towards the DCI's office. The door was ajar and he could see Russell sitting at his desk.

Detective Chief Inspector W. Stephen Christopher Russell was small for a police officer, and Handford, six foot one and wellbuilt, towered over him. Stature, however, was his only advantage — and not much of one at that, for Russell, educated at a public school then Cambridge, from where he graduated with a double first, conveyed an air of self-assurance that Handford found impossible to emulate. Everything about Russell, his presence, his bearing, his demeanour, even his office, ate into Handford's self-confidence and yet, if asked, he couldn't have explained why. Professional jealousy or pure dislike? Or perhaps resentment that in the modern police service there were those who gained promotion through their background and not their experience. Indeed, if it was experience that counted, then Handford would be sitting where Russell was now. He had twenty years versus Russell's ten. Twenty years in which he had caught more thieves, broken up more fights, questioned more suspects and run more inquiries than the DCI ever had. Handford wasn't as good at the paperwork, that he had to admit, but then Russell was an officer on a career path to the top, a route littered with

11

inspired paperwork. Was it any wonder that in the DCI's presence he saw himself as the archetypal northern plod?

At Handford's knock, Russell glanced up. 'Come in, John,' he said, 'sit down. I won't be a moment.'

Handford took the chair next to the triffid — a weeping fig so named because of the alarming speed with which it seemed to have increased in size since it was introduced into the station. How could anyone take seriously a DCI who surrounds himself with plants? Probably even talks to them. Gill wormed her way into Handford's thoughts: *Don't be so petty, John. Why shouldn't the man cheer his room up with some greenery if he wants?* Over the past year, she had become his conscience, restraining his anger and his bitterness. Handford smiled to himself; not many people could say they had a conscience they could make love to.

Cherishing the thought, he glanced around. As neat and organised as ever, the office reflected the chief inspector's personality — intelligent, efficient and methodical. The shelves behind the desk were filled with police manuals, a copy of Stone's Justices Manual, some other leather-bound books on the law, and carefully labelled box files. The glass-fronted shelves above the cupboards held silver sporting and academic trophies which, according to the dates, stretched back to Russell's schooldays, through university and on to police training college. Tastefully and mindfully hung where they could easily be seen were various certificates, including his First and

Master's Degrees. Equally carefully positioned on his desk was a silver-framed photograph of a woman Handford assumed was his wife: a slim, elegant blonde, with an engaging smile which flattered the perfectly formed teeth. There were no photos of children — children, Handford was sure, would have had a detrimental effect on the chief inspector's career plan. Otherwise it was much like any other room on the floor — except for the aroma of ground coffee, which constantly teased CID's taste buds. The DCI was never seen at the drinks machine, or using the electric kettle, mugs and jar of instant in the detectives' room; he percolated his own coffee each morning from freshly ground beans.

Russell signed the letter he was reading, placed it carefully in a brown folder, replaced the top on his fountain pen and looked at Handford.

'As I explained when I rang, the body of a young Asian woman has been found in Moss Carr Woods,' he said, without preamble. 'Unidentified as yet and quite a mess, by all accounts.' He paused, the silence effectively adding weight to the seriousness of what he was about to say. 'I needed to see you before you go up to the scene because when I spoke to Iqbal Ahmed he was not pleased you were to be the investigating officer.'

A leader in the Muslin community, Iqbal Ahmed was informed about any crime that affected the Asian population. Now, it seemed he expected to be consulted on the choice of investigating officer. But this was not the time to voice inappropriate opinions, so Handford

13

merely said, 'Right, sir,' to show that he had heard and understood.

Russell continued. 'I explained to him that we are overstretched at the moment, and also that the superintendent feels the time has come to ease you in to serious crime again — although personally I would have preferred a case a little less high profile.' He leaned back in his chair, considering his next words.

Handford waited.

'I want you to understand, John, that I've had to give Mr Ahmed my personal assurances that you learnt lessons from the fiasco after the Aziz murder. He made it clear that he would prefer someone else on the case but he has agreed, reluctantly, to give you the benefit of the doubt, for the moment.' Russell leaned forward. 'I need you to remember that it's not only your credibility on the line this time, it's mine as well. I cannot insist too strongly that you are careful, that we don't have a re-run of last year.'

Handford's hackles rose at the injustice. Why was it that they still blamed him? Didn't they realise what they had done, what the repercussions might have been to him personally had they succeeded? He had a house with a huge mortgage and two daughters who seemed to feel the need to keep up with every new fashion that hit the high street. Why couldn't they say: you got it right, Handford; it was the family and the community who got it wrong, and we're sorry? The answer was obvious of course: keeping the peace meant being Iqbal Ahmed's friend not his enemy. And keeping the peace also meant going

14

along with the DCI, not arguing with him.

'Of course I'll be careful, sir. I'm always careful; I was careful then, you know. It wasn't actually my fault it went pear-shaped.' His normally flat northern tones took on the stronger Yorkshire accent of his youth as his emotions took over. 'What still gets to me is that I was right — it *was* her brother who had killed her.'

'That wasn't the issue, and you know it. It was your attitude, John. The girl's parents insisted it was racial — you had to investigate it as that, but you didn't.' Handford opened his mouth to protest, but Russell went on. 'Not in their eyes, at least. To them you weren't prepared to listen.'

There was only so much a man could agree to. 'Oh, I listened, Stephen, believe me, I listened; every bloody day I listened, every time I picked up the bloody phone I listened, but if I'd taken any notice I would have arrested the wrong person. All the evidence, forensic included, pointed to the brother; there was none against the other boy. They were the ones who weren't listening.'

'I hear what you're saying, John. But the fact is you handled it badly.'

'I might have done, but that's all I did. Perhaps that warrants a slapped wrist, a bollocking even, but not an inquiry.'

'That's not for you to decide, Inspector,' Russell observed pointedly.

Back in his place, Handford said, 'No.'

The unfairness clouded still more the coffee-laden atmosphere and there was a moment's uneasy silence.

The DCI handed over a typewritten sheet. 'This is a list of detectives available at Central, plus a couple of DCs, Warrender and Appleyard, from Broughton.' Broughton was a police station in the southern subdivision of the city. 'I've also requested that Khalid Ali from there is brought in as your sergeant.'

Handford's eyes widened in astonishment. 'Why?'

'Because he will be a worthwhile addition. He's a good detective and — '

'We've good detectives here,' Handford broke in.

Russell gave him a hard stare. 'An Asian detective prominent on the inquiry will help diffuse any problems.'

'Meaning me,' said Handford bitterly.

'Meaning any problems that crop up which need someone who understands the culture to explain.'

'Community Liaison could do that, sir. It doesn't need Ali; you've brought him in to keep an eye on me, make sure I don't overstep the mark.'

The DCI's patience snapped. 'For goodness sake, John, stop acting like a probationer. If I thought you needed someone to watch over you, I'd do it myself, not bring a sergeant in from another district.'

Handford's eyes edged away from Russell's.

'I've discussed it with Community Liaison,' the DCI went on, 'and they've agreed it's a good idea. Think about it for a moment. Ali speaks Urdu, which does away with the need for an

16

interpreter. He is also a Muslim. In the present climate we need someone like him on our side. The families and the community will be more prepared to talk to one of their own than they will to us.'

But Handford wasn't prepared to let it go. 'I'd agree with you, sir, except word is that he's too fond of cutting his own path. He's well known for it. I've not worked with him personally, but I know others who have and he's caused them no end of trouble. I'd rather have a sergeant who doesn't go off on his own when the whim takes him. God knows what he could be doing.'

'Then it's up to you to make sure he doesn't. Spell out his parameters before you begin. I'm not arguing, John, unless you're telling me you can't work with him.'

Handford knew he was close to the edge. He backed off. 'No, sir, I'm not saying that.'

'Good.' Russell gave him a long look. 'Ali will come today, the DCs tomorrow. See me when you're back from the crime scene and we'll set up the policy. Oh, and John.'

'Sir?'

'Please don't swear in my office, however much you feel like it.'

Handford reddened. 'Sir.'

The northern plod had edged his way in again.

★ ★ ★

Sitting at his desk in Broughton's CID, Detective Sergeant Khalid Ali's eyes followed the copper-haired man as he strolled into the room, his

17

hands deep in his pockets. He was a stranger to the sergeant, but then, even though Ali was officially a member of the team, he tended to be more peripatetic than permanent, and was rarely able to build up more than a passing acquaintance with most of his fellow officers. In the eighteen months he had been on the squad, he reckoned he could count on one hand the number of cases he had taken part in from this station. For the rest he had been seconded to investigations around Bradford's other sub-divisions, wherever and whenever they involved the Asian community. Although he had always been greeted warmly, he was under no illusions that the real reason for his being there was to fend off any suggestions that the police were deliberately under-performing because the victim was Muslim or Sikh.

He knew he would not be back at Broughton long enough to get used to his chair and desk again, and sure enough by midafternoon he had been ordered to join a murder team at Central Police Station, the victim a young Asian woman.

The DI in charge was John Handford who, if his memory served him correctly, had been exonerated from a charge of racism about a year ago. Ali couldn't recall the exact facts of the case because at the time he'd been on one of the long courses officers on accelerated promotion were often sent on. His own rise through the ranks had certainly accelerated. He'd waved au revoir to Broughton a DC and returned a DS. But that was a year ago and he was eager now to move on to inspector rank.

Ali didn't know Inspector Handford, but it concerned him that he might be working with a DI who at best bore a grudge against Asians and at worst was a racist who had been lucky. Ali didn't want his career blighted by such an officer.

As the copper-haired detective passed him, their eyes met and Ali smiled a greeting, but the man ignored him and walked over to one of the others.

'Who's the Paki, Chris?' he asked, making only a scant attempt to lower his voice.

Chris Appleyard frowned a warning. 'DS Ali,' he said, his voice low.

'A DS? Well, that's positive discrimination for you.'

At his desk, Ali studied the paper he was holding, trying to pretend he hadn't heard. But he could feel the man's eyes on him as he went to turn off the steaming kettle. He poured water into the mugs, then shouted, 'Coffee's ready.' He turned and directed his gaze again towards Ali.

'Oh, sorry, Sergeant,' he said, 'I only made five. Didn't see you over there in the shadows. Did you want a coffee?' He picked up the milk carton and shook it. 'I'm afraid there's no milk left. Still, I expect you prefer it black.'

'Leave it, Warrender,' Appleyard hissed.

But Warrender was not to be silenced. 'I'm just asking if the sergeant wants a coffee,' he said. 'Pity there's no milk left. Too many in here now.'

Holding on to his anger with difficulty, Ali scraped back his chair. He didn't have to take this. He said evenly, 'Are you talking about detectives, Constable . . . Warrender, isn't it? Or

19

sergeants — or Pakis?'

Warrender shrugged. 'Take your pick, Sarg. Take your pick.' And he moved away to a desk where he sat down, forcing the chair backwards so that he could lift up his legs to rest them on the litter of papers.

Ali followed him, unsure of his next move. He would have loved to drag him off to the divisional commander, but he knew it would be a waste of time. Warrender would plead that he had been misunderstood; it had been no more than a genuine offer of coffee.

He felt Appleyard's restraining hand on his arm. 'Don't take any notice, Khalid. He's just a loudmouth. It's jealousy talking, he missed out on sergeant again.'

'And when he sees a sergeant who is an Asian, he feels the need to comment, I suppose,' Ali said bitterly.

'Like I said, don't take any notice.'

Ali pulled himself away and returned to his desk. It had been smoothed over, but he couldn't help feeling he had lost. He slumped in his chair. He could kill for a coffee, but he'd do without before he'd give Warrender the satisfaction of watching him drink it black. Moodily, he flicked at one of the memos he'd been reading. It skidded across the desk and onto the floor. He bent down to pick it up, blowing at the fluff that had attached itself to it. If only the detritus of racism could be so easily blown away. But the Warrenders of this world were always there with their comments, some obvious, some covert. And he was weary of it.

20

A voice from the door roused him. 'The DI wants a word, Sarg.'

'Right.' Ali walked across the room, stopping only at Warrender's desk. He stood, holding the man's gaze for what seemed an age. 'One day, Constable,' he said eventually, his tone icy, 'you'll take a step too far, and I shall be there. And then I'll have you off the force.'

Warrender smiled. 'In your dreams, Sergeant, in your dreams.'

'That's right. It will be.'

★ ★ ★

Handford strode into his office. Slightly smaller than Russell's, it was not so immaculate, not so formal and not so contrived to flatter the ego. There were one or two books appertaining to police training, some box files containing handouts from the various courses he had been on which had seemed interesting at the time but which he had hardly ever looked at since, and a couple of books describing walks in the Lakes and the Dales that he liked to flick through when he was not too busy. The only photographs were those of a local brass band to which he had once belonged but now had no time for, and one of his first drum set, well-loved but long gone after Gill had refused to have it in the house. His degree certificate was at home with all the others in an envelope marked 'Education.'

He slumped into his chair, still smarting from the interview with Russell and at the thought

21

of working with Ali. Handford had nothing personal against the man, he didn't know him, but
he had heard senior officers complain that he
acted alone and would follow up leads without
telling anyone. And if there was one kind of
detective Handford didn't need, it was one who
thought he was more important than the team.

That was the problem with officers like Ali,
young graduates on accelerated promotion, they
considered themselves better than anyone else.
Handford's views on fast-track coppers didn't
coincide with those of the establishment and his
opinion was exacerbated by the fact that the
scheme hadn't been in operation when he joined
the force. Had he been a few years younger he
might have used his degree to give him the same
opportunity. As it was, he adhered to the view
that good detectives and promotion equalled
experience, not pieces of paper. And whatever
else, Ali was not experienced. Placating the
community rather than building the best team
was about as bad a reason as you could have for
selecting officers for a murder investigation.

Handford picked up the phone and dialled the
front desk. 'I'm going up to Moss Carr Nursing
Home. When Sergeant Ali arrives, tell him to
meet me there.'

He had stepped over to the map on the wall to
locate the precise whereabouts of the nursing
home when he heard footsteps.

A voice from the door said, 'Khalid Ali, sir.
I've been told to report to you.'

Handford turned. He was tall, but the man he
faced was some two inches taller — and slimmer.

Slightly irritated that Ali had neither heeded his instruction to meet him at the scene nor bothered to knock, he said, 'Sergeant Ali. No, leave your coat on. The body is in Moss Carr Woods. I'll fill you in as we go.'

★   ★   ★

'Whoever did that, meant it,' Handford said as he scanned the dead woman's battered features. 'What a mess.'

Her body had not yet been moved and wouldn't be until she had been photographed and videoed from every conceivable angle. Although it was only half past four, darkness was closing in and the area was enveloped in an unnatural silence, made all the more macabre by the artificial brightness of the mobile lighting.

Violent death always came as a shock to Handford. Whether it was the sight of the injuries or the knowledge that one person could crush the life out of another in such an extreme way, he wasn't sure. Whatever it was, it made him desperately sad and he knew that when he left the scene, he would leave a small part of himself there too.

His eyes met the police surgeon's. 'How long has she been dead?'

'Well, it's cold and it's been raining, but at a guess she died late this morning or early this afternoon.' He gazed at the corpse, then at the inspector. 'I do hope, John, for your sake that this case doesn't cause the sort of problems that cropped up last year.'

The skin furrowed above Handford's eyes and his heart rate stepped up a beat, but he offered no comment. He glanced at Ali busy making notes and wondered how much he knew of the events of last year — and what his slant on them was.

'Do we know who she is?' he asked.

The uniformed constable answered him. 'Janet Turner, the manager up at the home, seems to think she's a health visitor with Dr Haigh's practice, sir. That's the one on Palin Road. Says she recognised the description of the dress.' He flicked at the pages of his notebook. 'Her name's Rukhsana Mahmood and she'd be up here to see her aunt who's recuperating from an operation. According to Mrs Turner, Mrs Mahmood drops in to visit whenever she can and she thinks she saw her arrive around lunchtime. Also one of the cars in the car park is registered to her so I've taped it off until the scene of crime officer can check it.'

'Thanks, Constable, you've done a good job.' Handford turned to Ali. 'Go up and talk to the manager and the chap who found the body. And Ali, go easy on him. I'll be up in a minute.'

He watched as the sergeant picked his way carefully up the banking, holding on to clumps of wet grass as he went.

Handford turned back to the uniformed officer. 'Any weapon?'

'There's a stone missing from the boundary wall, sir,' said the constable. 'It could have been that. It's up here.'

Handford followed the man through the taped

path to where the large coping stone was lying. He bent down to take a closer look. 'Could be.' His eyes wandered along the ground. 'There doesn't seem to be much else here to give those kind of injuries. But I can't see any blood, and there must be some. Still, if the killer dropped it rather than threw it, the blood would be underneath. Who found her?'

'Nathan Teale, sir. He's employed by the nursing home as a general handyman.'

'Is this where Teale was when he said he stepped on her?'

'More or less, sir. A couple of feet to your right, I think.'

'Right, then we'll assume for the moment that this is roughly where she was killed, and until we know any different we'll assume this is what was used. What do you think it weighs? Thirty, forty pounds?'

'Could be more, sir.'

'So, we're looking for someone with strength. I doubt if I could budge it, let alone pick it up.' He turned. 'Come on, let's leave it to forensics.' They began to pick their way gingerly down the path. 'Tell the duty inspector I'm going up to the nursing home, Constable. Let me know when SOCO and the photographers arrive. And find out what's happened to the tent — I want her covered before the press gets here. And let's have some more lighting. We won't be able to see a thing soon.'

2

A journey into drunken oblivion would have suited Nathan Teale fine at that moment. Instead he was slumped, stone cold sober, in the manager's office at Moss Carr Nursing Home, wallowing in a plethora of self-pity and a series of 'if onlys'. If only Janice had insisted he stay in bed with her, if only Turner hadn't made him sweep up the leaves, if only the brush handle hadn't broken, if only, if only, if only.

He still felt sick. Each time his mind formed a picture of the dead girl, his stomach lurched and his throat filled with bile. And as if that wasn't enough, he was being grilled by a detective sergeant who seemed to be all but accusing him of the girl's death.

Sliding down in his chair, he clutched at his stomach, hoping the sergeant would take pity on him, but he was studying his notebook and didn't seem to notice. It was all right for him, he was probably used to seeing dead bodies, probably saw them every day.

'Do we 'ave to go through this again?' he pleaded wearily. 'I've told you what happened.'

'Yes, we do, I'm afraid,' Sergeant Ali said. 'I don't understand why you didn't notice the body. You've said it wasn't covered and it was right in your path, so you couldn't have missed it.'

'Well, I did. Until I stood on it I didn't know it

26

was there. I've told you umpteen times I don't look where I'm going in those woods; I don't need to, I know me way around. I wasn't on a treasure hunt, yer know, I was only at the top end. And the light's dim with all those oak trees. All I had to do was pick the stone up, put it back on't wall and get the gatepost mended.'

'That stone must be very heavy. How do you think it got onto the ground?'

'Kids, I suppose. I don't know. I'm always having to put those top stones back.'

'A bit heavy for children, I would have thought.'

'Well, all right then. It wasn't kids, it was grown-ups. How should I know? All I do is mend it when it needs mending.'

'You can lift them, the stones?'

Nathan let out a long breath. 'I've just said so. It's drystone walling; they fall off and I put 'em back on.'

'You're strong then?'

'Yes, I suppose so. I like to keep fit, do a bit of weight-lifting.' He glanced warily at Ali. 'What's me being fit got to do with anything?'

'The victim may well have been hit with that stone, Mr Teale. And whoever did it is strong and fit and perhaps does a bit of weight-lifting. Did you hit her with it, Nathan? Push her down the banking, then realise what you'd done and make up the story about finding her?'

Nathan stared at the detective. He'd just endured what had been, without a doubt, the worst experience of his life and this fool thought he'd brought it on himself. He'd had the

27

strangest sensation ever since it had happened that he was standing outside himself, watching a drama unfold in which he had played no real part. Now, suddenly, he was the central character.

'I *found* her. I didn't kill her! I'd never kill anyone. Why should I kill her? I hardly know her.'

Next time he would stay in bed with Janice. A telling-off from Mrs Turner for a fourth bout of flu would be nothing compared with this. He drew his hands over his face, then turned pleading eyes on the sergeant. 'I promise you, all I did was find her. I'm sorry I didn't see the body. I'm sorry I stood on it. But all I did was find her. You've got to believe me.'

'We do, Mr Teale.' The voice came from somewhere behind him. He turned to see an older man. 'I'm Detective Inspector Handford,' the man said, showing his warrant card. He turned to the Asian. 'I think Mr Teale's had enough for one day, Sergeant, so let's leave it for the moment. You have his address?'

'Yes, sir.'

'You go off home, Mr Teale. We shall require a written statement, of course, but that can wait until tomorrow. In the meantime we would like the clothes you're wearing — just for elimination. Do you have any here you can change into?'

Nathan shook his head.

'In that case, a driver will run you home, you can change there and he will bring those back with him.'

Relieved and too tired to protest, Nathan

pushed back his chair and stood up. The movement made his head spin and he clutched at the desk to steady himself. Handford grasped his arm.

'Come on, Mr Teale,' he said, handing Nathan over to the waiting constable. 'It's been a long day and you must be exhausted. Go home and rest.'

As Handford closed the door behind him, he turned, the expression on his face hardening as he approached the desk.

Ali slid his chair back and stood up.

Attempting, without success, to keep the steel out of his voice, Handford said, 'I told you to go easy on him. So why so aggressive?'

Ali took a deep breath. 'I didn't think I was being aggressive, sir. It just seems odd to me that he didn't see her body. According to him there'd been no attempt to hide it. I was trying to find out why he missed it.'

'No you weren't, you were badgering him. A few minutes longer and he would have admitted killing her for a bit of peace and quiet. I agree a quick arrest would be nice, but I'd rather it was the right person, Sergeant. Nathan Teale has just found a body, slipped on it, touched it, looked at it. And she's not exactly pretty, is she? He's in shock, Sergeant Ali, and you don't badger a man in shock.'

'But if he's the one who killed her, sir — '

'We've no evidence to suggest that he killed her — not much evidence of any kind yet. Let's just wait and see what forensics his clothes give us. Did you check his hands?'

29

'Yes, but they're an odd-job man's hands, soiled and grubby — and he says he grabbed her, so any tissue under his nails could be easily argued away.'

'We'll send someone over to have them tested anyway. If he killed her, we'll find out, but let's do it properly. And Sergeant,' Handford emphasised his words, 'when I tell you to go easy on someone, you do just that, do you understand?'

Ali dropped his eyes. 'Yes, sir.' His embarrassment was momentary, however. 'You have to admit though,' he said, 'he is strong enough to have picked up that stone and hit her with it.'

'For goodness sake, Ali,' Handford said tersely, 'stop chasing shadows and start thinking like a detective, will you?' He took a step closer to the sergeant and held up his hand, counting on his fingers. 'One, we don't know for sure that the stone is the weapon. Two, we haven't had the body positively identified. And three, if she is who we think she is, we don't yet know of any link between her and Nathan Teale.' Handford walked over to the chair vacated by Teale and sat down. 'Now, if you think you can manage it without arresting one of the doctors, go to the surgery on Palin Road and talk to Dr Haigh. See if they've got a photograph of Rukhsana Mahmood. We want to be sure the dead girl is who we think she is before we go round upsetting her husband. Also, find out where she's been this morning and where she was expected to be this afternoon. Take someone with you. There's a Special outside the door, take her.'

'Sir.' Ali closed his notebook and pushed it into his inside jacket pocket. He didn't look at Handford as he strode out of the room.

★   ★   ★

Handford was back at the scene when Ali returned. He was relieved that Gill had understood about the meal out, because it was already half past six and providing Ali had brought back a positive identification of the victim, they still had to notify the relatives. He stuffed his hands deeper into his pockets and stamped his feet to ward off the cold. The earlier rain had turned to a steady drizzle and a freezing mist was clothing the woods. He wasn't sure how long the men here would be able to carry on working.

His eyes roamed the scene. More lights had been set up to illuminate the area and the body had been tented but would be removed to the mortuary before the end of the evening. Scene of crime officers clad in white, protective clothing were measuring, photographing, bagging anything that could be considered evidence. The press had got wind of the story and were crowding against the nursing home gates, demanding to know who had been killed. The uniformed constable, safe on the other side, had told them there was nothing to see and to go home. 'A statement will be made when we're ready,' he said. But the journalists and photographers had heard it all before and stayed where they were. Handford had to admire them for their stamina if nothing else.

He saw Ali picking his way carefully towards him.

The sergeant blew on his hands. 'They have photographs of all the staff at the practice, sir, on a board as you walk in the waiting room. I don't think there's much doubt that the victim is Rukhsana Mahmood. Dr Haigh gave me a copy of her photograph.' He handed it over to Handford who looked at it carefully.

'Yes, I think you're right, Sergeant.' He sighed with regret. Now that the victim had a name, it gave her a family, parents, husband, possibly children, on whom he was going to pour so much grief.

'According to Dr Haigh,' Ali said, 'she had visits this morning, but was supposed to be back at the surgery for a baby clinic this afternoon. She never turned up. The midwife took it on her own. She said she was worried about Rukhsana because it wasn't like her to miss a clinic without letting someone know, but thought perhaps she'd been held up somewhere and there was a problem with her mobile. I've got Rukhsana's address. She lives close to here with her husband, Amajit Mahmood. He works for the council, apparently — in the planning office, Dr Haigh thinks. I've also got a list of her morning visits. It was a bad time to talk to them because the surgery was crowded and they were very busy. I said we would go back tomorrow. Barring emergencies, Dr Haigh says he will make sure everybody is available after morning surgery, if that's all right, sir?'

'Yes, fine.'

A smile played on Ali's lip. 'And I've left the practice intact sir — not one doctor arrested.'

Holding up his hands in a conciliatory gesture, Handford said, 'I know, I know. I'm sorry. I do tend to descend to sarcasm when I get annoyed. My wife is always telling me off about it. She says it was one of the reasons why I was no good as a teacher.' He put the girl's photograph in his pocket and glanced at his watch. 'Come on, there's not a lot more we can do here until forensics have finished. We'll go and see the husband; break the bad news to him.'

★   ★   ★

Amajit Mahmood couldn't understand why his wife was not home. He was late himself — the planning meeting seemed to have gone on for hours. Rukhsana's car wasn't parked in its usual spot and there were no lights on in the house. Perhaps she'd been called out. He shivered in the cold of the November evening. Someone let off a firework further down the street and it startled him. A dog barked. Amajit looked around and wondered, not for the first time, if he and Rukhsana would ever have enough money to buy a house in a better neighbourhood. He hated it here. Bordered on both sides by long rows of dingy terraced houses, the street never saw the sunlight, even in the summer. Tonight the sky was illuminated by the orange fluorescence of the city lights and from the back of the house he could see the glow from the nursing home, but here in the street, the lamps that were working could do no more than throw smudged patches of light onto the ground, leaving the rest of the road in darkness.

He let himself in and switched on the hall light. If Rukhsana had had to go out, there should be a note propped up against the telephone, but he couldn't see one. He rang her mobile and waited. It was turned off and there seemed little point in leaving a message.

Drawing the curtains, he noticed that the distant glow from the nursing home stretched out into the woods. Perhaps one of the residents had gone missing and they were looking for him or her. He hoped it wasn't Rukhsana's aunt; perhaps that was where Rukhsana was — up at the nursing home. He'd try the surgery first, then ring there.

It was after hours at the practice and a taped message informed him that there was no one to take his call; if he needed a doctor urgently then he should ring 736978. The doctor on call answered immediately and in response to his question said he hadn't needed Rukhsana at all that evening and couldn't say where she was. Amajit would have liked to call the nursing home straightaway but decided to leave it for a while. If they had a problem with one of the residents they would be busy and not thank him for disturbing them.

He went into the kitchen and switched on the kettle. If she wasn't with the doctor and not at the nursing home, where could she be? He thought back to breakfast; had Rukhsana told him that she would be late? That she was spending the evening with a friend perhaps and he had forgotten? He was about to pick up the address pad when he heard a knock at the door. This must be her, she had lost her key again; she ought to have one of those lengths of coiled plastic attached to a ring to secure it to her person. He would buy her one next time he was in town.

Ready to tease his wife, he turned the knob of the Yale lock and pulled open the door. His smile faded as he looked into the serious faces of two strangers, one white and one Asian. Both were smartly dressed, their heavy winter coats buttoned against the weather. Salesmen perhaps.

'Mr Mahmood?' the white gentleman asked. He was the older of the two, the more well-built, his hair greying at the temples. And as Amajit looked into his eyes he saw a tinge of sadness lurking there.

'Yes,' he said.

'Detective Inspector Handford and Detective Sergeant Ali.' Amajit looked at the identity cards held up for security. 'Can we come in please, sir?'

Amajit stood back to let them through into the narrow hall. 'What is it?'

He squeezed past the two men and switched on the light in the sitting room. They followed him in as he moved across to the window to draw the curtains, shutting out the darkness of the night. The Asian detective stood by the door. He was younger, less careworn than the other, his long, thin face bordering on handsome, his colour lighter than many of his nationality, and he seemed ill at ease rather than sad.

The inspector spoke. 'Is your wife's name Rukhsana Mahmood, sir?'

'Yes. Why?'

Gently, he took hold of Amajit's arm. 'I think it would be better if you sat down.'

Amajit did not move. 'Is something wrong? She isn't home yet.' He felt panic welling up. 'Has she had an accident?' In his mind's eye he saw her car a crumpled wreck. His eyes flashed from one policeman to the other. It couldn't be a car accident, uniformed officers came with that kind of news, not those in suits. Fear replaced panic. 'What is it?' he asked again.

The white man nodded at the Asian detective, who came towards him. He stood close, his angular features tightening as he swallowed hard, and he frowned. He seemed to be searching for the right words. When finally he spoke it was in Urdu.

'I'm sorry, Mr Mahmood, but the body of an Asian woman was found this afternoon in the woods bordering Moss Carr Nursing Home. We think it's your wife.'

Amajit tried to focus on his words but although they penetrated his consciousness, they were so awful that they were pushed to one side by more rational thoughts. It was a joke, a cruel joke — the kind some people play on Asians. These men were not real detectives, they were . . . Amajit looked from one to the other and as their eyes dropped away from his he knew they were telling him the truth. Words uttered in his own language, which would have meant the same in any language.

He shuffled backwards, his hand feeling for the arm of the chair. Finding it, he sank down. Needing to do something that was normal, to cut through the confusion, to break the awful silence, he said, 'Rukhsana dead? In the woods? What was she doing in the woods? Are you sure it's her?'

Handford took the chair opposite him. Rukhsana's face smiled down from a photo frame on the mantelpiece. He said, 'I'm sorry, Mr Mahmood, we're as sure as we can be. We need you to identify her, but yes, it's almost certainly your wife.'

Amajit stared at the space in front of him. 'The lights.' He looked up at Handford. 'The lights up at the nursing home, are they for her?'

'Yes, sir,' Handford whispered. 'Yes, they are.'

'But . . . ' Amajit was finding it difficult to take in the information. 'But how did she die? Did she fall?'

'No,' Ali replied, this time in English. 'I'm sorry, there's no easy way to tell you this but she appears to have been attacked. She was hit about the head . . . '

Amajit trembled. He made an attempt to pull himself together, but his hands wouldn't stop shaking and he had to control one with the other.

'Hit about the head. But who would do that . . . ' Then the awful truth struck him. 'You mean she was murdered?'

'Yes, Mr Mahmood. I'm sorry.'

Amajit lowered his head. Half an hour ago

37

he'd been looking forward to a normal evening, and now . . . It didn't make sense. They had to be wrong. They wanted him to identify her; he would do that, prove they were wrong.

'You said something about me identifying her. Do you want me to come with you now?'

Again the inspector spoke with kindness. 'Tomorrow will be soon enough, sir. We'll send a car for you in the morning.'

'Tomorrow, why tomorrow? Why not now? I can't wait until tomorrow to know for sure.' The man didn't seem to understand. He turned to Ali. 'You understand, don't you?'

'Yes, yes, of course I do and so does Inspector Handford. But she's still up at the scene.'

'Then I'll go there.'

'No.' The sergeant's voice was firm. 'It would be better for you to see her when she's been taken to the mortuary.'

'And when I've identified her, I can bring her back with me? I can bury her?'

Handford answered. 'No, sir, not immediately, I'm afraid. The coroner will release her body as soon as possible. He'll not keep her any longer than necessary.'

Amajit looked up at him, his eyes fearful. 'But tradition . . . '

Handford shook his head. 'I'm sorry.'

Ali crouched down and placed his hand on Amajit's. 'We do understand,' he said. 'But if we are to find out who killed her, she needs to be with us a little bit longer. I promise you, the coroner will not keep her any longer than he has to.'

There was nothing more Amajit could say. The room, which had been their own private space, his and Rukhsana's, suddenly seemed cold and empty. The furniture they had chosen together, the decorating they had done, it was no longer of any importance. What was he going to do? How could he live without her?

He didn't want to be with strangers; he wanted the detectives to leave.

'I would like to ask you one or two questions, Mr Mahmood,' Handford said. 'If you feel up to it.'

Amajit tried to concentrate. 'What can I tell you? I've been at work. I haven't seen my wife since this morning.'

'You work at the planning office?'

Amajit nodded.

'Have you been there all day?'

'I went out on site with an architect this morning.' He hesitated, trying to recall the day. 'I was in the office all afternoon and this evening I was at a planning meeting. I haven't long been home.'

'Just one more question, sir, then we'll leave you in peace. Can you think of anyone who would want to do this to your wife? Did she have any enemies?'

Amajit stared into space, grief and shock etching his face. What did he know about enemies? Friends, enemies, family. They could all be enemies if the circumstances were right. The police would find out the truth soon enough, but at the moment he couldn't face the explanations, and the terrible feelings of disloyalty. 'No, she had no enemies.'

Handford nodded. 'Is there anyone you would like us to tell? Her parents, perhaps?'

'No. Yes. No. I'm not sure. We're estranged from her parents, from both sets of parents. Perhaps you had better tell them, I don't think they will talk to me. I'll get you their address. They live in Killinghall Road. It's in the east of the city.' He saw a frown spread over the sergeant's face and he knew that he knew. He wasn't surprised by his next question.

'Why are you both estranged from your families, Mr Mahmood?' Ali asked.

Amajit looked first at Ali then back to Handford. 'Your sergeant already knows the answer to that question, Inspector. He knows that where Rukhsana's parents live is the Sikh area of the city.' He turned back to Ali. 'You're right, Sergeant, I am Muslim, and my wife Sikh. We married without our parents' knowledge and outside our cultures and our religions.'

There was a silence in the room for a moment. Ali could not meet Amajit's gaze, and although he said nothing, he was clearly trying to contain his disgust.

Amajit felt tears prick his eyes. He was tired of having to explain to those he knew would never understand.

'Don't judge me, Sergeant,' he said wearily. 'It happens. It happened to us and we suffered for it. Perhaps this is our ultimate punishment.' Suddenly he felt drained. He could take no more. He needed time. 'Please, Inspector; no more, not just now.'

'Yes, of course, sir. We'll leave it for the moment. Is there anywhere you could stay tonight? Or can we get someone to be with you? We can bring in a family liaison officer if you wish.'

Amajit shook his head. 'No, no more strangers. I'll ring my cousin. He'll come.' He looked pleadingly at Handford. 'You couldn't be mistaken?'

Handford shook his head once again. 'I'm sorry.'

Amajit covered his face with his hands and began to weep.

★ ★ ★

Handford and Ali drove to see Rukhsana's parents in silence. They'd assumed she was Muslim, dressed as she was in a shalwar kameez; the fact that she was Sikh put a new complexion on the inquiry and threw up additional cultural problems, adding inevitably to the list of suspects, not to mention the horrendous possibility of a revenge killing.

The heater in the car had been keeping the two of them comfortably warm, but now Handford began to sweat. His mouth became dry and his stomach clenched. The memory of Jamilla Aziz and of a mass of sneering, jeering faces, of abuse, of flying glass from breaking windows threatened to overwhelm him. He saw himself sitting in front of senior officers, trying to explain why it had all been allowed to happen, defending in vain the fact that he had come to

41

the right conclusion and that the riot which ensued had had its own agenda and could not be wholly attributed to the death of a girl and the arrest of her brother.

'Sir!' The urgency in Ali's tone jerked Handford back to the present and he realised he was straying across the road. A horn blared and lights flashed, and he swerved back on course.

'Sorry,' he said.

Ali was holding on tightly to the door's armrest. It pained Handford to admit that he needed his knowledge and experience now. The family members would talk to him, knowing that he understood the shame of such a marriage and the reasons why they did what they had — whatever that was. If this was a family or a revenge killing, Ali would know where to begin to tease the information out of them.

But Handford was still worried. He'd seen the sergeant's reaction at Mahmood's house, and it had angered him, although he knew the importance of culture and religion to the Muslim community. But if Ali could barely hide his disgust when they'd just told a man that his wife had been murdered, how reliable — and objective — would his judgement be? A police officer couldn't afford to allow his beliefs to spill over into an investigation, or to affect the way he dealt with potential suspects. In theory it shouldn't be a problem; they'd all had to answer the question early on in their career, 'Would you arrest your brother, sister, mother, child if the need arose?' and no doubt they had all answered 'yes', assuming that because they knew their

42

brother, sister, mother or child, it would never be an issue. But what they had come across this evening involved religion, culture, family honour and pride — or rather, in this case, family shame. Handford understood this, but Ali lived it and therefore might not be able to separate it from his working life. He'd watched Ali's expression change when Amajit had told them he'd married outside his religion and culture. Amajit had seen it too, and even in these awful circumstances, he had felt the need to plead with the sergeant not to judge him, to ask his forgiveness — or so it had seemed to Handford.

The question was, did he leave it to Ali to work out or did he bring it out into the open? Had it been one of his usual team with a similar dilemma, he would have had a quiet word and tried to help, if necessary. But he knew how they operated, how they thought — he would have felt at ease with them. With Ali it was different; he neither knew him nor was at ease with him, and he hadn't made the best of starts working with him.

'Next right, sir.'

Handford manoeuvred the car off the main road and into the darkened street where Rukhsana's parents lived. Edging up against the pavement, he stopped and pulled on the handbrake. In the time it took to do that, he made the decision that he had to treat Ali as he would any other team member. He shifted his position to face the sergeant who was unfastening his seat belt, unaware of his gaze — or perhaps just ignoring it.

Handford tried to make his question seem friendly. 'This mixed marriage, Khalid, how do you feel about it?'

Ali let the seat belt slip through his hands. It clunked against the metal surround of the door. For a few seconds his head remained bowed, then he lifted his eyes and met Handford's gaze. 'I hate this part, sir. Can we get it over with?' Then he opened the car door and climbed out. Without waiting for Handford, he turned up the collar of his coat against the rain and set off to the house.

Handford pounded his hand on the steering wheel.

'Damn! Hell and damnation!' he said out loud.

He'd lost it, his clumsy attempt to get through to Ali had failed completely. Now it was too late, the moment had passed. Or perhaps Ali had made sure that it had passed, he didn't know. With a sigh, Handford unclipped his seat belt, opened the door and pulled himself out of the car.

★ ★ ★

Barry Penistone was drunk. He had been downing pints of beer and whisky chasers for the best part of the evening and now, a minute or two before closing time, he was lolling over the bar, his chin immersed in spilled booze. Leaning his head to the right in the hope of focusing more clearly, he peered at the line of glasses swaying in time to the music in his head. And as

44

he listened, he caught the sound of his name, first quietly, then more loudly.

'Come on, Barry, lad. It's near on closing time and you should be on your way home.'

As the words echoed round his brain, he felt himself gripped under his armpits and lifted upwards. The landlord's voice was closer now. 'It's work in the morning.'

Barry flailed his arms. 'Ger'off. Give me another drink.'

'No more for you, Barry me lad. Not tonight. You're going to wake up with a blinder tomorrow.'

He tried to stand, but instead felt his body drift downwards and the room float into darkness.

The landlord's knees gave way under his charge's weight. 'Come and help me,' he shouted to the barman collecting dirty glasses at the other end of the snug. 'Let's get him over to one of the benches. I'll ring a taxi, although God knows who'll want to take him in this state. I haven't seen him as drunk as this since he came out of prison and found Donna shacked up with that butcher.'

Barry roused from his stupor. 'She shouldn't 'ave done it,' he moaned. 'She shouldn't 'ave done it. It's all 'er fault. Give me another drink.' He banged on the bench. 'Give me another drink!' he persisted.

The landlord shook his head. 'He's off again. Forget the taxi, let's get him outside. The rain'll probably sober him up.'

For a second time Barry was grabbed by both

arms and hoisted to his feet. He tried to protest as the two men shuffled him round the beer-swilled tables, upturning chairs and stools as they went. But no one was listening to him. When the door was within reach, the landlord pulled at the brass handle. He held the door open with his foot and he and the barman forced Barry through. 'Come on, you bugger, get outside.'

Once outside, they grabbed hold of him again. 'Right, now lean him up against the wall.' The landlord was out of breath. 'God, he's bloody heavy.'

Barry made a move to go back into the pub, but an arm restrained him. 'No, you don't. You stay right where you are.'

He was wrenched round to face the other direction. 'Right, George, see him across the road and then point him towards the park. He'll find his own way home from there.'

Barry turned his head and looked at the landlord. 'It's all 'er fault. You believe me, don't you?' Shifting his position, he placed his hand on the landlord's shoulder. 'I know you believe me. It wouldn't 'ave happened if it hadn't 'ave been for her.' His voice rose to a crescendo. 'Donna, I want Donna.'

The rain was drenching their heads and shoulders. 'For God's sake get him across the bloody road, George.'

George had had enough too. It was late, he was tired and he wanted to get home himself, preferably before midnight. He grabbed Barry hard by the shoulders and propelled him towards the edge of the pavement. 'Right, lad. We're going across that road and you're going home. Then I'm going home. Do you understand?'

Purposefully, the barman manoeuvred Barry across the deserted street, hoisted him onto the pavement, rotated him ninety degrees, made sure he was as well-balanced as was possible in the circumstances and gave him a shove. Then, without so much as a backward glance, he returned to the pub.

Barry swayed gently as he looked round to see where the barman had gone. The rain was beginning to sober him up. He didn't want to be sober. Sober meant remembering and he didn't want to remember. He was on his own and he didn't want to be on his own. He wanted Donna. He needed Donna. He sank to his knees and curled his body into itself. His elbows rested in a puddle and as the water seeped through his jacket, he cradled his head in the crook of his arms, his hands pulling the hair on the nape of his neck.

'It's all her fault,' he wept. 'None of it would 'ave happened if it hadn't 'ave been for her.'

3

Karen Penistone opened the curtains and shivered. She stood for a moment looking out. It was still dark and the murky haze that had settled overnight stretched beyond the houses opposite, obscuring the small garden from her view. An amber glow from the street lights bruised the gloom, but balked at illuminating the deserted streets. The clock on the mantelpiece said almost ten to seven. Just time for a cigarette. She shivered again and crossed her arms tightly over her breasts, pulling the old candlewick dressing gown more firmly around her to keep in whatever warmth was lurking between it and her body. The gas fire was dark and cold, so she flicked the switch to set the red electric flames spiralling over the fake coals. She didn't turn on the gas; it was too early, she'd put it on in a bit so that the room would be warm enough for Danny when she brought him down. No point wasting money on herself.

Curling up on the settee, the harshness of the corded material pricked at her legs and she tucked her dressing gown underneath them. A cigarette packet and box of matches rested on the arm. Stretching backwards she scooped them up and dropped them onto her lap, hesitating a moment before she pulled out a cigarette. The match flared as she struck it against the side of the box and as she held it against the tip, the

48

tobacco glowed red. The flame from the match slowly subsided, turning from yellow to blue and finally metamorphosed into a tendril of grey, spiralling upwards. Drawing in the smoke, she savoured it as it burned the back of her throat. A moment's glow of pleasure and then nothing. For the umpteenth time she decided not to buy any more; she'd finish this packet because there was no point in wasting them, then she'd put the money on one side, order a new suite from her friend's catalogue and pay for it a bit a week.

Karen ran her eyes over the room, surveying it with distaste. It could do with something new to brighten it up. She'd tried her best to make it look good when she moved in, but there'd been no place to start; it didn't matter what she did with it, it remained what it was — a shabby mess. There wasn't a piece of furniture that wasn't second-hand. It wasn't even good second-hand. She remembered how the beige suite, which had been too big to be stored inside the dingy shop in the High Street, had stood outside on the pavement for weeks, open to the traffic, the weather and the kids who played on it. She would have preferred not to give it house room, but when it came down to it, it was all she could afford. 'There's a buyer for everything, that's what I always say,' the greasy-haired man had remarked as she handed over the money. He licked his fingers, then counted the notes slowly before rolling them up and stuffing them in his trouser pocket. 'Can you get someone to pick it up, love?'

Karen thought back to how she used to

49

fantasise about a home of her own; what she would do with it, how she would look after it; it wouldn't be posh, but neither would it be anything like this dump. Closing her eyes she imagined her dream semi, built on a private estate with a garden that ran down to a footpath planted with almond trees, the blossom pink in springtime and in summer the leaves a rich burnished copper. For a short while she lived in another world, the world she had wanted, even bragged about, before all of this. She drew on her cigarette again and breathed the smoke out slowly. One day, when Danny was at school, she'd get a job, not any old job, but the one she'd always wanted. She wanted to be a hairdresser and when she eventually was one, they'd be able to live somewhere better than this.

Karen flicked cigarette ash into the hearth in front of the gas fire. Who was she kidding? What right did she have to such dreams? What right did she have to expect any more than her mother had? She was just gone eighteen with a two-year-old kid. Too right she was bitter and fed up, because like everything in her life, she didn't even do that right. Danny hadn't been conceived in love. The first time ever and she hadn't wanted it or enjoyed it. She would have had an abortion, but left it too late. No one knew who the father was, except him and her, so people thought she was a tart who slept around. She heard the comments. 'Doesn't even know who the father is.'

But she knew, all right. She could still remember every detail of the sex, and of the fight there'd been when she'd finally plucked up the courage to tell him she was pregnant. He hadn't wanted to know, but she'd seen the look on his face. He was scared. He'd sneered at her, calling her a tart and a whore and she'd screamed at him that it was his fault she was expecting and had hit out at him with her fists, but before they could connect with his body, he had caught hold of them and held them tight, threatening to do her over if she ever told. She'd known he meant it and had kept quiet.

Her baby was born with deformed feet — club feet, her mother said. Probably the way he'd been lying inside her. When he was born, the doctor at the hospital told her that she would have to do exercises with him, and his legs would need to be strapped up to put them right, then later he would wear special shoes. Eventually he'd had an operation, which had helped, and now he was trying to walk. He needed a lot of encouragement though, and had it not been for Rukhsana Mahmood, her health visitor, who had visited her daily to begin with and now popped in at least once a week, more if she could, she would never have coped.

Karen liked Rukhsana; she didn't look down on her like the women at the DSS. Rukhsana encouraged her, even urged her to train as a hairdresser. She could do it at the local college, she told her, where there was a crèche, and by the time the new year started next September, Danny would be old enough to go to it. Karen had argued that with all she had to do for him it wouldn't be possible, but Rukhsana had said that

51

the nursery nurses at the crèche were well-qualified and would cope with him — and she would be on hand to help and give advice if necessary.

Finishing her cigarette, Karen bent down to turn on the gas fire. She had just begun to enjoy its warmth when she heard the rattle of the bottles as the milkman swapped the empties for the full ones. At the same time the mantelpiece clock struck seven; she sighed, she would have to stir herself. Wrapping her pink candlewick dressing gown even tighter round her body, she shuffled into the cold hallway, took the key from the small table and unlocked the front door. Leaning out into the dismal morning, she made to pick up the milk. As she bent down, she smelt the vomit splashed around the doorpost. She grimaced and, avoiding the mess, stepped outside to look up at the small bedroom window. The curtains were closed. Barry must have come in drunk last night and she hadn't heard him. Barry always bedded down at her house when he'd been drinking; it was nearer the pub than his mother's. It was funny, she thought, that no matter how drunk he was, he always closed the curtains.

Karen took the milk into the kitchen, then tiptoed upstairs. She glanced into her room towards Danny's cot. He was flat on his tummy, still fast asleep. Moving cautiously towards the door of the small bedroom, she listened but could hear nothing. Perhaps this time Barry had choked on his own vomit.

In the bathroom Karen regarded herself in the

cabinet mirror. What kind of a person was she becoming, she wondered, to think like that — to wish her brother dead? Peering closer into her reflection, she felt sad as she thought of the old Barry. What had happened to him? Once he had been the big brother who had looked after her, who wouldn't let anyone harm her. She remembered when he had stopped his father from hitting her when she had come home after an all-night rave, and then again when he had stood up to a gang of Asian boys who had surrounded her and taunted her.

She undressed, turned on the shower and stepped under the lukewarm spray. Shampooing her short curly hair and her body with the all-in-one gel, Karen tried to focus on the old Barry. He hadn't always been bad; true, he'd always had a temper, but never towards her — not until he came out of prison. Eighteen months inside had changed both of them. He had become more vicious, more aggressive — but what had happened to her? Was killing someone in your mind as bad as killing them in fact? She wasn't sure what kind of a person he had made her into, but she knew for certain that if drinking himself to death got Barry out of her life, then it was all right by her.

She was pulling on her sweater when she heard Danny cry. He was generally a placid baby, and only made a fuss in the morning when he woke up and couldn't get out of his cot. Within minutes of Danny's first wail, there was movement in the small bedroom.

'Shit! What a bloody stupid place to put a

chair.' Barry's voice went up a notch. 'Will you shut that kid up! He's doin' me 'ead in!' The child began to cry even louder. 'Shut 'im up, I tell ya. If you don't, I will.'

'Aw, shut up yourself, ya drunken sod. And clean that mess up outside.'

'Clean it up yerself and get me some tea.'

Karen ignored him and went to calm Danny. She picked her son out of the cot and carried him downstairs into the kitchen, kissing him through his mass of curly brown hair as she went. Holding him close, she dragged the high chair towards the table and put him into it, carefully manoeuvring his legs to each side of the strap and then busied herself getting his breakfast. She placed a bowl of Rice Krispies in front of him and handed him a spoon which he immediately banged up and down into the cereal, squealing with pleasure as the drops of milk splashed onto his face and over the edge of the table.

'Will you keep 'im quiet!' Barry pushed his way past the high chair and flopped down onto the kitchen stool. A cigarette hung out of the side of his mouth.

'God, you look rough. Had a good night, did you?'

Her sarcasm was lost on him. Barry took the cigarette from behind his dry lips and flicked the ash onto the lino. 'None of your business.'

'It is my business when you throw up over my front step, then let yourself into my house and sleep in my spare bed. And use an ashtray, will you?'

'Where's the tea?'

'You're not having any tea until you clean up that mess outside.'

'Aw, come on, Kar, I'll throw up again if I've got to do that. Get me me tea and then I'll do it.'

'Oh yeah, I've heard that one before.' Barry glanced up at her. His pale unshaven face and crumpled clothes said it all. He was a disgusting slob, and if he felt bad he only had himself to blame. But in spite of herself, Karen softened. 'All right, you can 'ave your tea, but I want that step cleaned afterwards.'

'Oh, God!' Barry groaned, rubbing his temples with the heels of his hands. 'What the fucking 'ell 'ave I done.'

'For Christ's sake, Barry, play another tune. You've done what you're always doing. You got drunk and now you're feeling sorry for yourself like you always do.' Karen took a step towards her brother and tentatively placed her hand on his shoulder. 'You've got to stop this, Barry. I know you're still fretting after Donna, but she's gone; she doesn't want you any more, not after what you did to the man in the pub, and getting drunk like this isn't going to change anything.'

Barry wrenched his shoulder from beneath his sister's hand 'What do you know?' he moaned. 'You know nowt.'

'I know it was your own fault. It was your fault she left you.'

'Get lost, will you!' Barry shouted, standing up and kicking the stool away. It fell noisily to the floor. 'Get lost!' He raised his hand and made to hit her face but Karen ducked down and sideways. Barry's fist resounded loudly against the wall cupboard.

'Get out!' she screamed. 'Get out!'

There was blood on his hand and on the cupboard and Barry sucked at his knuckles as he pushed his way past her. 'You fucking bitch!' he shouted. 'You fucking bitch.'

Danny, who had been watching his mother and uncle with guarded interest, began to cry. Karen picked him out of the high chair and held him close, her tears mingling with his curls. 'It's all right, Danny,' she sobbed. 'It's all right.'

★ ★ ★

Warrender was making his feelings known to the man next to him as Handford entered the incident room.

' . . . the one who set off those riots last year? Thought he'd been sacked. That's all we need, a duff DI and a Paki sergeant.'

'Shut it,' whispered Appleyard, throwing a warning glance at the door.

Handford stepped towards them. 'You have a comment to make, Warrender?' he asked, a touch of menace in his voice.

'No, guv, no comment.' Warrender didn't seem fazed.

The general buzz of conversation amongst the ten or so detectives subsided and Handford allowed the silence to deepen. His eyes remained steady on Warrender's for a few moments, before he manoeuvred his way through the tables to the other end of the room. It was early and the officers who had been called on to make up the murder team were stretched out on chairs or standing in small groups, drinking coffee and eating sandwiches. Noticeably, Ali was on his own, heavily involved, it appeared, in scrutinising the sketch map of the crime scene that had been pinned up on the wall. Handford didn't know whether the sergeant had caught Warrender's remark or not.

Chatting broke out again, but the earlier mood of excitement and expectancy was muted now; no one was quite sure what was going to happen next. Handford didn't need this; there was too much riding on it for him to have to put up with the kind of shit Warrender was handing out. He'd have to do something about it, but not now; there were more important things on the agenda.

'Right, let's get on.' The sharpness of Handford's tone sliced the air and he let the papers he was carrying drop onto the desk. There was immediate silence. When he spoke again his voice was quietly controlled. 'Sorry about the unearthly hour,' he said, 'but yesterday's killing is likely to be high profile and we have to be seen to be getting on with it.' He turned to Ali. 'For those who haven't met them before, this is DS Khalid Ali, and over there are DCs Warrender and Appleyard, all three assigned to us from Broughton for the investigation.'

There was a murmur of recognition and greeting from those who knew them. When it had subsided, Handford referred them to the buff folder each detective had been given. It contained the surgery photograph of the victim, maps of the nursing home and surrounding area, and a sketch pinpointing the original location of the body and its final position after Nathan Teale had pulled it with him down the embankment. There was a copy of a hastily written report from the police surgeon, which described in cold medical language the injuries sustained to the head and body and the damage to the hands and forearms, indicating the last terrifying moments of Rukhsana's life when she struggled with her assailant, and the final fruitless efforts she made to defend herself.

The DI pointed to the photograph pinned on the board. 'We're still waiting for formal identification to take place this morning, but there's little doubt that the victim is Rukhsana Mahmood, twenty-seven, health visitor with Dr Haigh's Palin Road practice, married to Amajit Mahmood, a planning officer at the town hall. She was found yesterday afternoon in the woods bordering Moss Carr Nursing Home grounds by the odd-job man, Nathan Teale. She'd been beaten about the head, probably with a coping stone from the boundary wall. I'm sorry there are no photographs of her at the scene yet, I'll pin them up as soon as I get them. We know very little about her so far, except that she was Sikh and her husband is a Muslim. I'm sure I don't need to explain to you the kind of problems that would cause them.'

'And us,' Warrender said.

Handford ignored the comment and the

murmur of agreement that followed it. Warrender was right, but Handford didn't want to dwell on it.

'Amajit Mahmood asked us to break the news to both sets of parents,' he continued, 'and when Sergeant Ali and I called on Amajit's, they denied the couple's existence, said Rukhsana had never been their daughter-in-law and since his marriage Amajit had ceased to be their son. They could see no reason to offer him support just because she was dead. Or to help us with our inquiries. Her family was obviously upset, but maintained that, in spite of many attempts to persuade her to leave the marriage and return home, she hadn't done so and had therefore brought much shame on them. Her father said that her death was her punishment. So, we can't overlook the possibility of a revenge killing by members of one or other of the families, but we mustn't be blinkered by it, we have to investigate all other possibilities.' Handford calmly met Ali's stare.

'Rukhsana was at the nursing home to visit an aunt who is a patient there, that much we know; what we don't know is why she went into the woods. Given the time of year and the weather yesterday, we can discount a walk to get some fresh air. The woods are some distance from the home, so there has to be a reason she went there. To be alone, to think something through? If so, what? To meet someone? If so, who? Friend, lover, family, drug dealer? She had nothing much with her. Her bag and mobile phone were found in her car. The phone was turned off, and her bag, as far as we can tell, was intact.' Handford paused to give time for everyone to assimilate the information.

'At the moment we don't have a suspect. Amajit appears to have an alibi; he says he was out on site with an architect during the morning, in the office all afternoon and at a planning meeting in the evening. Allen, I want you to check it out. The families also have alibis, and I'm going to leave them to Sergeant Ali and we'll see where we get. In the meantime, the sergeant feels that Nathan Teale is a good bet.' He glanced at Ali who shifted his position.

Warrender moved his head towards Appleyard. 'Anything to take the limelight off one of his own,' he said in a low voice.

'If you've something to add, Warrender, let's all be hearing it.' The DI's tone was hostile.

'No, guv, nothing.' Warrender stared back at him, his expression a mixture of contempt and mockery.

'If it was the coping stone that killed Rukhsana, Teale's certainly got the physique and probably the strength, but we've nothing from forensics yet and at the moment there is no obvious connection between the dead woman and him; but we can't rule him out. Davies, you and Jordan take his statement and find out all you can about him. We have his clothes and the boots he was wearing yesterday and SOCO has found a boot print of sorts near where she was killed. We'll know soon if it's his.'

He was interrupted by a telephone ringing. The detective closest to it picked it up. 'Incident room, Detective Sergeant Hewitt speaking.' There was a silence, then Hewitt said, 'Yes, thanks, I'll tell him.' She turned to Handford. 'Message from forensics, sir. She was definitely killed with that coping stone. They've found traces of the victim's blood, hair and skin on it. And the postmortem's scheduled for nine this morning after she's been formally identified.'

'Right, thanks. OK. Davies and Jordan, leave Teale until later. Davies, I want you with me at the PM, and WDC Jordan, you can go with Sergeant Ali to see Rukhsana's parents and then Amajit's. Get a full breakdown on family members, find out how they handled the marriage. Go into it in depth, don't let them wriggle out of it. We need to know a lot more about those two families. Ali, you and I will meet up here at about ten and then pay a visit to Amajit. Graham and Clarke, here's the list of Rukhsana's visits yesterday morning; go and see everyone on it, find out what time she arrived and what time she left and how she seemed — you know what questions to ask. Then follow that up with a visit to the surgery. Barring emergencies, the doctors will be there for us after morning appointments. Get some background on the victim, what she was like, were there any problems that anyone knew about, did she have any enemies, you know the kind of thing.' He pointed to a clutch of officers at the back of the room, 'I want you lot on site to help with the fingertip search. Wilson is exhibits officer. And DS Hewitt over there is office manager. Any questions so far?'

'Could it be drug related, sir?' Clarke asked. 'You know, killed for any drugs she might have been carrying, or dealing even.'

'I don't think health visitors carry drugs, which would mean she was killed because she didn't have any and we're looking at amateurs. Dealing? It's always a possibility and might explain why she was in the woods. Warrender and Appleyard, you get out and question all known addicts, and Clarke, ask which drugs, if any, she would have been carrying when you go to the surgery.'

'Sir.'

Handford could feel the adrenaline running. This was more like it — an investigation he could get his teeth into for once.

'I want three of you to start questioning the nursing home staff this morning. Get a list of their visitor records. There was a bus strike yesterday so given that Moss Carr is so isolated, anyone visiting had to have had transport. Find and check every vehicle registration number. If they have security cameras at the home, pick up the tapes as well, specifically those that cover the car park. Now door to door. First the Mahmoods' neighbours. They live in a predominantly white area, probably because of the marriage. They would have been ostracised or worse had they lived close to either Muslim or Sikh families. It makes our job easier but it does beg the question as to why they lived in Bradford at all. You would have thought that would have been the last place they would have chosen. We need to find the reason for that. If the families agreed to let them live in peace, then it makes some kind of sense, otherwise they were leaving themselves wide open to abuse, probably danger. Uniforms will make preliminary inquiries up there, but once their initial reports are in, I want you to dig a bit deeper. Who were their friends? What was their lifestyle? Did they socialise or keep their own company? Did they have many visitors, together or separately? Did they have any money worries? Did they have enemies? Did they appear happy? Anything and everything. In the meantime, you do house-to-house in Killinghall Road where Rukhsana's parents live and Tallow Road where Amajit's family live. Make sure you're partnered man with woman.' This was followed by comments and wolf whistles. 'Yes, all right, all right. I've arranged for some WPCs in civvies, so if you haven't got a partner, see the duty inspector. It'll be easier and quicker all round if a woman knocks on the door and the man stays in the background.'

'Quite right, guv. Keep them in the background where they belong.'

The light-hearted banter continued for a moment or two. Handford allowed them their fun, then banged on the table. 'Right, that's all from me. Sergeant Ali, is there anything you want to say?'

'Sir.' Khalid stood up and walked forward to stand next to the DI. His voice, when he spoke, was confident, but he kept his eyes away from both Handford and his Broughton colleagues, focusing instead on the men and women in the middle of the room. 'You will find that most of the women living in either area can't speak English with any fluency, but if their children are there, they will be able to translate and in my experience they do so faithfully, particularly the older ones. If you are at all concerned, make a note, let me know and I will do a follow-up visit. The main alibi will probably be that they were at the mosque or the gurdwara — that's the Sikh temple. Check, check and double-check. The neighbours will understand the feelings of the respective families and will stand by them — and may well suggest that we have no right to interfere with what they consider to be purely family business. Don't let that put you off.' He waited a moment for anyone to make comment or ask a question, and then stepped away.

Handford took his place. 'This isn't going to be easy, but remember we have a young woman who has been viciously bludgeoned to death. Currently the only obvious motive is a revenge killing by one or other of the families, but we don't dwell on that until we get the evidence. I can't repeat often enough that we mustn't be blinkered. Finally, we treat everyone the same, and we try to get the information we need.' He paused briefly. They were all experienced detectives; he shouldn't need to say what he was about to say, but for his own peace of mind he had to. 'I don't want any incidents. Don't go in expecting trouble. No leaning on people. Concentrate only on the information we want and give no aggro, even if you get it. We shall meet for a briefing tomorrow morning at ten thirty.' He looked round the room. 'No one, and

I mean *no one*, misses briefings without my permission, and I don't give that easily. If you need me or Sergeant Ali in the meantime, you can get us on our mobiles. Right, get to it.'

The sound of chairs scraping along the floor mingled with an outbreak of chatter which soon faded as the squad left the incident room. Only Handford, Ali, WDC Jordan and DS Davies remained. Handford moved back to the board where a photograph of the dead woman was pinned. He scrutinised it. Her black hair glistened under the photographer's flashlight and she was laughing, which was crimping the delicate skin under her eyes and deepening the creases that fanned from the outer corners of her eyes. The light accentuated her sculpted cheekbones. There were no photographs of her up at the scene as yet, but Handford carried the image of her as he had seen her for the first time, the left side of her face pulped beyond recognition. Why should anyone want to kill a woman like her in that way? Whoever it was must have been wild with fury. What had she done to get someone in a state where he would pick up a heavy coping stone and beat her brains out? Drugs? It was unlikely that she carried them with her, but she would have had access to them. There was a big drug problem in the city; could she have been part of it? Killed because of it? Or was it because of her marriage to Amajit? Could that be it? After two years? Or was it something closer to home? About to leave her husband for someone new perhaps? Whatever it was, she had suffered for it in her last few minutes.

'Poor thing,' he sighed. 'She must have gone through every kind of hell before she died.'

Ali, who was collecting up his things, glanced at him and then returned without a word to what he was doing.

Handford hadn't missed the expression of contempt on Ali's face. He thought at first that the sergeant was scornful of his sympathy for the victim. They all had to distance themselves from what had happened otherwise they couldn't do the job, but surely Ali didn't expect him to be completely detached. Certainly Ali hadn't shown indifference when he had passed on the news to Amajit in Urdu; Handford had seen his consideration, heard his concern. Perhaps his contempt was directed at him, at his ineffectiveness in curbing Warrender, or at his ham-fisted attempt to discuss the Mahmoods' marriage the previous evening.

He turned to Davies and Jordan. 'Go get yourselves a coffee in the canteen. We'll be down soon.' The two detectives, uneasy at the atmosphere which was building in the room, exchanged glances as they walked away. Handford waited until they had disappeared and closed the door behind them.

'What's the matter, Sergeant?'

Ali continued with what he was doing. 'Nothing, sir.'

'Don't bullshit me, Ali. I haven't the time. You've been acting like a two-year-old since you came in this morning.'

That got his attention. Ali's resentment flared. He flung himself round to face Handford full on, his brown eyes glistening. 'You had no right to question my commitment, my judgement or my loyalty last night.'

'Oh, but I had,' Handford said evenly. 'If I think for one minute that your judgement is likely to be impaired, I have to question it. And last night Amajit saw the disgust on your face when he explained that he is Muslim and Rukhsana was Sikh, and so did I. And you might remember that I'm the DI and you're the DS and therefore I'm the one who carries the can if anything goes wrong.'

Ali remained silent.

'I tried to talk to you in the car,' continued Handford, 'but you weren't having any. There was a problem and I needed to check that you could handle it. I would do the same with any officer on my team who gives me reason to think there's a conflict between the job and their beliefs.'

'The circumstances of their marriage isn't an issue.'

'Yes, it is. It was an issue for them, and it's an issue for us and for you. Like I said, I saw the expression on your face, Ali.'

Ali's eyes dropped away. There was silence for a moment, then, his voice taut as a violin string, he said, 'You don't need to question my judgement or my loyalty, sir. I'm a police officer and I know what that means. And the expression on my face wasn't disgust.'

'No? What was it then?'

'I don't know, but it wasn't disgust.'

4

Her face contorted with distaste, Karen threw water onto the vomit around the step and brushed it vigorously into the soil border surrounding the cheerless square of grass that passed itself off as a front lawn. With each swift movement she snarled her desire to propel Barry into the next world in the most tortuous way she could think of, preferably by his balls.

'You can be arrested for thinking things like that, love.'

Two men in raincoats were standing, one behind the other, about a foot away from her, each carrying a folder.

Coppers!

Looking around, she saw no sign of a police car, marked or otherwise, but these men were coppers; they looked like coppers, they smelled like coppers. Karen was an expert on coppers; she'd had the training. As a child she'd opened the door to them so often that she knew most of them by their Christian names. Any burglary within a five-mile radius of the Penistones and it was almost as if there was a tape feeding from the victim's house to theirs. The police had turned up on the doorstep so often that they might as well have been given their own key so that they could search without disturbing anyone.

Stepping back to the bucket, she picked it up

and with an unnecessarily wide swing flung the water onto the mess still floating on the path. The younger and larger of the two policemen jumped backwards to avoid the stream.

'Sorry,' she said, 'I was just cleaning up some sick,' and she gave the water a final brush towards the men, picked up the bucket and turned into the house.

The men grimaced as they moved over to the fence side of the path, careful to avoid the puddles. 'Can we have a word, love?' the grey-haired one said.

'Depends who you are and what it's about.'

He pushed aside the lapel of his raincoat and put his hand into the inside pocket of his jacket. 'Detective Constable Clarke,' he said, pulling out his warrant card and holding it up for her to see. He pointed to the man behind him, who was busy drying his shoes with a handkerchief. 'This is Detective Constable Graham.'

'Right. What do you want?' Karen walked into the house and through to the small kitchen where she placed the bucket in the sink. It had to be about Barry. He was using her as an alibi again. There was no other reason for coppers to be at her house. Well, this time he could forget it; after this morning he could whistle for his alibi.

Taking her question to be her agreement that they should follow her into the house, the men wiped their shoes on the threadbare doormat and walked along the hallway. Danny, now dressed, was in his high chair in the kitchen, playing with the toys she had put on the food tray. He regarded the two men with interest, then dropped one of his cars onto the floor.

Clarke picked it up and gave it back to the child, who squealed with excitement and immediately dropped it again. The policeman bent down once more to retrieve the car. 'We're making inquiries about an incident in the grounds of Moss Carr Nursing Home,' he said.

Karen relaxed. It was unlikely to have anything to do with Barry if whatever it was had happened up at the nursing home. She turned on the tap and began to swill out the bucket. 'What incident? What would I know about what goes on up there? It's miles away.'

Clarke ignored her questions. 'I understand that Rukhsana Mahmood visited you yesterday.'

She put the bucket in a cupboard under the sink and stood up. Turning to face the men, she rested her body against the kitchen unit. 'Yes, she comes every week.'

'What time did she arrive?'

'About eleven o'clock. Why?'

'And what time did she leave?'

Karen shrugged her shoulders. 'About quarter to twelve. Yes, it must have been, because she said she'd made me her last visit because she was going to see her aunt.'

'She told you that?'

'Yes, although I would have known anyway because she was wearing Asian dress.'

Clarke raised his eyebrows. 'And that was unusual?'

'She only ever wears it when she's going to see her aunt. The rest of the time she wears trousers and a blouse or jumper. She said her aunt was

70

very traditional and didn't approve of her flouting custom. So to please her she always wears Asian dress when she goes to see her. I think it's nice.'

Clarke smiled. 'Yes, it was. So when she was here, was she her usual self? She didn't seem worried or upset or anything?'

'No, she was like she always is.'

DC Graham, who had taken over the job of playing with Danny, spoke. 'Do you get on well with her?'

'Who, Rukhsana? Yes, well enough. She's my health visitor and she helps me with Danny. Look, why are you asking me all this? What's happened?'

'Can I sit down, love?' Clarke's voice was gentle. 'Perhaps you'd better as well.'

Karen moved from the sink and sat on the stool at the other side of the table. Her heart was beginning to drum. Since they still hadn't mentioned him, it couldn't be anything to do with Barry, but whatever was wrong was serious, that much she could tell. 'What's wrong?' she asked again.

Softly Clarke said, 'I'm sorry, love, but we found a woman's body up at the nursing home yesterday. She'd been murdered. We think it's Rukhsana.'

Karen stared at him for what seemed an age, then stood up and went back to the sink. She needed to do something whilst she got her head round what he had just said. 'I'm going to have a cup of tea. Do you want one?'

'Go on then, make a pot and we'll all have one.'

Karen resumed her seat while the kettle boiled. 'Does that mean she'll not be able to help me again?' What a stupid question, she didn't know why she'd said it; the cops must think her a real moron.

She stood up. 'I'm just going to get a cigarette. They're in the other room.'

Graham felt in his pocket. 'Here, have one of mine.'

'No thanks, I'll get my own.' Squeezing past Danny's high chair, she made for the door, then stopped. 'You said you think it's Rukhsana. Does that mean it might not be?'

'No. It just means she hasn't been formally identified yet.'

'Who does that?'

'Don't worry, love, it's not you. Her husband is going down to the mortuary this morning. In fact,' he glanced at his watch, 'he's probably already been.'

'Poor Amajit,' she said quietly and disappeared into the hallway.

When she had gone, Graham leaned over the table towards Clarke. 'You're getting soft,' he said in a low voice.

'Yes, I know,' Clarke whispered. 'But I've met kids like her before. A single girl on her own, probably only fifteen or sixteen when she had her baby. It can't be easy for her.'

'I'm sure she copes.' The kettle switched itself off and Graham went to fill the teapot. 'Tea's ready.'

A moment later, Karen reappeared, a cigarette between her lips.

'You know Rukhsana's husband then?' Clarke said.

Karen took three mugs from the worktop and began to pour the tea. 'Yes, I met them in town once and she introduced me. Then one day she asked me and Danny to have a meal with them. It was Eid and they were on their own, so Rukhsana thought it would be nice if Danny and I went.' She passed a mug to each of the men, then sat down again on the stool. 'I imagine Eid's a bit like Christmas — you know, for children. They don't have any — children, I mean — so I expect she thought a baby in the house would make it more Christmassy. We had a lovely time. He's nice, they're both nice.'

'Why was she still visiting you?' asked Graham, spooning sugar into the mug. 'It's not usual. My wife hardly saw our health visitor after the first few weeks.'

'She helps me with Danny. He's got something wrong with his feet. He wears special shoes and should be all right eventually, but he still can't walk properly so she comes to help me with him, that's all.'

'Well, if I were you, I'd go down to the surgery and ask if someone else can help you. It's a lot to cope with on your own. Kids are hard work at the best of times, but when there's something wrong . . .'

'Tell me about it,' she said. Turning to Clarke, she said, 'Do you think I could go and see Amajit? Do you think he'd want to see me?'

'I'd leave it a bit. There are a lot of questions we have to ask him yet, and our governor said he

73

was in quite a state last night. Give him a day or two.' The detective stood up and put his papers back into the folder. 'Right, love, that's all for now, but if you think of anything else, ring me on this number.' He gave her a small card. 'Good luck with the little lad.'

Karen smiled at him. 'Thanks.' She made to pick up Danny.

'No, leave him where he is,' said Graham. 'We'll see ourselves out. And thanks for the tea.'

She followed them anyway, it was second nature never to trust coppers, never to take your eye off them. They were outside and she was just about to close the door when Clarke turned round to face her. 'Who was sick, love?'

'Sick?'

'Yes, you said you were cleaning some sick up when we arrived.'

'Oh, that. It was my brother. Got drunk last night and threw up all over the step. But it's muggins who has to clean it up.'

'Does he live with you, then?'

'No, just turns up when he's had a skinful.'

'Well, that's brothers for you. Thanks again, love.'

Karen closed the door behind them. Still holding the knob of the Yale, she rested her forehead on her hand. Panic swept through her. How would she manage without Rukhsana? She'd relied on her — more than she would ever have admitted. And she was a friend, one of the few Karen had. She let go of the lock and leaned against the adjacent wall. Danny began to cry; he was missing all the attention of the last few minutes.

Karen groaned. 'For God's sake, Danny, shut up,' she shouted. 'Why is it always you? Can't you give me a minute?' But Danny continued to wail and Karen, putting her hands over her ears, sank to the floor. 'Shut up, Danny,' she pleaded. 'Please shut up.'

★ ★ ★

Zombie-like, Amajit followed his cousin Faysal into the front room. The events of the past eighteen hours had aged him. His once handsome features were drawn and haggard, and the blood had drained from his cheeks, giving them a discernibly ashen appearance.

His mind could not imagine the last few moments of Rukhsana's life, but the image in the mortuary he had just left was frighteningly clear. He had looked at his wife, her body covered with a white sheet, a bandage concealing the left side of her face. She was not his wife, yet at the same time she was. He wanted to go to her, touch her, take her into his arms like a baby and tell her everything would be all right. But she was on the other side of a glass window, and the man in the room with her was a stranger.

Her death had been the lead story in the early edition of the local paper and despite the steady drizzle, journalists and photographers were beginning to congregate on the road outside his house. Flocking around the car as it pulled up, they had bombarded him with questions, but their words were unintelligible and he could make no sense of what they were asking. The police officer tried to move them on, but one of them shouted, 'How are you feeling, Mr Mahmood?' That question penetrated, detonating an explosion of uncontrollable fury in his brain. He wanted to shout and scream at them not to ask such bloody stupid questions, but the surge of anger had taken all his energy and he stood in silence while his cousin unlocked the door to let them inside.

'I'll make us a coffee.' Faysal disappeared into the kitchen. Amajit didn't really want one, but he didn't have the energy to argue and accepted the mug from his cousin when he returned.

Faysal sat down opposite him. 'Amajit, we've got to talk about this.'

'What is there to talk about? She's dead. There's nothing to talk about.'

'You know what I mean.' Faysal put his mug on the floor by his chair and dropped forward onto his knees. He placed a hand on Amajit's shoulder. 'If there's any chance that this has anything to do with the family, we've got to decide what we are to do, what we are to say to the police, and we've got to decide now before they start to question you.'

'To do with the family?' Amajit looked at his cousin in horror. 'No, Faysal, it couldn't have been them, not after two years.'

'It might be two years, but you know as well as I do that Kamal and Jahangier have never stopped swearing revenge on Rukhsana. You turned your back on the wife your parents had found for you and instead you married a Sikh

76

girl. Can you imagine what that did to your brothers? You trashed your culture and your upbringing, Amajit, you brought shame on everyone. Rukhsana turned your head and your soul. She had to be punished, you know that.'

'By killing her?'

'By whatever means necessary. She shamed our family. And except for shaming our religion, there is nothing worse.'

'For God's sake, Faysal, we loved each other,' Amajit pleaded. 'I loved her.' His voice dissolved into a whisper and he put his hands over his eyes to stem the tears.

'Did you? Do you understand love? You're supposed to love your parents, but you've brought shame upon them. You should never have come back here. By doing that you added to the family's shame. That's what none of us could forgive.'

Amajit shook his head. 'You don't understand, Faysal.'

'I don't need to understand. I am Muslim and I accept my religion and my culture. I don't need to understand.'

They remained as they were, in silence, a frozen tableau. Then Faysal stood up. 'If this was anything to do with your brothers, then it's a family affair and that's how it has to stay. I mean it, Amajit. You cannot bring any more shame on us by telling the police. Leave the family out of it.'

'I can't, Faysal, they know already. They couldn't understand why I wasn't able to tell our parents of Rukhsana's death. And the sergeant

77

who came last night is one of us, from Pakistan. He realised, even if the Englishman didn't. When I told them, his face showed his hostility.'

'Then he understands; we talk to him, explain, he will see it our way. He will know that those who defile our culture must be punished. And he will understand that it's nothing to do with them, that it's family business.'

'He's a policeman, Faysal, of course he won't see it our way. He has a duty to his work. And anyway, I doubt the other man will let him.' Amajit slumped back in the chair and stared at the mug in his hand. 'They wouldn't let me stay with her, I couldn't even touch her, let her know that I was with her.' After a few moments he roused. 'Please, Faysal, I've got to know who did this to her. Whoever it was has to be punished.'

Faysal bent over his cousin, his hands grasping the arms of the chair. 'No, Amajit,' he said. 'You listen to me. We grew up together; we've always been more like brothers than cousins and in spite of your father's anger, I have tried to be here for you. But I'm warning you, if you utter one word to the police about Kamal and Jahangier, you will lose me too.'

Amajit raised his head, pain defined in each deep crease of his face. He knew Faysal wanted him to give an assurance, but he couldn't.

A sudden loud knock on the door startled him. 'Oh no,' he breathed. 'I can't talk to the journalists.'

'I'll get rid of them.'

Amajit heard the door open and voices, then Faysal came back into view. 'It's not journalists,

78

Amajit, it's the police.' He stood to one side to allow Handford and Ali into the room.

'Good morning, Mr Mahmood,' said the Englishman. 'I'm sorry, I know how you must be feeling, but we really do need to talk to you now.'

★ ★ ★

Karen went about the washing-up like an automaton. No one understood her and Danny's needs like Rukhsana; she would have no one to talk to, no one to comfort her, no one to encourage her. With Rukhsana gone, she would never pluck up the courage to go to college. Grief, dread and acute loneliness consumed her physically and mentally, and she cried aloud. Danny, startled, began to wail, his din mingling with hers.

'Stop that racket!' she shouted at him, throwing the mug in her hand back into the soapy water which splashed over the work surface and onto the floor. She stood for a moment, hanging on to the edge of the sink, then she slumped onto the stool and without thinking picked up the packet of cigarettes and took one out. Disgustedly she threw it down. 'Look what you're making me do,' she yelled hysterically at the child. 'I was going to give these things up.' Then, overcome by love and shame, she lurched over to him and plucked him out of his chair. Clinging to him with her wet hands, she sobbed until she could cry no more. 'I'm sorry,' she whispered. 'I'm sorry. It's not your fault.'

79

When both she and the child were calmer, Karen carried him into the hall. Dragging his dark blue anorak off the banister, she sat on the threadbare carpet of the bottom step and with him on her knee, pulled his arms roughly into the sleeves, straightened it around him and, with a final tug, closed the zip. Expertly, she lifted him onto her hip and held him there while with her free hand and one foot she unlocked his pushchair. She sat him in it and covered his legs with a checked woollen blanket.

She had to get out of the house — away from the smell and the dirt and the shabbiness. Not that she had any idea where she would go, there was nowhere to go that was any better — not her mother's, not her friend's. There was no doubt in her mind where she wanted to go. She wanted to go to Amajit's where she could share her grief. Never mind what the coppers had said, she could sit with him and feel with him and neither of them would be alone.

Outside, the mist had hardly lifted, it was drizzling and the cold clung like static. Danny, oblivious of the temperature, fell asleep with the movement of the chair, his cheeks reddened by the icy air. It was quite a distance to Amajit's, but Karen couldn't be bothered with the fuss of getting on and off a bus, not this morning, so she walked. When she arrived, she found a clutch of journalists and photographers outside the house and a policeman trying to move them on. There was a car alongside the pavement, which although unmarked she sensed belonged to the police. As she approached the house door, the young officer asked her where she was going.

'I wanted to see Amajit,' she said. And feeling the need to offer more of an explanation, she added, 'I knew Rukhsana.'

'Perhaps later then, love, the detectives are with him just now. Come back this afternoon.'

Without a word, Karen turned the pushchair round and set off towards the town. There was no way she was going back home, not yet. She'd have a coffee somewhere and stay in town until she could come back to Amajit's.

★ ★ ★

It was getting on for ten thirty when Handford and Ali were shown into Amajit's sitting room. Following the early-morning briefing, Ali and Jordan had visited both sets of parents but had made little progress. Separated though they were by their religions, they were of one mind in rejecting Rukhsana and Amajit as members of their respective families and the detectives had come away with little more information than they had gone in with. Rukhsana's parents had refused to discuss the marriage which had brought such shame on them, and although her mother talked a little about her daughter as a child and was plainly distressed at her death, no useful information was forthcoming.

'They have an alibi of sorts,' Ali told Handford. 'They insisted that they were at the Langar.'

Handford raised his eyebrows. 'The Langar?'

'It's the Sikh community's free kitchen, sir. They said they were there preparing and serving

81

food until well into the afternoon.'

'The men as well?'

'Yes, everyone helps. We called in on our way to Amajit's parents, and those we spoke to backed up their story.'

They had had, Ali admitted, even less success with Amajit's parents who were not in the least upset at Rukhsana's death and even less interested. They knew nothing, they said, about their daughter-in-law and nor did they want to. It was enough that she was dead; the how and the why were of little concern to them.

'His father insists his wife was at home and he was at the mosque at the time of the murder,' Ali reported. 'The imam who led the prayers agreed that Mr Mahmood was there. Mrs Mahmood was at home between twelve and one when she said the younger boys came from school, but after that she was alone. And that was all they would say. We're not going to get anything more out of them unless we have more to go in with. It wasn't a question of letting them wriggle out of anything, they just weren't prepared to talk.'

'Never mind. I'm sure you did your best.' Handford hoped he was right; he hoped Ali had been able to separate the Muslim from the police officer.

'We could bring them into the station to question them,' said Ali. 'Away from their own home, somewhere a bit more institutional might make them talk.'

'No, there's no need for that, we might alienate them even more.' Handford paused. 'What about other members of the family?'

'There are six. One sister is married and in Birmingham, the other away at university. The two youngest boys were at school. I'll check their attendance for yesterday, but they're only twelve and fourteen, so I can't see them being involved. The other two, Kamal who's seventeen and Jahangier, nineteen, haven't got jobs, but they weren't around, and no one seemed to know where they were, so I haven't had a chance to talk to them yet. But I suspect that any information we want on the relationships within the families we are going to have to get from Amajit. We could try the community leaders, I suppose. They might tell us something.'

Handford, too, had little more to pass on about the circumstances of Rukhsana's death than he had given out at the briefing. He had gone with Davies to the postmortem but had not stayed long. He disliked them intensely. He could never rid his nostrils of the smell, or find a way of distancing himself from the person on the slab.

'She doesn't seem to have been sexually assaulted,' the pathologist told him. He pulled away the sheet which covered her. 'As you can see, she has nasty defence wounds on her hands where she tried to ward off the blows. The bruising to her forearms is substantial, although the sleeves of her dress prevented any lacerations. The blows to the upper arms are less severe, probably due to the sleeves of her coat riding up and protecting her as she lifted her arms. But her right elbow was almost shattered.'

He looked at Handford. 'She put up one hell of a struggle, poor girl.'

'Anything beneath her fingernails?'

'Nothing from the killer. I doubt she got close enough to him. She'd be more concerned with avoiding the weapon.'

'So, no DNA then?'

'Not unless we find some elsewhere.'

After that Handford had left Davies at the mortuary, with instructions to ring him if anything of immediate interest came up, and made his way back to the station to catch up on paperwork and wait for Ali. So by the time they met up, they had very little more to go on, and even less to tell the journalists waiting outside the house, eager for an update. Handford said only that they would get a statement as soon as there was anything to give them.

'Is Rukhsana Mahmood's murder going to cause you the same kind of problems as that of Jamilla Aziz, Inspector?' one journalist asked.

Handford stopped in his tracks. He turned slowly, levelling an icy stare at the man. 'I'm not here to answer questions about previous cases, Mr Redmayne,' he said sourly. 'And as far as this one is concerned, we will issue a statement when we can. Now if you will excuse me . . . ' and he strode to the door.

Handford felt rather than saw Ali's eyes on him. He could have turned round to read the sergeant's expression, but didn't. And Ali said nothing. Handford wished his sergeant would speak his mind, then at least everything would be out in the open.

Amajit's cousin let them in and led them into the front room. Traces of the delicate perfume which marked Rukhsana's one-time existence were still detectable, but now the walls, the carpet, each piece of furniture exuded an atmosphere solid with grief; the sense of loss was palpable. Amajit, dressed in a dark suit and tie, was slumped in a chair. He forced himself out of it as they entered and introduced his cousin, who wore jeans, a sweater and designer trainers. The heavy gold watch and ring he sported suggested a man of some means.

They sat down, Amajit and Ali on the settee, Handford in a chair opposite them. Faysal moved away from them, and sat at the table in the corner by the window, but in direct line of Amajit's gaze.

'How long were you married to Rukhsana, Amajit?' Handford asked gently once they were settled. The man in front of him was in no fit state to be interrogated, but it had to be done.

'About two years.'

'Had you known her long before you married?'

'We met when I was at university and she was in the final year of her nurse's training.' He stared at the floor, lost in his memories.

'Sir?' Handford prompted.

Amajit roused himself. 'I had broken my leg playing football for the university. It was a bad break and I needed an operation. I was in hospital for almost three weeks. She worked on the ward.' He glanced at his cousin, who sat quite still, his lips set in a hard line, his expression unyielding.

85

'We became friends and when I left hospital she came to visit me. It just seemed to develop from there. There didn't seem anything we could do to stop it.'

'You should have come home. That would have stopped it.' His cousin's control was beginning to fracture.

Handford tried to read Ali's reaction, but the sergeant steadfastly kept his gaze on his notebook. Without turning to look at Faysal, Handford said, 'Please try not to comment, Mr Hussain. Go on, Amajit.'

'We both stayed in London after we qualified. She remained at the same hospital until I got a job with Lambeth Council and she moved as a practice nurse to a health centre close to where I was. She became interested in becoming a health visitor while she was there.'

'And you decided to get married while you were in London?'

'Yes.'

'Didn't you have a marriage arranged for you by your family?' Ali asked.

Handford glanced at him, but the sergeant's expression was quite neutral.

'Of course he did.' Faysal stood up before Amajit could answer. 'What kind of Muslims do you think we are?'

This time Handford faced him. 'Please, sir, I must request that you do not interrupt, otherwise I shall have to ask you to leave.' He turned back to Amajit. 'Your family had arranged a marriage for you — and Rukhsana's as well?'

Amajit's head was bowed. 'Yes,' he whispered.

'Yet you married her anyway?' Ali interjected.

'Yes.' Once again, Amajit Mahmood pleaded with the sergeant. 'We were in love, we couldn't live without each other.' Amajit turned to Handford. 'Are you married, Inspector?'

'Yes, I am.'

'And you married because you were in love?'

'Yes.'

'Then why not us?'

Faysal stood up again and made towards Amajit. 'Because he married one of his own, and because he's a white man and you are not, that's why.'

'For the last time, Mr Hussain,' warned Handford, his tone brooking no argument.

Faysal remained motionless for a moment, then snatched at his anorak which lay over the back of a chair. He walked towards the door. His hand on the knob, he turned and looked directly at Amajit's bowed head. 'Explain to them. Explain what you have done to your family. And when you've done that, explain the shame and why we all feel that Rukhsana is better off dead.'

The front door took the brunt of Faysal's anger and for a while after he had gone, the house seemed to vibrate with the ferocity of his passion.

What was the biggest crime in this family, Handford wondered, the marriage or the murder? He felt sorry for Amajit, both because he had lost his wife and because he had no one with whom he could share his grief.

He gave Amajit a little time to collect himself,

then asked, 'What was the reaction of your families?'

'They disowned us.'

'Was that all?'

'Wasn't that enough?' Amajit said bitterly.

Handford said nothing and waited again while Amajit struggled to regain composure.

Amajit coughed to clear his throat. 'Rukhsana's family sent one of her brothers to see her, to try and make her change her mind and return to the Sikh community. But she said no. He said the family would not rest until they had got her back.'

'What do you think that meant?'

'That they might send someone to kidnap her maybe.'

'And your family?'

He knuckled away the tears that were gathering in his eyes. 'They said I had brought shame on them and that I was no longer their son.'

'Any threats?'

Amajit hesitated. 'No, not really.'

Ali exhaled impatiently. 'Are you sure about that, Mr Mahmood?'

Handford glanced towards Ali, but before he could speak, Amajit said bitingly, 'Perhaps you have never done anything to torment your family, Sergeant. Although I doubt it. You are a police officer, after all, and I know what that means in our community.'

There was silence. The comment had touched a nerve in Ali. Handford was aware that the Asian community did not think the police service a suitable profession for their sons.

Perhaps Ali, too, had defied his father.

Handford said, 'I think it's time for a coffee, Sergeant.' It seemed the best way to diffuse the situation.

Ali threw him a furious look, but got up anyway and left the room.

'I'm sorry, Inspector,' said Amajit. 'I'm not thinking straight. I'll apologise to him.'

'No, leave him. He's used to worse than that. Now, you have brothers and sisters, how did they react to your decision?'

'My sisters said little. My younger brothers were sad; the older ones, Kamal and Jahangier, were angry.'

'How did they show their anger?'

Amajit avoided the question. 'They were just angry.'

'How did they show it?' Handford persisted. 'With threats?'

There was no getting away from it. 'They threatened Rukhsana.'

'Not you?'

'No, they blamed her for everything.'

Handford pushed harder. 'What kind of threats did they make?'

'They said they wanted to exact revenge for the family.'

'How?'

'By punishing her.'

'In what way?'

'I don't know.'

'Physically?'

'Possibly.'

'By killing her?'

'No.' The word came out as a strangled cry, and Handford knew that Amajit did not believe it any more than he did.

Ali returned with three mugs of coffee on a tray and handed them out.

'You have no children?' he asked as he gave Amajit his.

'No,' he said, 'we decided to wait a while.'

Handford took a sip. 'Did you have a happy marriage?'

'Yes, I think so; we were satisfied with our life together. Rukhsana was a good wife and we got on well. She was fun to be with, intelligent, we would spend hours just talking — we were a good match. But we were in a no-man's land — no longer part of any community. We had to be strong for each other. If we hadn't loved each other I don't think we would have got through.'

'So there were no problems — other than those with your families?' Handford asked.

'No, Inspector, no more than in any other marriage.'

'Why did you come back here? I would have thought it would have been easier for you to stay in London.'

'Good jobs came up for both of us at the same time, so we decided that we would come back. It wasn't easy for us, even in London. Our communities have built up quite a network of friends and family in all parts of the country over the years. It's hard to escape anything. So why not come back? We got a house in a white area, lived away from both families, tried to keep ourselves to ourselves.' Amajit leaned his head against the back of the settee. He closed his eyes for a moment.

Handford let him rest in silence then said, 'Let's go through your movements yesterday in more detail. You work at the planning office in the city?'

Amajit opened his eyes and wearily raised his head. 'Yes.'

'What time did you leave for work? Before or after your wife?'

'Before, about seven thirty. I wanted to get in early yesterday. I had a site visit and I needed to look over the plans to refresh my memory.'

'Where was this site visit?'

'Over the other side of the city, the new Parkway Estate just off the ring road. I was meeting the architect, Mr Craven of Craven, Jones and Medway. I got there about nine thirty and left about half past eleven.'

'Were you with each other the whole time?'

'Yes, and the builder joined us for about half an hour at quarter past ten.'

'So you left the site at eleven thirty. What did you do then? Return to the office?'

'Not straightaway. I called in at a takeaway for a sandwich then went back.'

'Which takeaway?'

'One in the city centre.'

'What time did you arrive at the office?'

'I suppose about midday. And I stayed there until I had to attend the planning meeting at four thirty. It was a long one and it finished about six. I came straight home after that.'

'And — ' Handford's question was interrupted

by the highpitched tone of his mobile phone. 'Excuse me a moment, will you?'

He was out of the room for only a few minutes. When he returned, his face was serious. He spoke to Ali.

'That was Davies,' he explained. 'He's at the mortuary, following the postmortem.' Then he turned to face Amajit. 'Why didn't you tell me, Mr Mahmood, that your wife was twelve weeks' pregnant?'

5

Handford and Ali sat in the car outside Amajit's house.

'She must have known she was pregnant,' Ali was emphatic. 'She must have.' He paused while he considered. 'Although,' he mused, 'you do hear of women who are unaware of their pregnancy until the baby's practically on its way.' He shook his head. 'I can't see it myself. My wife knew straightaway.'

'So did mine,' said Handford. 'And Rukhsana was a health visitor. She of all people should have known. Twelve weeks — of course she knew.'

'So why didn't she tell her husband?'

'I don't know. He certainly looked dumb-founded when I told him, so either he's a good actor or she really hadn't said anything. Maybe she was planning a termination.'

Ali looked horrified. 'She wouldn't do that, surely?'

'Probably not under normal circumstances, but you heard what Amajit said. By marrying they'd put themselves in no-man's land. Maybe she thought it was no place to bring up a child.'

'Even so, I can't believe she would consider an abortion, it would be totally against her religion.'

'So was marrying a Muslin but she didn't let it stop her.' He glanced at Ali. 'Sorry.'

'No, no, you're right. It didn't stop either of them.'

For a moment they didn't speak. The sergeant

93

was pensive and Handford sensed a lessening of tension between them.

'That marriage caused a lot of grief one way and another,' he said at last. 'His cousin certainly held it in contempt and the brothers put the whole of the blame on Rukhsana. Could it be a punishment killing?'

'I'm sure both Amajit and Faysal believe the brothers might have carried out their threat. But they're not going to admit it; to tell us would be letting down the family.' Ali hesitated. 'What worries me . . . ' He paused.

'Go on.'

'A punishment killing would be premeditated, planned. I would have expected a shooting or a stabbing, running her down with a car even. Beating her to death with a coping stone seems more like a rage attack. Someone in a fury.'

'Faysal showed a vicious temper this morning.'

'Yes. But Amajit seems to trust him; after all, he asked him to stay overnight and to go to the mortuary with him. He wouldn't have done that if Faysal had gone along with the rest of the family in disowning him. In fact, given what we saw of his attitude towards Amajit, I wonder why Faysal didn't disown him. It's got to mean something, I'm just not sure what.'

'Well, mull it over, and if you come up with anything, we can see Amajit again.'

'I wonder if we ought to talk more about the pregnancy. But not at home, bring him down to the station.'

Handford sat without speaking, cross-referencing what he had learned with what he knew and what he surmised, compartmentalising the snippets of information in his memory while at the same time trying to fit the pieces of the picture into some kind of frame. 'Let's see what today brings first. We'll leave him to stew until tomorrow, let him think about things.'

Ali looked dubious. 'He might be more forthcoming when he's had time to think but he's in a very vulnerable state. If Faysal gets a chance he could persuade him of anything.'

'Nevertheless, I'd rather we leave him for a while.' Handford sat silent for a moment, then asked, 'Who was Rukhsana's GP?'

'I'm not sure, sir. Do you want me to find out?'

'No, I'll do that. Who's at the surgery?'

'Graham and Clarke.'

'Right, drop me off there. Nip back to the station and pick up whoever has finished what they were doing, then go back to Amajit's parents and have a word with Kamal and Jahangier. They've been too elusive so far. If they're still not at home, find them. I want you to put faces to names and check their alibis for yesterday. But don't be too heavy. I don't want any aggro, I'd rather know more about them first. Once you've talked to them, check into their backgrounds, see if there's anything known. And don't mention the pregnancy — we'll keep that to ourselves for as long as we can, I think.'

★ ★ ★

Amajit had barely stirred since the two policemen let themselves out of the house.

Slumped in the corner of the settee, he stared into space, thoughts flitting in and out of his mind like darting moths, his body incapable of movement. The gold carriage clock on the mantelpiece chimed the hour and he roused momentarily. It had been Rukhsana's clock; she'd seen it in a jeweller's shortly after they were married and had instantly loved it. He had bought it for her as a surprise; he remembered bringing it home and creeping into the small sitting room in their flat while she was still in the kitchen preparing the evening meal. He had set the time for two minutes to the hour and when it had chimed she had realised immediately what it was and, without stopping to dry her hands, had run to the mantelpiece and with a cry of delight picked it up. Afterwards she had hugged him and kissed him until he could hardly breathe.

He lifted his fingers to caress the cheek she had kissed, recalling the lightness of her breath and the touch of her lips. Slowly, imperceptibly, the memory was replaced by the image of Rukhsana beneath the white mortuary sheet. Lifeless, his hand slid onto his lap and he gazed at the empty space on the settee where she often curled in the evening, reading a book or watching television. What consciousness there was in him alternated between the desire to wrap himself into a ball, safe and secure, and the need to scream out loud to release the pain. But he did neither. From time to time he thought of Faysal and the way he had stormed out of the house when the police were here. He would have to ring him, let him know how grateful he was for his support. But not straightaway. He was still trying to come to terms with the news Handford had given him and the last thing he needed were his cousin's platitudes and diatribes on family loyalty.

Why hadn't she told him she was pregnant? She must have known. Twelve weeks — three months — she *must* have known. Handford had asked if all was well with their marriage and he had answered yes, but the truth was that things hadn't been easy over the past few months. Rukhsana had been busy, he had been busy, and they hadn't seen as much of each other as he would have wished — as either of them would have wished. But they'd been all right, nothing major, nothing to tell the inspector about.

He recalled that recently she'd appeared preoccupied, and when he'd commented, she'd said simply that she was tired. He'd wondered then, fleetingly, if she was pregnant, but hadn't pursued the thought. Even though they would have loved a child, they had both known that having one would be hard, deciding whether it would be brought up Muslim or Sikh, helping it to fit into a family without a family. And anyway, they'd agreed they needed to get away from this house first, into something bigger in a better neighbourhood. Perhaps that was why she'd said nothing. She thought he might be angry that their plans had been spoiled. Surely she'd known him better than that; he could never have been angry with her, no matter what she'd done. He loved her so much and a baby could only have cemented their relationship. His pain intensified.

Now he had lost them both, the wife he adored and the baby he never knew but for which he nevertheless felt a deep love.

A rap on the door startled him. For a fleeting second he thought Rukhsana had forgotten her key again, but the pleasure was shortlived as the pain of her loss flooded over him. He stayed where he was, not wanting to see anyone. The visitor was persistent, knocking more loudly this time. The police again perhaps. He hoped not. Wearily he pulled himself off the settee and made his way to the door, his hand pushing against the wall, giving him strength to walk the short distance. Opening the door, he saw, standing in the steady drizzle, a young girl in blue jeans and black anorak. Her head was uncovered and her curly hair glistened with the rain. At her side was a baby in a pushchair. She would want Rukhsana. Oh, no. Please not that.

'Hello, Amajit,' she said softly.

'I'm sorry?'

'It's Karen, Karen Penistone. I came at Eid.'

Amajit tried to understand her words, to clear his tired mind.

'Eid?'

'Yes, don't you remember? Rukhsana invited Danny and me.'

The vaguest of recollections trickled into his mind. 'Eid . . . yes . . . Eid.' Then he forced himself to say, 'Rukhsana's not here.'

'I know, the police came to see me.'

'The police?' He wished he could clear his head of the confusion. 'It's raining,' he said, 'you'd better come in.'

Karen manoeuvred the pushchair through the door and into the narrow hallway.

'Why did the police see you?'

'I suppose because she was with me yesterday, before . . . ' Her voice trailed away.

'Yes, before . . . '

'Oh Amajit, poor Rukhsana. How could anyone do that to her? She was so nice.' And she put her arms round him, holding him tight. For the first time that day, he allowed his grief full expression. Encircling her with his arms, he buried his head in her hair and wept.

★　★　★

It was almost lunchtime and the waiting room at the Palin Road surgery was quiet. A couple of patients flicked through magazines as they waited to be seen. Dr Haigh had been called out on an emergency and would have to be interviewed later, but as promised everyone else was in the building.

Handford sent Graham back to the station, then listened patiently while Clarke updated him. Two pieces of information were of immediate interest. The first was that Rukhsana had recently changed doctors.

Clarke explained. 'Her original GP was Dr Berridge, but when Elinor Copeman joined the practice about two months ago, she asked to go onto her list. Said she preferred a woman.'

'That seems reasonable enough, Asian women often prefer female doctors,' Handford said.

Clarke lowered his voice. 'But that may not

have been the only reason, guv. One of the girls in the office told me that Rukhsana was particularly friendly with Dr Berridge and she reckons that's why she changed.'

Handford raised his eyebrows. 'Friendly?'

'As in spending a lot of time together. The office staff reckon they were having an affair.'

'Anything to substantiate the claim?'

'No, it's just gossip. But, as the receptionist said, they're not blind, and let's face it, this place is too small to miss something like that.'

'You've discussed this with Dr Berridge?'

'No, and I haven't seen Dr Copeman yet either. They still have one or two patients to see and the receptionist won't let me interrupt them.'

Handford was just about to remonstrate with the woman when the glass window of the receptionist's office slid back and a plumpish lady wearing a bright orange, yellow and red jumper which made her look like an over-ripe peach peered through.

'Mr Clarke,' she called. 'Dr Copeman will see you now. Dr Berridge has one more patient, but will be available in about five minutes.' And she slid the partition closed.

In Dr Copeman's consulting room, Handford introduced himself and Clarke. As he shook hands with the attractive young woman who came from behind the desk, he decided sadly that either he was ageing fast or doctors were becoming more youthful. His eyes traced her slender frame and he wished he was ten years younger. Her shoulder-length auburn hair

100

framed her face with deep waves and dressed as she was in a midnight-blue suit and dove-grey blouse, she radiated an air of elegant efficiency.

'How can I help you, Inspector?' Her voice held a faint Norfolk accent.

'I'm investigating Rukhsana Mahmood's death, Dr Copeman, and I need to ask you some questions.'

Elinor Copeman indicated the chairs next to her desk and they sat down. 'Of course,' she said.

Handford began. 'Mrs Mahmood joined your list about seven weeks ago, I understand.'

'Yes, she preferred to be treated by a female doctor, not an unusual request from an Asian woman, even one who is in the medical profession. Dr Berridge had no objections so I accepted her.'

'Have you seen her as a patient since?'

'Yes, though I'm not sure that I ought to discuss our consultation with you.'

'Dr Copeman, Rukhsana Mahmood is dead, there is nothing you can tell us that will damage her right to confidentiality.'

'No, I suppose not.'

'Had she been to you regarding her pregnancy?'

The doctor was unable to hide her surprise. 'You know?'

'From the postmortem,' he explained and wondered what it was about the question that had caused her surprise.

She relaxed a little. 'Of course,' she said. 'Yes, Rukhsana came to me a month ago to have her pregnancy confirmed. She was about eight weeks, but . . . ' She hesitated.

101

'Yes?'

'She was quite distressed at the thought of being pregnant.'

Handford glanced at Clarke. 'Did she say why?'

'Just that the time was not right.'

'Did you believe her?'

'I had no reason not to.'

'Did she ask for a termination?'

'No.' Elinor Copeman hesitated again for a moment, then said, 'She insisted that no one was to know, not even her husband, which was why it came as a surprise when you asked me. She was quite adamant about it.'

'But she didn't give a reason?'

'No. And I didn't push her; it was nothing to do with me.'

'Not even as a friend, a colleague?'

'I was her doctor as well and I kept her confidence as I would with any patient.'

Handford changed his line of questioning. 'Did you get on well with her?'

'She was friendly, pleasant to talk to and an excellent health visitor, but I didn't know her well socially.'

'Do you know anything about her relationship with Dr Berridge? I understand that their friendship went beyond that of colleagues.'

'I don't listen to gossip, Inspector.'

'No. But had you heard the rumours?'

'It's a small practice, it's impossible not to. If you want to know if I thought there was any substance to them, I have no idea. You'll need to ask him.'

★ ★ ★

Dr Ian Berridge leaned back in his chair and ran his hand through his unruly mop of shoulder-length brown hair before he answered. 'Rukhsana was a colleague. She worked with some of my patients — of course we saw quite a lot of each other.' His voice was cultured but there was no mistaking the soft Irish burr which bubbled gently beneath his words.

Handford let his eyes rest on the doctor's face. He had disliked him from the outset. The man was insincere. His explanation, his smile, even his handshake as they had entered the room lacked warmth. But that didn't mean Berridge was Rukhsana's lover or her killer, and since the rules demanded he kept an open mind, he pushed forward.

'And that's all, doctor? Your relationship was no more than that of colleagues?'

Berridge straightened and picked up the fountain pen on his desk. He toyed with it, twisting it in his fingers, giving himself the means to shift his gaze away from the detective. 'No, of course not.'

Handford smiled as though he fully accepted the denial. 'I know she was a patient at this practice, but who was her actual GP?'

'Dr Copeman.'

'Dr Copeman's only been here a couple of months. Who was her previous GP?'

Berridge looked uneasy. 'I was.'

'So, why change to Dr Copeman?'

Ian Berridge put the pen down and his dark

103

eyes held the inspector's gaze. 'It was nothing personal; she preferred to have a woman treat her. Some women do.'

'And that was the only reason?'

The doctor picked up his pen again and scrutinised it carefully as though for flaws. When he finally spoke, his voice trembled slightly. 'Yes, that was the only reason.'

Handford turned towards Clarke who read his boss's eyes. The man opposite them was lying.

★   ★   ★

Ali sat huddled in the car outside Amajit's parents' house, the heater blowing warm air around his legs. Pulling a second cigarette out of the packet on the passenger seat, he lit up. It was a habit he had picked up at university, but one he only ever indulged in private. In fact he wouldn't be considering it now if Handford hadn't sent him up here. He was perfectly capable of questioning a few doctors and it would have done Handford good to come out and face the community.

Lowering his window to let out the choking combination of heat and cigarette fumes, he felt the cold air bite into his cheek and lift his coat collar. He held it secure with a gloved hand while he waited for the two younger Mahmood boys to come home from school.

He was alone, and the boys' mother had refused to let a man on his own into the house. At his knock, a veiled face had appeared at the adjacent window and a hand had waved him away. He glanced at his watch: twenty past twelve. It would be just his luck that the boys ate lunch at school. He'd give it another quarter of an hour, then he would have to find a female officer to join him.

The street was deserted, the door-to-door inquiries had finished and he castigated himself for not having checked that out before he came. A WPC could have waited for him, knocked on the door for him, got him inside, saved a lot of time. A stupid mistake, the kind of mistake the DI would pick up on, comment on, particularly as he had been told not to come alone. In fact he had returned to the incident room as requested but found Warrender the only officer available.

'Can I do anything for you, Sarg?' the man had asked, a smirk of contempt sliding along his lips.

Ali hadn't bothered to answer. To sit in the car with Warrender and his comments was not his idea of fun, nor was he prepared to risk the kind of wisecracks he knew the DC would make when faced with the Mahmood brothers. Warrender wouldn't care that he was there; in fact he would revel in his discomfort and carry on doing and saying what he wanted. Ali leaned his head back on the rest and imagined Handford's censure when he found out that he had ignored his instructions. To hell with it; it wasn't the DI on the receiving end of racism, it was him, and he would deal with it in his own way.

The image of Handford remained with him. There was a chameleon character if ever there was one. One minute pleasant and professional, the next caustic and dictatorial. A duff inspector? Perhaps. There was no doubt he was marking time on this investigation, avoiding issues which could be considered racial and therefore not getting to the heart of what had been going on. The families were using language and culture as an excuse for not answering questions, and Handford was letting them do it. 'Go easy on him. Don't be too heavy. Leave them alone for a while.' It was as if he didn't want to upset anyone. He'd even apologised for commenting on Rukhsana marrying a Muslim. Why should he do that? The marriage was a fact. That she was Sikh and Amajit was Muslim were facts. What was the point in tiptoeing around the facts in a murder inquiry? Or tiptoeing around the witnesses and suspects for that matter? Upsetting people was built into the job. Getting in, breaking them before they had a chance to polish their story. Well, now he had his chance; he had been told to question the brothers and that was just what he was going to do — no creeping around, just good hard questioning.

Kamal and Jahangier were contenders for the murder — their motive for wanting Rukhsana dead was powerful, even Amajit had admitted as much. That they had blamed Rukhsana for the marriage wasn't in doubt, nor was their threat to punish her. But still Handford's instructions had been to go easy with them. Why? What was wrong with the man? Ali thought back to the discussions they had had prior to meeting Amajit, and afterwards when they had been considering the pregnancy. They had been professional, civilised, friendly even. But at other times it was as though Handford had to pick a fight with him just to show his authority — up at the nursing home and at the end of the briefing for instance. Ali was sure Handford's attitude had something to do with the case last year, and up to a point he could understand why the DI was touchy about it. It was a pity he'd been away when it had all blown up, because he had only the sketchiest of details. When he had time, he would delve into it a bit more. At least then he might be able to understand his boss a bit more.

He stubbed out his cigarette and was fighting his conscience on whether or not to have another when he saw the young brothers sauntering home. Scruffy, jackets unbuttoned, shirts out of trousers and ties hanging from their pockets, they jumped sideways when Ali opened the car door.

He showed his warrant card. 'I want to see your mother, lads. I need to know where Kamal and Jahangier are,' he said before they had time to get their breaths.

'They'll not be here, they'll be at Battle's.'

When Ali looked blank, the smallest said by way of explanation, 'The snooker hall off Thorn's Road.'

★   ★   ★

Battle's, it turned out, was one of six or seven halls which had sprung up in the rundown back streets off the city centre. Bought and furnished by speculators during the recession, they were a

107

favourite haunt of small-time drug dealers who backhanded their stock inside and prostitutes who hung around outside, smoking and waiting to pick up clients. Occasionally, they were raided by uniformed police, but generally and unofficially the halls and the surrounding streets were considered no-go areas.

To lessen the chance of losing wheels, stereo and anything else easily lifted, Ali left his car at the Central Police Station car park and walked to the hall. The back streets were quiet, the weather too cold for most of the women. One or two of the hardier ones were working and offered him a good time, which he turned down. 'Go on then, yer miserable bugger,' one of them called after him, but he kept walking until he reached the illuminated neon sign, muted in the murky dullness, and turned into the building.

Apart from the glow of the canopied lights over the tables in use, the room Ali entered was dingy and cheerless. Counters around the perimeter were littered with plastic coffee cups and overflowing ashtrays, as was the bar at the far end. Sellotaped onto the heavy green flock wallpaper were large, handwritten notices warning clients not to take their drinks to the snooker tables. The room stank of stale cigarettes, dope, beer and sweat, and as Ali approached the heavily made-up woman in the pay booth, he had almost decided to accept Handford's judgement and ask only essential questions. He didn't bother to say who he was but merely inquired if the two men were there. Without removing her cigarette from between her lips, the woman pointed them out. 'Over there,' she said. 'Table three.' Then she leaned through the small hatch and called, 'There's a copper for you, Jan. Been naughty boys again, 'ave you?'

And she and they laughed.

Ali approached the two men at the table. Taking his warrant card from his pocket, he introduced himself. As he drew closer, the smaller of the two hit the cue ball sharply. They watched as the white ball cannoned into the red one, propelling it across the green baize with such force that it hit the surround and ricocheted noisily across the table several times. Eventually it lost impetus and came to rest next to the yellow.

Only then did he glance at Ali. Turning to his brother, he muttered, 'Who let him in? There's a real bad smell in 'ere, Jahangier.' Not the most original of comments, but observing the man swagger over to his can of drink resting on the table's edge and put it to his mouth with a 'what yer going to do about it?' smirk on his face, Ali doubted that he was capable of anything more original.

Jahangier was bending over the table to take his turn. 'What do you want?' he asked abruptly.

'To talk to you about your sister-in-law's death.'

'We're busy.'

Ali forced a brittle smile and as Jahangier drew his cue back to slice the white ball, he scooped it up sharply from the table. 'You can be busy when I've finished,' he said curtly.

Menacingly, Kamal took a step towards the

detective and as Jahangier raised his cue, Ali feared that he was going to strike him with it, but instead, with a sneer, he laid it carefully on the table and said, 'You can have two minutes. What do you want?'

'When did you last see Rukhsana?'

'You've spoken to Amajit?'

'Yes.'

'Then you'll know the answer to that. We don't see her; we've never seen her. She's nothing to do with our family. Anything else?' Jahangier picked up his cue.

Ali turned to Kamal. 'What about you?'

'I'm fussy who I spend my time with.' Ali didn't doubt it. 'She was a whore, a tart and she's where she should be. Whoever killed her did us all a favour.'

'A whore and a tart? That's not the impression we have of her from those who knew her.'

'They didn't know her like we did.'

'But your brother said you never saw her. So how can you know she was a whore and a tart?'

'We just know.' And for effect, Kamal added, 'It's a good job for her that somebody got to her before we did.'

Ali smiled at him. 'Well, let's see if that is so, shall we? Where were you both yesterday, between eleven and two?'

'None of your business.'

'I think you'll find it is. Where were you?'

'I've just said, it's none of your business.'

'And I've just told you it is, so stop wasting my time. Here or the station, it's your choice.'

Kamal took another drink while he mulled

over his choices. 'Get on with it, then,' he growled.

'It's common knowledge that you blamed Rukhsana for the marriage and that you've threatened her more than once since she and Amajit were married. So where were you yesterday?'

Jahangier slowly placed his cue back on the table then looked the detective up and down, his eyes filled with contempt.

Ali ignored him and carried on. 'My understanding is that you wanted to punish her. What does punishing mean in your book, Jahangier? Running her down, knifing her, or getting her in some quiet spot — woodland, perhaps — and beating the hell out of her with a coping stone? Did you punish her? Either of you? Both of you?'

Jahangier took a step towards Ali, his fists clenched. Ali kept tight hold of the white snooker ball. His adversary got in close, so close that when Ali looked down he could clearly see the acne scars that covered his nose.

'She brought shame on our family, she deserved whatever she got. If you were really one of us, you'd know that and you wouldn't be wasting our time or yours.'

Neither of them moved. Jahangier was breathing heavily, his anger close to the surface, ready to explode.

'So, did you carry out your threat?' The ball was still tight in Ali's hand.

Kamal swaggered round to the other side of the table, breaking the tension. 'We could have

111

done it any time we wanted. Now we don't have to; someone's done it for us. And good luck to him.'

Ali turned to Kamal. 'Where were you both yesterday?'

Kamal had regained his confidence. 'That's none of your business.'

Ali should have brought Warrender with him, if only to stop him assaulting the little shit. Warrender would have loved it, the power of deciding which of the Pakis he would help and which he would manhandle.

He met Kamal's gaze. 'For the last time, where were you yesterday?'

Ali's tone persuaded Jahangier to take over from his brother. Still breathing heavily, he glanced up at the detective, then, pushing Kamal out of the way, he said, 'Here, we were both here, we're always here — every day. You can check if you like, it won't be difficult — not for a clever man like you.' He turned round and yelled to the woman in the booth. 'Mandy, where were we yesterday?'

'Where else would you two be but 'ere?' she answered.

Ali turned towards her. 'Were you here yesterday?'

'No, love, it was me day off.'

Ali couldn't help smiling. He faced the brothers. 'Not your best witness,' he said. 'Is there someone else who can confirm that this is where you spent the day?'

Kamal shrugged his shoulders. 'Anyone who was here.'

'Names?'

'You're the detective.'

He walked over to Mandy. 'Do you keep records as to who comes in each day?'

'They sign in and out, yes, but I wouldn't say they were records.'

'With times?'

'Yes.'

'Have you a list of members?'

'Somewhere.'

'Right, get it for me. And I want a copy of who signed in and out yesterday.'

He walked back to Kamal and Jahangier, bouncing the white ball from hand to hand. The atmosphere was oppressive, but Ali hadn't finished.

'Have you seen your brother since it happened?'

'No, why should we?'

'Because he's your brother, and because his wife has just been killed and because he probably could do with all the support he can get just now.'

'Are you stupid or have you become so much the white man that you really don't understand?' Jahangier moved back close to Ali. 'Let me spell it out to you, white man. She wasn't one of us and our brother chose to break out of our culture, so we want nothing more to do with them — ever! We don't care that she's dead and we don't care what he's feeling. She deserves it; he deserves it. So go away and leave us alone.'

Ali looked at them with contempt. 'No one deserves what happened to her. Whatever she'd done, whatever they'd both done, she didn't deserve to have her skull caved in with a coping stone; and he didn't deserve to see her like that. And if you think she did and he did, then your lack of compassion says that you're the ones letting the culture down.'

'Get lost, copper. Just fuck off.'

Ali smiled. 'I've finished for the moment, but I'll see you again. No doubt this is where I'll find you, since you spend all day here. I assume neither of you have a job.'

Jahangier gave a derisory laugh. 'What planet do you live on? Pakis don't get jobs, not in this country — unless they're pigs of course,' he added with venom.

Ali didn't rise to the bait. 'I shall want a proper statement. At the station, tomorrow morning, half past eleven.' He dropped the cue ball onto the table. 'Enjoy your game,' he said and, turning his back on them, went first to Mandy, who handed him the lists, and then out of the hall.

★   ★   ★

Amajit carefully carried the two mugs of coffee into the sitting room. He handed one to Karen who was on the floor playing with Danny. Not knowing what to expect or how long she was likely to stay, she hadn't thought to bring any toys with her. Amajit had said he would check if Rukhsana had anything in the boxes she always carried with her, but Karen hadn't wanted him any more distressed than he already was and had told him that Danny would be happy with anything that he could push around. They had finally found an empty cardboard box and a few small tins from the pantry, and he had played quite happily with them. And as they watched over him they talked about Rukhsana, about Amajit, about their marriage and life together, but mainly about Rukhsana. Then, when he could talk no more, Amajit had gone to make a coffee.

'Thank you,' said Karen as she took the mug from him and sipped at the hot liquid. It was more bitter than she was used to, but she drank it anyway.

They sat in silence for a moment. Then Amajit said, 'I'm sorry.'

'What for?'

'For . . . earlier. I just couldn't help it.'

'Don't be daft.'

'You're the first person to care.'

'No, that can't be right, everybody liked Rukhsana.'

'Not everybody.'

'Well, everybody I know who knows her likes her.'

Amajit smiled at her naivety. She looked so young, and yet she had a child of two. A single mother, no husband — he ought to abhor what she had done, what his family would have said she was. But he couldn't. She was kind, she cared, and she had come in the rain to tell him of her sorrow. His own family hadn't done that. Nor would they.

'What?'

Amajit realised he was staring at her. 'I'm sorry. I didn't mean to stare. I was just thinking . . . '

'Thinking what?'

'How considerate you are — to come all this way, with a baby, in this weather.'

'Not really. I just wanted to let you know I was sorry about what had happened. The policemen told me to wait a few days, that they had lots of questions to ask you. But it wouldn't have been the same.' She paused for a moment and then said, 'Do they think you did it — kill her, I mean?'

'Do you?'

'No, of course not.'

'I don't know whether they do or not. I expect I'm on their list of suspects. But they haven't said so in so many words.'

Danny, who was pushing the box around the room, got it caught against a chair leg and began to shout. Karen moved over to him to dislodge it.

'Rukhsana was pregnant, you know. Twelve weeks.'

Karen put her hand up to her mouth. 'That's awful. Well, not awful but . . . in the circumstances. She never said.'

'No, she didn't. She didn't tell anyone. I didn't know until the police told me. They found out at the postmortem.'

'That's awful,' Karen said again. 'Finding out that way, I mean.'

'I don't think the police believe that I didn't know.'

'She used to talk about having a baby sometime — when the time is right, that's what she used to say.'

'Yes, we wanted to move from this house before we had a baby.'

Karen looked round the room. Bright and clean, the wall lights reflected off the cream paintwork. The sage-green suite, lightly patterned with browns and beiges, contrasted with the darker carpet and curtains. 'Why should you want to move?' she said. 'It's a lovely house.'

'We'd have liked one somewhere else, a bit bigger, with a garden for the children to play in.'

'I've got a garden. But the house is a dump, the estate is a dump. I don't think I'll ever let Danny play in my garden, people throw all sorts over the wall: needles, used condoms, even dead animals. A garden doesn't make everything all right, you know. It's the people around you and the people inside the house that make things all right, and it's what's inside the people that really decides whether things are all right or not.'

Amajit looked at the girl sitting cross-legged on the floor, expressing the obvious with such simplicity, and wondered at her insight. She knew about life, her eyes said so. He turned to Danny, who regarded him with curiosity but was unconcerned about him because he was safe with his mother. His eyes were filled with innocence, trust, total belief in the adults around him. But not Karen's. Her eyes revealed her perceptions; eyes of experience, eyes that shrouded secrets and bad memories. The trust that showed in Danny's eyes, that she too had probably known as a child, was gone, replaced by a bleakness that spoke of unhappiness, damage, bruising. Rukhsana often talked about the messages eyes held, if you only wanted to read them.

'You're doing it again.'

'What?'

'Staring at me.'

'I'm sorry,' he said. 'I was thinking about Rukhsana.'

Only half a lie. A half lie that should have been the whole truth. For those few moments Rukhsana had not occupied his thoughts, she had entered later. Ashamed, he looked away. Grief, interlaced now with guilt, hung in the air, so tangible that he could have grasped it, held it close to him, forced it back into his mind and his heart, so that Rukhsana's presence would not be allowed to escape him again.

The silence was broken by the chimes of the carriage clock signalling the hour. Danny giggled at the sound and pointed a small finger in its direction.

'God, is that the time. I'm sorry Amajit, I shall have to go. Danny will want his tea.' She got up and walked over to the window. The curtains were open and she looked out into the November evening. It was dark, very dark, but in the headlights of passing cars she could see the rain falling, heavier now.

'Come on, Danny,' she said and picked him up. 'The buses will be packed, it'll be better to walk.'

Amajit roused himself. 'No, I'll run you

118

home.' It was the least he could do.

Karen glanced out of the window again. 'Are you sure? It would be nice.'

She began to gather together the box and the tins which Danny had been playing with and Amajit bent down next to her to help. 'I'll do this, you get Danny ready.'

While he was tidying up, Amajit watched her coax Danny away from his makeshift toys, and then dress him, patient, not minding that he wriggled, that he wanted to get down to carry on playing.

'Karen,' he said hesitantly, unsure how to put his request into words, wondering if it was appropriate to ask and how she would take it if he did.

'Yes?' She looked up at him, and then away as she struggled to get Danny's arm through the sleeve of his anorak.

'Will you . . . will you come back here . . . tomorrow?'

6

Had Sergeant Khalid Ali not been hunched against the November weather, eyes down, collar up, as he walked back along the dank street to the city centre, he would have noticed, parked opposite Battle's, a brand-new Porsche, retailing at a large five-figure sum, and a man in the driver's seat. Had he not been so intent on getting away from the covert violence of the snooker hall, from the towering buildings with their murky, urine-soaked doorways, menacing in the fading light, and from the sad, crabby women who continued to offer him a good time, and back to the orange brightness of the city, Sergeant Ali might have recognised the driver and marvelled that the restaurant business was so lucrative that it furnished the owners with such expensive luxuries. But then, being a detective with the cynicism that goes with the job, he would have questioned what Faysal Hussain was doing in a vehicle like that in this sort of neighbourhood and it wouldn't have taken him long to work out that Hussain was probably not only in the restaurant business, but was providing for other tastes as well, and that that was far more lucrative.

As Ali returned to his protected and protective patch of ground, Faysal Hussain remained where he was, warm and comfortable in the plush cream leather seat, listening to Bangra music on his CD player and mouthing the lyrics which described all policemen as ignorant, underdeveloped morons. As he watched the sergeant, he felt the strength of his own invincibility and of his special relationship with fate, which never put him in the wrong place at the wrong time. Had he arrived at Battle's a few minutes earlier, for instance, he would surely have bumped into Ali.

When the detective had disappeared into the obscurity of the afternoon, Faysal stepped out of the Porsche and walked towards the hall, half turning to press the electronic key fob to lock the doors.

The gloom of the snooker hall matched the gloom of the street and his eyes were able to penetrate the smoky haze. Glancing round, he made out the familiar silhouettes of his cousins and watched them as they argued vehemently with each other. He didn't have a very high opinion of the two men — thought them weak, pathetic even. Of the two, Jahangier was the most sensible, the most cunning, but so close were they in age, they came as a pair, and on the whole the elder kept the younger in check. Had they not been family Faysal would have had little to do with them, but they were family and because they would do whatever he asked, generally without question or comment, they were useful to him. That they looked up to him, he didn't doubt — he had done something with his life, was a respected businessman within and outside the community, he had money and the things that money could buy. They particularly respected his extra-restaurant activities and the way he conducted them under the noses of the police without a whisper of suspicion.

Faysal walked over to Jahangier and shook his hand. 'What did the copper want?'

'To know if we killed Rukhsana.'

'And what did you tell him?'

'What do you think?'

That hardly answered Faysal's question, but it would do for the moment. If he knew for sure that they had killed her, he would be obliged to get them out of the country and it didn't suit his purposes to have to do that at this moment.

Kamal swaggered round the table. 'I told the pig that we could have killed her any time we wanted to and good luck to whoever did it.'

Faysal, his long, angular face set like granite, fixed his penetrating brown eyes on his younger cousin, but his words were directed to Jahangier. 'Was he born stupid, or has it come with practice?' His gaze menaced Kamal for some seconds before he turned towards the elder. 'For God's sake, Jahangier, keep him quiet. And keep him away from the cops.'

'Can't do that, Faysal, we've to go to the police station tomorrow, half past eleven, to give a statement. They're bound to split us up; and you know him, he'll say anything if he thinks it makes him look big.'

Faysal stared at Jahangier for a moment longer, the latter making no movement except to run his tongue over his lips, the only visible sign of his fear. At last Faysal dropped his eyes and turned to lean against the table, arms folded.

'Look, I've got a job for you,' he said. He

would have preferred to have given it to someone more reliable, but he didn't have any other choice if he was to keep Kamal quiet and out of the way, and make sure that family business stayed where it was meant to be, in the family, and more importantly that his own well-oiled business stayed where it was meant to be — securely in his own hands.

Jahangier grinned. 'Another rave?'

'No, not another rave. This is different and it'll mean you staying well out of the way of the cops. I can't risk him opening his big mouth.'

Jahangier's courage returned. 'It'll cost you, Faysal. I'm not working for nothing, not if it can get us into trouble with the cops.'

'I just want you to keep an eye on Amajit — without him knowing.'

'Why? He can't do nothing to us.' Jahangier lit a cigarette and drew hard on it. Slowly he blew out the smoke.

Faysal wafted the fumes away from his face. 'For God's sake, do you have to?' He stared hard at Jahangier, until he felt obliged to stub out at least four-fifths of his cigarette. Leaning forward, Faysal kept his voice low. 'I don't trust Amajit; he's not one of us any more, no loyalty, not since he married her, and now that she's dead . . . At the moment he can't think who killed her, can't imagine it could be one of the family, but it won't take him long to point the finger at us, even if he can't prove it. And then he'll be talking to the police quicker than it took to do away with her. I don't want any interference in our affairs, Jahangier, and I don't want the police snooping closer to us than him. So don't let him out of your sight, see who goes to the house, who he talks to, follow him wherever he goes, and let me know.'

'I've said, it'll cost yer,' Jahangier repeated. 'I'm not doing this for nothing.'

'Don't worry, you'll be well paid and you'll have a car.'

A grin stretched across Kamal's face. 'A car? Great.'

Faysal's eyes held a mixture of contempt and loathing. 'He drives!' he snapped, pointing at Jahangier. 'You sit back and do as you're told. Got it?'

Unnerved by his cousin's tone, Kamal backed off.

'I take it we don't keep our appointment tomorrow,' said Jahangier, ignoring his brother's mortification.

'No. In fact I think it would be as well if everyone thinks you're in Pakistan. That you've gone to do a job for me there. Go home, pack a bag and pick up your passports. Tell my uncle that you'll be away for a while, you don't know how long.'

Jahangier exchanged glances with his brother. 'What about the police?'

Faysal shrugged his shoulders. 'Forget them. They'll get the same story when they ask. They can't do much about it.' He took the cue from Kamal's hand, bent over the table and sliced the black ball into the far pocket. He straightened up. 'You'll need somewhere to stay. You can have the flat above the restaurant.'

'But don't you use that for — '

'Yes, so don't get in the way and don't mess it up, and don't let anyone know you're there. Nobody! Everyone has to think you are in Pakistan, particularly Amajit.'

★　★　★

Amajit dropped Karen off outside her front gate, helped with Danny and the pushchair and waited until she was safely at the door before driving away. Although he dreaded returning to his own empty house, he had declined the cup of tea she had offered him, saying that he needed to get back, there were things he had to do. He thanked her for being there when he needed someone and said he was glad she had agreed to come over the next morning.

In spite of the sadness of the day, Karen's spirits were high. Amajit's concern that she shouldn't get wet had pleased her, as had his invitation. And she appreciated being driven in such a fine-looking car. It was only small and a few years old, but it was clean and well cared for and she had felt like a princess sitting in the back with Danny on her knee. She could see Amajit's profile as they passed under the street lights, and she'd been able to make out his hair, curling slightly at the ends, neatly shaped to the nape of his neck, and below that the darkness of his flesh shading into the paler shadow of his shirt collar which protruded above the clean knife edge of his jacket. He hadn't said much, but when he did speak his voice was soft, a strange mixture of accents, the Asian lilt and a trace of Yorkshire, both tempered by three years at university. The memory of his tears and her holding him while he wept made her want to touch him again, transfuse him with her strength. She had felt a shiver run through her body and it had added to her feeling of well-being. No one in her family had ever owned a car, and although Barry could drive, he always used his friend's, and that only occasionally. The shabby old green Volkswagen Beetle had seen better days, the rust along the door edges was gradually creeping up the body, and the boot cover, damaged in an argument with a motorbike, had been replaced by a bright orange one from a breaker's yard, which they hadn't bothered to match up to the rest of the paintwork. Karen hated to see it parked outside her house even for a short time, as it had been yesterday. It wasn't easy to lower the tone of the area any further, but as far as she was concerned that Volkswagen managed it.

As she walked up the path to her house, Karen saw the front room curtains were drawn, the window an opalescent square in the misty darkness. Icicles formed in her stomach. Barry. Trust him to spoil things. This morning he'd tried to hit her, called her a fucking bitch, yet here he was, back again, the arrogant, moronic sod that he was. He wouldn't have come to apologise, that much she knew. You didn't apologise when you believed everything you did was right, whatever it was, and he'd always had an inflated belief in his own righteousness.

He was sprawled on the settee watching

126

television and didn't move when she looked in at the sitting room door.

'What you doing here?' she snapped.

'Watching television, what does it look like I'm doing?'

Karen glanced towards the screen. 'But that's the news. What you doing watching the news?'

Her derisory tone was lost on Barry. 'It's local news,' he said.

'So?'

'There'll be last night's match on. I wanted to see the highlights.'

Karen disappeared into the hall to take off Danny's coat.

'What's wrong with your own television?' she muttered, low enough for him not to hear.

'What you doing coming home in a taxi?' Barry's voice floated through to her.

'I didn't.'

'Then what was that car?'

She didn't answer, but came back into the room, carrying Danny. Putting the child onto the floor, she turned to Barry. 'Make yourself useful and watch him,' she said, 'while I sort out his tea.'

Without taking his eyes off the flickering screen, he retorted, 'What do you think I am, a flaming nursemaid?'

The newsreader, who had been smiling a few moments before, became serious as he turned to face an adjacent camera. 'A fullscale murder hunt has begun after the body of Mrs Rukhsana Mahmood was found in woods near her home yesterday.'

Karen stopped and looked at the television. She moved back into the room and perched on the arm of the settee.

'The twenty-seven year old health visitor had been beaten around the head with a heavy object,' the newsreader continued. 'Her body was identified this morning by her husband, Amajit Mahmood, a planning officer with the local authority.' A picture of Rukhsana appeared on the screen, followed by images of the woods where she was found and of the nursing home, and then of the scrum outside Amajit's house on his return from the mortuary. 'Detective Inspector John Handford, leading the investigation, declined to speak to journalists when he arrived at Mr Mahmood's home this morning,' and there were pictures of the backs of the inspector and another detective as they disappeared into the house. Finally the camera cut to an exterior shot of the Central Police Station where, in a few moments, the newsreader said, they would be joining their reporter at the police press conference. In the meantime they would take a short break. The programme's jingle sounded and the man's face faded into the TV company's logo.

Barry leaned back into the settee. He fiddled with the controls, muting the sound as he did so.

'Poor Rukhsana,' Karen murmured, sadness furrowing her brow.

Sharply, Barry looked up at her. 'Poor nothing. Good riddance, more like. They can get rid of 'em one by one for all I care, or better still put 'em all on a plane back to where they came from.'

'Give up, Barry. Rukhsana was nice. She didn't think I was a waste of time just because I'm on my own with a baby.'

'Nosy bitch. There's none of them no good.'

'Yes they are. She was. I'm sorry she's dead. It was a horrible way for her to die. She didn't deserve it, no one does.'

'No? Paki tart. That's all any of 'em's good for.'

'You racist pig! You don't know what you're talking about. She was no different from us, not underneath. It doesn't matter what colour her skin was, she's still dead. I'd be just as dead if the same thing happened to me.'

'Well, at least it's put a stop to her nosing in our business.'

'She never did. She just cared. Me and Danny were the people she was interested in and she wanted to help.'

'Yeah, to see how much information she could get out of you. I know what they're like, no different from probation officers and social workers, prying into what doesn't concern them.'

'What would you know about what she did?'

'Enough to tell that doctor to get rid of her, to tell him that we didn't want 'er in this house any more,' he declared.

Karen stared at her brother. 'What? When? You'd no right. When did you do this, Barry?'

Barry snorted but didn't reply. He leaned forward and increased the volume as the TV screen filled with the picture of a room inside the

Central Police Station.

The camera closed in on the three officers seated at a table. The smaller of the three was speaking; his name, Detective Chief Inspector Stephen Russell, appeared across the bottom of the screen.

'. . . that the Broughton station has assigned Sergeant Khalid Ali to us and I am sure that his presence will be welcomed by the Asian community.' The camera cut to the Asian detective who tried to appear solemn, but succeeded only in looking embarrassed.

'Trust them to get a bleeding Paki in,' Barry scoffed.

'Shhhh.'

'Any suspects yet, Inspector Handford?' demanded one reporter of the other white police officer.

'Not as yet, but we believe she may have known her killer.'

'Any motive?'

'We're following up various leads, but as yet we don't have a specific motive for Mrs Mahmood's murder.'

'Could it be racial?'

'There are no indications at the moment that her death was racially motivated, but we don't rule anything out.'

'Was she sexually assaulted?'

'We shan't know that until we have the results of the postmortem.'

Another reporter stood up. 'Inspector Handford. The last time an Asian girl was murdered feelings ran very high within the community. Are you concerned that this might happen again? I'm referring to the murder of Jamilla Aziz, sir, and the subsequent riots.'

'I know very well what you're referring to,' Handford said. He sounded tetchy, Karen thought, and his expression had hardened. 'And I think I told you this morning, Mr Redmayne, in answer to the same question, that I see no reason for there to be any problems, except those you would expect in any murder inquiry. So the answer to your question is no, I'm not expecting trouble. Indeed, ladies and gentlemen, rather than concentrating on difficulties that might or might not arise, I would like to ask members of the public to help us by coming forward if they saw Mrs Mahmood after eleven forty-five yesterday morning. We don't yet know why she was in the woods and would like help in tracing her movements from her leaving her last patient in Saxton Avenue to her arrival at the nursing home to visit her aunt, and particularly after she left her aunt at about twelve thirty until she met her death somewhere between then and two p.m.'

The camera cut back to the senior officer. 'This was a particularly barbaric killing,' he said. 'And I do not use the term barbaric lightly. Mrs Mahmood was brutally beaten around the head and had tried in vain to defend herself. The killer is a dangerous man. If anyone has any suspicions at all as to his identity or indeed if there is any information you have, however insignificant it seems, please contact the incident room at the Central Police Station. We promise you complete confidentiality. Thank you for your time.' A contact number was flashed up at the bottom of the screen as he was speaking.

The picture faded as the three detectives rose from their seats.

'I don't know why they're going to all that trouble for a Paki.' Barry slumped back, grabbed the packet from the arm of the settee and flicked out a cigarette. Gripping it between his teeth, he held the orange and blue flame of his lighter against the end until it glowed, then snapped the lighter shut, inhaled hard and slowly released a series of smoke rings towards the ceiling.

Karen continued to stare at the screen, hardly noticing the reporter introduce the next item or the pictures of a mud-caked footballer sliding along a saturated pitch in the hope of getting a touch of the slimy, slow-moving ball. 'They think Amajit did it,' she said.

'Did what?'

'Killed Rukhsana.'

'How do you know?'

In the split second it took her to assimilate his words, Karen roused from her thoughts and almost simultaneously froze; it would have been better to keep her mouth shut, not to bring Amajit's name into it. Given her brother's violent prejudice against Pakistanis, she had never mentioned her growing friendship with Rukhsana or that she had been to her house at Eid. And it had not been her intention to disclose today's visit. So she remained silent and prayed to God that his suspicions would lie dormant.

But suspicion was part of Barry's nature and since he had come out of prison he had regularly proved himself adept at adding two and two to make five. This time, however, his calculations were more accurate and as realisation dawned, the skin tightened around his eyes. For a moment he stared at her intently, anger flooding his face, washing into his eyes, a red flush bruising his neck and cheeks. Slowly he pulled on his cigarette, savouring the smoke, allowing it to pace his aggression as he would an orgasm, until it engulfed him. Not taking his eyes off Karen, he removed the cigarette from his mouth. She watched as he pinched hard on the lighted end, propelling specks of burning tobacco onto the settee as he crushed it between his first finger and his thumb. Finally he flicked it into the hearth.

She attempted to limit the damage. 'I . . . I just assumed; I mean they usually suspect families, don't they?'

Barry remained perfectly still, his expression a mixture of mockery and contempt.

Sliding her gaze away from his, she said, 'I've got to get Danny's tea,' and made to stand up. Instantaneously, like a serpent capturing its prey, Barry's hand shot out to grab her by the wrist.

'How do you know?' The words were paced, controlled, brutal.

She tried to wrestle free, but his grip was too strong. If she told him the truth he would lash out at her, hit her, not stopping until either his strength or his anger had evaporated. If he thought she was lying he would do the same.

133

She'd seen it, experienced it all before. Her insides coiled and recoiled and when she spoke, her voice wavered precariously on the edge of her breath. 'I don't know, Barry.' She tried to prise his fingers from her arm, but he pushed them deeper, harder into her flesh, until they threatened to burrow into her bones. Then he pulled, twisting her round until she was on her knees below him.

'That was him, wasn't it? That was his car. You've been to his house — you've been to that Paki's house.'

Karen's head sank down onto the carpet, one arm still held. 'Barry, please. Please don't. You're hurting me.' She was crying now, fear and pain mingling with the tears and the mucus streaming from her eyes, nose and mouth.

He pulled again on her arm. 'You've been to that Paki's house, haven't you?' he brayed, digging his nails deeper into her flesh as he enunciated each word. The smell of cigarette on his breath and the sweat from his unwashed body made her want to heave, spew it all out, be free of it.

'Yes,' she screamed. 'Yes, yes, yes.'

He straightened up, lifting her off the floor until she was standing unsteadily in front of him, then he let go of her arm and hit her hard across the face. Karen staggered, her feet tripping over Danny still playing on the rug. She slid sideways and fell, hitting her head against the corner of the mantelpiece, and then again as she dropped onto the cold of the hearth. Danny cried out, frightened and hurt where her feet had caught him. Hearing his cry, she tried to pull herself up, teetering on the edge of unconsciousness.

The last words she heard before she passed out were Barry's. 'You bitch, you don't go to that house again. Do you hear me? You go nowhere near that Paki.'

★ ★ ★

As the press conference ended, John Handford caught sight of Peter Redmayne moving in his direction through the ruck of journalists. Heaven preserve him from self-appointed, moralistic newspapermen. One more comment about the Pakistani riot and he wouldn't be responsible for his actions. He glanced to one side to see if he could make his escape, but Ali was surrounded by journalists who were blocking the way through to the left, and at the other side the cameramen were packing up their equipment. He sighed.

'Inspector Handford.'

He attempted what he hoped was an obliging smile. 'Mr Redmayne. How can I help you now?'

'Just a point of information, Inspector. Faysal Hussain. Is he a relative of Amajit Mahmood?'

'Cousin.'

'Have you met him, Inspector?'

'Briefly, this morning. Why?'

'I might have some information for you.'

That's got to be a first, thought Handford, Redmayne giving me information. Usually it was the other way round. As crime reporter on the local paper, the man was constantly on the phone demanding confirmation of one story or another.

'What information?'

'Not here. I need to get back to the office, get my copy in, and I can see your DCI coming in this direction. I'll be in the Globe from about seven. See you there.' And he pushed his way through the crowd around Ali and walked out of the room.

'John.' Russell stood at his side.

'Sir?'

'Went very well, don't you think?'

'Extremely well, sir.' Handford forced a second smile in as many minutes.

'Sticky question about last year, but I thought you handled it well.'

Another first. 'Thank you, sir.'

'What did Redmayne want?'

'I'm not sure. He asked me if I knew Faysal Hussain, Mahmood's cousin, and then said he might have some information for me. I'm meeting him in the Globe at seven.'

'Well, make sure he's the one giving out the information and not you. He's a good journalist, clings like a ferret. Can't think why he's still working for a local newspaper.' He bent down to pick up his document case. 'Natasha's invited a few friends over for the evening so I'm going home now. You can get me there if anything important crops up. Otherwise, see you tomorrow.'

Only Russell would have a wife with a name like Natasha. Probably brought a small fortune into the marriage, maybe even an Honourable.

Having a few friends over for the evening — the Assistant Chief Constable? The Lord Lieutenant?

Handford glanced at his watch. It was nearly half past six; he would check what, if anything, was coming into the incident room before he went to meet Redmayne. Russell was right, Redmayne was a good journalist, didn't stop until he had what he wanted. So whatever he had on Hussain must be worth having.

Handford hadn't thought much about Faysal Hussain, except as Amajit's cousin; perhaps now was the time to start. An invisible hand clutched at his stomach. This was becoming more and more a family affair.

With a sigh he picked up his papers from the table and looked round for Ali who was over the other side of the room, in earnest conversation with his mobile phone. Handford walked over and waited for him to finish. 'Anything?' he said.

'No, sir. Nothing important.' Ali seemed on edge and struggled clumsily to replace his phone in his pocket.

'Right,' Handford said dubiously. 'Did you see the brothers?'

'Yes, sir. They were at Battle's, one of the snooker halls just off the centre. A nasty pair, and there's no doubt they hated Rukhsana.'

'Enough to have killed her?'

'Oh, yes. Although to be honest they're all talk and no action, at least, Kamal is; Jahangier is a bit more circumspect.'

'Alibis.'

'They said they were at Battle's all day. I've

got the records such as they are, but I wouldn't put much faith in them. I'll check some more tomorrow. I've told them to come into the station at eleven thirty to make a statement. We might get more from them separate than together.'

'Leave it until tomorrow then,' Handford said. 'I'm going back up to the incident room now, then I'm meeting that journalist, Redmayne. Says he has some information for me on Mahmood's cousin. Have you thought any more about him since this morning?'

'I haven't come up with anything new. He's arrogant, angry, against the marriage, but not against Amajit. Didn't want our interference, or what he saw as our interference.'

'Do we know anything at all about him?'

'Not a lot, except that he's successful. He owns the big curry house in the city centre. It's quite good actually, I've eaten there a few times. I think maybe he has others dotted up and down the district. From what I hear he's well thought of within the community. Do you want me to have him checked out properly?'

'Yes, it wouldn't do any harm. Quietly and carefully, mind. If anything vital comes out of my meeting with Redmayne, I'll give you a ring at home, otherwise I'll see you tomorrow. Then we'll talk to Hussain.'

'Sir!' DS Clayton stood at Handford's shoulder. 'I've had a call from the pathologist's secretary. The preliminary postmortem report is ready. She said she'd send it over tomorrow in the internal mail, but I suggested that Khalid picks it up on his way in.' She looked at her fellow sergeant. 'You don't mind, do you?'

'No, of course not, it's on my way.' He turned to Handford. 'Well, if that's all, sir, I'll see you tomorrow.'

'Fine, Khalid, goodnight.'

Clayton got into step with her boss as they walked together up to the incident room.

'Anything from the press conference yet?' Handford asked.

'Quite a bit. But you know what it's like, most of it from cranks who say they killed her and people who think they've seen her anywhere but where she was — Sheffield's the furthest away so far, I think.'

Handford smiled. 'That figures.'

'There was one though, sir. A woman who had been up to the nursing home said that she saw Rukhsana in the car park at about one o'clock arguing with a man. She was taking photographs for a new brochure they're producing, although I can't imagine why they would want pictures of the home in November.'

'Did she know who the man was?'

She checked her notebook. 'Yes, sir. She's pretty sure it was Dr Berridge.'

7

Slowly Karen came to, a vortex of mist whirling in her brain. Behind her closed eyelids a haze of minute glow-worms shimmered in the darkness. She tried to raise herself, but the movement sent her swirling and she lay back, closing her eyes again. With her fingertips she explored the area where her head hurt the worst. The skin seemed to be pulling tight over the right cheekbone and as she felt above and around the eye, her fingers indented the flesh, forcing aside the cushion of fluid.

After several moments she trawled her memory for any recollection of what had happened. Rukhsana's smiling face came to her through the haze, then Amajit's and finally Barry's. His eyes narrowed as he came into close-up, and she registered the gleam of hatred and felt the sting of the back of his hand striking the side of her face, the blow sending her reeling against the fireplace.

She was on the settee, a cushion beneath her head and a duvet cover over her. The light was off, but the room was not completely dark, for a triangle of subdued light fanned out across the carpet and up the wall opposite the door. As her other senses began to return, she caught the sound of movement from upstairs and the stale aroma of toast percolated her nostrils. She felt sick.

Her brow furrowed as she tried to establish whether it was morning or evening, for the room was dark enough to be either. From a distance she could hear Danny's cry. A recollection of trying to stay conscious long enough to get to her son slid into her memory, but she couldn't retain it. She called out his name. 'Danny!' The resonance of the word echoed inside her head, vibrating each nerve, yet rejected the sound waves which would carry it to the child.

She dragged the duvet away from her and made to swing her feet onto the floor, but the movement was enough to send the room spinning and nausea coursing through her body. For a moment she remained as she was, head down, eyes closed. A floorboard in the hallway creaked and she caught the sound of a man's voice whispering outside the door. Gingerly opening her eyes, she looked in its direction. The swatch of light expanded, and a figure stood, silhouetted in the half darkness.

'Oh, good,' he said. 'You're awake. I've fed Danny — a boiled egg and some toast. It's about all I can do, but he ate it all. And he's had 'is bath and I've brought him to say ni-night.' Barry crouched down so that the child could give his mother a kiss, but Danny only looked at her, his eyes questioning what was happening, why she was there. Then abruptly he turned towards his uncle and fastened his arms tightly round his neck.

Karen stared at her brother. 'You hit me, Barry. You knocked me out.'

Barry stood in front of her, looking for all the

world like a caring, loving uncle, a towel over his broad shoulder and Danny in his arms.

'Yes,' he said. 'You got me mad. But you're all right now and I'm going to stay with you tonight so you won't need to worry about Danny. Just stay where you are and keep warm. I'll put 'im down, get you a cup of tea and then we can watch telly.'

★   ★   ★

Handford was cheered by the heat from the log fire as soon as he walked through the lounge door at the Globe. It was a few minutes before seven and the place was practically empty, most people preferring to stay at home with cans or a bottle of wine than venture out in such weather. The rain was coming down more heavily now. There was the likelihood of a real storm before the night was over. Handford looked round appreciatively, deciding that at least Redmayne showed a reasonable taste in pubs. Usually he met police informants in less congenial places, but then most of his informants were not well-suited to a detached pub with garden in a residential area on the better side of the city. The aroma wafting through from somewhere behind the bar suggested that it also proffered a passable restaurant and menu of bar meals. For a few moments he toyed with the idea of ordering, but decided against it — Gill would not be best pleased at freezing yet another meal because he had already eaten.

When he had first become a detective, she'd

fed the girls and waited for him so that they could eat together, but that was a long time ago. Now that she was back teaching, she ate with the girls. She couldn't mark essays on an empty stomach, she said. Initially, if he was late, his went into the fridge to be warmed up later or, if he'd already eaten, into the freezer. But even that had got too much and a few weeks ago she'd complained about his thoughtlessness.

'This is the last time, John. If you can't be bothered to let me know that you've already eaten, and I have to cook and freeze yet another meal, then I shan't do it any more. You'll have to fend for yourself.'

He knew she was right. He had been thoughtless; most detectives were when they were involved in an investigation. It took over their whole lives. He was lucky his wife only complained; many took the children and left.

So, instead of ordering, he bought himself half a bitter and a packet of cheese and onion crisps.

Redmayne was late and while Handford drank his beer and ate his crisps in a booth close to the fire, he gave himself permission to relax. The deep red carpet, the dark oak furniture, the beamed ceiling carrying along its length four large, eight-spoked wheels which held, where the spokes met the rim, small candle-shaped light bulbs and their shades, and the roaring log fire gave the lounge bar an ambience which was pleasing to Handford's tired mind. Along the walls were framed photographs of actors in various Shakespearean roles. He lingered on one of a young Lawrence Olivier as Hamlet, holding

143

up Yoric's skull, and his thoughts returned to Rukhsana and her skull, caved in by person or persons unknown. He hoped with all his heart that one of those persons was not a family member.

'Inspector.' A voice broke into his reverie. 'Sorry I'm a bit late. Took me longer than I thought to get my copy done.'

The bespectacled man standing over him was quite unlike the popular concept of an investigative journalist. In his mid to late thirties, he was slight and angular, with dark bushy hair which looked as though it hadn't seen a comb in years. Beneath the uninspiring exterior, however, Handford knew there was a brain as sharp and disciplined as any academic's. His writing was well-reasoned and literate as well as hard-hitting and persuasive.

'Not to worry, Mr Redmayne,' Handford said as he stood to greet the man. 'Can I get you a drink?'

'Please. They do real ale here, so I'll have a half of Black Sheep, if you don't mind.'

'Right.' He pulled himself out of the booth.

The barman took his order without comment and in less than a minute Handford had returned from the bar, placed the glass of amber liquid on the table and sat down. 'Quite a nice pub,' he said.

'Yes, it's my local. And I knew it would be quiet.' Redmayne took a long drink.

'Faysal Hussain, Mr Redmayne, you said you had some information.'

'Peter,' Redmayne offered, then bent down for

his briefcase. He took a spiral notebook out of it, replaced the case on the floor by his foot and flicked the notebook's pages over one by one. 'Before we begin, if anything comes of my information, I want the exclusive.'

What else? Journalists never gave anything for nothing. Handford nodded his agreement. 'If anything comes of it, I'll make sure you get the story first.'

'Right then. I'm doing a piece on performance-enhancing drugs for one of the sporting magazines, and — '

'You mean anabolic steroids?'

'Yes.'

Handford was surprised. 'I wouldn't have thought there was much call for those around here — it's not exactly the sportiest area in the country.'

'No, you're wrong that there's not much call for them around here. And it's a myth that they're used solely by sportsmen. Lots of men in the street use them; it's an easy way to look tough, to look good for the fortnight in Majorca, to pull the girls.'

'What has this to do with Hussain?'

'He supplies them. To just about every gym, snooker hall, disco, youth club, and nursery in Yorkshire — and probably beyond. They're rife in the city, in the whole district come to that. At a conservative guess, I would estimate about six, seven thousand users, some of them as young as fifteen.'

Handford groaned. What was wrong with people? Couldn't they do anything without the aid of a pill? He had drummed into Nicola and Clare the dangers of drugs, now there was another one to add to the list, even if it wasn't as dangerous as some.

'The majority have no intention of taking part in body-building or sporting competitions,' continued Redmayne. 'They just want to look good, and they think this is an easy way of doing it. They haven't a clue about the risks to their health. Kidney and liver damage, heart disease, even HIV.'

'HIV?' Handford was unable to hide his surprise.

'Yes. Users more often than not inject straight into the muscle. That means shared needles.'

'And Hussain is supplying? You're sure?'

'Oh, yes. I've seen him at it. Makes a nice living out of it, I shouldn't wonder. He sure as hell didn't get his Porsche from the profits of the restaurants.'

'And you've seen him?'

'Mainly at the flat above the restaurant. He doesn't live there, he has a house on that new private estate over the other side of the city. You know the one near the museum and the park. I haven't seen many people at his house, but he gets lots of visitors at the flat. I think they're his distributors. I've followed one of them a few times, seen him pass over the gear.'

'But you've not actually witnessed Hussain passing anything over?'

'I haven't been in the flat, if that's what you mean. I haven't actually seen him hand them over. And he doesn't distribute them round the city himself; he wouldn't want to get his hands dirty. He employs others to do that. He's the supplier, the salesman, if you like. Occasionally, he visits the various establishments, and you can take it from me he's not there to do the catering. He was at Battle's this afternoon. Your sergeant would have noticed him too if he'd been looking.'

'Sergeant Ali?'

'Yes. Hussain was in his car outside, waiting for Ali to disappear before he went in himself. Your sergeant was in too much of a hurry to get away — not that I blame him.'

Handford tried to moderate his tone, avoid showing his annoyance. 'He was on his own?'

'I think so, I didn't see anyone with him.'

Ali was obviously living up to his reputation, thought Handford grimly. He had told him quite clearly to take someone with him when he went to see the older Mahmood brothers, it was common sense to do so, yet the sergeant had ignored the instruction. Handford pulled a crisp out of the packet and popped it into his mouth. Russell had said it was up to him to make sure Ali toed the line, yet at this moment he felt as though he'd have as much chance of persuading his packet of crisps to do as it was told as Ali.

Redmayne drained the dregs of his drink and stood up. 'Same again?' he asked.

Handford handed over his glass and the newspaper man threaded his way to the bar. The pub was beginning to liven up and Redmayne exchanged pleasantries with some of the regulars. Resting against the hard back of the booth settle, Handford wondered about Faysal Hussain, wishing he had taken more notice of him while he was questioning Amajit. As Ali had said, the man clearly didn't want police involvement, and he'd assumed that it was because he didn't want them knowing the family's business. But it could have been because he didn't want them delving into his own private business. Did Amajit know what was going on? Was he part of it? Had Rukhsana learned of it somehow, perhaps through the practice where she worked, from patients suffering the side effects of the steroids, and Hussain had found out and killed her? Or even Amajit?

Redmayne returned with the drinks. He sat down. 'I followed Faysal Hussain to Hull once. He went on board one of the vessels, the . . . ' he flicked through the pages of his notebook, 'the *Belgrade*, a Croatian fishing vessel sailing under a British flag. It had come from the North Sea — officially. I don't know what he was doing, but he seemed very pally with the captain. It's my guess they had the steroids — probably fake — on board. And Hussain was buying.'

Handford looked puzzled. 'Just a minute, go back a bit. He owns a string of restaurants. He could have been in Hull because he wanted fish. Why should you think it was steroids he was after, or that they were fake?'

'Because there's a flourishing market in Europe and most of the fakes are produced in underground laboratories in Croatia, Bosnia, Czechoslovakia. It's a nice little earner for people coming out of Russia or the former Yugoslavia.

148

And Hussain always gets his fish from the wholesalers' market — Snaygills, to be precise. His vegetables come from the same market, most of his meat is halal and comes from a halal supplier, the rest from Goodwin's butchers, his spices from a Pakistani supermarket and the bread from — '

'Yes, all right, Mr Redmayne.' Handford smiled. 'You've made your point.' He considered his next question. 'Where did you get this information?'

A grin played on the journalist's lips. 'I've seen the delivery vans.' Then conscious of the look on Handford's face, he held up his hands. 'Sorry.'

'So who told you about the drugs?'

Redmayne shook his head. 'Come on, Inspector, you know better than that. I can't divulge my source.'

Handford sighed. He hadn't expected he would, but it was worth a try. 'You'd make a statement, though, if necessary?'

'Yes, if necessary. But no names except those you already know.'

Handford wasn't sure how Redmayne's information figured in Rukhsana's murder, if at all, but it wasn't wise to let anything slip by. After all, money was a powerful motive.

'OK,' he said. 'Let's suppose you're right. How much does Hussain stand to make from steroids?'

'A lot if you consider that some of the hauls made over the past year or two had street values of between thirty thousand and several million pounds.'

149

Handford whistled. Against his better judgement he was beginning to feel a real sense of
admiration for Redmayne.

'Does Hussain deal in any other substances, as
far as you know?'

'Ecstasy certainly, and again I'm willing to bet
some are fake. There's a lot about, and most kids
taking them for the first time don't know the
difference between the real and the phoney.
Amphetamines, probably. They're used a lot by
people in the catering industry — to keep the
chefs and restaurant staff awake.'

Handford glanced round at the scene in this
middle-class pub, customers talking, laughing,
drinking, eating, and wondered if any of them
knew, or cared, what might be going on in the
kitchens behind the bar, apart from the cooking.

'In fact,' Redmayne went on, 'I'm pretty sure
he can get anything if he's asked — probably got
a warehouse if it could be found.'

'Heroin, crack?'

'He'll be able to get it, but I've never seen any
evidence that he's dealing in a big way. Why
bother? It would mean muscling in on the main
suppliers' trade *and* having the police on his
back. They're not worried about steroids.
They're only a category C drug, not a priority
and hardly worth their time. Hussain is no fool.
He's into making money and he gets a very good
living from steroids, the big dealers aren't
bothered and the police don't care. He's got
status in the community. Why change anything?'

'Why indeed? Anything else?'

'I don't have the same evidence, but I'm fairly

150

sure he's into organising raves — you know, those ticket only ones. You get your ticket by ringing a phone number advertised in the paper.'

'Yours?'

'Oh, yes, I'm sure. Not that you'd know from the advert, they're usually quite innocuous.'

'Busy man. You'd think he'd have enough on his hands running restaurants.'

Redmayne drained his glass. 'Well, that's my addition to your inquiry, for what it's worth. What will you do with it?'

'Have a chat with a colleague in the Drug Squad, see if they have anything on him. Like you said, they'll probably not be too interested in him if he's not into the heavy drugs, so I shan't be straying into their patch. File it away, keep an eye on him. It could have something to do with Rukhsana Mahmood's murder, or nothing. I just wish I'd taken more notice of Hussain when we were at Mahmood's house.'

Redmayne looked surprised. 'You don't know him then?'

'No, should I?'

'I would have thought so. He was the man who organised the riots after the Jamilla Aziz murder last year.'

★   ★   ★

When Khalid Ali drove home from the station that night, a frown blighted his handsome features. He was worried and puzzled. Worried because the call he had taken after the press conference had been from Amajit Mahmood,

151

asking him to visit him the next morning, and puzzled because he didn't know why he had avoided telling Handford about it.

Amajit hadn't said exactly why he needed to see him, but if it was to do with his reaction to the marriage, then the last person who needed to know was the DI. If on the other hand it was about Amajit's family's desire for revenge or even their part in Rukhsana's death, then obviously he had to talk to him. And since a white police officer couldn't begin to understand the Muslim concept of shame and honour, who else could Amajit talk to. Indeed, wasn't that the reason he had been brought in to every investigation involving the community? So that he could talk Asian to Asian, Muslim to Muslim. That didn't need permission from the DI, that was why he was here. So he hadn't said anything.

Yet in spite of his confidence in his decision, an invisible hand grabbed his stomach and squeezed; that hadn't happened since he was at school doing something that he knew he shouldn't be but doing it anyway.

★   ★   ★

It was there again, that doom-laden sensation which had been invading his gut throughout this investigation, this time brought on by Redmayne's words. Handford tried to believe that it was the beer settling badly on his empty stomach, but he knew differently. All the doubts about his abilities and the insecurities with which

152

he had lived over the past year had returned with renewed vigour.

He drove in silence, the cassette player turned off.

The rain had stopped for the moment, but the full moon which should have given some illumination was shrouded in thunderous clouds.

The darkness seemed interminable, limitless. A car swept by, throwing up a sheet of spray, momentarily blotting out his view. The wipers rasped across the water and grit. Mud and stones had slid down the waterlogged hillsides to gather across the road and a lorry travelling in the opposite direction caught one of the pieces of granite and flipped it against the driver's door of Handford's car. The sound as it hit triggered memories of the hollow impact of stones and bricks on police shields and vehicles. Handford's knuckles were white as he gripped the steering wheel and tried to rid his mind of that terrifying riot, of the petrol bombs bursting on the ground and, behind them, the silhouetted anonymity of the youths throwing them, their faces swathed in scarves to avoid recognition.

Drops of rain began to fall against his windscreen, first gently and then heavily, streaming across the glass. Suddenly sheet lightning lit up the landscape in front of him and a few seconds later a clap of thunder rocked the car.

As it resonated through him, the images retreated, leaving only the thread of fear that would forever tie his past to his future.

★   ★   ★

Handford replaced the receiver. 'His mobile's still turned off,' he said. 'What the hell is the man playing at?'

Gill handed him a glass of whisky. 'I'm sure he'll ring eventually. His wife's bound to have given him your messages.'

He sat down next to her and took a sip of his drink. 'That's not the point, Gill. I should be able to contact him at any time, not just when he feels like it. We're on a murder inquiry, for God's sake.'

'Perhaps his battery is down.'

'Then he replaces it; he has another.' Handford sighed. 'He knows as well as I do that we have to keep in touch. He was aware I was going to see Redmayne and that the meeting had something to do with the case. He needs to know the outcome; in fact I would have thought he would have wanted to know it.'

'How important is it that this man is supplying anabolic steroids?' Gill asked.

He pushed the books his wife had been marking to one side and placed his glass in the space on the small coffee table. 'I don't know yet, it might have nothing at all to do with the investigation, but equally it might have everything to do with it. If Rukhsana knew about the anabolic steroids, perhaps through patients with side effects, and she decided to shop Hussain, he may well have silenced her. Ali needs to be aware that we at least have knowledge that could tie him in.'

'But not,' Gill ventured, 'that he instigated the riots last year.'

154

Handford glanced at her. 'That's not necessary; that was last year, it has nothing to do with now.'

She gave him a sideways look, but made no comment.

He averted his eyes, picked up his glass and took a long drink. The answer was shallow, he knew. He didn't believe it himself, for the implications of the information had curled in his brain all evening. If Hussain instigated the riots last year when he had had nothing to do with the case, then what would he be capable of when he was involved, maybe even the killer? Handford didn't want to think about it, let alone talk it over with Ali — or Gill, for that matter.

He felt the pressure bearing down on him and turned the conversation away from himself and back to Ali and the need for him to be kept up to date.

'It's not just Hussain and the steroids, Gill,' he said. 'Shortly after Ali left the press conference, Hewitt told me a witness had called to say that she had seen Rukhsana up at the nursing home just before her death, arguing with a man. He needs to know things like that; and not tomorrow, now.' Handford smiled at his wife. 'If I die in the night, he'll have to take the briefing, so he has to have everything I have.'

Gill moved closer to him and put her arm through his. 'Don't worry, darling, if you die in the night, I'll make sure he gets the message.'

Handford laid his hand on hers. 'You know,' he said thoughtfully, 'I actually believed that he and I were getting on better. He's a good

155

detective, perceptive and thoughtful and sometimes surprisingly easy to talk to.'

'Then perhaps that's what you should be
focusing on.'

'I do when we're discussing case information.
It's other things, like the issue of the Mahmood
marriage. He really hated the idea of Amajit
marrying a Sikh and it showed on his face. We all
saw it, yet when I tried to talk about it he
ignored me and changed the subject and then
this morning suggested that I was in the wrong
for doubting his professionalism.'

'And do you?'

'What, doubt his professionalism? No, I don't
think so. But I do need to know if he can handle
the cross-religion marriage. Last night it looked
as though he couldn't.'

'What has he said about it?'

'That he can.' Handford grinned. 'In no
uncertain terms, actually.'

Gill considered. 'You know what I think, John.
I think the poor man has suddenly realised that
he's not only on the receiving end of prejudice,
he's perfectly capable of feeling it too. That's why
he's so angry with you.'

Handford doubted it. 'I think he would
dispute that, Gill. I think he would say that what
Amajit did was wrong because he went against
Islam and that his own views have nothing to do
with prejudice.'

'I'm sure he would, which is why it's easier to
blame you than face up to it. You've got to talk to
him, and talk to him properly. If he's as
perceptive and thoughtful as you say, then he'll

come to his own conclusions about what he really believes. He may even be talking it over with his wife at this very moment.'

Handford shook his head. 'I doubt that very much, Gill. Ali is far too proud to let out emotions that might put him in a poor light.'

★ ★ ★

But for once Handford was wrong, for that was exactly what Khalid and Amina Ali were doing. After his evening meal he had visited his father to discuss the mixed marriage; now he was doing the same with his wife.

What he had not been able to do, indeed *would* not do, was to admit to Handford that the idea of the union had disgusted him. He had had to admit it to himself, however, and he knew that if he was to continue on the case, he had to deal with it. That was why he had gone to see his father. It disturbed him that he had been overtaken by the need to judge, that his initial concern for the victim had been flushed aside by a sudden resentment of who she was. And that the person he had suddenly found himself to be was affecting his perception of the inquiry.

Amina had stayed up to wait for him. She'd taken two calls while he had been away, both from Handford. When he had first rung she'd said that her husband was out but had his mobile with him. The second call had come within minutes to say that the mobile was switched off and would she please ask him to ring as soon as he came in.

Ali groaned when she told him this. He was tired. More than likely all the DI wanted to talk about was his meeting with the journalist; anything else and he would have left a more detailed message. It could wait until first thing in the morning.

'Are you going to ring the inspector, Khalid?' Amina asked.

He made a play of scrutinising his watch. 'No, it's late. I'll see him first thing tomorrow.'

'Then please make sure he knows that I passed on his messages. I don't want him blaming me because you're not following instructions.'

He placed his arm round her waist. 'Don't worry, Amina, I'll tell him. It's enough that he's permanently angry with me, I won't let him turn on you as well.'

She stroked his face. 'You look tired. Let me make you a coffee.'

He was dozing on the settee when Amina brought the tray in. She touched him on the shoulder. 'Do you want this, or would you rather go straight to bed?' she asked.

He sat up. 'No, I'll have it.'

Amina poured the coffee. 'How's your father?'

'He's well. As hard on me as ever, of course. Not interested in my concerns or worries. After all, he did try to persuade me to stay in the solicitor's office but I wouldn't listen. So since a career in the police force was my choice, taken against his wishes, I alone will have to suffer the consequences. You know the sort of thing.'

Amina put her cup down and turned to face

him. 'Do you want to talk it over with me instead? I promise I won't be as hard on you as your father.'

He smiled at her. 'I'd like that, Amina, although I'm not sure I'm sufficiently aware of my own feelings to discuss them rationally.'

'Try. Start with Inspector Handford. Are you getting on any better? I must say he sounded very nice on the phone.'

'I imagine he did. He can be very nice. My trouble is, I never know for how long he's going to be nice. One minute he's discussing the investigation quite reasonably, letting me have my say, the next he's chewing me up for something he imagines I have done, like putting pressure on Nathan Teale.'

'You were, though,' his wife commented candidly. 'You said as much yourself last night.'

'Perhaps I was,' Ali replied defensively. 'But the fact is he could have killed her, Amina; he's the only person we've met so far who has the strength. He needed a bit of pressure.'

Amina remained silent.

Khalid met her silence with a grin. 'All right, so I was wrong, perhaps I deserved the DI's rebuke.'

She indicated her agreement with a slight nod, but again made no comment. After a few moments she said, 'But that's not it, is it, Khalid? You've put up with being reprimanded for going your own way before; it's not that that's worrying you. This time there's more to it, and whatever it is, it's affecting your relationship with Mr Handford, as well as tearing you apart.' She

159

placed her hand on his. 'Don't keep it to yourself, Khalid, tell me.'

For a moment he fought to find the right words. 'He wants me to discuss my feelings regarding the marriage between Amajit and Rukhsana Mahmood. I can't do that because his concern is probably because he wants me off the case. Why should I give him the satisfaction? He'd never understand why I feel what I do.'

'On the first count, I think you're wrong, Khalid. That's just an excuse so that you don't have to come to terms with the fact that your beliefs can sometimes trip you up in a job that no one wanted you to take. On the second, I think he might understand. You've got to give him the benefit of the doubt at least.'

The muscles along Ali's jaw tightened, and when he spoke again, there was a bitterness in his voice that he had hoped to avoid. 'It's not the marriage itself, my thoughts on that are easy to explain. It should never have been allowed to happen. It's more — ' He stopped again, knowing that once he articulated his feelings, he would have to accept that his beliefs were affecting the way he wanted the inquiry to go, and that he might purposely push it in that direction. He wanted Amajit guilty; he wanted him punished.

He looked at Amina, and saw in her eyes the encouragement he sought.

Taking a deep breath, he said, 'It's more how I'm handling those thoughts that is so hard to explain.'

'You mean it has affected your perception of the case?'

Ali sighed. He had reached the point of no return. 'And of Amajit. As soon as he told us, I felt my compassion for him dissolve. I wanted him punished. And it obviously showed on my face, for he asked me not to judge him and afterwards and this morning the DI wanted to know if I could handle the marriage.'

'What did you say?'

'That I knew what it meant to be a police officer and that he had no right to question my judgement or my loyalty.'

Amina smiled at him. 'Oh dear,' she said.

He smiled back. 'I know. That was my arrogance showing.'

'I rather think, my dear, that that was your guilt showing. It just came out as arrogance.'

She was right, as always. He did feel guilty. 'So what do I do?'

'As far as I can see, you have two options. The first is to ask to be relieved of the case, which will mean giving reasons. You could blame Mr Handford, I suppose, but although it would be easy, it wouldn't be true, and you're too honest a man for that. That means you're left with giving the real reasons.'

'Yes. I know.'

'So face up to them, talk them over with Inspector Handford before it becomes a bigger issue between you than it already is. He knows some of it anyway, just fill him in with the rest. But you've got to talk to him and talk to him properly.'

161

Ali leaned over and kissed his wife. 'You're right of course. It seems so easy when you say it. You know, Amina, the world thinks that it is the man in the Muslim marriage that is in control, the one who makes the decisions. They're wrong. It's the woman. You're much wiser than I am, and if I'm honest, I don't know what I'd do without you. I'll do as you suggest, I'll talk to the DI tomorrow.'

★   ★   ★

Karen slept badly that night. Her head ached and the painkillers she had taken had not had much effect. The thunderstorm had done little to clear the air and the atmosphere in the room was heavy. Even though it was November, she was sweltering under the duvet and threw it off. She would have liked to get up, walk around, make herself a drink, but staying where she was kept the throbbing pain in her temples to a minimum and the nausea at bay.

The rest of the house was silent and she missed the familiar sound of Danny's breathing and occasional whimpers as he slept in his cot, since Barry had insisted that he should spend the night in his room. He had made a great ritual of dragging the cot across the landing, eager to demonstrate in physical terms his concern for his sister and to make amends for what he had done. He had said very little, not apologised or shown any remorse, and Karen knew that his actions were the nearest thing to an apology that she was likely to get. It was something that he hadn't

162

walked out on her and had stayed to look after Danny.

He had a soft spot for the child, always had had; sometimes it showed, but mostly it didn't. He wouldn't have wanted his mates to think he was a pushover where a kid was concerned — that would tarnish his image. And there were other things he wouldn't have wanted them to know. But Karen kept her counsel on those. This time he'd only hit her; if she told what she knew he would probably kill her.

★ ★ ★

Ali awoke with few bedclothes over him and the distinct feeling that he had been hit by a truck. He had had a bad night, having tossed and turned for what seemed an age, sleep evading him until the early hours. Amina had snuggled close to him like she did with the children when they were restless. It had helped, but then he had slept heavily and woken with a start as the alarm shrilled in his ear. Pain spread from the base of his skull, filling his head and hammering to get out. Analgesics hadn't helped.

A watery sun, low on the horizon, teased the blue sky. The car was sluggish in starting and he cursed himself for not having put it in the garage for the night. But eventually the engine spurted into life and he made his way through the early morning traffic to the pathologist's office to pick up the postmortem report. From there he drove across the city to where Amajit lived.

The man looked wretched and Ali hoped he

would never have to feel the kind of pain Amajit was experiencing.

'How are you?' he asked, a question to break the ice, for he did not expect an answer.

Amajit shrugged his shoulders. He led the way into the sitting room and indicated that Ali should sit down. 'Coffee?' he asked.

'No, no thanks.' Ali paused for a moment. 'Why did you want to see me?'

'I'm not sure. I . . . I just needed to talk.'

'I'm not really the right person for that. We can still appoint a liaison officer if you wish.'

Amajit ignored the suggestion. 'Do you think I did it? Killed Rukhsana?'

Ali knew he should stop right there. He should say, 'I'm sorry, I can't discuss the investigation with you.' But Amajit's tortured features prevented him. 'We don't know who killed her,' he said. 'But we have to go through a process of elimination.'

'It's often family, isn't it?' Amajit said.

'Quite often, yes.'

Amajit studied his hands, then ran them through his hair. 'Faysal thinks that it may be someone in my family.'

In spite of himself, the expression in Ali's eyes hardened. 'I expect he does.'

'You don't approve of me, Sergeant, do you?'

Ali stiffened. 'It's not my job to approve or disapprove, sir,' he said.

'Nevertheless . . . '

Neither man spoke. It was cold in the room and Ali shivered. 'Can I change my mind about that coffee?'

164

'Sure.'

While he was waiting, Ali stood up and stepped towards the mantelpiece. Rukhsana smiled at him out of a wooden frame. The clock chimed the hour. It had been a mistake to come, Amajit had nothing to tell him, he wanted a shoulder to cry on, and his was not, could not be, that shoulder.

Amajit carried two mugs carefully into the room and gave one to Ali, who returned to his seat. 'Tell me about Faysal.'

'He's my uncle's son. He will marry my eldest sister when she finishes her degree next year.'

'But he hasn't gone along with the rest of the family in disowning you?'

'He would have nothing to do with Rukhsana, but I've seen him from time to time. He doesn't approve, though he's been there for me when I needed him. We are close in age and grew up together, went to the same schools. We were hardly apart.' Amajit smiled slightly at the memory. 'My parents said that we were more like brothers than cousins. I suppose that kind of relationship is never really broken.'

'You've been lucky, then.'

'Yes.'

'You said Faysal thinks that someone in the family may have killed her. Did he say who?'

'He thinks,' Amajit hesitated, 'he thinks . . . possibly Jahangier and Kamal.'

'And do you agree?'

'They're my brothers, how can I agree?'

'They blamed Rukhsana and swore revenge, you said as much yourself.'

Amajit closed his eyes. Ali watched him, noting the desperation in his face. He tried to make it easier for Amajit.

'It isn't enough that Faysal thinks they may have done it. We need evidence, and when I spoke to them they said they had been at the snooker hall at the time she must have been killed.' Ali's stomach clenched; he was doing it again, passing on information that he shouldn't.

Amajit opened his eyes. 'So, they couldn't have?'

'Well, I have to check their alibis, but if they were where they say they were, then no, they couldn't have done it.'

'So why has Faysal sent them to Pakistan?'

Ali looked up sharply, his eyes wide. 'When?'

'Last night. He came over to see how I was and told me.'

Ali didn't need this; two possible suspects whom he had already interviewed going off to Pakistan. He could hear Warrender's comments: 'Isn't that what they always do at the first sniff of trouble, run back to Pakistan. Wouldn't be surprised if Ali didn't help them on their way.' He pushed the thought from his mind.

'Did Faysal give a reason?' he asked.

'He said he wanted a job doing and he was sending them over to do it.'

'What job?'

'He didn't say.'

'Is he in the habit of asking them to do work for him in Pakistan?'

'Occasionally, although usually only when they're going anyway, to visit relatives.'

166

'Did he say when they were going?'

'They've gone — last night.'

'And you think the real reason is because he suspects that they had something to do with Rukhsana's death?'

Amajit's face was grey with grief. 'I hope — I pray that he is wrong, but yes, I think that is what he thinks.'

★ ★ ★

Ali glanced at the clock on the dashboard. There wasn't time to check where Faysal was and talk to him, but he could go to the Mahmoods' house, find out if the brothers had indeed gone to Pakistan the previous night.

The city was well into its working day now and it took him a good half hour to manoeuvre his way through the slow-moving traffic, crawling engine to boot along the crammed streets.

Pulling up at the house, he prayed that Mr Mahmood was there and he would not have to contend with a wife who would refuse to let him over the threshold. Luck was with him, his first that day, but the information Mr Mahmood gave him was not what he wanted to hear. Yes, Kamal and Jahangier had gone to Pakistan the previous evening, yes they were helping out their cousin and no he didn't know how long they would be away. He wasn't even sure exactly where they were going, but Faysal would let the family know when they had arrived. Mr Mahmood agreed to inform Ali when he had news of them, although he

167

couldn't see the purpose of doing so.

Ali stepped out through the front door then turned back. 'It was rather sudden, Mr Mahmood. Does Faysal often expect them to fly halfway round the world at such short notice?'

'Faysal is a businessman and there are times when he has to move quickly. Sometimes he asks my sons to help out.'

'Your nephew owns restaurants in this country. What possible business can he have in Pakistan?'

'Faysal does not discuss his affairs with me. He is an ambitious and well-respected member of our community, Sergeant. It was inevitable that eventually he would take his business into Pakistan. He wishes my sons to help him.'

Ali knew little about Faysal Hussain but he was sure that he was too astute to employ the Mahmood brothers to help him set up businesses in Pakistan. Amajit, possibly, but not Kamal and Jahangier. They hadn't struck him as likely candidates to get the best deal for their cousin. No, the reason for their sudden departure was much more likely to support Amajit's fears — that they had killed their sister-in-law.

Any hopes that Ali could keep his visit from Handford were now firmly demolished. At least he couldn't be blamed for the brothers' departure, and they had the information earlier than they would have had they waited for the two men to show up at the station to make their statements. He decided to see Handford before the briefing. 'God, the briefing.' His watch gave him a quarter of an hour to get there — he could just about do it, if the lights were for him and he ignored the speed limit.

His fingers were numb with cold and it took him a moment or two to fiddle his car key into the door lock, and then into the ignition. Settling himself in his seat, he turned the key. Nothing. The engine was silent. He tried again — still nothing. Telling himself not to panic, he prayed as he tried once more, but his God was not listening and the vehicle remained comatose. Angrily, he dragged himself out of the car and walked round to the front. He lifted the bonnet, releasing the smell of warm engine oil, and scrutinised the interior. He didn't know why he had done this because the machinery meant nothing to him. He couldn't tell what was working and what wasn't. Or why it wasn't.

Slamming down the bonnet, he returned to slump down into the driver's seat. For a moment he stared into space, panic rising, then grimly, in desperation, he dragged his hands over his face. His fingernails clawed his cheeks as he accepted that he was not going to make the briefing — Handford's briefing that no one ever missed without permission.

8

In spite of his promises to Gill, Handford's pent-up anger erupted as soon as he saw the sergeant. 'Where the hell have you been?' he said, his voice as cold as the morning.

The briefing was over as Ali had expected it would be. He had hoped to slip into the station unnoticed, spirit himself into CID and spend a few minutes collecting his thoughts before he put his head into the DI's office to say that he was sorry he was late, but his car had broken down. He had rehearsed the lines on the way back in the pick-up truck so that they were matured to exactly the right tone. But, colliding with Handford in the corridor a few strides from the door of the incident room as he did, he lost the opportunity to wait in the wings and was catapulted instead straight onto centre stage.

He wanted to take his coat off. The warmth of the station compared with the temperature outside was making itself felt and he was beginning to sweat. He could feel his cheeks smarting and his fingers were tingling with the renewed flow of blood.

'My car broke down.'

'And your mobile's on the blink as well, I suppose?'

Ali's stomach lurched sickeningly. 'No, sir, I don't think so.'

'No, it's bloody well turned off, Ali, like it was last night.'

'Because I went to see my father.'

'And that's a good enough reason to turn your mobile off?'

Ali didn't answer. There was no point him trying to explain; Handford wouldn't understand.

His fingers had ceased tingling; now they were throbbing.

The corridor was throbbing too, like the city centre on a Saturday afternoon. At the far end, a uniformed constable pushed open the doors and walked towards them, murmuring, 'Excuse me, sir,' as he passed by.

Ignoring him, Handford barked, 'What the hell are you playing at, Ali? Where've you been?'

Ali looked around him. He couldn't explain here, in a brightly lit corridor, sandwiched between the clutch of offices. But Handford was waiting.

'I was on inquiries,' he said. Then, 'Perhaps we could . . . ' He was about to say 'go into your office', but was interrupted again by the doors banging open and a couple of plainclothes officers appearing in the corridor, sharing a joke.

Handford seemed not to have noticed. 'What inquiries?' He spat out his words. They were standing close and Ali could see the veins in Handford's neck pulsating above the blue striped shirt collar.

The detectives passed by, averting their eyes, their laughter silenced. Ali said nothing. He moved sideways and leaned against the wall, his hands behind his back. The coldness of the paintwork penetrated his palms and he looked down, scrutinising the toes of his shoes. He was trying to stay calm, but as he asked himself if Handford would have spoken to a white detective in this way, he began to feel arrogance taking over, like a sharp-toothed animal gnawing at his emotions.

Once more the double doors banged open, and once more Handford seemed not to notice.

'What inquiries?' he repeated.

Ali's arrogance suddenly erupted into a surge of anger and resentment. How dare Handford — anyone — speak to him like this in an open corridor? He pushed himself off the wall and began to stride away.

'Where are you going?'

'To your office.'

'Stay just where you are, Ali, and answer my question!'

'In your office.'

'Now!'

Ali stopped walking and turned to face Handford. He swallowed hard. 'No. Not until we're in your office.'

They stood for a moment, their eyes ablaze. Not inspector and sergeant any more, but enemies challenging each other across an expanse of anger, mistrust and hatred.

Ali suddenly felt the weariness of years of trying to fit into an organisation which was made for white men. What was the use? He slapped his hand at the air as though swatting at an insect, exhaled and shook his head. He moved forward towards the door of the incident room and caught hold of the handle to push it open. A telephone rang; a woman's voice shouted for a report; the photocopier buzzed; a man was humming loudly. The sounds of activity suggested indifference to what was going on outside the door, but Ali knew that the men and women behind it would have heard. He didn't need their comments and their ridicule. Handford's groupies, who would be glad to see him get what they thought he deserved. He turned abruptly and set off down the corridor.

Handford's angry voice followed him. 'Come back here, Sergeant!'

Ali walked on, ignoring the order. Driven by his fury and his frustration, pride had linked arms with arrogance and they were walking away together.

Another voice took over. 'Back here, Sergeant.' It was Russell. An icy blast blew down the corridor. Ali had never heard him shout before, never heard his cultured tones raised in anger. The sound pierced him between the shoulder blades. He stood quite still, closed his eyes momentarily, then turned. He would have preferred to keep going until he got back to Broughton, but knew that if he did he would arrive there in uniform, changing as he went, and before nightfall he would be a PC back on the beat. He didn't want that, he wanted to stay where he was, be a detective, be accepted as one of them. And in the back of his mind he could hear Warrender's snide comments and see the look of derision on his face. Suddenly the pride and the arrogance of a moment ago died like flies in a haze of insecticide. He swallowed hard and walked towards the DCI, his heart hammering in his chest.

'Wait in Inspector Handford's office, Sergeant.' The tone of Russell's voice was enough to freeze the entrails of the most hardened of coppers. The image of a teacher Ali had had at school loomed in front of him. She had been small, slight, and ought to have been a pushover; but one word from her, even one as innocuous as his name, was enough to keep his head down for the rest of the day. He wouldn't have dared disobey her. He didn't dare disobey Russell.

'Sir.' He kept his eyes off the senior officer and away from Handford. As he opened the door, he heard Russell say, 'My office, now, Inspector.'

★   ★   ★

The word 'now', said with such force, registered with Handford. Ali was not the only one in trouble. 'Now' meant a carpeting. Handford followed the DCI into his room, knotting his tie as he went, not sure that he was prepared to be told off by someone who was in short trousers when he was at university.

But the choice wasn't his and at a nod from his boss he closed the door. The aroma of ground coffee beans caught at his nostrils and his mouth watered.

Russell turned on him. 'Don't ever do that again.'

Handford kept his eyes on the DCI's tie. It

was an elegant tie, patterned with tessellating cubes in pale lemon, grey and black and he had an irrational urge to ask him where he had bought it.

'You are an inspector, a rank with responsibility.' Russell's tone was icy and his words paced and uncompromising. 'You're supposed to have some sense of what is acceptable and what isn't. What on earth got into you?'

'Ali . . . ' Handford's voice came out as a high-pitched note and he cleared his throat. 'Ali was late; he missed the briefing. I just lost it when he sauntered in as though he couldn't give a toss. And when I asked him where he'd been, he dug his heels in and wouldn't tell me.' He lifted his gaze away from the tie to focus on Russell's face. 'I know,' he said, holding up his hands in capitulation. 'I should have waited, had it out with him in my office. I'm sorry, sir,' he ended lamely.

The DCI's eyes bored into him. 'At the very least, Inspector, I expect you to have some control over your temper.'

'Yes.'

'Or is it that you're incapable of rational behaviour where Ali is concerned? I thought you could work with him. I asked you, if you remember, and you said you could.'

'I can, sir.'

'No, John, not can, will. And amicably. Do you understand?'

'Yes, sir.'

Russell moved to the chair behind his desk and sat down. 'I've got community leaders on my back demanding to know whether there is to be an arrest. Am I to tell them that there is never likely to be one because the two senior officers on the case can't see eye to eye?'

'No, sir, of course not.'

'You're sure of that, are you?' Russell spoke quietly, his voice treading a knife edge. 'Because, given that one of the officers is an Asian, they'd be shouting racism before I'd finished speaking, don't you think?'

'Probably.'

'And it would be your blood they'd be baying for. And don't be under any illusions, Inspector, it will be your blood they will get. I don't care what Ali has done, you sort it, and do it now. Because if you don't, you'll be off the inquiry and I'll put someone else in.' He leaned forward. 'Do I make myself clear?'

'Yes, sir.'

'Right.' Russell indicated that Handford should take the chair opposite him. 'So why did we have to put up with that exhibition?'

The smell of coffee was becoming overpowering. It was too much to expect that Russell would offer him a cup.

'I have no idea where Ali was this morning or what he was doing,' he said. 'He wasn't at the briefing, in fact he's been nowhere near the office until a few moments ago.'

'Does he have an explanation?'

'His car has broken down, he says.'

'Perhaps it has; it happens.'

'So why didn't he ring in to let us know? His wife said he left at eight. It was after eleven when he got here. He could have walked it twice in that time. We tried to contact him but his mobile was off and he ignored his pager.' Handford was warming to his argument. 'The same happened last night; I couldn't get in touch with him then either. I wanted to talk to him after I left Redmayne. He wasn't at home, I couldn't contact him on his mobile, so I left messages with his wife for him to ring me but he made no attempt to get back in touch — I waited up for long enough. For God's sake, Stephen, we're investigating a murder, I'd hardly be likely to be wanting him for a chat. I think I've good reason to be angry, don't you?'

Russell let out a sigh. 'Yes, John, I do,' he said. 'You're right, it's not what we expect from a sergeant. Send him through and I'll speak to him; blow him out of the water for you. Then you can find out what's been going on.' Russell leaned forward, senior officer once again. He looked at Handford, his eyes critical. 'And at the same time, Inspector, you can sort out your relationship with him. I am *not* having him taken off the case. If you can't sort it, then *you* go, not him. Do you understand me?'

'Yes, sir. I do.'

* * *

Handford sighed. There were times when he felt his age, and this was one of them. The aroma of coffee beans and his threadbare nerves had put him in need of caffeine and he made a detour to the drinks machine on his way back to his office.

Something stronger would have been better, but he didn't dare, not with Russell's views on drinking during office hours. Wearily, he walked back into his room, carrying the white polystyrene cup containing the muddy liquid that the machine described as coffee with milk, no sugar.

As he pushed open the door, he caught sight of Ali staring out of the window. The grey domes of the buildings on the other side of the carriageway loomed large against the blue of the wintry sky, and over to the west, dark rainclouds were gathering.

'It's your turn now,' he said, 'but come back here when you've seen him.' Without a word, the sergeant left. Handford put his cup down and shook drops of coffee from his thumb and wrist.

Ali's coat was draped over a chair. He took it and hung it next to his own, then sat down behind his desk. He pulled out the bottom drawer to rest his feet on and leaned back in his seat, arms clasped behind his head, staring at the ceiling. *Do I make myself clear, Inspector? Oh yes, sir, perfectly clear! So bloody clear you're transparent, sir.*

Stephen Russell was covering his own back; a sniff of discrimination and the DCI would make sure it was someone else's career that went down the pan, not his. Handford's argument with Ali was nothing to do with race; it was to do with the man's attitude, his apparent unwillingness to be one of the team.

I don't care what Ali has done. I'm not having him taken off the case. If you can't sort it, then you go, not him.

Handford closed his eyes and dragged both hands over his face, his fingers clawing at his features as he tried to blot out Russell, his words and his coffee-scented office. But the best he could manage was to replace them with the vision of himself and Ali together in the corridor — him raging, the sergeant seemingly calm. His intellect fought to rationalise the scenario but as he watched the re-run, his resentment against the DCI disintegrated. The bloody man was right. Without a doubt the events in the corridor had been his fault and no one else's. What had he been thinking of? How had he let it happen? Why had he reacted so emotionally? Why did Ali make him lose all sense of reason?

He'd let Ali annoy him right from the start, and once he'd started on that road of mistrust, he'd been unable to get off it. Last year he'd had a raw deal from the Asian community and he was still angry with them. Was he blaming Ali for that, using him as a punch bag because it was the first chance he'd had to get his own back? Was he taking his anger out on him because of his race? Or because the sergeant had been brought in as a result of Jamilla Aziz? He didn't know. He wasn't keen on either explanation. But what he did know, deep down, was that Russell was right; he shouldn't have bawled the sergeant out in an open corridor with people passing.

He sighed and dragged his feet off the drawer, swivelling his chair to sit square to his desk. His sense of remorse was all very fine, but it didn't help him solve the immediate problem. He was Ali's boss and he still had to concern himself

179

with Ali's attitude. In the short time they'd been working together, he seemed to have disregarded every instruction he'd been given. He'd even gone alone to interview the brothers. That was something else Ali was going to have to explain, Handford thought grimly.

He had warned Russell what the man was like when he brought him in from Broughton, but community relations had been more important than the dead girl and so Ali was on the team — as his sergeant. Now *that* had a lot to do with race, because the reality was that truth became invisible when only the perception mattered, and sadly it was the community's perceptions that mattered right now. And if he didn't come to some kind of workable truce with Ali, unfair as it was, it would be him off the case, not the sergeant.

He picked up the postmortem report which had been left on his desk and began to read.

'The victim died from a series of blows to the left side of the face and head. There were multiple fractures of the skull and severe damage to the brain. The frontal, zygomatic, sphenoid and temporal bones . . . '

Some ten minutes later he was still trying to get past the first paragraph when Ali knocked on the door. Handford put down the papers, picked up his now cold coffee and called, 'Come in.'

Had he not used up all his pity on himself, Handford would have felt sorry for the sergeant. His face was ashen, his features strained. There was little doubt that Russell had 'blown him out of the water', as he had put it.

180

'I think you'd better sit down, before you fall,' he said.

Gratefully, Ali pulled up a chair and slumped into it.

'We've both been given a hard time by the DCI this morning; I certainly was, and by the look of you, so were you.'

'Yes.'

'Well, I'm sorry, Sergeant, but it's not over yet. I'm going to ask you once more why you weren't at the briefing.'

'My car wouldn't start.'

'For God's sake, Ali, that's no excuse.' Handford could feel his temper rising again. He drained the dregs of cold coffee, then bounced the empty polystyrene cup into his waste bin. Catching the top edge, it rattled round the rim, before finally coming to rest amongst the rubbish.

'All you had to do was ring in and we would have sent someone for you, you know that. Where were you when your car wouldn't start? Not at the pathologist's, because Hewitt rang his secretary and was told you had left.'

'No, sir.' Ali cleared his throat. 'I was in Tallow Road.'

'Tallow Road?'

'Yes, sir.'

'Where Amajit Mahmood's parents live?'

'Yes.'

'Why? It's nowhere near the mortuary, and well off the route back to the station.'

'I went to see Kamal and Jahangier,' Ali said wearily.

No wonder he'd kept his mobile off, hadn't wanted to be contacted. Why couldn't the man do as he was told? 'I said that they were to be left alone until we had more information on them.' Handford leaned over the desk and bellowed, 'Do you never obey an instruction? Or is it just mine you ignore?'

Ali flinched. 'It wasn't like that, sir. I went because I had information that they'd gone to Pakistan.' His voice slid into a whisper. 'I wanted to check it out.'

'Pakistan? When?'

'Last night.'

'But you told me after the press conference that you had spoken to them. Didn't they say they were going away?'

'I don't think they knew. According to their father it was a sudden decision.'

'On whose part?'

'Faysal Hussain's.'

Faysal Hussain again! 'Why should *he* want them in Pakistan?'

Ali opened his mouth to speak, but Handford held his hand up to stop him. 'No, just a minute.' He picked up the phone and dialled the incident room. 'Sergeant Hewitt, it appears that Mahmood's brothers have gone to Pakistan . . . last night. Check the flights, find out exactly where they've gone . . . I don't know, Manchester probably, but it could be any airport. Yes, do that . . . thanks.' Replacing the receiver, he looked at Ali. 'Right, go on.'

'According to their father, Hussain is setting up in business there and has sent the brothers out to — I don't know exactly, to start negotiations.' The inflection in Ali's voice suggested that this was more of a question than a statement.

'How do you know all this?'

'Their father told me.'

'No, Ali, I don't mean that. Who told you the brothers had gone?'

Ali winced. 'Amajit Mahmood,' he said.

'Amajit Mahmood.' Handford sighed. 'So when did you see him?'

The sergeant's jaw tightened. 'This morning,' he said in a low voice.

'I thought we — you and I — decided *not* to see Amajit again until after today's briefing.'

Ali remained silent.

'Well, go on. Why were you with Amajit Mahmood?'

'He rang me, sir, yesterday evening, just after the press conference. He asked me to go and see him.'

'Why?'

'He said he wanted to talk.'

'And this came through after the press conference? That was the call you were taking?'

Ali nodded.

'Why didn't you tell me?'

'I don't know. Because . . . well, I suppose because I thought that since we'd decided to leave him alone, you might have said no and that would have made me look . . . ' He searched for the words. 'Inadequate, incapable of making decisions . . . I don't know.'

'The decision had already been made, Ali.'

183

'I know, but I just felt it was important that he knew that one of us understood his situation.'

And there was no doubt as to who that was going to be. Handford wasn't sure what he had sitting on the other side of his desk — an overambitious sergeant who wanted to be liked, or a man more loyal to his race than to his job. Although after his reaction yesterday, he would have thought that Ali was the last person to have understood Amajit's situation, as he put it.

Ali was still talking, attempting an explanation. 'I thought that once he realised we didn't suspect him, were on his side so to speak, he would be more truthful. I honestly didn't think it would matter; he does have an alibi which puts him out of the frame.'

'You told him that?'

'More or less.' Ali's voice was now barely a whisper.

Astonishment mingled with anger in Handford. Whether or not Ali was overambitious or had divided loyalties, one thing was certain — the man was a fool.

'More or less? Out of the frame? On his side? What kind of language is that? What the hell are you playing at?' Handford paused, grappling with his temper. 'We're not on anyone's side, Ali. Certainly not on Mahmood's. Nor is he out of the frame, as you would know if you'd been at the briefing instead of playing social worker. How do you know he has an alibi? You just take his word for it, do you? Well, let me tell you, Sergeant, Amajit Mahmood does *not* have an alibi. He lied to us. He didn't get back to his office until after two; that means there are nearly three hours unaccounted for in his movements between half eleven and going on two thirty. I don't suppose he told you that?'

Ali shook his head. 'No.'

'He had plenty of time to meet up with Rukhsana at the nursing home, kill her, go home, change his clothes *and* get back to the office.'

Ali tried to retrieve some credibility. 'But he doesn't have a motive.'

'I think we can assume he has. His wife may well have been having an affair with Dr Berridge. Something else you would know had you been at the briefing. Perhaps the baby was Berridge's. Perhaps she told Amajit and he killed her. After all, he lost everything when he married her, his family, his friends, his respectability, even his religion. Can you imagine what it would do to him, learning that his wife was having an affair and expecting her lover's baby? You said yourself that the killing was more like a rage than a premeditated murder.'

The realisation of what he had done spread over Ali's features and he sagged visibly. His eyes closed for a second. 'I'm sorry, sir.'

'I should bloody well hope you are. Not that that's anywhere near good enough. Thanks to you we have Amajit Mahmood thinking we're on his side; what's he going to feel when he finds out that not only are we not on his side, we've put him at the top of our list of suspects? Christ Almighty, Khalid, if we have to put him under caution, we'll get more 'no comment' answers from him than Russell has beans in his coffee grinder.' Handford picked up the postmortem report, then threw it down again.

'Why do you think you're here, Sergeant? To investigate a murder or placate the Asian community? I don't know what you were told when you were assigned, but as far as I'm concerned you're here to investigate Rukhsana Mahmood's murder. If the fact that you're Asian helps gain the community's confidence, that's all to the good obviously, but you are *not* here to be their friend or their ally.' He paused for a moment, watching Ali, whose eyes seemed to be fixed on the rim of the desk.

'You do not,' Handford continued coldly, 'rush off as the whim takes you; you do not pass information on to anyone, let alone a possible suspect; you do not break agreements we've made; you do not ignore your pager and you do not turn off your mobile so that you can't be contacted. I left messages with your wife for you to ring me last night when you got in. I assume she gave you them.'

Ali nodded.

'I stayed up until the early hours waiting for a call. Nothing. I tell you to go easy on someone — you don't; I tell you to take an officer with you when you go to talk to the brothers — you go alone.'

Ali made to protest.

'Don't deny it,' Handford said, 'you were seen. You did go alone, didn't you?'

'Yes, sir,' Ali whispered.

186

'Why?'

'There was only Warrender available. I didn't think he was a suitable person to question Kamal and Jahangier.'

Handford could understand why, but this wasn't the time to be understanding. 'That was your opinion, was it?'

Ali remained silent.

'It's not up to you to pick and choose who you take with you to question suspects,' Handford snapped. 'You do it in pairs with whoever is available. I could instigate disciplinary proceedings over this, Ali, as well you know. One more step out of line and I will.' He leaned towards him. 'If I had my way, Sergeant, you'd be off this case. You've practised bloody awful policing, a probationer could have done better. I said this to you up at the nursing home and I'll say it again — you're a detective, start acting like one.'

There was silence. There seemed no more to be said. A brisk knock on the door broke the tension.

It was Hewitt. She glanced at Ali. 'I'm sorry, sir,' she said, 'but the lab's just rung. According to forensics the boot print is not Teale's. There *is* some of her blood on his jacket, but the spread of it is more consistent with him dragging her down the embankment than with bludgeoning her.'

Handford reined in his anger. 'Right,' he said, taking a deep breath. 'Then that let's him out, I think. Anything else?'

'Yes. They've found a cigarette burn on the victim's coat. It's fresh and might have come

187

from the killer. I checked with the exhibits officer and he confirmed that several butts were found, one near where the victim was killed. I thought we'd better eliminate her patients first, so I've got someone checking them out. We're starting with yesterday's list and working backwards.' She consulted her notebook. 'Oh, and forensics have sent the foetal tissue off for DNA testing. They'll try and rush it through, but it'll take a while.'

Handford felt calmer now. 'Good. Thanks, Liz. Anything on the Mahmood brothers?'

'No, guv, not yet.'

'OK. Is there some coffee going?'

'Just been made, guv.'

'Ask someone to bring us a mug, will you? I think Khalid could do with one, and you know me, I can drink it any time.'

As she turned to go, Handford saw Hewitt throw Ali an understanding smile, which he attempted unsuccessfully to return. The door closed.

'Right,' Handford said, 'the briefing.' He picked a file from his desk, opened it and cast his eyes over several of the pages before looking up at Ali.

'There's nothing of much use from the patients Rukhsana saw before she died,' he said, 'and I think the possibility that the killer was after drugs is a non-starter. However, a freelance photographer rang after the press conference to say that she'd seen Rukhsana up at the nursing home at about one o'clock, seemingly arguing with a man she thinks was Dr Berridge. She was taking photos for a new nursing home brochure and managed to catch Rukhsana and Berridge on film.' He handed an envelope to Ali, who pulled out several prints.

He scrutinised them. 'I haven't met Dr Berridge, but it certainly looks like Rukhsana.' He handed the photographs back. 'Could he be a suspect?'

Handford shrugged. 'We can't rule him out, although we need to be sure that he had a reason to kill her — like he *was* having an affair with her and he thought the baby was his. If she didn't want a termination, I suppose that could have angered him.'

'Enough to pick up a coping stone?'

'I don't know. I spoke to him yesterday morning, but he denied that he and Rukhsana were any more than colleagues. He was edgy, nervous even, so there's probably some truth in the rumours. Anyway, I'm going to see him with Clarke. Let's see what comes of that. In the meantime, I want you — '

The door opened and a detective came in with two mugs of coffee. He gave one to Ali and the other he placed on the desk. Handford could see that Ali's hands were trembling; he'd had a rough morning. He waited until the detective left, then continued, 'I want you to see Amajit . . . '

The skin round Ali's eyes tightened for a moment and he closed them as if trying to shut out the words.

'I'm sorry, Khalid, you made the mess, you can sort it out. We need to know how he accounts for those hours — it's a long time.

189

Graham did the check on Amajit, so he will go with you. Now, the other thing is my meeting with Peter Redmayne.' Leaving out Faysal Hussain's part in the Aziz riots, Handford told him of the previous evening's meeting. 'I'm sure the information is genuine but I'm not going to waste money on a full-scale surveillance; instead, uniforms will keep a discreet eye on Hussain. I checked with the Drugs Squad and they have nothing on him, so they're happy to let us keep him in our sights. They're not that interested in anabolic steroids anyway, too busy with heroin and crack dealers.' He paused. 'I don't suppose you've anything more on him?'

'No, nothing much, except that for some reason he hasn't disowned his cousin. Amajit puts that down to their relationship as children. Apparently Hussain thinks Kamal and Jahangier killed Rukhsana which is probably why he's sent them to Pakistan.' Ali drained the last of his coffee and put the mug on the floor beside his chair.

Handford shifted his position. He wasn't looking forward to this, but it had to be said. 'Look, Khalid, we haven't got off to the best of starts. I don't know whose fault it is, yours or mine, and I can't say I'm in the mood for finding out.' He attempted a smile. 'And I imagine you're not either. We can talk later, but just for the moment, let's call a truce, start again — whatever.' He stretched out his hand for Ali to take.

'Yes, sir, I don't have a problem with that.' He clasped Handford's hand.

190

'OK, let's get going. Your coat's over there, hanging up. Tell Clarke I'm ready when he is.'

Ali took his coat and opened the door.

'Oh, and Ali.'

'Sir?'

'I'm sorry about this morning. I shouldn't have bawled you out in the corridor.'

'No, sir, you shouldn't.'

Handford could feel himself blushing. In those four words, Ali had reprimanded him more successfully than Russell had with all his fine phrases.

★ ★ ★

'Have you talked to him?' Clarke asked.

'Talked to who about what?' Handford glanced at the silver-haired detective sitting next to him. They were driving through the midday traffic to the surgery on Palin Road.

'Ali. About last year.'

'No.'

'Why not? You owe it to him after this morning. He ought to understand why you've been such a bastard towards him.'

'Watch it, Clarke. Just remember who you're talking to.'

But Clarke wasn't to be put off. At forty-nine, he was the oldest man on the squad. Still only a detective constable, he had never been particularly ambitious, preferring legwork to decision-making. But over time he had become the mentor and father figure in the office and he took these duties seriously. He also knew John

191

Handford well; they had started in the job at the same time, had walked the beat together, and although he was older by some five years, they had been firm friends ever since. Handford knew that his rank didn't faze him at all; as far as Clarke was concerned, he was talking to a friend — and a friend who, he felt, needed to be told some home truths.

'Ali's feeling very raw at the moment.'

'So am I. It may have escaped your notice, but he wasn't the only one to be chewed up by the DCI.'

'No, but you had another go at him afterwards.'

'He deserved it.'

'Maybe. But it doesn't alter the fact that you got away lightly compared with him.'

'So, you're going to have a go at me now. Even up the score.'

Clarke sighed as an adult does when trying to deal with a teenager with attitude. 'Talk to him, John. How can he understand your position until you do? He's the only one of the team who isn't aware of exactly what happened, and if he asks about it, he could get hold of the wrong version — there are plenty of them around still. Tell him. Let him get it from you, not from somebody like Warrender.'

'I'll think about it.'

Clarke lifted his eyes to the roof of the car. 'Heaven preserve me from stubborn DIs.' He faced Handford. 'Think about it, John. He can never be one of the team if he's not privy to information that the rest of us have. Not when it impinges on the investigation.'

'It has nothing to do with this investigation.'

'It shouldn't have, but it does. We know, we're careful; he won't be because he doesn't know he has to be. You're walking on glass, John. One minute cutting yourself, the next cutting Ali.'

Handford didn't reply. Clarke was right, though he wasn't going to tell him that.

'I'll give you the rest of the shift, John. If you haven't told him by the morning, then I will.'

'I'll have your pension if you do,' Handford growled.

Clarke grinned. 'No, you won't.'

They pulled into the surgery car park. Handford turned off the engine and sat back in the seat. Whether Clarke was right or wrong, he didn't need this. He wished he was a child and could have a good cry; he was sure that would do him more good. 'All right, you win,' he said. 'I'll talk to him.'

'By tomorrow,' Clarke warned.

9

'I'm sorry, Inspector, I was only outside.' Ian Berridge strode into his consulting room where the two men were sitting waiting for him. 'Margaret should have told me.'

The two officers stood up. 'No problem, sir,' Handford said. 'Your receptionist told us you'd been cooped up here all morning and were out getting some fresh air. I must say she looks after you well.'

'Too well, sometimes. She's been here for years; kind enough, but rather protective — she shields us from the rigours of the clientele.' He laughed. 'She terrified me when I first came; I felt I had to ask her permission to go into my own consulting room.'

'I can imagine.' Handford observed Berridge as he indicated that they should resume their seats, then took off his coat and threw it onto the examination couch. With his youthful demeanour, he didn't seem old enough to be a GP, but then Handford was beginning to feel that no one was old enough to be anything any more. Tall and slim with shoulder-length brown hair which was surreptitiously creeping back from his temples, the doctor was singularly handsome. Analysed separately, his features were unattractive; the receding hairline and acute angle of his chin exaggerated the length and slimness of his face. His narrow eyes, large nose and small mouth fitted quite snugly into the bottom half, giving his forehead the caricatured effect of an intellectual. Yet, as a whole, the picture was one of roguish, sultry, boyish good looks, which veiled the hint of petulance hovering around his lips. He would have worked on those looks since childhood, perfecting them and exploiting them to give him what he wanted and to get him out of trouble. They would work well with the women in his life. And why not? thought Handford. Women fell for men like Berridge. Margaret would mother him, Rukhsana sleep with him and his female patients adore him. But boyish charm had its limitations; it would take more than that to get him out of this scrape.

Handford wasn't sure yet whether the scrape Berridge was in was professional or criminal. What he was sure about was that Berridge was edgy. Strain clouded his face, and he continued to make small talk, putting off the moment when the more formal questions would begin.

'To be absolutely honest, I'd gone out for a smoke, but don't tell Margaret that. It wouldn't go down well with her; she thinks all her doctors are above that kind of thing.'

'I'm sure.' Handford smiled. 'A doctor who smokes isn't the best example for the practice to set.'

'No, but I don't do it often; it's just my way of unwinding when I've had a stressful morning.' He gave a nervous laugh. 'Or when I'm waiting to be questioned by the police for the second time in two days.'

'We just need to tie up some loose ends, sir. Nothing to be concerned about.' There were times when Handford had attacks of conscience over his euphemistic language.

They sat, facing each other, Clarke and Handford opposite Berridge. The doctor broke the silence. 'Well, how can I help you, Inspector?'

'Are you married, Dr Berridge?'

Whatever he was expecting, it wasn't that, and the reply when it came was expressed more as a question than an answer. 'Yes.'

'Children?'

'Yes, although I don't see . . . '

Handford smiled. 'I like to know something about the people I'm talking to. It's not just their words I'm interested in, but who they are, so I build up background, try to understand where they're coming from.' He paused for a moment. 'How many? Children, I mean.'

'Three — two boys and a girl.'

'And how long have you worked here?'

Berridge thought for a moment. 'It must be almost four years.'

'Where were you employed previously?'

'I was a registrar in a hospital near Belfast.'

'So, what made you come over to England, and to this part of the country in particular?' The expression in Handford's eyes showed genuine interest, a look he had fostered over the years.

'I wanted to get away from the troubles in Northern Ireland, give my children a chance to grow up in peace. I'd decided on general practice and this job came up. It seemed to be just what I wanted. Being a GP means I get to know my patients, see them as people with lives, families, problems; you know, real people. You can't do that in a hospital.' Berridge made himself more comfortable, sliding down in his seat.

'Four years. So you were here when Rukhsana Mahmood joined the practice.'

'Yes.'

'How did you get on with her?'

'I told you yesterday; she was a good health visitor.'

'She was just a health visitor, not a *real* person?'

'She was a colleague; it's different.'

'Was she a friend?'

'She was a colleague, Inspector. Just a colleague.'

There was a pause while Handford seemed to consider the response. 'Yet everyone else I've spoken to seems to have liked her, thought of her as more than just someone they worked with.'

'Well, yes, of course I liked her. She was a likeable person.' Berridge straightened in his chair.

Handford often marvelled at the predictability of humans. The doctor's expression and body language registered his concern at the way the interview was going and his need to take control. Handford waited the few seconds that it would take for Berridge to make some comment about how he realised Handford was only doing his job, but . . .

'Look, Inspector, we all miss Rukhsana. It was a terrible thing to have happened, and it's hard

197

to take in. I know you have a job to do, but no one here would do that to her. Shouldn't you be out looking elsewhere?'

'We are, sir. I can assure you, we are. But you see,' he said, taking the doctor into his confidence, 'we have to build up a picture of Rukhsana: her life, her background, the person she was, and that means questioning the people she worked with.'

Ian Berridge raised a hand in capitulation.

'You said yesterday that you were her GP before Dr Copeman?'

'Yes.'

'Tell me again why she moved to Dr Copeman's list.'

Dr Berridge sighed. 'She wanted a woman doctor. Some women do, particularly Asian women. We didn't have one — a woman doctor, I mean, until Dr Copeman joined us. Quite a few of our female patients transferred to her list.'

'So while you were Rukhsana's GP, would you say she was in good health?'

'Yes, very. The odd virus, sore throat, but nothing major.'

'Sounds like my wife,' Handford said with a smile. 'I think the only times she ever sees her doctor seriously is when she's pregnant. And that hasn't been for a long time, thank God.'

Berridge appeared more relaxed. He was on his own territory. He returned the smile. 'A familiar story, Inspector. It's true that the only time I see some women is when they're expecting.'

'And Rukhsana?' An innocent question laced

198

with a small amount of surprise.

'I didn't see Rukhsana, she wanted Dr Copeman to oversee her pregnancy.'

There it was; Berridge had let his guard down.

'Rukhsana was pregnant?'

Berridge stiffened, realising his mistake. 'Yes. Yes — at least — I think she was.'

'You think she was? You're not sure?'

The doctor began to flounder. 'I think I may have heard it talked about, you know — surgery gossip.'

'Her pregnancy wasn't confirmed by you, then?'

'No.'

'So how did you know that she wanted Dr Copeman to oversee it? If you hadn't confirmed it, then at best the information was, as you say, no more than gossip.'

'I suppose I didn't know — not exactly. She — she'd talked about her and her husband wanting a baby and I suppose I got the impression that once pregnant she would rather be cared for by a woman doctor.'

'When exactly did Dr Copeman begin her work here?'

'Beginning of September.'

'And when did Mrs Mahmood transfer to her list?'

'I'm not absolutely sure, Inspector. I'll have to check that for you.'

'Please.'

Dr Berridge turned to his computer and tapped on the keyboard, then read from the screen. 'She left me halfway through September

— the eighteenth, to be precise.' He spun his chair back round to face his desk.

'According to the postmortem the foetus was approximately twelve weeks old when Rukhsana died,' mused Handford. 'That would mean she would have been about five weeks on the eighteenth of September.'

Berridge picked up his fountain pen and began to twist it round in his fingers. A ray of wintry sunlight glinted through the Venetian blind to catch the thin gold band on the third finger of his left hand.

'Yes,' he said.

'So why did you think she didn't transfer lists as soon as Dr Copeman took up her post?'

'I don't know.'

'She was a health visitor,' said Handford, 'she knew what pregnancy was about. Why wait? She must have conceived round about mid-August so would have had some idea by the beginning of September; she may well even have confirmed it with a home test. Why do you think she waited another two, nearly three weeks to transfer to Dr Copeman?'

Berridge offered no response.

Handford observed him for a moment, then, 'Are you sure she didn't mention the fact that she was pregnant to you at all as her doctor?'

'No, Inspector, I've told you she didn't consult me.'

Handford leaned forward in his chair. 'If she didn't consult you about the pregnancy, Dr Berridge, how did you learn of it? I don't buy surgery gossip. And it can't have been from Dr

Copeman, that would have been breaking doctor-patient confidentiality.'

'Yes. I mean, no, it wasn't Dr Copeman — of course it wasn't.' Berridge was becoming flustered. 'Rukhsana must have told the receptionists; I think it must have been one of them.'

'Can you remember which one?'

'No.' There was a moment's silence, then, in an attempt to regain control, he said, 'Does it matter who told me? I knew — it could have been mentioned by anyone at any time.'

'It wasn't Rukhsana herself, then?'

'No, it wasn't. I've told you that more than once.'

'You're sure, sir.'

'Yes, Inspector, I'm sure.' Berridge sounded weary.

Handford leaned back in his chair. 'I'm sorry if I sound persistent, but you see, what's worrying me is that Rukhsana told Dr Copeman that she didn't want anyone to know about her pregnancy; in fact she was adamant that no one should, not even her husband. And as far as we can ascertain, no one in the practice apart from Dr Copeman and yourself did know about it.'

The doctor's head jerked upward from his pen and his eyes darted from one detective to the other. Handford signalled, almost imperceptibly, for Clarke to take over.

'When I spoke to various staff members yesterday,' Clarke said quietly, 'they seemed to think that there was something going on between you and Rukhsana Mahmood, that you had a close personal relationship.'

Berridge's expression registered horror. The Irish accent became more pronounced as his voice climbed to a peak. 'Don't be ridiculous. She was a patient, for God's sake. I could be struck off for having a relationship with a patient. I can't imagine where you got that from. You can't believe I would do anything so stupid.'

'But she came off your list,' persisted Clarke. 'I could be reading more into that than there is, but did she come off your list because she was pregnant and preferred a woman doctor to treat her, or because she was having a relationship with you and she didn't want you struck off?'

The petulant streak broke from its moorings as Berridge threw down the pen he had been holding. 'I'm not having this. You're questioning my professionalism and my ethics. If that's the way the interview is going, I want someone with me.'

Handford intervened. He didn't want to alienate Berridge too much.

'Let's leave it then, for the moment. Yours is quite a stressful job, isn't it?'

Berridge threw a hostile look at Clarke, then turned to Handford. 'Yes, it can be.'

'A bit like mine. I usually set off walking when I feel the need to get away from things. I like walking, lots of fresh air; it blows the cobwebs away, helps me think clearly again.' He smiled. 'How do you wind down?'

'Play squash usually.'

'You don't go walking, then?'

'Not often. There are no decent places around here to walk.'

'Except Moss Carr Woods.'

Berridge picked up his pen again.

Handford said, 'It's just that I noticed a pair of walking boots in the corner there. Are they yours?'

'I use them in bad weather. Some of my patients live on muddy back lanes. I take them when I visit them.'

'Like at the nursing home?'

'Sometimes.'

'Right. I'd like to talk about your movements on the day Rukhsana was killed. Now, according to Margaret you had a very full list in the morning and didn't finish until going on midday.'

'If Margaret says so, then that's how it was. She'll be able to give you a printout of the patients I saw.'

'Yes, she said she'd get one for us. What time did you leave the surgery?'

'I had a coffee and a quick sandwich here, so it must have been shortly after twelve, about twenty past.'

'And where did you go?'

'I had visits. I was running late and wanted to get on with them. I had another surgery in the evening.'

'Did you visit patients up at the nursing home?'

'Not on Tuesday, no. You can easily check that with the manager.'

'So, you weren't up at the nursing home on Tuesday.'

'I've just said so.'

'No, Dr Berridge, you have said you didn't visit any patients. I wondered if you went up there at all.'

'No, I had no reason to.'

'I ask because we have a witness who claims to have seen you in the nursing home car park around one o'clock. According to the witness who contacted us after the press conference, you were having quite a heated argument with Rukhsana Mahmood.'

The last tinge of colour drained from the doctor's face. He stared first at Handford and then at Clarke. He shook his head. 'No, that's not true. Your witness is mistaken. It must have been another day. I wasn't there on Tuesday.' His voice remained steady, but panic was clouding his eyes.

'I'm sorry, Dr Berridge, our witness wasn't mistaken. She's one of your more healthy patients, but she knows you quite well. More importantly, she's a freelance photographer and was taking pictures of the home and grounds for a new brochure they're preparing. I've checked with the manager and it was definitely Tuesday she was there. Given the weather, she was pleased to see people out in the grounds and she caught you on film. She gave us copies.' Handford took a large ten-by-eight photograph from his folder and placed it in front of the doctor. A man and a woman stood close together, obviously in animated conversation. The man, who was tall and slim with shoulder-length brown hair, was wearing an overcoat, similar to the one Berridge had thrown

204

onto the examination couch, and on his feet were a pair of boots into which he had tucked his trousers. The woman was Asian. Beneath her coat the bright turquoise trousers of the shalwar kameez she was wearing were clearly visible.

'The photographer wouldn't have used the picture without your permission, of course, but that is you and Rukhsana, isn't it, sir?'

Fleetingly the doctor's eyes closed then opened; clearing his throat, he said, 'Yes, yes it is.'

Handford brought out another photograph, this time an enlargement of Berridge and Rukhsana. Berridge had a deep frown on his face; his mouth was open, his lips tightened as though he was shouting. Rukhsana seemed frightened and tears streaked her cheeks.

'It's not too clear,' Handford said, 'but the expression on your faces suggests to me that you weren't discussing a patient.'

'No.'

'You look quite angry, Dr Berridge. Were you having an argument?'

The doctor nodded.

'Mrs Mahmood seems to be crying.'

'Yes.'

'Would you like to tell me why?'

Berridge shook his head.

Handford waited for a few moments, then said, 'Let me help you, doctor. You tell me if I'm close. You'd been having an affair with Rukhsana Mahmood. She told you she was pregnant — perhaps on the day she was killed, perhaps before she transferred to Dr Copeman's list.

Maybe you just wanted to talk about it, persuade her that the baby was not yours, or maybe you wanted her to have a termination and she wouldn't. You knew she was going up to the nursing home to see her aunt — everyone knew that. We have statements from patients and staff who all say that the only time she wore Asian dress was when she visited her aunt. So, Dr Berridge, knowing where she was going, I suggest you followed her there to talk to her, perhaps to try to make her see sense. An hour or so later, she's found dead with massive head injuries. What conclusions would you draw, Dr Berridge? You had a good reason to kill her. At best you could be struck off, at worst you'd lose your wife and family as well as your job if any of this should come out.'

Berridge slumped back in his chair and covered his face with his hands. 'Oh God.' The words were barely audible.

Handford allowed himself an inward smile. It didn't always please him to catch a normally decent person out in a lie, but with Berridge it was different. He was willing to bet that lying was a way of life with him, that he did it with ease to rid himself of situations he had been instrumental in creating. His charismatic personality was his shield. It felt good to have pierced it.

'Right,' said Handford. 'Let's start again. You were having an affair with Rukhsana Mahmood.'

'Yes.'

'For how long?'

Ian Berridge lifted his eyes to meet the

206

detective's. The strain that had shown in them earlier had spilled over to form deep grooves on his forehead, and his pallor had deepened into an exhausted grey. Handford stared at him. He had seen many men and women in this position; some became defensive, some belligerent, and some, like Berridge, pathetic.

'About nine months. She's — was — an attractive woman, full of fun, lively, with a voice like sunshine. It was her voice I fell in love with first.' His tone softened and a sad smile caressed his lips. His eyelids flickered momentarily as he gulped down a mouthful of air to steady himself. 'We got on well; we liked each other.' He was twisting his pen more feverishly now. 'It was never meant to become an affair — it just happened.'

'When?'

'In May. We'd gone to a conference in Harrogate, to do with the care of geriatric patients. Stuart — Dr Haigh — thought it would be a good idea for us to go; the practice has a lot of elderly patients. But it was incredibly boring. We stood it for the morning but then decided to give the rest a miss and drive out into the country. You surely don't want details, Inspector.' He let out a deep breath. 'Call it love, lust, whatever you like; all I know is I wanted her so much it hurt.'

'And you always get what you want, Dr Berridge.' It was not a question.

Ian Berridge shrugged. 'She didn't argue.'

'And the affair continued?'

'Yes. We met when we could, at her house, at

mine. My children are away at school, my wife is a social worker and often works late, and her husband had evening meetings. It wasn't difficult.'

'Did Rukhsana see the relationship as permanent?' Handford glanced at Clarke; he was glad it was him he was with and not Ali. Even if they had called a truce, he still wasn't sure how the sergeant would take what they were beginning to learn. As far as Handford was concerned, they hadn't yet cleared the air regarding Ali's attitude to Rukhsana's marriage.

Berridge shrugged. 'She never talked about leaving her husband, if that's what you mean.'

'And you? Did you think it would go somewhere?'

'It couldn't. I was her doctor, she was my patient. It was a bit of fun, that was all.'

Fun! Handford grimaced. Why did some men look upon playing with women's emotions as fun? He wondered how often Berridge had done it before.

He forced himself back to the questioning. 'When did she tell you she was pregnant?'

'Before she went onto Dr Copeman's list; that was why she transferred.'

'And the baby, was it yours?'

'I don't know. I really don't. It could just have easily been her husband's.' He looked now as though he was about to burst into tears. Handford waited, giving him time to gather himself.

'What exactly were you arguing about?'

The doctor exhaled hard. He could probably

208

have done with a cigarette at this moment. 'I wanted her to have a termination. She was for it at first, then she seemed to change her mind and said she would think about it. Time was pressing. I knew she was going to the nursing home to see her aunt so I drove up there. She had to make a decision. But she was prevaricating, giving all sorts of reasons why she couldn't do it. First it was her religion, then what if it was her husband's baby, then she said she would have to have a private termination but couldn't afford it. I said that wasn't a problem, I would pay; but then she said she couldn't get rid of it because she'd already told her husband that she was pregnant, so it was too late.'

'Do you think she had told him, or was that an excuse to stop you putting pressure on her?'

'I don't know. I couldn't take the risk that she was lying. She said she had told him, so I had to believe her.'

'What did you do then?'

Berridge seemed lost and Handford knew that the doctor was acutely aware that the charm he always relied on was no use to him now. 'I shouted at her, called her names.' Berridge closed his eyes, as if trying to shut out the memory. 'I might even have hit her, I don't know. She began to scream at me, then to cry, not a sobbing kind of crying, more in anger than anything. That must have been when the photographer saw us. You've got to understand, everything seemed to be slipping away from me: her, my career, even my family. I just wanted her to see sense. But I didn't kill her, Inspector. I didn't kill her. I left her, I walked away and I didn't see her again.' He raised his eyes to look squarely at the two men. 'Did her husband know of the pregnancy?'

'It doesn't seem so; it appears he learned of it only after the postmortem.'

Berridge's eyes appealed to Handford. 'Does he know about the affair?'

'Not that I'm aware.'

Berridge ran his tongue over his lips. 'And will you tell him?'

'Probably, but not necessarily.' Let the man stew; he deserved it. 'At the moment he's grieving over the loss of his wife and his unborn child. I think that's enough for him to be going on with, don't you?'

Berridge lowered his eyes and scrutinised the pen in his hand.

Handford replaced the photographs in his case. 'I want a list of your Tuesday afternoon visits, Dr Berridge. Names and addresses and reasons for the visits.'

'I can't give you that, Inspector. You know as well as I do that kind of information is confidential.'

'Dr Berridge,' Handford's patience was beginning to wear. 'We can waste time while I go to a JP to get a warrant signed to give me access to that information or you can give it to me now. It's up to you.'

Berridge was beaten. 'Right,' he said wearily. 'I'll get Margaret to print one out for you.'

'I also want your boots and the clothes you were wearing on Tuesday. DC Clarke will go with you to get them.'

The doctor looked at Handford, his eyes beseeching. 'Does it have to come out? I really can be struck off for this.'

His future life, thought Handford, must be flashing in front of him like a past life of a drowning man. A future smashed like Rukhsana's skull, rendered into a pulp like her brain. Ian Berridge could be looking at the end of his career while still in his mid thirties. All the years of study, the hours of work as a junior doctor, the nights without sleep — for what? A fling with a woman who was not his wife and who was or had been his patient. There was no point telling him that he should have thought of the consequences before he began the relationship; it was too late for that. No one, not even a doctor, was immune from the strength of passion that one person can arouse in another. And Rukhsana, it seemed, had been capable of arousing such passion.

'Whether it comes out or not depends on who fathered the baby and who killed Rukhsana. We've sent foetal tissue for DNA testing. If the child is not Mr Mahmood's then we shall ask for a sample of your blood. You can refuse, although I've got to say that refusal could lead to only one inference. The analysis will take quite a while, so I'm afraid you'll just have to bear with us until we get the results. However, if you did kill her, Dr Berridge, I think you'll have more to worry about than being struck off, don't you?'

★ ★ ★

It was almost a quarter to twelve before Karen knocked on Amajit's door. She had promised to be there by mid-morning, and he had wandered backwards and forwards to the window in the hope of her arrival. He'd almost decided she wasn't coming.

The morning had been awful and he wasn't sure how he was going to get through the afternoon and the evening, or the next day or the next. His call to Sergeant Ali had been made on impulse. Talking with him hadn't helped.

If anything, it had left him feeling empty. The detective had been curt, more interested in asking questions than answering them and he hadn't seemed to understand that what Amajit needed to do was to talk about his wife, to understand why someone — anyone — would take her into the woods and beat her to death. Rationally, he knew that it was too soon for answers, it wasn't yet two days since it had happened, two days that had seemed like an eternity. He had tried but been unable to pull his memory back through the forty-eight-hour haze to the moment when he had called 'See you tonight' as he walked out of the front door. Everything had stopped, frozen somewhere around the time of her death, and his mind refused to move from that moment. His senses were heightened by his imagination; he heard the sickening thud of the stone as it beat down on her, the sound of her skull shattering and the screams as the pain tore through her. When he closed his eyes to shut out the sounds, he saw her blood saturating the wet leaves and earth, felt

the cold drizzle seeping through her coat, and he
smelt the damp, rotting odour of autumn.

And then there was the child. The child he
would never now know. He wasn't sure which
was the hardest to bear.

The sergeant didn't care about any of this
— why should he? To him, her murder was just
another investigation. So transparent had he
been in his disapproval of the marriage, he
couldn't even feel pity. If Rukhsana's death had
taught Amajit anything, it was that prejudice
stretches in many directions. That Ali would do
his job, he didn't doubt; but he wouldn't do it
with compassion or with tolerance. He was
probably the only Asian on the inquiry, doubtless
brought in because of 'the victim's ethnic
background', yet ironically he was probably the
least likely of all of them to understand. So he
would do his job, ask questions, root out the
facts, discuss him, his wife and his family and
rationalise the information, organising it into
pieces of a puzzle which may or may not lead
him and the rest of them in the right direction.
And if it didn't, then so be it, he could go back
to the beginning, killing Rukhsana, killing him,
all over again.

It alarmed him to think that a group of
strangers were delving into his past, and
Rukhsana's past, coming up with . . . with what?
He shuddered. They had known before he did
that his wife was pregnant. What else did they
know? What else would they learn?

Over the past few weeks, months even, there
had been something wrong with their marriage.

213

He had put it down to their jobs; they were always involved, always exhausted. Her patients wanted more of her time than he wanted her to give, and the councillors wanted more of his time than she wanted him to give. Public servants, that's what they had both been, servants to the public, but little to each other. Yet he would have done anything to make her happy, had been about to . . .

He glanced around the room. It was unnaturally quiet. He had been here without Rukhsana many times, but it had never seemed so silent before. Like a grave. Her perfume still lingered. It was surprising it had lasted so long; though he dreaded it fading, leaving him with nothing. He let the tears spill over. He yearned for his family: his father's strength, his mother's loving arms and his sisters and brothers there to form a cocoon about him until he was ready to face life without Rukhsana. But he knew it wouldn't happen. Perhaps if she had died naturally they might have come to him, but her death was too public and the shame he had brought on them was felt also by the community; they would not, could not, have anything to do with him. Faysal was the only one who came near, and he was critical, concerned that this was no one's business but theirs. But it wasn't; murder wasn't private — not in this country. In this country it was the property of the police, the press and the people. And they lived in this country.

The knock on the door, when it came, startled him. He opened it with unwarranted impatience.

Karen was bending down to unfasten Danny from his pushchair. As she stood up, Amajit gasped. The right side of her face was bruised a mottled purple, and the skin around her left eye, into her hairline and on her cheek was black and there was a long angry gash above her eyebrow. She was deathly pale and looked as though she would collapse right there on the pavement.

'My God, Karen, what's happened?'

She attempted a smile. 'I'm sorry I'm late,' she said. 'There's another bus strike. I had to walk.'

She was still struggling with the straps on the pushchair, but her hands were trembling. Tears were running down her cheeks.

'Never mind the bus strike. What happened to you? Come here.' Amajit bent down and placed his hands round her shoulders, lifting her gently into a standing position. 'Go on inside and sit down. I'll bring Danny and the pushchair.'

★　★　★

Kamal yawned. Of all the things that he and Jahangier had ever been asked to do, this had to be the most boring. And it was cold. The car had a heater, but if they used it, the chunter of the engine and the constant stream of exhaust fumes might cause someone to wonder what they were doing there. So they watched Amajit's front door, shivering, numb and bored, himself in the back seat and Jahangier in the front. That way they had space to duck if someone came snooping.

He snuggled up inside his coat, hoping that

215

what little warmth was trapped inside might make him feel better. God, it was boring. Nothing had happened since the Asian policeman had dashed out of the house and driven off in his car. That was the nearest thing to excitement they'd had all morning.

The car that Faysal had got for them was ace; nothing like the Porsche of course, but new enough and sleek enough to satisfy his vanity. He'd fancied getting out and having another look at it from the outside, but Jahangier had yelled at him from the front seat to stay where he was. 'Do you want to bring attention to us?' he'd shouted. 'Because that's what you will do if you keep hopping in and out.'

Kamal glanced through the back window at two girls walking towards them. It was a pity he wasn't in the front, preferably in the driver's seat, but if he wound his window down, the girls would see him sitting there and maybe like what they saw and come over. He imagined himself with them in the back of the car where he would give them the best time ever — both of 'em. But they passed by without a second look. He slid further down in the seat and folded his arms. Well, it was their loss.

He yawned again.

'For God's sake, stop it.' Jahangier lifted his eyes from the porno magazine he was leafing through. Closing it, he passed it backwards. 'If you want something to do, read that.'

Kamal opened it up at the centrefold. He sat up straight. Forget the poxy girls in this street, he'd rather have this one anytime. He thrust the page in front of his brother's eyes. 'Look at that,' he moaned.

But Jahangier was sitting up straight himself. 'No, look at that,' he said, moving the magazine aside with his hand. A girl with a pushchair had stopped outside Amajit's door. She knocked, then squatted down to unfasten the straps round the child. The door opened and Amajit came out. He spoke to her, bent down, wrapped his arms round her shoulders to help her up, then she moved inside and he finished unstrapping the child. He disappeared into the house with the baby in his arms, then reappeared to fold up the chair and carry it in. The door closed.

'He's got a white girl!' Kamal couldn't contain his excitement. 'First that tart and now a white girl. You saw, Jan. He's doing it again — first that tart, now a white girl. Let's go and get 'im.' And he made to open the car door.

'No!' Jahangier put a restraining arm on him. 'We stay where we are. That's what Faysal said and that's what we do.' He lifted the mobile phone from the front sill, tapped in a number with his thumb and put it to his ear.

'But you saw. He'd got his arms round'er. We've got to get 'im.'

'No, I've said we stay here.' Jahangier lowered the phone. 'He's not answering. I'll try again later.'

They sat in silence for a moment, then Kamal's voice burst out, more excited than before. 'I know her,' he said. 'I went to school with 'er. A fat bitch, she was. She had a brother, big, like a gorilla, he used to pick her up from

217

school sometimes — a right bully, you didn't pick a fight with him.' He turned to face his brother. 'Once, he — '

'Stop your yapping.' Jahangier didn't want to know. 'I need to think.'

Kamal frowned his resentment at his brother. Who did Jahangier think he was? Why was he the only one allowed to open his mouth? He slid down in the seat again, grumbling under his breath.

After a while Jahangier spoke. 'What's her name, the girl?'

'I can't remember; it's a long time ago. And I wasn't at school all that much.'

'Well, think. It's important.'

Kamal frowned as though he was trawling the corners of his memory — he had cultivated that look in lessons. It made the teachers think he was working. 'I don't know. It began with a K.' He said the letter as though it was the initial sound of a word.

'Christine? Clare? Kimberley?' Jahangier exhaled impatiently. 'Come on, think, you moron, think. I can't go on for ever trying to remember English girls' names. What about Carol? Karen?'

'That's it!' Kamal shouted excitedly. 'Karen — Karen, er, Penistone. That's it, Karen Penistone. A stupid name, Penistone. We used to call her stonewall.'

Jahangier shifted his position to stare at his brother. 'Anything to do with Barry Penistone?'

'Yes, that's right. That's 'er brother's name.'

'I know him. He works for Faysal — sells some of his stuff, sometimes works as a bouncer at the raves. Yeah, I know him; you're right, he is dangerous, got a real temper on him and a punch like a battering ram. He got eighteen months about three years ago for bashing someone in the face with a beer glass. Thought he'd been pawing his girlfriend and just hit him. So, what's his sister doing with Amajit?'

'What do you mean, what they doing? You know what they're doing. They'll be at it now, him and that white girl. The thing is, what are we going to do?' Kamal could see action ahead and was becoming impatient. 'We can't just leave them in there. I vote we batter the door down and catch 'em at it, then teach 'em both a lesson.' And he slapped his fist into the palm of his other hand.

'Don't be stupid. Go in now and that's the end of Amajit, the girl and us.' He gave Kamal a knowing look. 'We're getting paid good money for this — we need to string it out as long as we can. So he's fucking a white girl. So what? He's been finished a long time, has Amajit. Let him go on digging his own grave and we'll make a fistful while he's doing it. No, we stay here just like Faysal said. And we don't let either of them, Amajit or the girl, know we're watching them. There'll be plenty of time for some rough stuff later. You'll get your chance.'

10

Although it was not yet two o'clock, the curtains in the flat above Faysal Hussain's restaurant in the city centre were closed. When it came to his 'other business', Hussain was cautious, probably unnecessarily cautious, but since the rooms above the shops on the other side of the carriageway would make good observation points for anyone wanting to check him out, he felt caution was justified. Today was distribution day and the less anyone could see, the better.

For the moment, a telephone call had taken him a stride away from the man with him, but his eyes didn't leave him. He didn't trust anyone; some of his distributors thought nothing of pocketing the merchandise and then complaining that they had been sold short.

He listened to the caller without comment, but as he placed the receiver back on its wall rest, a smile curled along his lips, like surf running on the sea shore. He placed the first finger of his left hand lightly across his mouth as he considered the man crouching at the open box, checking its contents.

'Do you know Amajit Mahmood?' he asked.

The man didn't look up. 'He's a Paki. Why should I know him?'

Hussain stiffened. 'His wife was murdered a couple of days ago.'

A ray of liquid sunlight seeped through the

vertical slit where the two curtains failed to meet and particles of dust danced along the pale shaft which came to rest in a pool on the grey melamine of the table top. To one side of it were four more cardboard boxes and, opposite, a wad of twenty-pound notes.

Barry, satisfied that the contents were as they should be, closed the box up by alternately overlapping the four flaps, lifted it onto the table and placed it next to the others. He handed the money over. 'Are yer going to count it then? I've got to get back to work.'

Faysal pocketed the notes. 'I already have. Not that you're likely to doublecross me; you need me more than I need you.' He shrugged his shoulders. 'If you want the stuff, I'm the only person round here you can get it from.'

Barry threw him a look loaded with contempt, but said nothing.

Faysal's eyes strayed back to the telephone. 'You're sure you don't know Amajit Mahmood?'

'Why should I know the husband of some Paki tart who got 'erself murdered?'

'Because your sister knows him. She went into his house about a quarter to twelve this morning. That's what the call was about.' A smile of satisfaction played on Faysal's lips as he watched Barry's eyes widen, then burn. Who needed fists to knock Penistone down when a snippet of news like that did the job just as effectively?

Faysal walked towards the door. 'I'll leave you to get the stuff out to the taxi. You are using a taxi, aren't you? If it's that old tin can you're driving, be as quick as you can. I don't want it outside my restaurant any longer than necessary, it puts the customers off their curries.' He paused for a few seconds. 'You'll be at the rave? Remember it's two nights, Friday and Saturday.'

Still beyond rational speech, Barry made no reply.

Faysal said, 'I'll take that as a yes, shall I?' And when there was still no response, he continued, 'Somebody'll bring the other stuff up to the barn about half eight. Make sure you're there.' The door creaked as he opened it. 'Oh, and draw the curtains back before you go.'

Barry Penistone remained quite still, his breath rasping as though he had been stabbed deep in the chest. He watched without a word as the door closed then opened again slowly. Faysal reappeared, grinning widely. 'I don't think I mentioned, did I? They left Amajit's in an ambulance. She was the one on the stretcher.'

★　★　★

Graham glanced at Ali. 'Bad, was it, this morning?' he asked.

'If you mean being chewed over by Russell and Handford, yes, bad enough.'

They drove along in silence for a few minutes.

'It's common knowledge, then?' Ali said. He didn't want to talk about it, but he needed to know.

'Well, you can hardly keep a thing like that quiet,' Graham observed. 'The DI was well choked that you weren't at the briefing. You didn't stand a chance.'

'No, I suppose not.' He paused momentarily. 'I imagine Warrender had a lot to say.'

'Warrender always has a lot to say, none of it worth listening to.'

Ali pulled the sunshield down against a sudden ray of light. The brightness of the morning had just about lost its battle for supremacy as the rainclouds rolled across the sky, staining it a deep blue-black. But from time to time the sun pierced a fragile junction to shine directly into his eyes as he followed the ambulance along the back roads to the hospital.

They had arrived at Amajit's house to find it parked outside, and while experience told Ali never to jump to conclusions, his heart had slithered sickeningly into his stomach at the sight of the large white vehicle, its back doors open wide. An unpleasant image of Amajit and an empty bottle of paracetamol flashed into his mind and he could see himself having to explain to the DI and the DCI that the victim's husband had overdosed on a bottle of pills sometime after the early morning meeting. He didn't deserve this; he was feeling as guilty as hell as it was and he didn't need any more heaped on him.

It wasn't until the house door opened and Amajit backed out, holding a bag of what appeared to be saline solution in the air, closely followed by paramedics manoeuvring a stretcher through the narrow entrance, that Ali was aware that he had been holding his breath. He let it escape in a vaporous cloud as he pulled himself out of the car and hurried towards one of the men in green coveralls. Showing his warrant card he nodded towards the blanketed figure. 'What's happened?'

'Head injuries. We're taking her to the Royal.' He turned to Amajit, who was now in the ambulance. 'You coming with her, mate?'

Amajit handed the pliable bag of clear liquid to the paramedic and said, 'Yes. I'll just go and get the little boy.' Acknowledging Ali's presence, he jumped down and ran into the house.

'Who is she?' Ali looked down at the girl on the stretcher. Where her face was not discoloured with angry bruising it was ashen, and there was a thick crust of blood shielding a long gash over her eye. A drip ran into her arm and the paramedics had fitted a medical collar round her neck.

'Her name's Karen Penistone. But she's in no fit state to be questioned; she's had a hell of a bashing.'

'Do you know how it happened?'

'The usual, she fell down the stairs.' The paramedic raised his eyebrows to the heavens to register his disbelief.

'Did he do it?' Ali gestured back into the house with his head.

'Not if what he told us is right. He says she arrived here about twenty minutes ago and passed out in the front room. There's a bus strike and she'd had to walk from Saxton Road. Personally, I'm amazed she made it this far, the state she's in. She's more or less conscious now, but not lucid.'

Amajit emerged from the house, a young child in his arms, and Ali moved towards him. 'Look, I know this is a bad time, but I need to talk to you. Perhaps you can stay and we'll run you to the hospital later.'

'No, I'm going with her.' And to show that he would brook no argument, he pulled his key resolutely out of the Yale, climbed into the ambulance and seated himself opposite the stretcher. The paramedic closed the door. 'Like I said, we're going to the Royal, you can follow us down,' he said to the two detectives.

The casualty waiting room was hardly the best place to question Amajit but short of arresting him there was nothing the detectives could do but follow. Ali had lost control of the day, not a situation he liked to be in, nor one he was used to.

'Do you know who the girl is?' he asked Graham as they drove.

'Karen Penistone? Comes from a family of petty criminals, although as far as I know she's never been in any trouble — except for getting herself pregnant when she was still at school.'

Ali pulled the car up behind the ambulance which had stopped at the lights. 'There's no way she fell down the stairs with those injuries; that girl had been badly beaten. Do you think Amajit did it?'

'I doubt it, Sarg. It's much more likely to be one of her family. They're a violent lot, particularly Barry Penistone.'

But Ali was not prepared to let it go. 'A bit of a coincidence, though, don't you think? Two days ago Amajit's wife is found dead in a wood with severe head injuries and now another girl with similar wounds is carried from his house. I'm not sure I believe in coincidences.' Ali didn't want to let his personal opinions get in the way, but either Amajit had been downright unlucky or he was personally involved somehow. Either way, there was a link.

'Sarg, we're at green.'

Ali slid into gear and moved off. 'I wonder how she knows Amajit.'

'I don't think she does really know him. Rukhsana invited her to their house at Eid, she'd meet him then.'

'So you don't think there's anything between them?'

Graham's reasoning was phlegmatic. 'No, I can't see it. It's one thing marrying out of culture, but an affair with a young white, single mother? I doubt it. It's more likely she'd gone to see him to offer her condolences and help.'

Ali wasn't so sure. He wouldn't put it past Amajit. A Muslim who could marry out of his religion could easily take up with a white girl.

Keeping his thoughts to himself, he said, 'In that state? I don't believe it. There's more to it than that. When she's fit enough to be questioned, have a talk with her. See what you can find out.'

At the hospital the ambulance turned right to Accident and Emergency, while they were obliged to turn left to the car park. They followed the convoluted network of roads to the back of the building, and then the multitude of signs directing them through the hospital complex to casualty. Amajit was sitting at the

226

back of the waiting area, Danny fast asleep on his shoulder.

Ali approached him with what he hoped was an expression of sympathy on his face. 'How is she?'

'They've taken her to X-ray.'

Ali had a quick word with Graham then sat down on the chair next to Amajit. 'Look, I'm sorry, but I do need to talk to you. DC Graham's gone to find out how long they're likely to be in X-ray, and see if we can use one of the relatives' rooms. Do you want a drink while we're waiting?'

Amajit shook his head.

'Who is she? The girl?'

'She's — was — one of Rukhsana's patients.'

'Is this her child?'

'Yes.'

'Does she have any family?'

'I don't know. She lives on her own, but there may be some family. We haven't talked about her, only about Rukhsana. Although . . . ' He thought for a second or two. 'I think Rukhsana once mentioned a brother.'

At this moment Graham returned to say that Karen would be some time yet and yes, they could use the relatives' room. Giving Amajit no chance to argue, Ali took the sleeping boy from him and walked over to the door a nurse was holding open. He placed Danny gently on a two-seater settee. He stirred slightly, but didn't wake.

Amajit walked over to the window, rubbing the feeling back into his arm. He stared out onto the visitors' car park, busy even at this time of day. Then he turned and leaned against the sill.

Ali spoke. 'Why was she at your house?'

'She came to see me yesterday and I asked her to come again today.'

'Why?'

'Because she was kind and because I don't want to be alone — not that it's any business of yours.'

Ali ignored the comment. 'You don't know how she came to have those injuries?'

'No. Although I gather you think I might have done it. The ambulance man said you had asked if it was me,' he added by way of explanation.

It was a pity the ambulance man couldn't keep his mouth shut.

'Did you?'

'You really think I would hit a young woman — any woman?' Amajit fixed him with a hard stare. 'That wasn't the impression you gave me this morning.'

'It's not this morning any more,' Ali said icily. 'Rukhsana died from head injuries only two days ago, and I arrive at your house to find this girl leaving on a stretcher in a similar condition. I wouldn't be doing my job if I didn't wonder about that.'

'So you think I killed Rukhsana one day and then beat one of her patients unconscious the next? You'll have to do better than that, Sergeant.' Amajit's voice was steeped in sarcasm.

'Will I?' Ali said. 'You might give the outward impression that you're gentle and loving, but I know how single-minded you have had to be since you married your wife. It's probably not that big a step from getting your own way by determination to getting your own way by killing.'

Amajit's knuckles were white as he gripped the edge of the windowsill. 'I didn't kill my wife,' he said through gritted teeth, 'and I didn't push Karen down any stairs or beat her senseless. However small you think that step might be, it isn't one I have taken.'

'Well, we'll talk to Karen later, ask her. In the meantime, I want you to go over your movements on Tuesday again.'

Amajit turned back towards the window, but this time he didn't look out. Spreading his arms wide, he held on to the sill and bowed his head. Ali waited. Then Amajit pushed himself upright and moved slowly from the window to sit on a chair opposite the detective. 'Obviously you know.' He lifted his head. 'You know or you wouldn't be asking me again.'

'Know what, Amajit?'

'You know that I lied about where I was on Tuesday after the site visit.'

'So where were you?' Ali was surprised it had been so easy.

Leaning forward, his head sinking onto his chest, his elbows resting on his knees and his hands clasped together, Amajit took a moment to consider his answer, then he looked up and said, 'It had to be only a matter of time before you found out. Where I was, Sergeant, strengthens my alibi, but I'm sorry, I'm not prepared to tell you.'

'Well, I'm sorry too, Amajit, but you're going to have to tell me. There are at least two and a half hours unaccounted for and if you refuse to say where you were, then don't be surprised if I jump to the wrong conclusion.'

'You've already jumped to it.'

'Then tell me where you were.'

Amajit looked Ali squarely in the eye. 'It's not that I'm not prepared to say where I was, it's just that I'm not prepared to tell *you*.'

Ali couldn't conceal his surprise. 'Why ever not?'

'Because of your attitude towards me. You don't approve of me . . . ' Ali made to interrupt, but Amajit refused him the opportunity. 'Don't dishonour me even more by denying it. I know how you feel, and I know how you will feel when you find out where I was. You have a very expressive face, Sergeant, and you will show your disapproval just like you did on the day Rukhsana died. It's enough that I have to take it from my family and from the community, but I will not take it from a man I don't know who thinks he has a right to disapprove just because he's currently savaging my life.'

Taken aback by the onslaught, Ali sat quite still.

'You're on this case because you're one of us, right?'

Ali remained silent. He had lost control of the interview as well as the day.

Amajit stood up and walked away from the sergeant, then rounded on him. 'They think you will understand me, be a friend?'

230

Ali cleared his throat before he spoke. 'Not a friend,' he said, 'just someone who will understand.'

'Yet you understand less about me and my wife than anyone.' He pointed at Graham. 'I bet he has more awareness than you do. I bet he doesn't disapprove of me.'

'Nor me, sir. I'm not here to approve or disapprove — '

'I've only known you two days,' Amajit interrupted, 'and you must have said that to me at least three times. I don't believe you.' Then he added, 'And don't call me sir unless you mean it.'

Danny stirred again and gave a little cry. He opened his eyes and looked sleepily at Ali. Amajit moved towards him. 'Come on, little man, let's see if we can find your mummy.' He picked him up. Holding the boy close, he turned to Ali. 'I've nothing more to say. You tell your inspector I'll talk to him about where I was on Tuesday, but I want you nowhere near.'

★ ★ ★

Barry forced his way through the throng of women, children and old men milling around the reception desk.

He'd driven straight to the Royal after Hussain had told him about Karen. He knew she wouldn't be at any other hospital; the Royal was where his mother was brought each time his father gave her a good hiding. He looked round at the women with black eyes and bruises. They

231

always came here — every time.

He banged a closed fist on the counter. The harassed woman glared at him. 'Yes?'

'Ow long they gonna be? I 'aven't got all day.'

'It's a two-hour wait,' she said, pointing a well-manicured finger at the illuminated sign. 'They'll call when they're ready for you.'

'I'm not a patient, I'm waiting for my sister. She's back from X-ray, so what they doing?'

'They'll still call when they're ready,' she insisted.

Stupid bloody woman! He opened his mouth to tell her what she could do with herself, when he heard the sound of a child behind him. Recognising Danny's high-pitched cry, he spun round. He expected Karen, but saw instead an Asian man with the boy resting in his arms. Anger increased his adrenaline and he made a wild grab. 'What you doing with him? You bloody Paki; ger off him.'

The man, startled, moved backwards.

Barry jumped at him. 'You're that Paki she was with. What you done to her? You beat her up? You Paki bastard.'

Amajit tried to avoid the punches being thrown at him, and at the same time to hold tight onto Danny, but he moved too far and too fast and was unable to stop himself falling backwards onto the lap of a woman who, seeing what was going to happen, was attempting to flee her chair.

Barry sprang. 'Give 'im to me, he's mine.' He snatched at Danny. But Amajit was too quick and pushed the boy into the arms of a woman behind him.

The patients, who a moment ago had thought themselves too injured or too ill to move, scattered from the fighting men. Barry lunged for a chair. He lifted it above his head and made to throw it, but found himself caught in an armlock. He wasn't prepared for the ease with which the man who had come up behind him snatched the chair from his grasp. It bounced along the ground as his arms were pulled down and pinned behind his back and he was forced to the floor.

He struggled to free himself, but the armlock was too secure and the more he writhed, the tighter the hold. So he stopped squirming and lay still, his face contorted as it was pushed against the cold tiles.

'Well done, Sarg,' he heard a voice say. Then he was pulled upwards and pushed into a seat. 'Now, stay there.' Barry, his fury unabated, made to move, but the man pushed his hands into his shoulders. 'Stay there, or I'll cuff you.'

'Right.' The detective, breathing heavily, ran his fingers through his dishevelled hair, straightened his coat and pulled his warrant card out of his pocket. 'Sergeant Khalid Ali,' he said. 'And you are?'

Barry grunted, but said nothing.

'He's come for his sister,' the receptionist volunteered.

'Who is?'

'Karen Penistone. She came in with head injuries.'

'Thank you,' Ali turned to Barry. 'So, why the fight Mr Penistone?'

'What's he doin' with 'im?' Barry pointed at Danny, safe in Graham's arms. 'He's mine. No Paki touches him.'

'No, he's not yours, Mr Penistone. He's your sister's son. And Mr Mahmood is looking after him while she's being treated.'

'He's family, and he,' he glared at Amajit, 'he's not. He beat my sister up.'

'No, he didn't. If she's to be believed,' the inflection in Ali's voice suggested that she wasn't, 'she fell down the stairs. However, Mr Penistone, you did assault Mr Mahmood, we all saw that. And if he wants to press charges, then I shall arrest you.' He turned to Amajit, who was sitting in one of the vacated chairs, and raised his eyebrows inquiringly.

'No, no, Sergeant, I don't want to press charges.'

'Then, Mr Penistone,' said Ali, 'I suggest you go home and calm down. No doubt your sister will be in touch.'

Barry slouched towards the door. As he pulled it open, he turned and yelled, 'You watch out, Paki. I haven't finished with you.'

Ali turned to Amajit. 'I think he means you,' he said with a wry grin, 'but I suppose he could have meant me.'

For the first time that day, they both smiled.

A doctor appeared from a treatment room. 'Mr Mahmood?' Amajit stood up. 'Miss Penistone's X-rays show no fractures, but she is badly concussed. I would much prefer she was admitted, at least for one night, but she's adamant that she has to go home. She says

234

there's no one to look after her child. Do you know if there is anyone who can be with her? She really shouldn't be on her own.'

Ali raised his eyebrows in astonishment when Amajit said, 'That's all right, she can stay with me.'

★ ★ ★

Handford, a folder of papers in his arms, walked over to Ali's desk. 'I hear you got stuck in today,' he said. 'Quite a fight, from what I've been told. Graham was very impressed. He says Penistone is a mountain of a bloke.'

'Reflex action. I acted before I thought.'

'Not what I heard.'

'No? Well, there was a child involved.'

'Well done, anyway. But try not to make a habit of it. The team's not big enough for me to lose an officer to a hospital.' Handford grinned, attempting to allay any thought Ali might have that he was criticising.

There was a moment's silence, then Handford said. 'I gather you didn't get far with Mahmood.'

'No. He won't talk to me. Well, not about what he was doing during those two and a half hours. He's prepared to tell you, but he thinks I'll disapprove.'

Handford was tempted to comment, but instead said, 'It happens. I'll see him later this afternoon.' He placed the file on Ali's desk. 'In the meantime, look through that. It's the file on the Jamilla Aziz case last year. It doesn't have a bearing on this case — or at least it shouldn't, but it won't go away. It's only fair,' he glanced over at Clarke, who held his thumb up in the air, 'that everyone knows what happened. Read it, then come and ask any questions you want. I'll see you later.'

11

Barry stood in the small sitting room, his anger at his humiliation at the hands of Ali and Graham straining to overtake his concern for Karen, but not wholly succeeding. Where the hell was she? Still with that Paki? She'd get what for if she was. She should never have been with him in the first place. Hadn't he made that clear enough last night? With a kid to look after she should be at home, looking after him, not giving him over to some Paki.

A feeling of hopelessness swamped him. Why couldn't she be here? Where was she? Concern was winning. He tried to force his anger back to the surface, because anger pushed aside all those emotions he never wanted to feel. Emotions that hurt. Just like thoughts of Donna hurt. Donna and Karen; Karen and Donna. The two women he wanted most in his life were the two he was losing; one to a butcher and the other to a Paki. Donna had been like no other woman he had ever known, and Karen was the sister he loved more than any other member of his family. She wasn't like the rest of them. She was no looker, not even her best friends would say that. But she was bright, would probably make something of herself one day, or would have done if she hadn't had Danny. No one could consider intelligence a large part of the Penistone make-up — one brain cell between them, the teachers used to say

— except for Karen. A loose gene somewhere, one that had sneaked in. She shouldn't have been born a Penistone, she deserved better, and so did Danny because he was sharp like his mother. They both deserved something better than what they had; but not a Paki, not that Paki, not Mahmood.

The image of Danny in the man's arms rekindled Barry's anger. Finally it outpaced concern. Why couldn't she stick to one of her own? Why spoil things? Karen and Danny were his, not some Paki's. *He* should be taking care of them and no one, particularly that black cop, had the right to stop him. But coloureds swarmed everywhere, thinking they could run everyone's lives.

Well, not his, nor Karen's, nor Danny's. He would see to that. His father used to say they needed to be shown who was boss. 'They're in our country,' he used to say, 'and they've to be bloody well shown who's boss.' Then he'd laugh and dig him in the ribs. 'It's the eleventh bloody commandment, Barry lad, show the Pakis who's boss.'

In all his twenty-seven years it was probably the only commandment Barry had ever followed. He'd shown them who was boss all right, even in school — or at least he had until one of them had made him a laughing stock. One lunchtime he'd sought out the weediest kid he could find, cornering him against the gym wall, intending to thrash him, demonstrate who was top dog and who was nothing. But the boy had ducked as Barry rammed out his fist and instead of hitting him he'd slammed into the brick wall. Made a right mess of his hand but, worse, the Pakis had laughed at him. Groups of them taunted him every time they saw him and it was one of them who later, much later, had arrested him after he'd smashed the beer glass into the face of the man in the pub. That was the worst humiliation, the Paki clamping the handcuffs tight round his wrists and pushing him into the van, then sitting there, never taking his eyes off him, never letting the smirk leave his lips. In prison Barry had kept that image at the forefront of his mind so that his hatred of them could mature until it was fully ripened, so ripe that it was sweet to the taste.

And now his sister was spending time with one. Doing God only knew what.

In the bakery warehouse where he worked, his imagination wouldn't leave him alone. He'd conjured up a picture of them together, a picture which had adhered itself to his brain, like a sticky tape that he couldn't shake off, and his hatred had festered like a sore so that eventually he'd just left, gone back to the hospital to tell them that they'd got to stay away from each other. But she wasn't there; the woman with the long fingernails said she'd been discharged and gone home. Just showed, she was all right — that Paki'd had no need to stick his nose in.

And now he was back at the house and she wasn't here either.

The woman next door had said something about seeing a car outside earlier. 'I thought I saw a car, but I didn't see her. Course, there are those that just use the estate as a car park. The council should do something about it.'

She'd have prattled on endlessly had Barry not pushed past her to thrust his key into the lock. He was in no mood to listen to her drivelling on. As he closed the door, he caught the words, 'Miserable git.' From the security of the hallway, he signed his reply.

The house was silent. He'd shouted her name, but there'd been no answer. 'Come on, Karen; I'm not going to hit yer.'

The gloom of the November evening mixed uneasily with the murky staleness of the hallway and together they seemed to intensify the silence. He tried to shoulder away his unease, but a coil of apprehension squirmed its way through his body, the nerve endings shorting like loose wires as his concern for his sister emerged to crawl over them. Perhaps she wasn't with the Paki; perhaps she'd collapsed somewhere.

Feelings he preferred not to experience were edging into his mind; they smacked of guilt and he didn't believe in guilt. It implied that what had happened was all his fault and it wasn't, she'd brought it on herself, it was nothing to do with him, he'd just put her right, that was what you did with someone you loved, it was a way of showing them that you loved them. He forced himself to think of other more palatable explanations for her absence. She'd probably gone to do a bit of shopping — for Danny's tea. She'd be back soon.

That should have calmed him, but it didn't. His nerves jangling, he wandered the house. The kitchen was as he'd left it when he'd gone off to

240

work this morning — she hadn't even washed up. He picked up the half-empty bottle of milk and sniffed at it. Instantly he pulled his nose away as the rancid foulness percolated his nostrils. She needed putting right on a few things; he didn't want Danny brought up in a mess like this. She'd been too young to have a kid, that was the trouble. If she'd told him early enough that she was in the family way he'd have made her get rid of it; might have slapped her around a bit first, taught her a lesson, but he'd have helped her in the end. She was his sister and you didn't desert your sister, whatever she'd done. But she'd kept it to herself until it was too late, so Danny was born and now he was family and she had to look after him properly.

A sound startled him. Karen. He lunged into the darkening hall, peering into the shadows. There was no one there. No Karen, no Danny. What he had heard was the local evening paper dropping onto the mat. Leaving it where it had fallen, he returned to the sitting room and turned the knob of the gas fire to high. There was nothing to do but wait. To discourage any more unwelcome thoughts from churning him up, he switched on the television, then slumped into a chair. It was still the children's programmes, so he flicked the controls until he found something more to his liking. Some American chat show, better than nothing; but eventually the sound and the flickering images faded into the background. It couldn't be far off Danny's teatime, so where was she? Danny should be here now, playing with his toys. He

241

liked to watch Danny play with his toys.

Glancing over to the cardboard box which housed the playthings, suspicion shifted abruptly into certainly. It wasn't there. He hadn't noticed before, but it was gone. She'd taken Danny's things to that Paki's. The car outside had been his, just like it had been his the previous night. It was the only explanation; she couldn't be anywhere else. None of her friends had a home of their own and there was no way she'd be at her mum's, not with the amount of grief she was given there. So the Paki's was the only place she could be.

Anger erupted in a torrent of expletives and he dashed up the stairs and into the bathroom. Danny's bath things were gone; in the bedroom his cot was empty, there were no night clothes — and his blanket, that was gone too. She'd take that to help him sleep; he'd not sleep without that blanket.

Back down in the kitchen, Barry pulled open cupboards and drawers, pushing crockery and cutlery to one side, knocking over the milk bottle which spilled its curdled contents over the draining board and onto the floor. Danny's plastic dishes and spoon and fork were gone too.

He bolted back into the hallway and grabbed the newspaper off the floor. Snatching at each page he tried to find a piece on Rukhsana Mahmood's murder — it would say where she had lived. His eyes scanned the print. Nothing. Only what the cops had said on telly. Throwing the paper down, he flung himself round the door into the sitting room. Yesterday's newspapers

242

— there'd be something in them. He scrabbled about in the pile, finally finding the paper whose headlines screamed out the one word MURDER in large black letters. And down towards the bottom of the page was the name of the road where she had lived.

★ ★ ★

'So, what happened?' Faysal threw a couple of cans at the two men sitting at the table, then leaned up against the cupboards, arms folded.

Jahangier's can fizzed as he opened it and the brown liquid spurted out, spilling over the edge. He licked the splashes off his hand, then took a drink. 'Just what we told you. She turned up at the house with her kid. Amajit came out all friendly, put his arms round her, took her inside, then came back for the kid and the pushchair. About twenty minutes later an ambulance arrived and took her to hospital. He went with her. Just before they left, the Asian copper turned up, but Amajit wouldn't have nothing to do with him so he got back in his car and they followed the ambulance.'

'And there's no doubt it was Karen Penistone?'

'It was her all right,' Kamal said.

'Did you follow them down to the hospital? Find out what had happened?'

Jahangier answered. 'No, we couldn't take the chance we'd be spotted. It was like a fucking convoy, what with the ambulance and the police.'

'So, you don't know what happened to her?'

'Head injuries, according to the woman at the hospital. I rang on the mobile, said I was her cousin and had been told she'd been taken to casualty. I gave some guff about being on the motorway and being really worried about our Karen and she told me that she'd been brought in with head injuries.'

'How did she get them?'

'Somebody beat her up, I suppose.'

'Amajit?'

Jahangier laughed out loud. 'Can you see our cousin beating anybody up? He's far too nice for that, too educated.'

Faysal ignored the bitterness in his tone, he wasn't interested in Jahangier's jealousy. 'Then what happened?'

'Well, we hung about for a couple of hours until the ambulance brought them home.'

'Both of them?'

'Yeah, him and that tart.' Kamal was tired of being on the sidelines. 'She went in the house with him, and then a bit later they both came out and got in his car.'

'You followed them?'

'Yeah, he drove her to her house.'

'Where's that?' Faysal shifted his position.

'Saxton Road, on the Scargill Estate. Number one hundred and four.'

'And then?'

'They stayed there for about a quarter of an hour, then they came back out carrying some carrier bags and a box and went back to Amajit's.'

'She's gone to live with him,' Kamal broke in.

He could barely conceal his excitement. 'He's moved her in.'

'What, with her stuff in a few carrier bags?' Jahangier scoffed. 'I don't think so.'

Kamal strove to re-establish his credibility. 'They'll go back for the rest.'

'Yeah, with a furniture van, I suppose,' his brother retorted, his voice heavy with sarcasm. 'Don't be stupid!'

Banging his can hard onto the table, Kamal scowled at his brother. 'You think you're so fucking clever, you tell me what they're doing.'

For a moment the two of them stared at each other, their eyes locked together, neither giving way.

'Leave it,' growled Faysal, and Kamal picked up his can and took a long drink.

Faysal turned to Jahangier. 'He's got a point, you know,' he remarked. 'Why has Amajit got the girl in his house?'

Feeling more assured, Kamal smirked at his brother. 'One out, one in. And he's not fussy, anyone'll do.'

Faysal rubbed his hands over his face. 'You're sure it's Penistone's sister?'

'Yes.'

'Then we need to put a stop to it. Anyone else but Penistone's sister I wouldn't have minded; but *he* won't like it and he'll cause trouble.'

'We could go in and sort them out. Put them both in hospital.' Kamal could barely conceal his excitement.

'Don't be stupid. We'd have the fuzz crawling all over the place. Do what I told you to do.

Watch them and let me know what's happening. I'll talk to Amajit, sort him out. Now you go downstairs and get yourselves something to eat — in the kitchen, not in the restaurant.'

The aroma of the curries being prepared for evening clients was filling the upstairs flat, and both brothers were hungry. They'd spent all day in the car, with only sandwiches and a flask of coffee, and they were ready for a good evening meal. They were almost at the door when Faysal said, 'Just a minute, Jan.'

Jahangier turned back, saying he would catch Kamal up.

'Not in front of him.' Faysal indicated Kamal's disappearing form with his head. 'I want you to warn Barry Penistone's sister off. Make sure she keeps away from Amajit. Do whatever it takes, but warn her off. The last thing I need is Penistone on my back. And if Amajit's screwing his sister, that's what I'll get and I don't need it. He's trouble, is Penistone, and I don't want the cops around here because of him.'

★　★　★

'Please don't go on about it. I don't want the cops involved.' Wearily, Karen laid her head back on the settee where Amajit had insisted she rested. Danny was playing on the floor with his toys.

Amajit, squatting down beside her, shook his head. 'People can't go round beating people senseless. Look at you.'

'I'm all right.'

246

'No, you're not. You've been lucky. It could have been a lot more serious. You could have ended up like Rukhsana, on a mortuary slab.' Tears filled his eyes.

Karen stretched out her hand and stroked his cheek with her palm. 'I know, I know. But that won't happen. He wouldn't do that to me. He was just angry with me, that was all.'

'Who was angry with you, Karen?'

Without replying, she pulled her hand away from his face. Amajit held her gaze for a long moment, then said quietly, 'It was your brother, wasn't it? I saw what he was like when he came at me at the hospital. If Sergeant Ali hadn't been there . . . ' He shrugged. A frown creased his forehead. 'Why, Karen? Why would he do this to you?'

'Please, Amajit.' He heard the fear-laced weariness in her voice. 'I can't tell you.' She made to move from the settee. 'I can't stay here. I've got to go home.'

Placing his hands on her shoulders, he said firmly, 'No. You're staying here. No more questions, I promise. I told the doctor I'd be with you and I will.' He stood up. 'You rest, try to get some sleep. Just tell me what to give Danny for his tea, and I'll do it.' An expression of surprise nudged away the pain which blanketed her face. He laughed. 'Don't look at me like that. I do know what a kitchen looks like. I might not know much about children, but I can probably give him a bath as well if I'm pushed. Putting nappies on — well, that might prove a bit more difficult.'

247

'Anything then. Beans on toast, a boiled egg; anything like that.'

'Right. Don't worry about us. We'll be all right, won't we, Danny?' And he lifted the child and a couple of his toys from the floor and disappeared through the door.

Out in the hallway, he rested against the wall. 'What's happening, Danny?' he asked the child. Two days ago his life had been peaceful, ordered. Now, he seemed to be caught in a whirlpool of violence, spinning round, arms thrashing, trying to grasp first at Rukhsana, then at Karen, but still sinking. He held Danny close, felt the hardness of the boy's skull against his cheek. Its firmness gave him comfort. Tears wet the child's hair and he wiped them away with his hand.

'Who would hurt your mummy like that?'

Her brother? It had to be; she would have denied it if it hadn't been him. What could she have done to deserve such a beating? Come here to see him? At the hospital Barry Penistone had called him a Paki, hadn't wanted him to touch Danny. But to beat his sister because he didn't like Pakistanis . . .

Pushing himself off the wall, he gripped Danny. 'Come on, teatime,' he whispered in the boy's ear and walked towards the kitchen where he placed him carefully on the floor.

'There was no need to hit your mummy like that.'

The little boy's eyes stared up at him, as though taking in every word.

'He shouldn't have hit her, not because of me,' Amajit told him, and he bent down to trace the

248

child's cheek with his finger. 'I would never have done that to Rukhsana, whatever she'd done.'

⋆ ⋆ ⋆

'Thank goodness.' Amajit appeared singularly relieved to see Handford. He grabbed him by the arm and ushered him and Graham through the door. 'I don't suppose you know how to put a nappy on, do you?'

'Well, it's a long time since I've done it,' Handford said, 'but I imagine it's a bit like riding a bike, once learnt never forgotten.'

Graham followed them into the room, the hint of a smile hovering about his lips.

Handford sensed the constable working on the story he would convey back to the station. He turned. 'Don't even think about it!' he warned. 'One word; just one word . . . '

'I've given him something to eat and he's had a bath,' Amajit explained. 'But the nappy is beyond me. I'm not even sure which is the back and which is the front.' He raked a hand through his black hair. 'Karen's asleep upstairs and I don't want to wake her if I can help it.'

'How is she?'

'Tired and still in some pain. She ought to have stayed in hospital.'

Handford took his coat off and handed it to Graham.

'Is there any cream in that bag?' he asked, bending down towards the child who was sitting up on the settee. Danny had squirmed out of the towel that had been wrapped round him and was

249

completely naked. 'Come on, young man, let's see if I can still remember how.' Deftly, he laid him on his back, held up his legs with one hand and liberally spread cream over his buttocks and genitals with the other. Then he wrapped the nappy round him, pulled the tapes tight and fastened them down. He lifted the toddler up; the nappy stayed secure. 'Not a bad attempt, if I say so myself, although they're easier than in my day,' he remarked.

'You've saved my life.' Amajit wound the towel round Danny and gathered him in his arms. 'I'll get his pyjamas on and put him to bed, then we can talk. I imagine that's why you're here.'

'Yes.' Handford cleaned his hands with a baby wipe from the plastic box.

'Make yourselves a coffee, I won't be long.' Amajit moved towards the door. Twisting himself around to face the two strangers, the little boy's face lit up with a wide grin and he waved his fingers at Handford. The big man smiled and threw him a kiss. In spite of the situation, the murder, the violence, he was reminded of his daughters when they were babies and he felt a sudden surge of envy for Karen. She was the lucky one. He'd missed such a lot of his children's lives; they'd grown up almost without him realising it. It wasn't too bad while he was in uniform, but as a detective he'd hardly ever been at home, certainly not when the children were up. He left in the morning while they were in bed, and arrived home at night when they were asleep. And even when he was at home in decent time, he'd been so immersed in cases, reports and working his way up the promotional ladder that he might just as well have not been there.

Graham watched him with approving eyes. 'You've made a friend there,' he said. 'And that nappy, guv, a neat job, if I may say so.'

'Yes, and if it gets round the station, I'll know who it came from.'

'Not a word, boss; my lips are sealed.'

'They'd better be. And since I've done my good deed for the evening and all you've done is stand around and watch, you can make the coffee.'

Left alone, Handford let his eyes wander the room. Nothing much had changed; it was a little more untidy perhaps and dust was beginning to settle on the furniture, but that was all. He lifted the photograph of Rukhsana off the mantelpiece; she was quite beautiful, vibrant and colourful. It was a studio photograph, but for all that it was natural rather than posed. The deep blue of her dress glowed against the cream background. Black hair framed the swan-like neck and slender face. Luminous brown eyes shone with happiness, but it was the smile which caught Handford's attention and as he looked at her he wanted to smile with her. No wonder Amajit had fallen for her — and Ian Berridge for that matter. Handford sighed and wondered why such a beautiful woman who had risked all to marry out of her faith, had strayed so soon. Perhaps it was that she had found an independence that so many Asian women were not allowed. He knew from the race relations officers at Central that many second-generation

251

Asians lived a double life, partly in their own culture and partly in that of the West. Perhaps that was the reason for both the marriage and the affair. He would never know, but what was certain was that if Amajit knew nothing about his wife's relationship with Berridge, then sometime during this evening he would bring the man's world crashing down around him once again.

He replaced the photograph as Graham, three mugs of coffee in his hands, came in, followed by Amajit. Handford took one mug and turned to the chair. 'May I?' he asked.

Amajit nodded. 'I've put Danny in bed with Karen. Do you think he'll be all right?'

'I'm sure he will.' Handford paused for a moment. 'Why did you agree to have Karen stay the night? If you don't mind me saying so, it seems an odd thing for you to do, particularly in the circumstances.'

'What circumstances? Do you mean because my wife's just been murdered and I'm a man on my own, or because I'm Asian and a Muslim?'

Handford shifted uncomfortably. 'Well, all of those reasons, I suppose, but mainly I was wondering if you could cope. You've had a hard forty-eight hours.'

Amajit clutched his mug tightly with both hands. 'Sorry, I'm a bit touchy at the moment. You're right. It is odd and I've been asking myself the same question ever since I made the offer.' He paused for a moment, as if trying to understand his own reasons. 'Karen came to see me yesterday afternoon; she wanted to say how sorry she was about Rukhsana and she stayed, let

252

me talk, listened to me, didn't judge me. She liked Rukhsana, she wanted to grieve with me. I don't want to be alone, so I asked her to come back today and she did, in spite of her injuries. I just felt it was the least I could do, let her stay so that she would be looked after. She certainly couldn't be on her own, not in her condition.'

'Who did it, do you know?'

'Her brother, I think. She hasn't said so in so many words, but I think it was.'

'Do you know why?'

'Probably because she came to see me. He was at the hospital, you know. He tried to grab Danny from me. He hates me — well, not me particularly, but all Asians. He calls us Pakis, but I don't think he can distinguish an Indian from a Pakistani from a Bangladeshi. He just lumps us all together.'

Silence spanned the room. Handford broke it.

'Why did you lie about your movements on the day Rukhsana died?'

The abrupt change in topic and in the detective's tone caught Amajit off guard. Startled, his hand jerked, spilling coffee over the side of the mug. 'I'm sorry?'

'Why did you lie about your movements on the day your wife died?'

Rubbing at the brown liquid dripping onto his trousers, Amajit attempted to regain his composure. 'I'm not sure I did, exactly.'

'Come on, Mr Mahmood, you told us you had returned to the office immediately after you left the building site. Yet when we checked, we were informed that it was around half past two before you got back. Where were you?'

Amajit studied his coffee. 'I was in Leeds.'

'Leeds?' Handford glanced across at Graham. 'Why Leeds?'

'I went to see someone.'

'Who?'

Amajit's gaze was still concentrated on the mug of coffee, but the expression on his face was a contorted mixture of grief and shame. Then, as though he had come to a decision, he looked up, holding Handford's eyes. 'I went to the gurdwara — that's the — '

'Sikh temple, I know.'

'I went to talk to one of the elders there. I wanted . . . I'd decided to . . . I wanted to know if I could become a Sikh, change my religion.' The words tumbled out, as though the speed at which they were uttered would make them more palatable. 'I couldn't discuss it with anyone here, not where Rukhsana and I were well known, it would have caused too much trouble. So I went out of town.'

A silence developed which neither Handford nor Graham attempted to break. No wonder Amajit wouldn't tell Ali. It didn't take much imagination to guess at his reaction.

'Can I ask why you considered changing your religion? It's an awfully big step.'

Amajit grasped the mug with both hands and lifted it up against his cheek. It seemed to give him comfort and strength.

'I loved her, Inspector. So much. But it was hard for us, living estranged from our families, wanting a child, but knowing the difficulties for it and for us, arguing over whether it was a good idea, trying to come to a decision. I thought, I felt, that if I made this move, Rukhsana . . . ' his voice faltered and he paused to collect himself. 'Rukhsana could have returned to her family; they would probably have accepted her back. I also thought it would stop any arguments as to how our children were to be brought up and give them a chance to grow with parents who were at one. And I hoped, too, that just possibly her family would come to terms with our marriage and accept me. At least then our children would have *one* set of grandparents.'

'And your family?'

'It would hurt them.' Four words which were nowhere near adequate to describe the further anguish they would have endured. Amajit sank into himself for a moment, grief stalking but not breaching the boundary of his fragile sanity. No doubt he wished it would, then he would cease to feel; but he was too strong for that, had too many reserves to draw on. Pulling back from the edge, he fought to regain his composure. 'I've learned to live without them, Inspector,' he said quietly. 'I don't like it, but I could have gone on doing so.'

'I take it then that Rukhsana didn't know what you were intending to do.'

'No.' Amajit lowered the mug, dragging his gaze with it. 'I wanted to see whether it was possible before I mentioned it to her.'

'How did you get to Leeds?'

'By car.'

'You drove straight there after the site visit?'

'Yes.'

'So you arrived round about twelve, twelve fifteen?'

'Yes, about that.'

'You were expected?'

'I rang them a few days ago, asked to see one of their elders.'

'How long were you at the temple?'

'About three-quarters of an hour.'

'Do you have the name of the person you spoke to? We'll need to check.'

'I've got it written down. I'll get it for you. It's in the car.'

The two detectives waited until they heard the front door close, then Graham said, 'No wonder he wouldn't tell Sergeant Ali. It doesn't seem that much of a deal to me, but then I'm not the religious type, although I do know how the sergeant feels about being a Muslim.'

Handford didn't want to discuss Ali. 'If Mahmood left the temple around one o'clock, he would have been back at the office by a quarter to two, two at the latest, yet he logged on just after half past. He couldn't have gone straight back, he must have gone somewhere else first.'

The front door opened and closed and a few seconds later Amajit appeared in the room. He gave the piece of paper to Handford.

'I'm sorry, Inspector, I should have told you all this when you first asked.'

'It would certainly have saved us a lot of time.'

'I'm sorry.' He stood in front of the detective like a schoolboy in trouble.

Handford looked up at him from his chair.

'How long did it take you to drive back to the office?'

Amajit hesitated. 'Half an hour, three-quarters at most.'

'Are you sure?'

'Yes.'

Anger suddenly flared in Handford's eyes. 'Oh, come on, Amajit,' he shouted, startling both the man in front of him and Graham, who shot a surprised glance at his boss. 'Even if it took three-quarters of an hour you'd have been back by a quarter to two. You didn't log on until two thirty or thereabouts. Stop messing me around. Where were you?'

Amajit didn't reply immediately. His lips compressed as the muscles around his jaw line flexed. He inched backwards to his chair and eased himself into it.

Handford watched Amajit's eyes as they darted like moths caught in the light. 'Come on,' he said quietly, 'where were you?'

The calmer tones seemed to soothe Amajit and he leaned forward, letting his gaze drop to the carpet. 'I went up to the nursing home on my way back.'

The two detectives looked at each other. Amajit was there at the relevant time. He could have killed her. And if he knew about the affair, then he had the motive.

'Why? Why did you go to the nursing home?' Handford asked.

'Rukhsana was going to see her aunt, I was hoping she'd still be there.'

'Why?'

257

'To talk with her, tell her where I'd been.'

'Was she there?'

'I didn't see her.'

'Her car was in the car park.'

'I didn't go into the car park. I was halfway up the drive when I saw the odd-job man. I stopped to ask him if he knew where she was, but he said he'd seen her come out of the main building, so I assumed she'd left.'

'And then?'

'I carried on up to the front of the house to turn round and then I went back to the office.'

'Did Nathan Teale, the odd-job man, see you drive away?'

'No, he'd gone by the time I reached that part of the grounds.'

Handford rested against the back of the chair and rubbed his hand over his face. The smell of the baby cream still lingered. There was irony, he thought as he savoured its fragrance; Amajit couldn't put a baby's nappy on, but he could well have done the unthinkable and smashed his wife's skull with a coping stone. How much time would that take? Would half an hour, forty minutes, be long enough to kill her and get back to the office? It was all too loose, he needed to know exactly when Amajit had arrived at the temple, when he had left; what the traffic conditions were like, how long it would have taken him to get back.

'You realise what this means, Mr Mahmood?'

Amajit lifted his head. 'Yes, it means that I was up there round about the time my wife was being murdered.'

'It means, Amajit,' Handford said softly, his words paced and even, 'that there is nearly three-quarters of an hour unaccounted for in your movements. And unless you can fill those forty-five minutes for me, you don't have an alibi. You could have been the one up there murdering her.'

12

Amajit sprang from his chair and strode across to the window where he snapped the curtains shut, locking out the lights and sounds of the evening traffic. He turned to face the two police officers.

'I didn't kill my wife. I didn't!' He placed increasingly hysterical emphasis on each word.

'Why should I believe you?' Handford's voice was hard. 'You've lied about just about everything.'

'I haven't lied about being at the gurdwara, about wanting to change my religion.'

'Probably not, but it's taken a long time to get the truth out of you. You could have told me when I first saw you, you could have told Sergeant Ali earlier today, but you didn't. You might argue it was an evasion of the truth, rather than a lie, but it was still done to avoid the facts.'

Amajit spun round and faced Handford, his eyes gleaming. 'If you were in our situation, mine and Rukhsana's, you'd understand,' he said.

'Meaning?'

'Meaning that in our circumstances you learn very quickly that the only way to save face, to keep your self-esteem alive is to evade the truth, avoid the facts, as you put it. To be careful who you tell the truth to.'

'But not when we're trying to find out who killed your wife,' Handford pointed out quietly. 'What's pride worth then?'

Amajit offered no reply. Instead he sat down on one of the dining chairs near the window. Hunching his shoulders over the table, he contemplated his fingers as they picked up and played with an itinerant piece of fluff.

'What did you do after you left the nursing home, Amajit?'

'Nothing much. I drove a little way down the road, stopped the car in a lay-by and tried to think.'

'About?'

'About what I was doing; about my family and the effect my actions would have on them. About just how much more hurt I was prepared to inflict on them.' He rotated the fluff into a ball between the middle finger and thumb of his right hand and covered his eyes with the other, pressing hard against them to prevent his tears seeping through. 'I don't know . . . '

The man was exhausted and Handford felt deeply sorry for him. Amajit was carrying so much guilt. Handford knew he was being hard on him, yet it was important to bring the guilt out into the open. With Berridge it had been easy; his guilt, what there was of it, was on the surface and needed only scraping off, but Amajit's had gone deep and needed much more careful work.

'Go on,' Handford said gently.

Amajit dragged his hand away from his eyes, trying to wipe away the tears with it. 'I loved Rukhsana and I married out of my religion because of my love for her; I was considering deserting Islam for her. I needed to reflect on

261

what I was doing and why. I needed to be sure that my love for her was deeper than everything else, and that I would never blame her for what I was about to do.'

Handford threw a glance at his partner, a glance filled with sympathy, a glance that said that Rukhsana didn't deserve Amajit; and he didn't deserve what he was about to learn.

Amajit stared in front of him. 'I must have sat there for twenty minutes or more. I didn't reach any conclusions, because all I could think of was how much I loved her. I tried to fight my feelings, to let my head work out what was best but I couldn't do it because my love kept getting in the way.' He turned towards the two men and shrugged slightly. 'So I started up the car and returned to the office.'

'Did anyone see you?'

The prosaic nature of the question seemed to help and Amajit's voice gained strength as he answered. 'I have no idea, Inspector. I wasn't much interested in what was going on around me. I didn't take note of anyone, wave at anyone, talk to anyone.' His tone became tinged with desperation. 'So if you think I wasn't sitting in my car, if you think I was murdering my wife, you're just going to have to prove it because I can't help you any more.' He straightened up, heightened adrenaline giving him the energy to gain control. 'Now if that's all, I'd like you both to go.'

The sympathy Handford had felt a moment ago evaporated at Amajit's abrupt dismissal of them.

'I'm sorry, Mr Mahmood,' he said tersely, 'but I haven't finished yet. There are more questions.'

'And if I don't want to answer them?' Truculence couched his words.

'Then I'll caution you and take you to the station and we'll carry on there.'

'You're arresting me?' Consternation eclipsed the brashness.

'Not if I can help it, but I've enough to arrest you on suspicion.'

Handford wasn't sure whether Amajit believed him or not. He hoped he did, because if he did, he would see the sense in staying where he was. Suspicion sticks to a person who has been 'helping the police with their inquiries', particularly if that person is the victim's husband. He hoped Amajit would realise that. But in truth Handford was more concerned that arresting Amajit would mean his rights to a solicitor would come into play, the clock would start to tick and Handford would be under pressure. That was the last thing he needed, because this time he might be arresting the wrong person.

They waited for what seemed an eternity.

'All right, Inspector, ask your questions.'

Handford's relief was evident. Needing time, he edged away the moment.

'Perhaps another coffee first, sir. Detective Constable Graham will do the honours.'

'If you like. You don't mind if I just take a look at Karen and the little boy while we wait?'

'No, you go ahead.' Handford was glad of the break. It gave him time to collect his thoughts, to decide how he was going to tackle the next few minutes.

The chances were that Amajit had no idea what was coming. Handford wished he didn't have to tell him. In fact, he didn't *have* to. In spite of what he had just said, he could get up and go now, terminate the interview until another day. And why not? It was late, Amajit was tired, *he* was tired. But if he gave in, said to hell with it, let's go home, start again in the morning, Amajit would have time to regain his strength. The only way Handford would really know if the man was telling the truth would be to take him to the edge; put him where he was most vulnerable. Handford knew all about vulnerability; he'd been in its clutches for over a year.

The trick was to play it so that Amajit didn't become so insecure that he'd agree to anything to end the nightmare; rather, he had to get him to a state where he could pick at the truth, just as he had with Berridge. In the end the truth was what mattered — to everyone involved. And digging out the truth demanded that he ferreted about in other people's lives, foraged around in their present and their past, tainted the memories of those they loved and had loved. Soon the photograph in the frame would not be a comfort to Amajit; soon he would hate what he saw in it. And it worried Handford. It didn't matter a jot to him that he might bring Berridge down, because Berridge deserved it, but for some reason it did matter that he was doing the same to Amajit.

'Coffee, sir,' Graham announced.

'Thanks.'

'Do you think he killed her?'

Handford thought for a moment. 'No,' he said at last. 'If I'm honest, I don't, but we've got to be sure.' He took a sip of the coffee. 'I hope he didn't,' he murmured quietly.

Graham glanced at his boss. 'Why? Why do you hope he didn't?'

Handford sighed; Graham was not meant to have heard the last remark. 'Because I like him.'

'Not a very professional reason, sir, if you don't mind me saying so.'

For God's sake, what was it about his team that made DCs think they could lecture him? 'In my day, Graham,' he said, 'detective constables didn't question detective inspectors. They had more respect.'

Graham grinned. 'Sorry, sir. But even I know that lots of seemingly nice people kill.'

'Yes, all right, all right. Since you seem determined, I take your point. Now drink your coffee.'

Handford could feel the beginnings of a smile playing round his lips, but he wasn't prepared to give Dave Graham the satisfaction, so he stood up and walked to the window. The banter, he knew, had done them good. It was important every now and again to pull themselves away from the grief and the evil that surrounded them and act normally, even if only for a minute or two. He pulled the curtain to one side and peered out. It had begun to rain and the headlights of passing cars reflected in the puddles. He turned into the room.

'Tomorrow, I want you to check out Mahmood's alibi, particularly the times he arrived at and left the temple. Check with Traffic to see what the roads were like and how long would it have taken him to drive back from Leeds. Let's see if he did have time to kill his wife. Ask Warrender to question Nathan Teale again. Take him through his whole day, minute by minute. He didn't mention seeing Mahmood, so his mind needs jogging. If he forgot that, he may have forgotten other things. Bring him into the station if you have to.'

'Sir.'

'They're both sound asleep.' Amajit walked wearily into the room and slumped into the chair. Graham handed him a coffee.

'Thanks. I don't think I've ever drunk so much of the stuff. They say too much is bad for you.'

Handford wanted to get on. 'Let's make a start, shall we?'

Amajit gestured his agreement.

'Rukhsana went to visit her aunt at the nursing home regularly. Didn't that cause friction within her family?'

'I expect so, but her aunt is an independent old lady, she does what she wants, always has. Oh, she was hurt at the marriage, who wasn't? But she was forgiving and refused to disown Rukhsana, although she would have nothing to do with me.' Concern spread over his face. 'Has anyone told her about Rukhsana? I didn't think.'

'Yes, don't worry,' Handford said. 'The

266

manager at the home broke the news to her. She was obviously upset, but as you say, she's tough. One of my officers spoke to her this morning; he said she was coping well.'

'Good.' Amajit seemed genuinely relieved.

'Tell me about Rukhsana's friends.' Handford had drawn his metaphorical knife.

'She didn't have many. Most of the girls she knew at school, Muslim and Sikh, were forbidden to associate with her after we married. There were one or two she met in secret, but only occasionally.

'What about at the practice?'

'I don't think she looked upon the women there as friends, more as colleagues; she didn't talk about them much.'

'Did that include Dr Copeman?'

'Yes, I think so.'

'And what about Karen Penistone?'

'I don't know. She seemed to have built a good relationship with her. She said Karen was an intelligent girl but born into the wrong family, if you know what I mean.'

Handford nodded.

'Danny was born with club feet, so Karen has had to give him daily physiotherapy from the beginning. He had an operation when he was quite young, I think, but he still can't walk properly. Rukhsana dropped in as often as she could to help and give encouragement. She told me once that she was worried about who the boy's father was. Karen refused to name him, she was adamant she didn't want anyone to know, but I think Rukhsana had some idea.'

'Did she tell you?'

Amajit frowned. 'No, she wouldn't. Although she was intending to talk to Dr Haigh about it. I don't know whether she ever did.'

Handford drained his coffee mug and placed it on the floor next to his chair.

'You said that Rukhsana looked upon the women in the practice as colleagues. What about the other doctors?'

'The same; they were just the doctors.'

'I gather she was Dr Berridge's patient.' The knife played along the skin's epidermis, not quite drawing blood.

'At first, but when Dr Copeman joined the practice, she changed to her. She said she preferred a woman doctor.'

Graham, who had been sitting quietly, leaned forward in his chair. 'Are you with the same practice, sir?'

'Yes. I'm on Dr Berridge's list.'

'Are you happy with him?' Graham asked.

'I have no complaints.' Amajit seemed puzzled.

'How well do you know him?'

'Not at all, except as my doctor. Forgive me, but I can't see what my being a patient of Dr Berridge has to do with Rukhsana.'

This was decision time. Handford could either plunge the knife straight in or continue scratching the surface until the blood came. It would hurt either way. He decided on the former, to get it over with.

'Did you know your wife was having an affair with Dr Berridge?'

As Handford watched Amajit's expression

change, he knew for the first time the meaning of absolute horror. A host of emotions declared themselves one by one on Amajit's face. From disbelief to loathing. And the loathing, Handford knew, was for him.

And as the loathing penetrated, Amajit sprang to his feet, coffee spilling onto the carpet. 'Get out!' he yelled. 'Get out!'

Handford found himself being lifted by his jacket lapels. Graham made a grab for Amajit, forcing him to loosen his grasp, then pinned his arms behind his back. 'Sit down,' he barked and he pulled him back into his seat.

Breathing heavily, Graham turned to Handford. 'Are you all right, sir?'

'Yes, fine.' Handford smoothed his jacket and straightened his tie.

Amajit lay in a huddle, his tears forming a dark patch on the velvety fabric of the chair arm. 'How dare you! How dare you!' The words were just audible.

Handford returned to his chair. 'Mr Mahmood,' he said. 'Sit up straight, please.'

Amajit ignored him, spitting out the same words. 'How dare you? She would never do anything like that.' Then, looking up, he demanded, 'Where's your proof?'

'Dr Berridge has admitted the affair. He wouldn't do that unless it were true, he has too much to lose.' Handford paused. 'If you knew about it you would have had a strong motive for killing your wife.'

'If I'd known about it, Inspector,' he said, his voice muffled, 'it wouldn't have been my wife I would have killed.'

Handford forced himself out of his seat and wandered to the window. Unless other evidence came to light, he was fairly sure he had the truth now.

Amajit stirred. 'Why did you have to tell me?' The words were muffled. 'Why tell me?' He rocked backwards and forwards. 'Isn't it enough that she's dead?'

Handford turned. 'I'm sorry. I had to know how much you knew. And this was the only way.' He paused for a moment. 'Murder is a rotten business; it brings out the worst in all of us.'

Amajit fought for the words. 'The baby, was it his?'

'I don't know, not yet.'

Amajit doubled over, resting his forehead on his knees and wrapping his arms tightly across his stomach to stop the hurt. 'Will you tell me when you do know?'

'Yes, I will, when I know.' He squatted down beside Amajit. 'I promise.' He paused. 'I'm sorry,' he said at last. 'I know how it must hurt. Are you going to be all right?' A stupid question which deserved the look of derision it received.

Handford straightened up and Graham took over. 'Can we get someone to stay with you tonight?' he asked.

Amajit didn't want their concern; he shook his head. 'Just go,' he said.

They picked up their coats.

'Right, we'll leave you,' Handford said as he pulled his on, 'but we shall want to speak to you again. I'll give you — '

His voice was drowned out by loud and persistent knocking on the front door.

Handford turned to Graham, 'For Christ's sake, see to that,' he said, 'before whoever it is kicks the door down. Get rid of them.'

Graham had reached the sitting-room threshold when the sound of a boot impacting against the front door reached them, followed by the noise of wood splintering and the lock cracking open. A man Handford had never met pushed past and crashed into the room

'Where is she, Paki?' he yelled.

Oh God, thought Handford, taking in the man's enormous frame, I could do without this.

Graham made a grab for him. 'What do you want, Penistone?'

But Barry Penistone shook him off. He turned square on to Amajit who had moved from his chair and was backing towards the fireplace. 'Where is she, Paki?'

Handford took over. 'If you mean your sister, Mr Penistone, she's in bed. And if you want my advice, you'll leave her there.'

'Get lost, copper. This is between me and the Paki, it's nothing to do with you.'

'Then I'm making it my business. Karen needs to rest. In the meantime, you have broken down Mr Mahmood's front door and that's criminal damage. So if you don't want to be arrested, I would advise you to go home.'

Penistone sprang towards Handford, his fist raised towards the DI's head. For a man the size and build of Barry Penistone, the movement was smooth and very fast, and the detectives didn't

271

see it coming. Handford dodged smartly, instinctively raising his arm for protection. It took the full force of the ferocious blow which, even through the thick material of his overcoat, hurt like hell. He made a grab for his opponent's arm before Penistone could land another punch, missed and instead caught the blow full in the chest. The impact forced him backwards against the dining table. Penistone sprang at him again, but Handford rolled out of the way. Unable to get to the detective, Penistone turned towards Amajit, but Graham grabbed his arm, forced it downwards and twisted it behind the burly frame, at the same time pushing him down to the floor. Penistone thrashed and flailed around to break the hold on him, but by this time Handford had clambered over the furniture and had grabbed his head to bulldoze it into the carpet.

'Calm down,' Handford shouted at him. 'When you've calmed down, we'll let go of you.'

Eventually, his anger dissipated, Penistone stopped struggling and they pulled him to his feet. Handford shoved him towards Graham.

'Arrest him for assault and criminal damage,' he snarled, 'and call for a van to pick him up. In the meantime, get him out of my sight.'

As Graham pushed Barry out through the door into the hallway, Handford worked at getting his breath back; there was no doubt that he was growing too old for this.

As soon as he was able, he turned to the frightened figure behind him. 'Don't worry,' he said, still breathing heavily. 'He won't bother you again tonight.'

'Are you hurt?' Amajit asked.

Handford rubbed his arm ruefully. 'Broken arms mend,' he said. Then, 'No, I'm fine. I'll be able to show off my bruises tomorrow, though. God, he's a big man. And strong with it.'

A woman's colourless voice drifted in from the door. 'That's because he takes steroids.'

Amajit and Handford turned to see Karen, Danny in her arms, leaning unsteadily against the jamb.

'Steroids?'

'Yes, he's been taking them ever since he came out of prison.'

★   ★   ★

While DC Graham took Barry Penistone down to custody to be processed, Handford returned to his office to make two phone calls. The first was to Peter Redmayne. If Barry Penistone took anabolic steroids, then it was likely he had some dealings with Hussain. He needed to know whether Redmayne had seen Penistone at Hussain's flat.

'Peter? It's John Handford.'

There was a moment's silence at the other end. Then, 'Hello, John. I gather you want something.'

'Well, yes. I would like to ask you a question and possibly a favour.'

'Thought as much. You called me Peter, a sure sign you want something. I was Mr Redmayne in

273

the pub.' He let the comment sink in, then said, 'What can I do for you?'

'Do you know a man called Barry Penistone?'

'No, should I?'

'He's taking steroids, which probably means he's getting them from Hussain or one of his dealers.'

'What's he like?'

'A big bruiser of a man.'

'They're all big bruisers, the women as well. That's the point of taking steroids.'

'Yes, sorry. I'm a bit tired, I've just gone six rounds with him — at least it feels like it.' He rubbed at his arm and wondered whether he ought to have it checked out at the hospital. 'He's tall, six foot three or four, covered in what seems like sixteen stone of solid muscle. Face like a doughnut, eyes to match, dark hair, what there is of it; not quite a skinhead, but close.'

Peter Redmayne chuckled. 'My, he has caused you a problem, hasn't he? That's hardly the most prosaic description I've heard from a policeman.'

'If you mean I don't like him, then you're right,' Handford said, his tone vitriolic. 'He's a thug. But he hates Pakistanis, and if I can get a link with Hussain, I might be able to persuade him to shop the man — especially if I agree to drop the assault charge against him.'

'Any other form?'

'Yes, he's done eighteen months for GBH; came out about three years ago. Nothing much since has come to our notice, although there was an incident when he threatened the boyfriend of his onetime fiancée with a butcher's knife.'

274

'God, where did he get that from?'

'From the boyfriend, as it happens — he's a butcher. It seems Penistone was trying to get his girlfriend back and she wasn't having any, so he picked up the cleaver and threatened to use it on him. If I can't have you, I'll make damn sure he can't, kind of situation. Luckily someone heard the commotion and dialled nine, nine, nine. It didn't go anywhere in the end because they dropped the charges — didn't want the hassle.'

'Do you have a picture of him?'

'Yes, I'll fax it through to you.'

'Better send it to me here, at home. It's the same number. I'll see if I know him, have a ferret around, then get back to you.'

'Thanks.'

'Can I ask, is it likely that he has anything to do with Rukhsana Mahmood's murder?'

'I don't think so, we're not looking at him as a suspect. His sister was a patient of Rukhsana's, but as far as I know there's nothing to link him with the victim.'

'Just wondered. I'll get back to you on the steroids. And if anything comes of it, it's my story before it's anyone else's, yes?'

Handford stifled a sigh. 'Yes, Peter, it's your story before it's anyone else's.' He replaced the receiver. What the hell, better a friend than an enemy.

The second call was to Khalid Ali. Handford had wondered whether it would be better to speak to him face to face in the morning, but decided against it. He wouldn't have waited had it been any other officer and the sooner Ali knew

275

what Amajit had had to say, the better. If nothing else, it would give him time to sort out his feelings.

In the event, Ali's reaction was pleasing. 'I thought as much,' he said. 'It had to be something like that.'

'And you can deal with it?' Handford ventured. He was sure it wasn't as simple as that.

'Yes,' he said, 'I can deal with it. Today hasn't been the best one I've spent, but that and a long conversation I had with my wife last night has made me think about myself.'

Handford thought of Gill. 'You and me both, Khalid. You and me both.'

'Sir?'

'Yes?'

'Talking about my wife, she asked me . . . well, she wondered if you and your wife would spend the evening with us on Saturday. She thinks it would give us a chance to get to know each other — away from the job.'

'Why not? I think it's a great idea. I'll have to check with Gill first, make sure she hasn't got anything else fixed, but if she's free, we'd love to. I'll let you know in the morning.' The truth was that he wasn't sure it was such a good idea, but it would have been churlish to refuse, and Ali was right, it would give them the opportunity to get to know each other away from work.

He could almost hear Ali's grin on the other end of the phone. 'Right, sir, I'll see you then.'

'Before you go, have you read the file on Jamilla Aziz?'

'Yes, and I've talked to Clarke. I hope you

276

don't mind. He told me about the inquiry. I was on a long course during most of it, so he filled me in with the details.'

Handford could feel Clarke's smugness. 'No, I don't mind. He was the best person to ask.'

'He's very loyal to you, sir. He said you'd been badly treated. And if it's any help to you, I agree with him.'

'Thank you, Ali.' Handford suddenly felt very tired, it had been a long day. 'I ought to have told you before, but to be honest I couldn't get it out of my mind that you had been brought in to keep an eye on me. Stupid really. I'm sorry.'

'Forget it, sir. It's not important.'

'There is one thing, though. According to Peter Redmayne, the instigator was Faysal Hussain.'

'Amajit Mahmood's cousin?'

'The very same.'

'But why should Faysal Hussain start riots?'

'I wondered that too.'

'I could understand it if he was a relative,' Ali said cautiously, 'but he wasn't. So what was it to do with him? He strikes me as a person who wants to keep out of the limelight rather than risk being part of something as high-profile as a riot.'

'He wasn't that high-profile; I hadn't heard of him until this case, and had no idea about his involvement in the riots until Redmayne told me.'

'Nevertheless, I'd say it had little to do with the Aziz family, and more to do with getting rid of you. Perhaps he thought you were close to learning about his various dealings.'

'But why? His name never came into it.'

'He didn't know that though, did he? And he obviously wasn't taking any chances.'

'Are you saying that Jamilla's brother was somehow involved with Hussain and he thought I knew?'

'That would be my bet, yes.'

'You mean I've been through the hell of last year,' Handford said incredulously, 'because of an unconfirmed fear?'

'Looks like it to me. We'll need to watch him, sir, or he'll do it to us again.'

Handford was grateful for the 'us'.

'It's stupid really,' Ali continued. 'If he left well alone we'd more than likely turn a blind eye to his activities. It's only a category C drug, after all.'

'It might be,' Handford mused, 'but we've both had a taste of what it can do to users. When Penistone came at me, it was like being hit by a ten-ton boulder. I can't believe the strength of that man.'

Ali was quiet for a moment, then said, 'Strong enough to pick up a forty-pound coping stone, do you think, sir?'

Handford pondered the proposition. 'He's probably the only person we've come across so far who is.' He paused, turning it over in his mind. Wistfully he said, 'It's a nice thought, Khalid, but there's absolutely no link between him and Rukhsana as far as I can see.'

'Except Karen Penistone, sir. And his prejudice.'

13

'I've got to go,' Karen turned towards the sitting-room door. 'I have to find out what they're doing with him.'

Amajit made a move to restrain her. 'Karen, you're in no fit state to go anywhere except back to bed.' He pulled her gently towards him and, grasping her shoulders, bent forward so that his eyes looked directly into hers. They were filled with concern, but his face was pale and drawn. 'You heard what the inspector said. There's no point you going anywhere tonight. He'll be in custody.'

'Not if you withdraw your charges.' She didn't want to throw his kindness to her back in his face, but she couldn't keep the defensiveness, the accusatory tone out of her voice, as though it was his fault that she was here and that his door had been kicked in.

He hardly seemed to notice. 'Karen, even if I do, he assaulted a policeman. They're not going to let him get away with that.' He manoeuvred her gently towards the settee. 'Please, you still don't look well. Stay here.' He turned to the child who was fast asleep on the chair. 'Let me take Danny back upstairs and I'll bring a cover and a pillow and you can lie on the sofa for a while.'

Too tired to argue, she allowed herself to be eased onto the cushions and let her head fall back against the velvety smoothness of the settee. Amajit had switched all the lights on, so that there were no shadows in the room, no dark corners. It made Karen's head ache all the more and she closed her eyes against the stark, uncompromising brightness.

Danny hardly stirred as Amajit carried him out of the room. She could hear his muffled footsteps as he climbed the carpeted stairs. A bit different from hers where the pile was so worn that she might just as well have had bare boards.

The door creaked slightly on his return. 'He didn't move, just curled up as soon as I put him down. He'll be there till morning.' He placed the pillow on the arm of the settee. 'Come on, lie down.' She did as she was bid and he covered her with the duvet. 'I'll make some tea for us. Do you want a sandwich or anything?'

'No, just tea.' Her eyes met his. 'You look tired, Amajit. Was it awful with the police?'

The memories of the past couple of hours clouded his face and he slumped onto the nearest chair. 'She was having an affair.'

'Don't be silly.'

'That's what they said.'

Karen pulled herself further up the settee. 'I don't believe it. Who was it with?'

'They say it was one of the doctors at the practice. Dr Berridge. It's been going on for months. They think I found out and killed her. They think I picked up a coping stone and brought it down on her head; they think I beat her to death.' He kneaded his forehead with the heels of his hands, his fingers curled like claws. 'I wouldn't do that, Karen. I wouldn't. I loved her. Whatever she'd done, I wouldn't have done that to her.'

Pushing aside the duvet, Karen pulled herself towards him. She circled his shoulders with her arms and held him tight. 'I know, I know,' she whispered, kissing him through his thick black hair, as though he were a child needing comfort. He clutched at her, burying his face in her neck as the sobs wracked his frame. Eventually, slowly, the crying ceased, but they stayed where they were, entwined, until without warning he pushed himself away from her, the tears gone but the pain lurking deep in his eyes.

'I'm sorry,' he said. 'I shouldn't have put you through that. Just give me a minute and I'll get the tea.'

Karen's gaze followed him as he disappeared from the room. Clutching at the duvet, she lay back, pulling it tight under her chin. She didn't believe for a minute that he had killed Rukhsana, he wasn't capable. If only she could take away some of his pain, help him cope with the violence he had experienced, new to him but a bedfellow of hers. Over the years she had learnt to deal with it. But the passion of hatred and extreme anger was a stranger to him, Barry's kind of anger, the instant, intense rage which he fielded in a moment and then forgot just as quickly, as though it hadn't happened. Amajit knew nothing of that, didn't understand it, was afraid of it. She knew she couldn't help him with the anguish of his loss or of the affair, because although she understood, she didn't know, couldn't begin to comprehend his feelings, but if she could take some of the fire out of the other, it would give him room to cope with the rest. She closed her eyes. Pain was pain, but as much as it hurt, it was probably easier to live with the pain of Barry's beatings which in time faded than to carry on living with the kind of hurt Amajit was experiencing.

Her head was throbbing still, but more intense now, and she drew the back of her hand gently across her forehead. It was cool to the touch, but gave little relief. Sensing suddenly that she was not alone, she opened her eyes. Amajit was kneeling beside the settee, his face close to hers. She felt the warmth of his breath against her flesh. Unable to stop herself, she stroked his cheek.

'Are you feeling better?' she asked.

He took her hand in his. 'A bit,' he said. 'I'm so glad you're here, Karen. I don't think I could have coped without you.'

★ ★ ★

'Poor man, he doesn't look as though he's slept much since it happened.' Margaret whispered her comment to the receptionist next to her, and they both glanced over to where Amajit was sitting.

He'd come without an appointment, but Margaret had said she would get him in to see Dr Haigh as soon as possible. He'd give him something to see him through the worst, she said.

The worst! What was the worst? Two days ago he would have said it was the moment he'd been told his wife had been murdered; yesterday the realisation that he was a suspect, and that awful persistent questioning; then learning that his wife had been having an affair and that the baby she'd been carrying could have been her lover's and not his. Handford's words beat incessantly, rhythmically in his head: *'Did you know your wife was having an affair with Dr Berridge?'* until he thought he would go mad. Did Dr Haigh really have pills to get him over that?

He wasn't sure why he'd told Karen about the affair with Berridge. At first he'd intended to say nothing, try to keep his wife's memory sweet, but after the detectives had gone, torrid images of Rukhsana with Berridge kept swilling his mind and he'd just come out with it.

He'd seen so little of the doctor he could barely remember his face, but he could see their naked bodies, white against brown — entwined, writhing, passionate. He clenched his eyes in an attempt to shut out the picture. They'd been having an affair. Where? Where had they met? In her car? Some hotel? Here at the practice? In his bed? Anger and shame wracked his body. He could feel himself shaking, the tremors vibrating every nerve, goading each muscle to hit out, take everything in his path until he could endure it no more. Clinging feverishly to the chair arm, he forced himself to stay where he was, to hang on to the last vestige of willpower he possessed. It was Karen who had suggested he should get a prescription from the doctor, said he couldn't be

283

expected to cope with the shock he had experienced without something. He didn't have to see Berridge, he could ask for Dr Haigh instead. After all, he'd been very supportive when he'd visited the day after Rukhsana's death. Had told him that if there was anything he wanted, anything at all, he only had to ask.

So, he'd left her giving Danny his breakfast and had driven to the surgery. At first he'd sat in the car, not knowing how he could enter the building, observe the staff going about their business as though nothing had happened. But he was desperate to sleep without the nightmares and Karen was right, pills would help him do so. So he'd pushed open the door and walked like an automaton to the reception desk. Margaret had been very sympathetic.

He was sitting in a chair which faced Dr Haigh's consulting rooms, but from which he could also see Berridge's. He'd had no intention of going anywhere near his wife's lover when he came to the surgery, but between one patient coming out of the consulting rooms and the next one being called in, there was a minute or two when Berridge was alone and on impulse Amajit jumped up and thrust open his door.

Berridge was writing and he looked up, surprised at the interruption. When he realised who his visitor was the surprise turned to alarm and then to panic. He didn't move; he sat, paralysed, pen in hand, strain chiselled into his expression.

'Why? Just tell me why?' Amajit's voice cracked.

284

Berridge remained motionless and for a fraction of a second Amajit wondered if he'd got it wrong, if it had been a police trick.

'Mr Mahmood, I — '

Berridge's tone told him he'd got it right.

'You bastard, why?' he shouted. 'You're *my* doctor as well, for God's sake. I'm *your* patient; how could you have had an affair with my wife?'

Berridge said nothing. He sat with his head bowed.

Amajit moved to the open door, and pointed to the row of chairs. 'Do *they* know? Do all those people out there in the waiting room, do they know that you have affairs with your patients?' He stepped back towards the doctor and grabbed the lapels of his jacket.

'Please, Mr Mahmood . . .'

Amajit dragged Berridge, stumbling, into the waiting room, where he twisted the doctor round in front of him. Unable to keep his balance, Berridge fell forward onto his knees. Amajit grabbed at the long brown hair, pulling his head back.

'Look at him!' he yelled. 'Look at him. This is your doctor. Your doctor had an affair with my wife! He didn't care she was his patient, he didn't care that I'm his patient. He had an affair with *my wife*!' He pulled harder. 'Didn't you?' he rasped. And when there was no reply, he yanked the hair viciously. 'Didn't you?'

No one moved or spoke.

'Tell them! You had an affair with my wife.'

'Yes.' Berridge could manage no more than a whisper.

'Louder. I want them to hear you say it.'

'Yes.'

Breathing heavily, Amajit let go of the clump of hair and pushed Berridge down onto the carpeted floor. Then, drained of all energy, he sank onto his haunches beside him.

How long he was there he wasn't sure, but it could only have been a matter of seconds later that he felt strong hands on his shoulders.

'Come on, Mr Mahmood. Come with me.' The voice was filled with compassion.

Gently Dr Haigh helped him to his feet and led him into his room. 'Look after him,' he told a nurse. 'I'll be back in a minute.'

As the nurse guided him into a chair, the room began to spin. The last thing he heard before the mists closed in was Dr Haigh's voice. 'Someone see to Dr Berridge.'

★ ★ ★

'Thank God that's finished.'

Handford placed the budget file in his in-tray then stood up, stretched and glanced at his watch. Quarter past six. He'd give it another half-hour then he was off as well. After that they could page him. Tonight he would get home early, enjoy a meal, have a beer, watch some television — or more likely fall asleep in front of it.

Sounded good, so why did he feel as though he was bunking off? He'd been in the job too long, that was the trouble; long hours had become the norm. But there was nothing more he could usefully do here. The Mahmood brothers almost certainly hadn't gone to Pakistan; there were no bookings for them on any flight on Wednesday, Thursday or Friday, so they were probably still in the area and needed to be found. He'd left instructions for the detectives on duty over the weekend to question the family and Faysal Hussain again in an effort to find them. Nathan Teale and his wife were away until Sunday night, according to the neighbour who had been asked to feed the cat, so there was no chance of questioning him again until Monday.

Nor was there anything more to be gained by talking to Amajit since, apart from the half-hour or so in the lay-by, his alibi had checked out. The press office had issued a statement for the evening paper and the local TV and radio news requesting sightings of his car at the relevant time. It was becoming more and more unlikely he had killed his wife, but they could do with confirmation for the thirty minutes to tie it up nicely. Even without the confirmation, Handford knew their case against Amajit was weak, made up of conjecture and assumption, and if it got past the CPS, any halfway decent barrister would tear it to pieces in court. He wasn't sorry. At least he wouldn't have to face the wrath of the community — unless Kamal and Jahangier had indeed taken their long promised revenge. If they hadn't, that left Ian Berridge as the prime suspect.

Handford walked into the incident room and poured himself a coffee. Would a man who'd sworn to keep the Hypocratic oath kill so viciously? *Don't be stupid, John, of course he would. What about Shipman?* Berridge certainly had the motive and the opportunity, but did he have the strength? Nathan Teale and Barry Penistone had, but neither, as far as he could see, had any reason to kill her. So unless it was a revenge attack by a member of the family — and so long after the marriage that seemed unlikely — he was back with Berridge. A puny, ineffectual man, but a man who if he was angry enough might find the strength from somewhere — and Berridge had been angry.

'John?' Handford hadn't noticed Clarke at his desk. He walked over to him.

'I think I've got something on Berridge,' Clarke said. A half-smile played on his lips.

'Must be good, I haven't seen that twitch for a while.' Handford grinned.

'Well, it's juicy, I'll give you that. Quite a Lothario, our Dr Berridge.'

'Lothario? Now that *is* showing your age.' Handford pulled up a chair and sat down, stretching out his legs.

Clarke gave him one of his 'do you want this information or not' looks. 'I've spoken to a Detective Sergeant Jowett in Belfast,' he said. 'According to him, Berridge takes his instructions from below the waist when it comes to the ladies, particularly the young pretty ones.'

'Now why doesn't that surprise me?'

Clarke glanced at his notebook. 'He doesn't have a record, but a file was opened when the parents of a young patient accused him of

288

serious sexual advances towards their daughter. She was fifteen going on twenty and, according to school friends, sexually active. Berridge denied the accusations of course. He worked in gynaecology and said she'd mistaken examination for advances.'

Handford raised his eyebrows in disbelief.

'Anyway, nothing could be proved, it was his word against the parents, so it was dropped.'

'What about the girl?'

'When push came to shove, she changed her story. Said she'd made it all up. A teenage fantasy that got out of hand. The consensus was that he'd persuaded her one way or another to say that she'd misunderstood what he was doing. The family were obliged to drop their complaint and Berridge left the hospital shortly afterwards to come here — with excellent references, apparently. According to Jowett, the authorities were relieved when he left; rumours were rife that he'd had various affairs and wasn't above dating patients and young girls. His wife had been on the point of leaving him more than once.'

'So he sleeps around. That doesn't mean he killed Rukhsana.'

'No, but that's not all. During the police investigation it came out that Berridge was very likely responsible for getting a young girl pregnant the previous year. Again, she was his patient, not underage, but for a while chronically ill; in and out of hospital for months. Some gynaecological disorder.' He looked at his notes. 'Endometriosis.' Clarke sounded out the word, syllable by syllable. 'Something like that.' He stopped to look at the word again and shook his head in wonderment.

'Anyway, her name was Bethany Cantrell. Student, eighteen years old. Naive and, according to her college friends, madly in love with Berridge; talked about him non-stop. I don't think there's any doubt they saw quite a lot of each other. Eventually she went off to university and it was believed that the affair fizzled out.'

Handford crossed his legs. 'I don't quite see where this is going.'

'The thing is, guv, it came out later that it hadn't ended because Bethany went to university but because she'd become pregnant. She'd confided in a friend that he loved her and would stand by her. But he didn't, insisted on a termination instead. For her sake, of course. She was about to go to university, it would ruin her life, etcetera, etcetera. But she'd refused, didn't want an abortion, couldn't see how she was going to get one in Ireland anyway and couldn't afford to go abroad. He'd tried to persuade her, saying money wasn't a problem, he'd pay for it. But in the end she said she couldn't do it; she'd tell her parents and take her chances.'

Handford sighed. 'This sounds familiar.'

'What's more familiar is that within hours of that conversation she was in hospital with injuries to head and abdomen, and she lost the baby. She said at the time that she'd been mugged. Gave quite a convincing nondescript description of her attackers — tall, in their twenties, one dark, one fair, wearing denim

290

jackets, jeans — you know the type of thing. Not surprisingly, they were never traced. But the following year, when the investigation began, Bethany heard about it from a friend and contacted Jowett. Apparently she'd warned Berridge that if he ever hurt someone as he'd hurt her and she got to know about it, she'd go to the police. And she was as good as her word. Told Jowett everything, particularly that Berridge had been prone to hitting out if he didn't get his own way.'

'Had there been any suspicions prior to this that it was Berridge who attacked her?'

'None. Her original story stood until she heard about the girl and went to Jowett. I know this doesn't mean he killed Rukhsana, guv, but he's certainly not the kind, caring doctor his patients think he is, and he's got a temper.'

'*If* she's telling the truth.' Handford slid further down his chair. 'Can't be ruled out that all she wanted was revenge.' He clasped his hands behind his head. 'What came of it?'

'Nothing. It was her word against his and, as you said, it could have been nothing more than revenge on her part.'

'Where is she now?'

'London, Clapham; works for the BBC as a researcher. I can get in touch with Cavendish Road, ask them to question her, if you want.'

'Yes, do that. Get them to email the statement and a photograph too, if they've got one. I'll square it with the DCI.'

'Square what with the DCI?' Russell appeared in the doorway, his expression serious.

291

'Ask London's Cavendish Road to question a background witness for us.'

'If it's necessary and if the budget will stand it. Tell me about it later.' He turned to Clarke. 'Leave us a moment, would you?'

Clarke, exchanging a glance with Handford, gathered up his coat and walked out of the room.

The DI sat up straight. What now? Russell pulled up a chair. 'I have Dr Haigh in my office.'

'Sir?'

'It appears that Amajit Mahmood visited his surgery this morning where he attacked Dr Berridge. He says you told him that Berridge had had an affair with his wife.'

Handford's heart took a perfect dive into his stomach. He knew Amajit had been angry, but there was no need for that. Stupid bloody man. 'Yes, last night when we went to question him.'

'Why?' Russell's eyebrows lifted at the question.

'Because I needed to know if he knew. It would have been a powerful motive for killing his wife.'

'Is he a suspect, then?'

'I can't rule him out, sir. Not yet.'

'And Dr Berridge?'

'Nor him.'

'Well.' Russell let out a deep sigh. 'It's a pity you couldn't have been gentler with Mahmood, teased it out of him, instead of coming straight out with it. Bull and gate are two words that spring to mind, John.'

It was a moment before Handford spoke.

'If I'd thought for a minute that he knew, I

292

would have made him tell me. But it was obvious he didn't. And in the end it would have hurt him just as much, however I'd done it.'

'That's as maybe, but it's not the issue. A gentler approach might have prevented the fracas at the surgery this morning.'

It was done, the rap over the knuckles. Russell stood up and replaced the chair in its original position. 'You can come and appease Dr Haigh. As I intimated, he is not happy.'

Handford let the sigh he had been holding in escape.

'Don't worry, John, I'll back you.'

They walked through to Russell's office. Dr Haigh was sitting in a visitor's chair, comfortable with arms, a china cup and saucer resting on his lap. He was a homely looking man, grey-haired, rounded — a veritable Dr Cameron. Handford wondered if Russell was old enough to remember television's Drs Finlay and Cameron.

The DCI smiled at the doctor. 'You know Detective Inspector Handford, I believe.' It was amazing how that man's demeanour could change in such a short walk. He was the perfect host now, not at all the aggrieved chief inspector of a few moments ago.

'Yes.' Haigh raised himself slightly to shake hands. 'Inspector.'

'Sir.'

'A coffee, John?'

Don't look a gift horse . . . 'Thank you, sir.'

'Dr Haigh is rather concerned about the events of this morning,' Russell said, pouring a coffee from the percolator. He handed it to

293

Handford, then moved to sit down behind his desk. Handford remained standing, carefully balancing his cup and saucer in his hand.

'Yes, I can accept that, sir. Mr Mahmood was understandably upset.'

'I just wish you'd warned me that you were intending to tell him.' Dr Haigh took a deep breath. 'I could have made sure we avoided the whole worrying display. It was most upsetting, particularly for the patients in the waiting room.'

I'll bet! It'll be the topic of conversation for weeks. 'You knew of the relationship, sir?' Handford moved to lean against a filing cabinet; it had been a long day, he was tired and the least Russell could do was offer him a seat.

'I'd heard rumours, but when Rukhsana left Dr Berridge's list for Dr Copeman's and he was no longer her GP, it wasn't any of my business.' He took a drink. 'I didn't approve, but they were adults, able to make up their own minds. I just hoped that they would be discreet.'

Handford took a sip of coffee, then placed the cup and saucer on the cabinet. 'I understand Dr Berridge has been with you four years.'

'Yes, about that. He came highly recommended from Belfast. And he was an experienced gynae-cologist, an expertise we lacked here. He's a very good doctor, Inspector. I would hate to lose him. Which is why I am so angry about what happened. If rumours start . . . well, you don't know what harm they could do the practice.'

Handford wanted to suggest that if Dr Haigh had kept a tighter rein on the practice, none of this would have happened, but a sideways glance

294

from Russell warned him to keep his thoughts, whatever they might be, to himself.

Instead he said, 'Rukhsana was killed in the woods bordering the nursing home and we are curious to know why she was there. It was a miserable day; the woods are some distance from the building and the car park. Can you think of any reason why she would have gone down there?'

'Absolutely none, Inspector.'

'Was she worried about anything, do you know?'

'You mean her pregnancy?'

'You know about that?'

'I do now, after this morning's episode. Obviously I had to speak to Ian — Dr Berridge — and he told me; he was understandably worried that he might be the father. But as to whether she had concerns about it, I'm afraid I don't know.'

'Could there have been anything else?'

'No, nothing — not that she confided in me.' Dr Haigh placed his cup and saucer on Russell's desk. 'I'm sorry, I'll have to go, we're having a practice meeting after surgery. I don't like to do it on a Friday, but . . . ' He sighed his annoyance at being forced into a situation which he obviously considered Handford's fault.

Shaking hands with the DCI, he said, 'Thank you, Chief Inspector, it was good to meet you. I'm only sorry it was in such unfortunate circumstances.' He nodded towards Handford. 'Inspector.'

Handford moved to open the door. 'How is

Amajit Mahmood, doctor?'

'I took him home and gave him a sedative. He should sleep for some time. The poor man was exhausted. There was a girl there with a young boy. She said she'd stay with him.'

'Karen Penistone.'

The doctor halted in the doorway and turned to the inspector. 'So, that's Karen Penistone.'

'You know her, sir?'

'No, not personally.' He edged back into the room. 'I'm not sure it's relevant, I'm not even sure I should be telling you this but, yes, there was something else worrying Rukhsana — to do with Karen Penistone.'

Handford closed the door. 'Sir?'

'She came to see me one day, not sure what she should do. She was anxious about Karen's relationship with her brother.'

'Barry?'

'Yes, that's him. Apparently she's terrified of him. He's always at the house, often violent and rules her as though he owns her. But he adores the little boy. Tells her exactly how she should bring him up. Very prejudiced as well, he hated Rukhsana visiting. I remember he came to me once to tell me that they didn't want her as their health visitor any more.'

'What did you say?'

'I told him that she was his sister's health visitor and if she came to me to ask, then I would think about assigning her to someone else. She never did.'

'Was it that that worried Rukhsana?' Handford asked.

296

'No, something potentially more serious. The baby was born with the condition talipes. Both feet affected.'

'That's club feet, isn't it?'

'Yes. The heels were turned inwards and the rest of the foot bent downwards and inwards. In his case there was the added complication that the shin bones were also twisted. The condition can be genetic, Inspector. Karen's grandfather was affected in the same way, but it rarely reappears in succeeding generations — unless, that is, both parents are carriers of the gene. That's why Rukhsana was worried.'

14

It could have been any time when Karen was roused from sleep. The orange glow of the street lamp sifting through the finely textured curtains veiled the room in hazy particles of fragmented light but gave little illumination. She turned her head towards Danny. He was stretched out, fast asleep, one arm curled above his head, his hand locked in a small fist, the other out to his side, fingers spread as though caressing the edge of his tiny domain. Karen gently pulled her arm from under the duvet so as not to disturb him, and brought it towards her, screwing up her eyes in an attempt to read the time on her watch face; but it was too dark.

The house was silent. And cold. Drawing the duvet to one side, she eased herself out of bed and pulled on the dressing gown Amajit had lent her. Cautiously she edged her way out of the bedroom and along the landing, running her hand along the wall until she felt the plastic of the light switch. She flipped it downwards. The sudden brightness from the bathroom made her blink. Not wishing to disturb anyone else, she closed the door before plucking the toothbrush glass from its holder and filling it under the cold tap. Her mouth was dry and she swilled the icy liquid around it once or twice before swallowing, savouring its coldness as it went down her gullet and into her stomach.

Checking her watch, she saw it was ten past four. The element in the bathroom's heat and light glowed red and its warmth was beginning to penetrate the towelling gown. She leaned forward against the washbasin and examined her reflection in the mirror. It seemed a lifetime since she had done the same thing in her own small bathroom on the day she'd learned of Rukhsana's death, and wished for Barry's. How long ago was that? Two, three days? Such a short time for her life to have changed in a way she could never have anticipated and in a way, she had to accept, it couldn't be allowed to go on changing. If she didn't stop it, Barry would. In him hatred lay so close to the surface that, like a landmine, it needed only the slightest touch to explode.

The bruising on her face was fading. She traced it with her fingers, sketching as she did so the picture of her life — the beatings, the harshness, the bitterness, and the relentless uncompromising pain. Not the external pain that faded as the injuries faded, but the pain inside her, the pain that had been with her for two, almost three years since the night . . .

A shiver ran through her and she forced herself back into the present. It wasn't fair, but that was the life she understood and the life she knew she would have to return to in the morning. It was stupid of her ever to have considered that she could cross the city to Amajit's world and leave behind the dingy estate which housed the disruptive families and the ever-growing collection of single mothers.

With a sigh she rinsed out the glass and replaced it in its holder. Pulling the dressing gown more tightly round her, she left the bathroom, gingerly easing the door shut. The strip of yellow leaking from underneath snapped into darkness as she pressed the light switch.

The door to Amajit's bedroom was closed. He deserved to sleep, even if it was drug-induced; at least it gave him some respite from his grief. Tomorrow, when she was gone, he would have to begin to cope with it on his own. He had no one else. No family prepared to put aside their prejudice, no friends prepared to be seen with him. Perhaps in the end she was the one who was lucky, because whatever they were like, however cruel, however violent they were, her family would not do what his family was doing, they would not leave her to face tragedy alone.

She was about to enter her own room when she heard a sound, like muffled choking. It didn't seem to be coming from Danny, but she checked anyway. He was just as she'd left him. She could still hear it, though softer now. She strained to catch its direction. Earlier she had avoided turning on the landing light, but now she did. There was no movement downstairs, the front door was shut, the new lock fitted by the joiner the police had sent and the repairs to the jamb still intact. The sound, indistinct, was close by. Cautiously, she pulled down the handle to Amajit's door and eased it open. He was lying on top of the bedcovers, still wearing the kimono-style dressing gown he had put on when Dr Haigh had given him the sedative. He had curled himself into a ball, his head, as far as she could make out, buried in the pillow. As she tiptoed towards him, it became clearer that he was sobbing, but whether in his sleep or not she couldn't be sure. She crouched down to see him more clearly, then touched his hair, stroking it as she would Danny's. He didn't stir, so she continued, murmuring, 'Shh,' with each caress. How long she was there she wasn't sure, but at last he became silent and she pulled her hand away and pushed herself up from the side of the bed. She moved slowly backwards.

'Don't go.'

Karen stood quite still. 'I didn't mean to wake you,' she said.

'You didn't.' He turned his head towards her. 'Please don't go.'

Stepping back to the bed, she knelt down beside it. 'I'll stay until you go to sleep.'

Amajit pushed himself up to face her. His cheeks were wet with tears, his eyes red from crying.

'It hurts so much, Karen,' he said. A sob caught at his voice and he waited a moment until he was back in control, then, 'What am I going to do? How am I going to get through?'

Her hand embraced his cheek. 'I don't know, Amajit. I honestly don't know.'

'Hold me.'

She put her arms round him. He clung on, holding her so tightly that she was forced to edge herself onto the bed in order to support him. His body was tense, and it was some time before she felt him relax and his breathing become more regular. When she thought him calm enough, she roused him to suggest that now he might be able to sleep.

He lifted his head from her shoulder, angling it so that he was looking directly at her. As he moved closer, she felt his breath warm on her face. Enclosing her cheeks in his hands, he tilted her head closer to him until he found her lips and kissed her hungrily, his tongue searching her mouth hard, penetrating. She wanted to push him away, tell him no, and once or twice she tried, but each time something stopped her and she held on to him, returning the kiss with a fervour that startled her. She ran her fingers through his hair, clawing at his scalp as the passion surged through her body.

Pulling away, he gazed at her, tenderly, his eyes soft and gentle. Then he lifted her further into the bed and slowly untied the belt of the dressing gown. Gently, he manoeuvred her arms out of it, then lifted the T-shirt she was wearing until he revealed her breasts which he caressed first with his hands and then with his tongue. She released the belt from his kimono and as he knelt up, he shrugged the garment off, revealing his nakedness. He pulled her T-shirt over her head and lay on top of her. The fervour of earlier was replaced by tenderness as they explored each other's bodies, and when he penetrated her, he did so slowly and gently. At one time he called Rukhsana's name, but Karen didn't care; he needed her to soothe his pain and, for her part, she loved him. They had nothing to protect them but their own vulnerability, and it was that vulnerability that was refashioning in Amajit, at least for a moment, the peace that had been snatched away from him and creating in her a peace she had never known. They climaxed together and as he came, she felt his semen wash into her. It trickled between her legs as he withdrew and she could feel it beneath her, warm and sticky.

★ ★ ★

Barry stamped his feet. The grass squelched beneath his shoes and he sensed the dampness beginning to soak through their thin soles, cold against his feet. Tomorrow night he'd wear boots, whatever Hussain said. As it was, he'd ignored the Paki's instructions and was wearing his donkey jacket; it wasn't brilliant, but it went some way to protect him from the cold, and it was cold, bloody cold. Winter was an anathema to Barry — no warmth, no sun, just greyness and grief. It'd been like that in prison. Whatever the season, the sun had been lost to him, its rays fighting hard but never succeeding in squeezing through the small barred windows. Even the exercise yard and pitches were in the shadow of the high walls. For eighteen months the sun's brightness and heat had been no more than a memory, and now, every winter became his prison all over again.

Endeavouring to infuse warmth into his frozen limbs, he slapped his gloved hands together. Only Faysal Hussain would organise a rave in November; and only Hussain would expect his

303

bouncers to dress as though they were working in a city centre nightclub instead of a beaten-down old barn belonging to some farmer wanting to line his pockets. Still, the black jacket and bow tie made him look good — that and the steroids; helped to pull the girls, they couldn't get enough of him.

He turned his head, screwing up his eyes in an attempt to penetrate the gloom of the barn interior. It was cloaked in a murky, smoky darkness relieved intermittently by the rays of colour thrown out from the makeshift strobe lighting, some sparkling like loose wires, others fanning out in wide ribbons over the grey gyrating figures. The relentless beat of the music bounced in his ears. God only knew what it must be doing to the kids inside; they'd probably be deaf by thirty. Someone had said the police had had complaints from two miles away after the last rave, but then that'd been in a warehouse on the outskirts of the city, not perched on a godforsaken hillside in a field littered with cow clap. He'd never liked the smell of the country, even less when it had been churned with the rain and the cold. He couldn't rid his nostrils of it, even through the smoke, the dope and the sweat from the barn.

Not that any of that bothered the kids, nor did they seem to care that it was only a few degrees above freezing. Most of them were so pie-eyed on acid, amphets or Es that they wouldn't know what month it was, let alone whether it was hot or cold. A few were on scag, he'd seen at least half a dozen shooting up. Didn't touch the stuff himself, not to take, not to sell. Didn't need to, he made out well enough on the rest.

He shoved his hand in his jacket pocket and let his fingers trace the bundle of notes. They felt good. Not a bad night all round, in fact; even the steroids had gone well. They didn't need much selling, he found, almost sold themselves; one look at him and the young lads put their hands in their pockets, dreaming of the women they could pull when they imaged Mr Universe. They were right too, he'd never had any problem, not since he'd been using them. In fact he'd have a woman tonight; there'd been a couple who'd been smarming round him, he'd have one of them. If nothing else, it'd warm him up.

The headlights of a car manoeuvred their way into the field, bouncing as the car wheels hit clumps of grass. It was too dark to see, but at this time of night it would likely be Hussain. The car halted and the lights faded. A door closed and he heard the beeps and saw the orange side lights flashing as the vehicle was locked. A few seconds later the figure of Faysal Hussain appeared in front of him.

'I thought you were banged up. Kicked a door in and hit a copper, I'd heard.'

'Yeah, well, they let me out. Magistrates court in three weeks. They won't do nothing.'

'You hope.' Faysal pushed past Barry to look inside. 'Seems to be going well. Sold much?'

Barry stamped his feet again. 'Considering it's so fucking cold, you've got a full house.' He pulled the bundle of notes out of his pocket. 'I'm all out; this lot can't get enough.'

'Put that away, you stupid bastard, some of them up here wouldn't think twice about doing you over to get their hands on it.'

Barry shoved it back into his inside pocket. 'Fat chance,' he smirked. Not with his strength and his sharp little friend shoved down into his boot.

Faysal's gaze considered his bouncer's frame and refrained from comment. 'Any trouble?' He jerked his head in the direction of the village.

'No. Lights've been popping on and off like it's Christmas, but no one's sent for the fuzz — at least if they have, they're not coming.'

'Good. See you tomorrow. I'll bring the stuff up about eight. And tomorrow night lose that jacket. It makes you look like you've been crawling through shit.' He turned on his heel, not waiting for a reply.

Barry thrust his middle finger in the air as he watched him go. And you, you Paki git. A smothered giggle caught his ears and he turned to see two girls mincing in his direction. Smirking, he waited for them to get close to him.

★ ★ ★

Karen was already up and preparing breakfast when Amajit appeared.

'Do you want some toast?' she asked.

Without looking at her, he shook his head. He didn't have a tie on but he was dressed smartly in dark trousers and a crisp white shirt. Rukhsana must have ironed that, Karen thought

306

and wondered who would do it now she was gone.

'Coffee, then?'

'Please.' His voice cracked as he spoke and he cleared his throat to repeat the word.

She poured it out and handed it to him.

'Karen, I — '

'I think I'd better go home today. I feel a lot better and I've shopping to do and things to get for Danny.' The words fell over themselves. She knew what he was going to say and didn't want to hear it.

'Yes, of course.' Amajit clutched at the coffee mug as though it would fly away if he let go. 'I'll drive you.'

'Thank you.'

There seemed no more to say, and for a while they maintained an uncomfortable silence, Karen busying herself with she wasn't sure what, Amajit fixed like stone, staring at the contents of his mug.

'I'm so sorry, Karen.' The words were almost inaudible but she didn't need to hear them. She had known how he felt by the look in his eyes.

'Don't be.'

'Last night was unforgivable; I shouldn't have done it. What can I say?'

Karen perched on the edge of the chair opposite him and leaned forward to lay her hand on his arm. 'Nothing, because you didn't, Amajit — we did.'

'But I had no right to . . . to violate you in that way.'

Karen felt the tears well up in her eyes. 'You

307

didn't, Amajit.' She squeezed his arm. 'You didn't.'

'I betrayed Rukhsana. I've never done that, ever. You're used to it, but I'm not. I don't sleep with other women.'

For a few disorientating moments her mind reeled with his words. They spun round as she tried to grasp their significance and make sense of them. Had she heard him right? Seconds ago he'd been blaming himself and she'd been comforting him; now, suddenly, incredulously, it was her fault because she was — was what? Sliding her hand away from his arm, she stared at him.

'What do you mean, I'm used to it?'

Needing to put some distance between them, she pushed the chair away from the table, the feet scraping on the tiled floor, then she stood up and backed away. But her legs trembled and she had to turn towards the kitchen units to support herself, her hands flat and hard on the work surface, her back to him. Had he really said what he had said? Was that really what he thought? She turned.

'I don't sleep with other people, Amajit. How could you say that?' Her voice rose. 'I've never slept around. What kind of person do you think I am?' She pulled the chair nearer to her and sat down heavily, brushing away the tears which were beginning to spill over and run down her cheeks. How dare he? Who did he think he was to condemn her when he didn't even know?

'You're all alike,' she said. 'Just because I'm white and single and young, you think I'm easy.

308

Is that why you slept with me last night, Amajit? Because I'm white and easy? And here was me thinking that you made love to me, when really all it was was you screwing me because I'm easy.' The words were loaded with bitterness. 'Well, let me tell you, you bastard, I'm not easy, I've never been easy. My God, from what the police said, Rukhsana was easier than me; did more sleeping around than I've ever done.'

At the mention of his wife's name, Amajit's head jerked up. The expression of shame which had been veiling his face while she was speaking was replaced by a look of disbelief.

'Don't say that, don't ever say that,' he cried, banging the mug down on the table.

Hot coffee splashed over Karen. It cooled on her blue top before it penetrated, but she could feel it burning her hands. Acting on reflex, she pushed back the chair and darted to the sink to turn on the cold tap and plunge them under the flow of water.

His emotion spent, Amajit slumped over the table, the sleeves of his white shirt soaking up the pool of coffee which had spread over the pine surface and was beginning to slide over the edge and onto the floor.

'Don't ever say that.' His voice had slid into a whisper. 'Rukhsana wasn't a whore; she wasn't, she couldn't have been.'

'And *I'm* not a whore either, Amajit. *I* don't sleep around, not with anyone, and you've no right to say that I do.' Her voice unravelled, catching in the back of her throat as she tried to make her point. She pulled her hands away from the water. 'I've never slept with anyone. You're the first.' She picked up a dishcloth and began to scrub at the coffee stains on her sweatshirt.

'What about Danny then? What is he, the second immaculate conception?'

His sarcasm cut deep and suddenly she could take no more. The pleasure of last night slipped away and the hurt she had endured over the past three years surfaced. There was no strength left to hold on to the anger she had felt a moment ago. Her shoulders sagged and she turned to face him, tears still wet on her cheeks, her expression a curious mixture of contempt and grief.

'Quite the opposite, Amajit,' she said without emotion. 'There was nothing immaculate about Danny's conception. There's nothing immaculate about rape; nothing at all.'

★   ★   ★

The two detectives were alone at the table, relaxing in Khalid Ali's dining room.

The evening had gone well and Handford was feeling more at ease than he had for some time. The curry and its accompaniments of chutneys and nuts, cooked aubergine, okra, crisply fried sliced onions plus a raitha made with diced cucumber mixed with yoghurt, followed by sweet Asian desserts, had been superb, as had the company and Handford was glad that he and Gill had accepted Amina Ali's invitation. Any reservations he had had before had been swept away immediately they entered the house where the atmosphere was warm and welcoming.

The children, seven-year-old Hasan and five-year-old Bushra, had been in their night clothes when they arrived, but had been allowed to stay up to meet the English guests. After some initial shyness they had taken to Handford and had insisted he read them a story before they went to sleep. Ali had remonstrated with them, but Handford had brushed it aside, asked them to choose a book and been led upstairs by the hand.

Although apart in age, Gill and Amina had taken to each other immediately and they had talked for a long time about how Gill managed a job as demanding as teaching as well as a family. Then Amina had shown her round the house, until Gill had commented on the pale green and emerald shalwar kameez Amina was wearing, whereupon Amina had taken her to her wardrobe.

Feeling somewhat redundant, Ali sat at the piano and ran his fingers over the keys, then opened up some music and began to play.

'Amina has the most wonderful clothes,' Gill told her husband when he returned from reading to the children. 'And she makes most of them herself. She said she'll make me a shalwar kameez if I would like one. Do you think I'd suit one?'

'I think you'd look wonderful in one,' he said.

'Good, because we've already arranged the shopping trip to buy the material.'

Ali was still playing and Handford stood behind him, listening. Not only was his sergeant a good police officer, he was also an accomplished pianist.

'That's you booked for the Christmas party,' he said when the piece ended.

'You can do a duet with John,' Gill said.

Ali looked surprised. 'I didn't know you played,' he said.

'Not the piano, at least not as well as you. Trumpet and the saxophone, but I'm a bit rusty.'

Gill put her arm round her husband. 'Don't you believe it,' she said. 'Before detecting took over his life, he played in a brass band. He's good.'

'That's a date then, the Christmas party it is.' Ali pushed himself off the piano stool. 'If nothing else, it will surprise Warrender.'

The conversation through the meal covered all subjects from families to weather to putting the world to rights, but once Handford and Ali were alone, they reverted to discussing the case.

'You know, John,' Ali mused, 'given what Dr Haigh told you, Barry Penistone could be a suspect. 'If he is the father of Karen's baby, then he's not only guilty of an incestuous relationship, but since she can't have been more than fifteen when she conceived, he could be charged with unlawful sexual intercourse.'

'No, too late.' Handford argued. 'That's got to be done within the year.'

'Penistone may not know that. And if he thought for a minute that Rukhsana knew and was going to shop him he would quite likely have tried to stop her, violently if necessary. I really would like to spend some time checking on him.'

Handford had reservations, but this time he was prepared to go along with Ali's instincts.

312

Yesterday, he knew he wouldn't have.

'I still think you're wrong, Khalid. There's no sighting of Penistone at the nursing home at the relevant time, but check on him if you want. Remember, he'd need a car.'

The women came into the room and stood, arms crossed, listening.

'John, you promised,' Gill Handford rebuked eventually. 'No shop talk, no work.'

'I'm sorry, but don't blame me, Khalid started it.'

Amina walked over to stand at the back of her husband's chair. She placed her hands on his shoulders. 'In that case we'd better break them up. We've washed the dishes, Khalid can make the coffee.'

Ali leaned his head back to smile up at his wife. 'And here was me thinking I'd got away with it. You've been talking to John, haven't you? He's put you up to this.' He turned to Gill. 'Thanks to your husband, my wife is picking up on the fact that I get a lot of practice at making coffee; I do it all the time when we're out on inquiries.'

'Of course you do,' Handford said with a grin. 'That's what sergeants do when they go out with inspectors — make the coffee. Why do you think we take them?'

'In that case, I'll help you with it,' Gill said. 'You look after my husband for a while, Amina, and I'll have a nice long uninterrupted chat with Khalid and give him some hints as to how to get out of doing everything John tells him.' She threw Handford a spirited smile as she and Ali left the room.

'Let's go into the lounge.' Ali's wife indicated that they should go through the glass doors which separated it from the dining area. Neat as it was, there was no doubt this was a family home, with the ever-present signs of children — boxes of toys against the wall, music for the beginner on the piano. Heavy velvet curtains were drawn against the November evening and a coal fire burned brightly in the stone-built fireplace, adding to the homely, lived-in feel. On the sideboard were photographs of the children and displayed on the cream walls original oil and watercolour paintings.

'It's been a lovely evening, Amina,' Handford said as he walked towards one of the plush chairs upholstered in a rich burgundy Dralon. 'It was a good idea of yours. Khalid and I needed to get to know each other away from work.' He sat down, crossing one leg over the other.

'It's been fun,' Amina agreed, perching on a chair opposite. 'We don't get much chance to entertain, not with Khalid's job. You must find that too.'

'We all do. Long hours, always on call, even when we're on holiday. And it gets worse the higher up the scale you go. A policeman's life is littered with broken promises. It's no real surprise so many marriages flounder.'

'Yours hasn't. You've been married quite a long time, haven't you?'

'Nineteen years, or thereabouts. But I've been lucky. It was hard for Gill when the girls were young and I was rarely around, but the girls are twelve and fourteen now and she's returned to

314

teaching. She's done well, too, she made Head of English last year. I'm proud of her. But I accept it's not easy being married to a detective.'

They sat in silence for a moment until Handford said, 'What about you? How do you manage?'

'I manage. Khalid and I knew each other for a long time before we married. I was always aware of what he wanted to do with his life and as his wife it's up to me to make sure he has the freedom to do it.'

'Your marriage was arranged?'

'Yes, but as I said, we weren't strangers. We were both brought up not that far from here. And unlike many young girls from our culture, my parents were happy for me to complete my education at a university before the wedding; in fact they actively encouraged it. We married as soon as I had my degree, but I worked for a few years afterwards and gained my professional qualifications before the children were born. When they're old enough, in secondary school, I might go back — part-time at least. I was an accountant, it's the kind of work you can do part-time. In the meantime, I look after the home and the children and when I can find the time I do a bit of painting.'

'You've done these?' When she nodded, Handford stood up to examine the landscapes and portraits displayed on the walls. He stopped in front of one of his sergeant. 'This is very good, you know. You've really caught his likeness. His sense of humour is there, but it's mingled with, I don't know, a kind of sadness — no, not sadness, that's not the right word, more an unease, a disquiet that he always seems to carry about with him. Sometimes it's as though he has all the worries of the world on his shoulders.'

Amina came to stand next to him. 'Khalid told me what happened on Thursday.'

Taken by surprise at the turn in the conversation, Handford didn't reply, appearing to concentrate on the picture.

'He told me what you'd said.'

His eyes met hers. 'Did he? Yes, having met you I imagine he did. He's more straightforward than me, I'm not sure I would have told Gill.'

They moved away from the portrait, returning to sit on the settee, her in one corner, him in the other.

'He said you were reprimanded too.'

'Yes.' Her candour unnerved him.

'And you didn't talk to your wife about it?'

'Not in detail, no.' In fact all he'd said to Gill was that he'd had a bad day.

'You should have done, I'm sure she would have understood, supported you.' Ali's wife seemed to have the same knack of making him feel uncomfortable as her husband had had at the end of their interview.

Handford shifted his position. 'Probably, but I suppose I was embarrassed, didn't want to look bad. If I know Gill, she would have said I deserved every word.'

'That's what Khalid said — that he deserved every word you said to him.'

Handford thought back to the altercation in the corridor. 'Well, perhaps not every word.'

'Oh, I'm sure he did, John. I know my husband, he tends to act first and think afterwards. Usually he gets away with it; this time he didn't, and it serves him right.'

'You can't blame him entirely, it wasn't all his fault.' Handford would rather the conversation wasn't taking place and he wasn't sure why he was prolonging it, but Amina Ali's manner encouraged openness, confession even. She ought to have been a social worker or a counsellor, not an accountant. 'It was more to do with my perception of him. I didn't trust him, not because he's untrustworthy but because I wasn't sure why he'd been assigned.'

'Because of the case last year, the one where the boy killed his sister?'

Handford smiled at her. 'He's told you about that as well, has he? Do I have any secrets left?'

Her eyes twinkled. 'Probably not. You're right about one thing, though, my husband is trustworthy and honest and loyal. He wouldn't spy on anyone, least of all his inspector.'

Handford didn't reply; there was nothing he could say. What was it about the Alis? He'd never met anyone more able to probe so deeply into his conscience with so few words.

Amina leaned forward. 'I can understand how you feel, but last year was last year, you should let it go.'

'I know.' Handford sighed. 'But it's not easy. I was that close to losing everything I had worked for.' He measured the distance between the thumb and finger of one hand.

She copied the movement. 'That close? That's

where Khalid seems to be most of the time; that close to giving up.'

'What, to leaving the service? Why?' Handford furrowed his brow. Warrender? He knew there was trouble with Warrender, but he didn't think it had caused Ali an enormous problem.

Amina seemed to be checking her answer carefully before she replied. 'It's not easy being an Asian in a white man's world, even less so in the police force.'

So it was Warrender. 'Is he having trouble with someone on the team? He really ought to tell me, I could do something about it.' Not that I have up to now, even though I've known. He made a mental note to stop sitting on the fence and come down hard on Warrender when he next made a comment.

'No, it's not that. That's something he lives with; he doesn't like it but he lives with it.' She hesitated. 'Khalid's a proud man. He has a lot to prove, not just to you, but to himself and to his parents, particularly to his father. His father never wanted him to be a police officer; to him, as to a lot of his generation, there are only a few professions worthy of their sons. I am in one, the others are medicine and law, but as solicitors or barristers not policemen. Unfortunately, that was what Khalid always wanted to be, so much so that he applied and was accepted before he told his family.'

This was something with which Handford could empathise. 'That must have been very difficult for him. I do know that many Asian people think the police force is not a suitable

318

profession for their sons and daughters. But it's not only your people. My father didn't think it was for me either. He wanted me to be a teacher like him. Thankfully, when he realised that I hated teaching, he accepted my decision. I think he was quite proud of me when he came to the passing-out parade.'

'Khalid's father wasn't proud, he was grief-stricken; he sobbed — in front of him. And that's an image Khalid carries with him, all the time. It became easier when he joined CID — no uniform. But even so . . . '

'But he still sees his father?'

'Oh yes, as upset as he was — still is — his father didn't disown him, but Khalid can't talk about his work as he would like to; he tries, but his father feels that he has — how would you describe it — made his own bed?'

Handford smiled. 'So that's why Khalid turned his mobile off when he visited his father, so as not to upset him more, make things worse. I wish he'd told me.'

'As I said, John, my husband is a proud man.'

They were interrupted by the sound of the glass doors being slid back.

'Coffee,' Ali announced as he came into the room carrying a tray. He glanced round. 'Come on, you two, you haven't even got the small table out. Where am I supposed to put this?'

Handford jumped up to bring the coffee table closer to them. 'Sorry, we've been too busy talking.'

Ali put down the tray and began to pour. 'Help yourself to milk and sugar,' he said. He looked up at Handford. 'So, now you know all about me?'

Handford let his eyes meet the sergeant's. 'I know more than I did,' he said seriously.

'And I about you, sir.'

⋆ ⋆ ⋆

Handford glanced at his wife. He wasn't absolutely sure, but he could have sworn she was smiling.

'What are you thinking about?' he asked.

'My conversation with Khalid. He has a wicked sense of humour.'

They drove on in silence until Handford could stand it no more. 'Well, aren't you going to tell me?'

'Certainly not. It would be breaking a confidence.'

'Gill!'

'No, John.' Then with a giggle, 'But it was funny.'

Handford changed gear as they turned off the main road onto the avenue. 'I'll get it out of him when I see him next,' he said petulantly.

'I doubt it.' She turned her head to look at him, the smile gone. 'He's a good man, John,' she said. 'He has a lot of respect for you, you know.'

Handford sighed as his memory trawled the events of the past few days. 'I doubt it,' he said. 'If I'd treated me as I've treated him, the last thing I would feel is respect.'

He negotiated the steep drive and brought the

car to a halt. He pulled on the brake and turned off the engine. The security light had come on and they sat for a moment, bathed in its brilliance. Gill broke the silence.

'Why didn't you tell me what happened between you?'

'I did.' He stared through the windscreen at the garage door.

'Hardly. And certainly not in any detail.' She turned to face him. 'You can talk to me, you know.'

'Yes, I know, I'm sorry.' Stretching out his arm, he felt for Gill's hand and covered it with his own. He picked it up and drew it to him, kissing it gently. 'I do love you, Gill Handford.'

'Yes, I know you do.' She smiled at him and pulled their hands towards her own lips. 'I just wish you could love yourself a bit more.'

15

The police took them by surprise on the second
night of the raves. They came in convoy and
must only have been a hundred yards or so from
the gate when the blue lights flashed on, then
moments later the sirens. The metallic scream
reverberated through the darkness, merging yet
competing with the pulsating beat of the music
which pounded the walls of the barn.

Somebody from the village had complained.
Obviously. Inevitably, to Barry's way of thinking.
He'd warned Hussain that a rave over two nights
was pushing it round here. Bridgeden was
riddled with businessmen, councillors and
wealthy sods who'd nothing better to do with
their money than buy new cars every year, and
houses too big for any normal family. These
people had clout and were sure enough of their
position to wield it. But no, Hussain knew better.

The kids in the barn were oblivious, too far
gone on drugs or too mesmerised by the lights
and music to distinguish police sirens; but as
Barry saw the first blue lamp eddying along the
rough stones of the wall, he knew what was
happening and what he had to do: get rid of the
knife and the notes.

For the second night running he'd sold out
and soon he'd have enough saved to start dealing
in his own right; then fuck Faysal Hussain, fuck
everybody. One day he'd be as rich as those

bastards who lived in Bridgeden, rich enough to buy a house there. He'd already seen the one he fancied — a large bungalow in its own grounds that stood well back from the road — near the bus stop. Not that he'd need the bus stop, because when he could afford the house, he'd be able to afford the car to go with it — a Porsche like Hussain's. In fact he might even buy Hussain's.

Perhaps Karen and Danny could live with him. He'd like that. Take Karen's mind off that Paki, if nothing else. Not that he objected to her shacking up with someone, or even getting married if that was what she wanted. But to his mind there were some you lived with, some you married and some you didn't do either with. As he thought of what Mahmood might be doing with his sister, he felt his hatred and jealousy surge. If he wasn't careful he would explode, his emotions were slashing at rational thought like a scythe through grass. Like when he'd hit Karen.

As the police cars entered the field, the headlights shone like searchlights, jerking him back to the present. Come on, Barry, get rid or there'll be no house, no nothing.

Despite his bulk, his movements were cat-like. Keeping low and in shadow, he scurried across to the green Volkswagen. The police drivers were desperately trying to prevent their vehicles from bogging down in mud as the wheels channelled deep furrows in the marshy ground. Barry squeezed on the handle and opened the front passenger door. Lifting the matting, he dropped the money and the knife into the dust, smoothed

323

the black rubber back in place, then swept the rubbish from the seat onto the floor. Thirty seconds later, he was standing back at the barn entrance watching the coppers struggle out of their Pandas. He smirked at the lack of physical fitness of the modern police officer. Perhaps he ought to try and sell them some gear. Not tonight though, even if he'd had any left. Tonight he wanted out as soon as possible, so he'd wait for them, shout at them, give them a bit of a fight, then allow himself to be taken down to the nick. He couldn't stop that, but they wouldn't keep him there long, there was nothing they could charge him with — no drugs, no money, no knife. He'd be back to pick up the car before daylight.

An officer stood in front of him. Barry scrutinised the man's form. He could have swatted him like a fly had he wanted.

'Who's the organiser?'

Barry rubbed the silver pips on the man's shoulder. 'Bloody 'ell,' he said. 'Whoever it was grassed us up must have some clout. Never seen so many pips at a rave. You want to be careful, this field's full of crap. Wouldn't like yer to get yer shoes dirty.'

A clutch of policemen scuttled past him into the barn, the darkness of their uniforms transformed by the rays of colour fanning the room. Screams and swearing flooded into the night. Suddenly, the doorway was crowded with youngsters struggling to get out, to get away before they were caught and their parents were called down to the police station. Parents who would realise for the first time that their offspring were not where they had said they were going to be, and that although they could never get them out of bed in the morning, they could gyrate the night away aided by ecstasy and amphetamines.

The coppers stationed outside tried to catch hold of them as they fled past; many, the lucky ones, slipped their grasp.

The inspector swatted Barry's hands off his shoulder. 'Who's in charge?' he barked.

'How should I know? I'm just the doorman. Keeping out the undesirables.' He leaned towards the officer as if to make his point more clearly. 'Look, tell them coppers to stop touching up those lasses.'

The inspector ignored him. 'You're the bouncer?'

Without taking his eyes off the girls skirmishing in the doorway, Barry said, 'Doormen, we're called doormen.' He made to jump forward to pull a policeman away from one of the girls, but the inspector grabbed him.

'Oh no you don't.'

Barry's donkey jacket tightened round his bulk as he was dragged back to the door of the barn. That wisp of a man was stronger than he'd thought.

The inspector shouted for one of the officers to come over.

A fresh-faced policeman, who looked to Barry as though he hadn't started shaving yet, strode up. 'Sir?'

'Search the bouncer.'

'Sir.'

Barry glared at them. 'You've no right.'

'Oh yes we have if I suspect you're carrying drugs. And I think you're carrying.' The inspector indicated that the officer should begin.

Smirking, Barry held up his arms. The young copper felt along his body, dipped his hands in the pockets of his donkey jacket and monkey suit.

'Hey, just watch where you're putting your 'ands,' Barry told him.

The young man's cheeks reddened visibly in the lights from the barn. 'Nothing, sir.'

'Take him to the car.'

'You're nicking me?' Barry feigned surprise tinged nicely with anger. He was quite proud of the way he was handling things.

'Just helping us with our inquiries, sir. You might find your memory's better at the station; you know, actually remember the name of your boss.' The sarcasm in the inspector's voice suggested he was fast losing patience. Probably thought himself too important to be raiding raves in the middle of the night.

For a fleeting moment, Barry wondered whether in fact this might not be the right time to grass up Hussain. He'd already saved a good few thousand, probably enough to set up on his own if he was careful — and with Hussain banged up, the territory would be his. He might never get another chance as good as this.

'That's him.' A girl's voice sliced through his thoughts. She was standing with another policeman and pointing over at Barry.

'The bouncer,' the officer prompted.

'Yes, 'im.' It was the girl from last night, the one with her friend, the one who'd gone behind the barn with him. She hadn't been the best fuck he'd ever had, but better than none at all. She'd come to him again tonight, but he'd told her to piss off. He wanted somebody who'd had a bit more practice against barn walls, who could position herself right. There were plenty of them around; a few years of working at raves, you got to know who they were. It was just a matter of being patient, and his had soon been rewarded.

Half turning, the officer whispered in the inspector's ear. The girl's middle finger punched at the air in Barry's direction. What was the silly bitch playing at?

Satisfaction spread over the inspector's face as he looked at Barry; an expression that said 'Got yer!' He turned to the girl. 'Are you sure, miss? It's a serious allegation.'

'Course I'm bloody sure. It was him, he was the one who 'ad 'is mucky hands up me blouse and in me knickers.'

★ ★ ★

Khalid Ali was restless. Sighing, he placed the Sunday paper next to his plate and pushed his chair away from the breakfast table. 'I'm going down to the station,' he said.

'Oh, Khalid, no!'

'Not for long; I need to check on something.'

'Not today, Khalid, please. The children were looking forward to having you home. Can't it wait until tomorrow?'

'Don't argue with me, Amina. I've said I shan't be long. There'll be plenty of time for me to play with the children.'

His wife flung the tea towel onto the work surface. 'I've heard that before, Khalid. They'll be lucky if they see you before bedtime.'

'I'll be back.' Sincerity swathed his words, like a sheath of bubble wrap, and before Amina had time to utter one of her well-chosen comments, thereby stripping them naked, revealing their falseness, he had grabbed his coat and the car keys and walked out of the door.

The drive down to the station was not a comfortable one. But that was what happened in his job, you became good at making promises that you knew you couldn't or wouldn't keep. He didn't have to go in, it could wait until Monday, everything that had to be done was being done. Twenty-four hours without him would be unlikely to affect the progress of the case, while it would make all the difference to his relationship with his children. Handford had detectives working on whatever was needed and no doubt would pop in himself, or at least be at the end of a phone if anything important cropped up. Ali sighed; only last night he'd complained to Gill Handford that he saw nothing of his family, blaming the job and his bosses who sent him all over the district, keeping the community sweet. The thought tasted bitter. For a few moments, his duty as a husband and father fought the policeman in him, but as always the policeman won. He persuaded himself that until he'd at least made a start on checking out Penistone, he'd be no use to anyone at home. The man was niggling away at him, like an itch just out of reach. Call it instinct, call it what you will, he had a gut feeling about him, and the only way to relieve it was to go back to the office and work on it. For his own peace of mind, it couldn't wait until Monday.

Nor could his curiosity regarding Faysal Hussain's involvement in the Jamilla Aziz case. It had been nothing at all to do with Hussain. He hadn't rated a mention in any statement, either as a witness or a suspect. Yet for some reason he'd lit the fuse that had sparked the violence. Why? Was it racial? Police hatred? Or was it personal against Handford? If it wasn't to happen again, the questions regarding Hussain's part in the riots needed answers.

CID was all but deserted when he arrived. The usually busy corridors were empty and in the incident room there was only one officer, his legs resting on his desk, eyes closed as he listened to his Walkman.

Ali pushed at the man's legs. 'Nothing to do, Warrender?'

Warrender glanced up at the face above him and pulled the earphones roughly from his head, leaving them to dangle like a stethoscope round his neck. The music continued to throw out its tinny beat.

'I was thinking,' he said abruptly.

Ali scanned him. The detective had draped his jacket over the back of his chair. The top button of his shirt was undone and his tie loosened, but

329

not discarded. He didn't blame the man, for cold though it was outside, the warmth in the building was over-powering. His eyes came to rest on Warrender's face. 'Thinking about what?' he asked.

'About me wasting my time trailing around following up dozens of reports of sightings of Mahmood's car; and about why I've spent half my weekend trying to talk to the family when they don't understand a bloody word I'm saying — or pretend they don't. It's a waste of time. We all know it's family who've killed her. It always is with that lot. We should bring 'em in, tell 'em to stop buggering us around and force it out of 'em.'

Ali could feel his anger mounting. With no one else to hear, Warrender was making the most of his opportunity and loving every minute of it.

The sergeant's voice was cold. 'Slap them around a bit until they confess, is that what you mean?'

'Why not? It's probably the only thing they understand. They think nothing of beating each other up. Tell me, Sergeant,' Warrender inclined his head to one side, 'do they really think bruises won't show? There was this girl last year, in a hell of a state, blacker than ever by the time her brother had finished with her. And all she'd done was speak to a boy who was at school with her.'

'And that doesn't happen in white families?'

'You quote me one case.'

There was a prolonged silence.

'You see, you can't.'

'Barry Penistone and his sister is the one that

330

springs to mind immediately,' said Ali. He pondered for a moment, watching the detective's expression change from one of derision to one of contempt. He pushed home the point. 'And if, as you say, it only happens in the Asian community, perhaps you can tell me, Warrender, why we have an overworked Domestic Violence Unit, and why most of the women they deal with are white?'

Warrender pressed the stop button of his Walkman and ejected the tape. Turning it, he fitted it back in the machine. 'What are you doing here, anyway? I thought it was your day off. That's the trouble with you lot, always working.'

'And who exactly do you mean by 'you lot' '

Warrender looked up at him and smiled. 'Fast trackers,' he answered amiably. 'Who did you think I meant?' He waited for an answer. When none came, he said, 'Come on, Sergeant, I don't have to spell it out. You lot can't wait to make superintendent. Working all hours, especially when you don't have to. Why don't you just stay at home on your day off?'

'Well, Warrender, this morning I beat my wife, so I thought I'd give her and me a rest, come and do a bit of work before I go home and beat her again.' His voice was fashioned in steel. 'Does that answer your question, Constable?' Ali's eyes lasered into the man, noting with satisfaction that the detective had the grace to blush. 'I'll take that as a yes, shall I?' he said.

He walked over to the kettle and switched it on. Realisation that for once he had bitten back had left his mouth feeling like a sandpit. He could leave it there, get on with what he came in for, but he knew he had to do more than make a point, he needed to stamp his authority on the situation. His tongue flicked over his lips as he turned to face Warrender.

Swallowing hard he said, 'Since you appear to have nothing to do but listen to that thing, I've got a job for you.'

Warrender made to argue but Ali stopped him. 'Don't even think about commenting, Constable, or I'll report you to the DI and then to the DCI. I've got plenty: racism and laziness for starters.'

'You can try. There's only the two of us here, it'll be my word against yours. And after the bollocking you got, your credibility will be nil.'

'Maybe or maybe not. But think on this, Warrender. Had you done what I did, you'd probably have been back in uniform. Not me. I'm the token Asian on this inquiry. I'm the brown-eyed boy of the team, brought in to make the whole investigation credible. Russell refuses to take me off the case no matter what, and last night I had dinner with John Handford and his wife. So you see, at this moment, of the two of us I'm the one more likely to be believed; I'm the one with the clout. If you want to risk challenging me, feel free, but I wouldn't if I were you.' Ali let his words sink in, hoping that Warrender couldn't see his hands trembling. He'd never fought back like this and he didn't believe a word of what he'd said; he only hoped that Warrender did because he had nothing more to offer.

The silence deepened, and when he felt that he had control, he said, 'I want you to find out as much as you can about Faysal Hussain and Barry Penistone. With your skills, you should be able to rake up some muck on Hussain. He seems particularly prone to inciting riots and I need to know why. Penistone, on the other hand — '

'There's something in the night book about Penistone.' Warrender stood up and walked over to the front desk. He opened the book. Ali watched while his finger traced down the lines. 'Yes, he's been arrested for indecent assault on a girl up at a rave which was raided in the early hours of the morning. I don't know whether he's still in custody.' He paused. 'Do you want me to find out?' he asked ungraciously.

'Yes, and how long they're likely to be keeping him, then check him out to the last detail, but don't tread on any toes. I don't want the duty inspector on my back.'

'Shouldn't worry about it, Sarg. You said yourself, you're the brown-eyed boy; no one will dare.' Warrender closed the book and dropped it on the table. He returned to his seat and sat down. 'Is he a suspect for Mahmood's murder?'

'The DI doesn't think so.'

'And Hussain?'

'Well, you said yourself, it's quite often family.'

Warrender, regaining confidence, returned his feet to the papers on the desk. 'It's always family. It's not worth anyone's time bothering with Penistone.' He replaced his earphones and

333

leaned back in his chair, cradling his hands behind his head.

'You're probably right.' Ali bent over the detective, pressed the stop button, then pulled the earphones out. 'I'm going to find Penistone's sister. I expect you to have something by the time I get back.' And with that he moved off, sensing the man's eyes boring into his back as he walked the length of the room.

At the door, Ali turned. 'And Warrender.' The detective, who had been pushing the Walkman into his desk drawer, looked up. 'Don't even think about leaving until you've seen me first.' He tapped the corner of his right eye. 'Remember the brown eyes.'

★ ★ ★

It took Ali longer than anticipated to find Karen Penistone. There was no one at Mahmood's house. The murky weather gave the morning a good impression of dusk and lights illuminated the windows of most of the houses. Amajit's was in darkness. Ali knocked loudly then stepped back to look up at the bedroom window. The curtains were open, so he was unlikely to be in bed. He knocked again and waited; no answer. Nor was there any sign of his car.

There weren't many places they could be. Amajit would hardly have gone to his parents. He might be visiting Hussain, but certainly not with Karen. It was possible that she was back at the hospital, although Handford said she'd seemed better when he'd seen her a couple of days ago. Nevertheless, to be sure, Ali rang through to casualty to be told that they hadn't seen Karen Penistone since she was discharged.

The only likely place left would be her own house, probably picking up some clothes — or maybe she'd decided to go back there and wasn't with Amajit at all; she couldn't stay at his house indefinitely. Unsure of her address, he rang Warrender.

'One hundred and four Saxton Road, it's on the Scargill Estate,' Warrender said when he came on the line. 'By the way, while you're on, Penistone was released on police bail at about eight o'clock this morning. The girl is still sticking by her accusation and he's still denying it. No surprise really; I doubt it'll go the whole way, it's just her word against his and there's no evidence. He agrees he had sex with her at the first rave on Friday, but not last night. He admits to sex with another girl, but says he doesn't know her name. He says the Ms Friday's dropping him in it because he told her she was useless at it and to piss off. And since she isn't saying he had sex with her, just that he touched her up, there'll be no forensics. Apparently there were boot prints in the mud by the barn where she said it happened, and Penistone was wearing boots, but it still doesn't mean she was the girl he was with. And anyway, the prints will have been well obliterated by now.'

'Has a scene of crime officer been up there?'

'Doubt it, there won't be any forensics; I told you, it's indecent assault, not rape.'

'Who's the SOCO on duty?'

Warrender was puzzled. 'You're not really interested in this, are you, Sarg?'

'Not in the allegation, no; but I am in the boot prints. There was a partial one in the wood, close to where Rukhsana was killed. And so far, we've no idea whose it is.'

'You're grabbing hold of whatever moves, Ali.' Warrender's voice was tinged with scorn. 'You don't want it to be family, so you're trying to pin it on anyone. Why not some over-sexed white thug who's left a boot print in the mud? He's as good as the next person.'

Ali refused to be drawn. 'Who is the duty SOCO?' he repeated.

'OK, if you insist. Alison Morand. Do you want her number?' He read it out. 'You're wasting her time and yours, you know.'

'We'll see.' Ali broke the connection.

His inclination was to go straight up to the field, but since Penistone was on bail the chances were that he had gone to find his sister, and Ali wanted to make sure she was all right. He had no doubt that the injuries to her face were from her brother's fist, even though she wouldn't admit it. He couldn't understand why women who were beaten so viciously insisted on protecting the person who had done it, or what was so bad that it could prompt such an attack in the first place. He'd ridiculed Warrender when he had spoken about beating up Amina, but domestic violence was no joke. Karen Penistone had been lucky; she might not be quite so lucky next time, and Ali was fearful that next time might be right now. The field and the prints could wait.

The estate was a warren of streets and cul-de-sacs and it took him a while to find Saxton Road. He drove slowly, glancing around, grimacing in distaste. There were some awful, rundown estates in the city, but this had to be the worst. Drab houses lined the even drabber streets. The dinginess of the cement rendering on the council houses merged with the dinginess of the day, so that in the distance the one could not be distinguished from the other. Paint was peeling off doors and windows, and the gardens, such as they were, lay grimy and bare. Refuse filled the gutters — polystyrene cartons that held the remains of takeaway food, thick brown liquid that had probably been curried sauce oozing onto the road; squashed chips; carrier bags; beer cans. Streets ran off streets like a maze, all names similar, but not the same — Saxton Crescent, Saxton Avenue, Saxton Lane, Saxton Brow. Ali kerb-crawled so as not to miss Saxton Road. Eventually he found it. Halfway along, he saw Amajit's car, drawn up outside one of the houses, a clutch of people standing on the pavement by the gate of 104. Karen's house. Women stood, smoking, talking, children in their arms; the men further away, looking up towards the front of the house. Neither Amajit nor Karen were in evidence. Ali's first thought was that he was too late, Barry Penistone had been there, seen the two of them together and beat her or both of them up again. Ali parked the car and ran over.

'What's happening?'

One of the women in the crowd pointed up at

the house. The walls were scrawled in graffiti, deep red letters, some capitals, some not, all different sizes stretching across the rendering and the windows. Tears of paint ran down the wall, as though lamenting each word. The message was clear. WHITE WHORE. OUT. OUT. OUT.

'Where's Karen Penistone?'

'She's inside,' one woman informed him. 'She's in a right state. Crying and ranting and raving. That coloured fellow's with 'er, trying to calm 'er down.'

Ali pushed through the women. He ran up the path and without knocking dashed into the house. Amajit met him in the hallway.

'Is she all right? She's not hurt?'

'No, just upset. She's in the front room.'

'Who did it, do you know?'

'No, but I could make a wild guess.'

'Have you called the police?'

'One of the women outside has, but that was ages ago.'

Ali made to go through into the sitting room, but Amajit grabbed his arm.

'She's upset and she's frightened, Sergeant,' he whispered, 'but she won't hear a word against him. Insists it's not him.'

'When was it done, do you know?'

'It wasn't here when I dropped her off yesterday, and the man next door says it wasn't here when he checked round the two houses last night. Does that every night, apparently. He's got quite a bright security light and says he would have noticed if there'd been anything. It was the milkman who saw it, round about quarter to eight this morning.'

Ali shook his head. 'Barry Penistone was acting as a bouncer up at the rave in Bridgeden until going on half past one and then in the cells at Central Police Station accused of indecent assault. He wasn't released until eight o'clock this morning. So whoever did this, it wasn't him.'

16

Kamal sat in his usual place in the back of the car pondering his paint-speckled hands.

'What they doin' now?'

'Still looking up at the wall.' Jahangier craned his head to take in the whole scene. 'They gotta be wondering how it got there, seein' as nobody heard nothing.'

'That copper still there?'

'He's gone inside.'

'Amajit too?'

'Haven't seen him for ages.' Jahangier yawned. They'd finished the job late last night and he was tired. He was also annoyed — all that work and for what? For her to ring Amajit and for him to come running. Hadn't the message been clear enough? It was supposed to warn them off each other, not to bring them together.

Well, if she couldn't understand a gentle warning, they'd have to try something with a bit more bite to it. Give it a few days, see if it penetrated; if it didn't or she was acting dumb, then they'd give her one she couldn't ignore.

★ ★ ★

As soon as he saw her, Ali knew there was little to be gained by questioning Karen about her brother. Her tear-stained face told him that. She was sitting in a chair, her arms tight across her,

340

her gaze fixed on a point beyond him, although he doubted she was actually seeing anything. Amajit sat opposite, his demeanour suggesting that he was unable to offer much in the way of comfort.

Ali approached and, crouching down, placed his hand on her knee. 'Don't worry,' he said quietly, 'we'll find out who did this.'

She directed her eyes onto his. 'Who would want to do that to me?' she demanded wearily.

Since Barry's alibi was unimpeachable, he could think of no one. 'I don't know,' he said, standing up and taking a step backwards. 'Do you?'

'No, although there *are* those who think I'm a whore.' Her voice cracked as she threw a look of hostility towards Amajit; he caught it and lowered his eyes.

'That's not true, Karen,' he said, the words stabbing ineffectually at the compacted atmosphere.

Her expression softened suddenly and tears welled in her eyes, but she refrained from a reply, her gaze settling back into the distance.

Ali watched them, perplexed. What was happening here? Tension strained between the two of them, rather than between Karen and an unknown graffiti artist. What had happened warranted anger, hostility even, but not the anguish that was feeding into the air. The word 'whore' was the catalyst, and yet Ali was willing to bet that, however unfair the description, it wasn't the first time she'd been called it. Whatever the problem, there was more to it than words daubed on an outside wall.

'All I did,' Karen's voice, firmer now, broke into his musings, 'was to go to a friend's house to show some sympathy and to help him out.'

And stay three days. Ali swallowed the thought; there was no point alienating either of them Karen was the victim here, not the perpetrator. She needed support, not condemnation. Nevertheless, Ali couldn't rid himself of the feeling that she wasn't on the outside of the events of the past few days. The beatings and the graffiti might not connect her directly to the murder of Rukhsana Mahmood, but somehow, somewhere, there was a link, of that he was certain. Rukhsana, Karen, Barry Penistone, Ian Berridge, Faysal Hussain, Kamal and Jahangier — they all connected, and the thread was Amajit.

Ali turned to him. 'A word,' he said and indicated that he should follow him into the hallway.

'What's going on?' Ali asked.

Exhausted, Amajit leaned against the wall. 'I don't know what you mean.'

'No?' Ali was sceptical. 'There's an atmosphere here you could cut with a knife. What's happened?'

'You've seen what's happened. She's got graffiti scrawled over her wall.'

Ali shook her head. 'That's not it, at least not all of it. The tension's between you two. Something's happened that you're not telling me. You know who did it, don't you?'

Amajit shook his head. 'If it's not her brother,

342

and you say it can't have been, then no, I don't know.'

'Your cousin, perhaps?'

Amajit's eyes widened. 'Who, Faysal? I doubt it.' He was unable to keep the derision out of his voice. 'Can you see him up a ladder daubing a house with paint?'

Ali had to admit it was unlikely. 'He could have got someone to do it for him. Kamal and Jahangier perhaps.'

'Probably, if they were here. But they're not. They're in Pakistan.' Amajit seemed to have gathered energy from somewhere. Inclining his head close to Ali's, he said contemptuously, 'Tell me, why would you assume it's someone from our community who's done this? Why not a white?' He moved closer. 'You condemn me, Sergeant, yet loyalty's not your strong point either, is it?'

Ali let the comment ride then changed the subject. 'What do you know about Barry Penistone?'

Amajit hesitated and took a step backwards. 'I hardly know him.'

'You haven't talked to Karen about him? I find that hard to believe. He beat her up badly enough for you to have her stay with you only two days after the death of your wife. And when he knew she was with you, he broke down your door and would probably have assaulted you had not Inspector Handford and DC Graham been there to stop him. So don't tell me you haven't spoken about him.'

The muscles around Amajit's jaw line

tightened. Ali stiffened, preparing for a repetition of the scene at the hospital, but it didn't come. Instead, Amajit seemed to lose himself in the silence and it was some time before he was able to wrench himself back to the present.

'Not here,' he said, pushing himself away from the wall. 'Can we sit in your car?'

Without a word, Ali led him outside. The neighbours who had gathered earlier had returned to their own lives, to do whatever they did on their Christian Sabbath. He made his way to the passenger door, pushed the key into the lock and turned it. The sound of the central locking clicking open was distinct in the mist. They seated themselves in the front and Ali turned on the ignition to allow warm air from the heater to circulate.

It was a while before Amajit spoke. Whatever it was he wanted to say, he was obviously finding it difficult. 'Barry Penistone's a thug, Sergeant, and he's a racist. He beats his sister up, probably more often than she lets on.'

Was that it? He'd brought him outside for that? 'None of this is new, Amajit. If she won't report him, there's little we can do except wait until he harms her in a way that we can become involved.'

Amajit sighed. 'She won't report him, she'll not risk him going to prison.'

'Then we can't help. She's got to make the first move.'

The silence deepened again. Ali had had enough and signalled his impatience by turning to open the car door. 'If that's all there is,

Amajit, you needn't have dragged me outside.'

Amajit placed his hand on the sergeant's arm. 'No, it's not all.' Shifting his position, he turned to face Ali square on. 'Look, I'm not sure I should be telling you this, but . . . '

'But?' Ali urged.

'You're right, we have talked about him. On Saturday morning, at length.' He hesitated again. 'Look, what Karen told me was in confidence, and she'll not thank me for breaking it . . . ' Amajit scrutinised his hands. 'Karen's little boy, Barry is his father.'

The words, spoken in a whisper, echoed around the car. Ali felt his excitement rising. What Amajit had just said bore out what Dr Haigh had told Handford about Rukhsana's suspicions. And, as he'd already suggested to the DI, if Penistone knew of them, which was possible since he'd demanded that Haigh keep Rukhsana away from his sister, then they had proof of motive.

'Are you sure of this?' he asked.

Amajit looked up. 'Of course I'm not sure, but why would Karen tell me if it's not true?'

'So why did she tell you?'

Amajit's eyes dropped. 'She told me, that's all. She just told me. And I believe her.'

Ali let his gaze wander over Amajit's frame until it came to rest on his lowered eyelids. 'You're saying that she's having an incestuous relationship with her brother?'

Amajit's eyes bounced up, his face flushed with anger. 'No, I'm not saying that. She's not like that. It happened once, when she was fifteen;

and it wasn't her fault.'

The reaction was unexpected, disproportionate. Ali frowned. Why had the question so upset the man? All he had wanted was confirmation that he had understood him correctly. There was more to Amajit's relationship with Karen than was outwardly apparent, of that he was sure. Perhaps it was more deep-rooted than either of them cared to admit. And if so, how long had it been going on? Earlier, Handford had suggested Rukhsana's affair with Berridge as a motive for Amajit to kill his wife. If he had been having an affair with Karen, then there was a combination of circumstances that could easily end in murder. After all, his alibi wasn't solid, there was still more than half an hour unaccounted for while he was supposedly in the lay-by.

'What do you mean, not her fault?'

'She was . . . forced into doing it. He was drunk. He raped her.' The words spewed from Amajit's lips.

Ali felt as sick as the man opposite him, but he had to play the police officer, show no emotion. He placed a hand on Amajit's. 'Just tell me what she said happened, as calmly as you can,' he said quietly.

Amajit took a moment to compose himself, then said, 'He was engaged to a woman called Donna Harrison. According to Karen he was mad about her but very possessive and when he thought a man in a pub was interfering with her he punched him in the face with a beer glass.'

'Yes, we know about that. He got eighteen months.'

'Yes, well, by the time he came out of prison, Donna had broken off the engagement and was living with another man. Karen said that Barry just couldn't accept it was over and a day or two after his release, he went to see Donna. It took sometime, apparently, but eventually she and her new man managed to persuade him that she wanted nothing more to do with him and that he was to leave her alone. However, that's not Penistone's style, leaving people alone, and if he couldn't have her, he said, he'd make sure her new boyfriend didn't either, then he picked up a meat cleaver and attacked him with it. A neighbour heard the girl screaming and called the police. Barry was arrested, but when Donna said that neither she nor her boyfriend wanted him charged, they had to let him go. He must have left the police station and spent the rest of the afternoon and evening in a pub, because by the time he got back home he was very drunk. Karen was in bed, but not asleep. She said she could hear him downstairs, bumping into things and swearing and cursing; but it didn't particularly worry her, because it wasn't the first time he'd come home drunk, and she assumed that eventually he'd go to bed to sleep it off. But this time he didn't. He pushed his way into her bedroom instead, yelled and screamed at her for a while, then made to get into bed with her. She tried to kick him off, but her feet got caught up with the covers. She said it was like being caught in a fishing net, not being able to get the sheets off her; the more she fought, the more tied up she became. She said she knew what he was going to do, and she couldn't stop him. In the end, drunk as he was, he raped her.' Amajit stopped for a moment, his breathing laboured, the expression on his face registering the effort needed to keep his emotions in check.

Ali understood his distress. There was something about rape as a crime that was more abhorrent to him than almost any other. Each time he listened to a victim's experience, his objectivity as a detective seemed to drain away and disgust take its place. And this time, although the story was second-hand, was no exception.

Amajit continued, 'Karen said that when he'd finished, Barry rolled off her and fell asleep as though nothing had happened.' He shook his head. 'It's difficult to accept anyone raping a woman, but he was her brother.' He looked up at Ali. 'What made it even more difficult for her to take was that the next morning he carried on as though nothing had happened. *She* couldn't tell anyone what he'd done because he would have denied it and probably given her a beating as well. And Mrs Penistone wouldn't have believed her anyway, because she dotes on Barry. In her eyes he can't do any wrong; he's the man of the family and she relies on him totally, for money, support, everything.'

'Karen could have come to us, told us.'

'She was fifteen, Sergeant. Fifteen and terrified that no one would believe her. She's a Penistone. No one believes a Penistone, least of all the police. And even supposing on this occasion they had, in the end it would have been

348

her word against his and she would have gone through a lot more grief for nothing. There'd have been little or no evidence since she'd washed it away. She said she scrubbed herself sore to try and rid herself of him. So she kept quiet. Even when she found she was pregnant she refused to say who the father was. And when she finally told Barry, he said she ought to have been more careful. Can you believe it? And then he threatened her with a good slapping if she ever told anyone what had happened. From then on she was on her own. But now, according to her, Barry loves Danny and tries to do the best he can for the both of them.'

'By beating her up and almost hospitalising her,' Ali said bitterly. And Warrender thought only the Asian community did things like that. Perhaps he ought to get him down here to listen to this.

Amajit shrugged. 'It's what she knows; she's used to it. At least that's what she says. Although how you ever get used to it . . .'

The men sat in silence for a few minutes.

'If she's so frightened of what Penistone will do to her and has kept this to herself for so long, what made her tell you — and in such intimate detail?' Ali ventured.

From the silence that followed, he knew he had hit a nerve. Something deep, something that it was unlikely Amajit would acknowledge. That they were lovers and had been for some time? Perhaps. But not a question for today. That was one for Handford. Today Ali had a more pressing question.

349

'Did Rukhsana know any of this?'

'She may have done; but if she did, it would have been confidential and she would never have told me.' Amajit's relief that Ali wasn't pursuing his earlier question was short-lived. Horror filled the gap it had left. 'You think she knew and Barry Penistone killed her to keep quiet?' He grabbed at Ali's lapels. 'You do, don't you?'

★   ★   ★

Bitch! Bitch! Bitch!

It was the only word Barry Penistone had uttered since he left the police station. And now, as he drove the Beetle back into town, he banged his fist on the steering wheel each time he voiced it. Even finding the money and the knife intact had done little to relieve his resentment against women in general and the one at the rave in particular. Why had she done it? He hadn't touched her, not last night. Wouldn't have touched her with a barge pole. Hadn't he told her that? What the fucking hell did she think she was playing at dropping him in it like that? Thanks to her, he'd spent most of the night and part of the morning at the police station. In the end they'd had to let him go — 'to make further inquiries', that poncy inspector had said. What inquiries could they make when he hadn't done anything? Now if it had been the other one who'd complained they'd have inquiries worth making. He smirked. God, she'd been good; but the first one . . . bloody little bitch, she needed some lessons.

Bitches, all of 'em. Donna, the girl at the rave, and — his hands grabbed at the wheel, his knuckles showing white with the pressure — and that black bitch, the dead one. The one whose husband was letting Karen live with him, who was taking Danny from him and who had to be screwing his sister or else why would she be staying there?

The bitch!

★   ★   ★

'Thanks for coming, Alison,' Ali greeted the woman feeling her way gingerly across the muddy field.

The damp mist overnight had kept the earth soft and made the furrows from the police vehicles even more treacherous to cross.

'No problem,' she said, testing the ground in front of her as though any minute she might sink into its boggy depths. 'I love spending Sunday morning up to my eyes in muck.'

Slipping on a patch of mud, she grabbed at a tuft of grass to save herself. Her forensic bag fell from her hand and as she tried to save that, she sat down heavily. Looking up at Ali, she said, 'You owe me one, Khalid Ali, and I won't let you forget it.' She grabbed at the hand he offered her and, when upright, peered round to check the seat of her trousers. 'And a dry-cleaning bill,' she observed drily. 'Now, a boot print, wasn't it?'

Ali led her to the side of the barn. The ground near the door and beyond had been churned by the exodus from the rave, but very few of the ravers had run round the side, believing, no doubt, that the quickest way to freedom was in a straight line.

'There's not much of it left, but you might be able to get enough to make a comparison with one found close to where Rukhsana Mahmood was murdered. We don't know who owns that boot, but I've got a feeling it could be the same person who owns this one.'

'I hope you've got a bit more than a feeling to go on, because it'll be a big coincidence if the two match,' the scene of crime officer remarked. 'We're expensive, you know, us forensic people. Still, if you don't mind a bollocking for wasting my time and your murder budget, I'll check it out for you.'

★ ★ ★

It was well past lunchtime when Ali arrived at the prison. He could hear Amina's words, soft against the churning of the engine. *They'll be lucky if they see you before bedtime.* Perhaps he ought to give her a ring, tell he where he was and what time he expected to be back. He glanced at his passenger. On second thoughts, perhaps not. Not with Warrender by his side to overhear.

Until Warrender had told him about the arrest and the boot print, his sole intention had been to check out Penistone's background, see if there could be a link between him and the murdered woman, and then go home. Now that Amajit's information had provided both link and motive, the print and the fact that Alison Morand was duty SOCO was too good an opportunity to miss; she owed him a favour from way back and this had been as good a time as any to call it in. That only left Warrender's information and he could hear that and then go back to his children. Unfortunately or fortunately, depending on how you looked at it, what Warrender unearthed was good: Faysal Hussain, it seemed, used students to sell his gear — students like Mohammed Aziz, Jamilla's killer.

There was no way Ali could let that lie until the next day; not if it linked Hussain and his steroids to the riots and even, if he was very lucky, to health visitor Rukhsana Mahmood. Given the new information, Barry Penistone was Ali's prime suspect, but it would be irresponsible to rule out Hussain. If he set up the riots to make sure he couldn't be implicated in the Aziz murder, then perhaps he would go even further and kill his cousin's wife if she threatened to tell the police what he was doing. After all, he was into a lucrative business, and in this case he'd be doing not only himself a favour but his family also, by exacting revenge on the woman who had shamed them.

It had been worth a try and Ali had rung the prison where Aziz was serving his sentence, talked to the liaison officer and been granted permission to interview Aziz. Luckily, the hard bit, getting authorisation, had been made all the easier because the uniformed chief inspector on duty was being harassed by a deputation from Bridgeden when Ali approached him. Even though it was Sunday, the group had obviously decided to make their irritation known at the earliest possible moment and had enough authority between them to gain an audience with a policeman of substantive rank. The chief inspector had been stressed and hardly heard Ali's request, murmuring as he signed the authorisation, 'God protect me from middle England.'

Ali parked the car in the car park some distance from the prison and the two detectives walked towards the door in the shadow of the outer walls.

'These places give me the creeps,' Warrender complained.

'Well, at least you're coming out again, you'll be home for tea.'

'I would have been home for dinner if you hadn't decided to play detective on a Sunday.'

'Yes, and no doubt claimed overtime for a full day. I've got the measure of you, Warrender, so watch it.' Ali couldn't help feeling smug; for the first time he'd grasped and kept the upper hand. He didn't expect it to last, but it was a good feeling, nevertheless.

Once through the security procedure, they were escorted to an interview room.

'How's Aziz doing?' Ali asked as they walked.

'Good as gold, no trouble at all. It was a bit much for him at first, because of his colour and trying to get off the drugs, but now he's clean he's settled down. He began an OU degree at the beginning of the year. He's an intelligent lad.'

The officer held open the door to let Ali and Warrender through. 'Wait here, I'll get him for you.'

Warrender looked round the sparsely furnished room. 'Some of us don't have the time to do an OU degree.'

'You'd like a degree then?'

'I'm not that bothered, it's the time I'd like. Perhaps it's better to be one of the dregs, they seem to get all the privileges.'

Ali sat down on one of the chairs behind the table. 'You know, Warrender, you're carrying a big load on your shoulders. Why don't you shed it and give yourself a chance. Use the time you waste feeling badly done to and you might even find you can fit a degree in.'

Warrender threw him a look of contempt. 'Thanks, Ali, but I don't think I need your advice.' He sat on the chair next to him. 'I can sort out my own life; I don't need one of you lot telling me what to do.'

Ali smiled; the upper hand was slipping, but not too much. He was about to tell Warrender that the job was about relating to others and in that area he was sadly lacking, when the door opened and the prison officer walked in accompanied by Mohammed Aziz. An untypical image of a killer, he was small, slightly built, probably not much more than nine stone. Barry Penistone could have blown him over with a puff of his breath. His eyes shifted from one detective to the other, then he glanced at the man who accompanied him, as if appealing for him not to leave.

'I'll be just outside if you want me,' the prison officer said. The comment was for the detectives, but as he patted the boy's shoulder, Ali saw Aziz relax a little.

He walked round the table to offer the boy a chair. 'How are they treating you?' he asked.

Aziz shrugged. 'It's not too bad now; they say I might be moved from here soon to a less secure prison.'

Warrender reached in his jacket pocket and pulled out an unopened packet of cigarettes. 'Do you smoke?'

When the boy nodded, he threw it over to him. 'They tell me you're doing an OU degree. What in?'

Aziz opened the packet and pulled out a cigarette. He put it between his lips and bent forward across the table as Warrender offered him a light. 'Computer science,' he said.

Ali watched the scenario with amusement. This was a new side to Warrender. The man didn't smoke, in fact his dislike of smoking was second only to his dislike of Asians; he had to have bought the cigarettes specially.

Ali sat back down. 'You're not in trouble, Mohammed, you're not under caution or anything like that and we're not recording on tape. DC Warrender here will take a few notes, but that's only so that we remember accurately what you say. Is that all right?'

Aziz nodded.

'Do you remember when you were arrested, there was some trouble outside the police station?'

'My father told me, but I didn't see it. It wasn't anything to do with me.' He seemed suddenly nervous and looked round to see if the officer was still visible through the glass in the door. He pulled hard on his cigarette.

'No, we know it wasn't any of your doing, but we need to know if you know who set it up.'

Aziz began to twist the cigarette in his fingers. 'Why should I?'

Warrender leaned back on his chair. 'The officer outside seems to think you're doing well here.'

'He's OK, not like some of 'em.'

'He told us you were clean now — off the drugs.'

'Yeah.'

'What were you on?' Warrender's voice had taken on a sympathetic tone; as if he empathised with the boy, understood what he had gone through.

Aziz was warming to him. 'Amphets, ecstasy, steroids.'

'Nothing stronger? Heroine, crack?'

'A bit of crack sometimes.'

Warrender leaned over the table. 'Who sold them to you?'

Aziz shrugged.

'What about the steroids? Who did you get those from?'

'They're not illegal.' The boy's voice took on a defiant tone.

'No, of course they're not — not to take.'

Defiance turned to alarm. 'Not to sell, that's what he said.'

'That's what who said, Mohammed?'

Aziz glanced round as if looking for a way out; the officer beyond the door stiffened, ready to move in.

Ali spoke. 'I promise you, you're not in any trouble.' He tried to emulate Warrender's level of reassurance. 'Before all this happened, did you have a job?'

'Not full-time, I was at college.'

'Doing computer science?'

'Yes.'

'What did your father think about your choice?'

Aziz chafed at his bottom lip. 'What do *you* think? He wanted me to do law or medicine or something. I'd have been useless, all that reading, all those essays.'

'But you went to college, so he must have helped you out with money.'

'Not my father. He said if I wanted to study computers, I'd have to pay my own way.'

'And you found some work?'

'Yeah, in a restaurant, as a waiter.'

'Where?'

'The Curry House in the city centre.'

'The one owned by Faysal Hussain?'

Aziz nodded. He pulled on his cigarette for the last time and stabbed it out in the ashtray.

'Well-paid, was it, the job?' Warrender's tone suggested that he understood it wasn't.

Aziz picked up on it. 'Only if you worked all hours. I'd start at about half past six and finish anytime after midnight, six sometimes seven nights a week.'

'Couldn't have given you much time for college work.' Warrender leaned back in his chair again.

'No, it didn't. I'd stay at college until lectures

were over, do as much as I could in the library, then go off to work. But then one day the boss . . . '

'Meaning Mr Hussain?'

'Yes. He said that he could see how tired I was getting and if I wanted I could work less hours in the restaurant and have more time for college, if I . . . '

'If you what, Mohammed?'

Aziz let his shoulders sag. He had walked right into Warrender's trap and he knew it.

'If I sold steroids to the kids in college,' he said, his voice down to a whisper.

Warrender let the front legs of his chair drop back onto the floor. The sound echoed triumphantly around the room. He shot a look at Ali, a look which said: 'And there's your link between Hussain and the riots and the reason why he'll set them up again if he has to.'

17

Ali had arrived home last night to a cool reception from Amina. The children were already in bed.

'You have to stop letting them down, Khalid. They're too young to understand.'

He had apologised profusely, but although Amina had been brighter this morning, he was fairly sure it was a brightness put on for the children, and that she had still not forgiven him.

Sitting at his desk, he read through Faysal Hussain's statement regarding his movements on the day of the murder. He was, he had said, buying a property on the outskirts of the city where he intended to open another restaurant. It had been an old cinema, and he had spent the bulk of the day with architects, planning officers and builders to check the feasibility of the proposal before putting in a bid.

He called over to Warrender. 'Find out how much of Hussain's statement has been checked. If it still needs doing, do it yourself.'

Warrender pulled a face.

'Oh, come on, Constable,' Ali said. 'You know how much you'll enjoy it.'

With Hussain out of the way, Ali could concentrate on Penistone.

He'd tried to see Handford, but he'd been with Russell ever since he came in, and so Ali hadn't been able to talk over yesterday's

360

developments with him. He was in a quandary: should he wait until Handford was free, wait until he got the results of the boot prints from SOCO, or take a chance and question Barry Penistone straightaway?

A call from Peter Redmayne decided him. The call was actually for John Handford, but when Ali told him that the inspector was in a meeting, Redmayne asked him to take a message.

'John asked me what I knew about Barry Penistone. Tell him that I've asked around and there is no doubt the man is dealing steroids for Hussain. And he's definitely one of those who visits the flat above the Curry House every Thursday. I recognised him from the picture John faxed me.'

'Do you know where he's doing his dealing?'

'Probably the gyms in the area, youth clubs maybe. He isn't one of the dealers I've followed. He may well work for Hussain at the raves though, probably as a bouncer, but he's bound to be selling as well.'

'Thank you, Mr Redmayne. I'll pass your message on to the DI. He'll no doubt be in touch.' A thought occurred to Ali. 'Before you go,' he said quickly, 'how does Penistone transport his drugs, do you know?'

'Probably by taxi. There are usually a lot of them around the restaurant on Thursday afternoon. Hussain has quite a few of the drivers in his pocket.'

'Right, thank you; I'll pass your message on.'

Ali replaced the receiver. Dealing drugs at the rave was what he needed to give him a legitimate

361

reason to question Penistone. He wouldn't know that it was nothing to do with CID — one copper was no doubt very much like another to him.

. It was out of his way, but Ali took the route round by Moss Carr Nursing Home to Penistone's workplace. It would give him some idea of the minimum time needed to get from the bakery to the woods where Rukhsana was killed. The roads were busy, leading as they did to the motorway or to the ring road and from there into the outskirts of Leeds. Semi-detached houses built in the sixties stood along one side of the route to the bakery, their gardens offering some protection against the relentless hum of the traffic. On the other side, long rows of terraced dwellings stretched away at right angles from the road and far into the distance, terminating abruptly where the valley met the edge of the Pennine range, trapping them in the shadow of the steep hillsides.

There were still signs of the thriving area it had once been. Buildings which had housed engineering companies in an era when workers were told they'd never had it so good stood dismal and deserted. Pounded by a recession which was none of their making, the owners had laid off some of the workers, then more, then eventually surrendered to the inevitable and pulled out, leaving vast edifices to stand as testimony to their betrayal. Some had been demolished, leaving acres of veined concrete, sporadically carpeted by grasses which had found refuge in the weathered fissures. Others,

362

abandoned but still standing, provided shelter of sorts to the homeless and the addicts.

Ali turned left into a road that dropped away steeply. Here entrepreneurs had bought up the land and were busy building leisure centres or supermarkets. Incongruous amongst such modernity, the bakery sprawled in its own acreage, a one-storey building of cream concrete and red brick, surrounded by a stone wall topped with green plastic-coated netting.

The girl at reception was helpful, but it took some time to locate Penistone.

'He could be anywhere, Sergeant,' she apologised. 'Everything goes to the warehouse first and he stores it or delivers it. So he might be in the works or in the offices.' She gave Ali a wide smile. 'I'll tannoy him if you want.'

Ali returned the smile. 'That would be very kind,' he said.

She disappeared into a back room. 'Barry Penistone to reception. Barry Penistone to reception.' The tannoy echoed through the lobby.

'There,' the girl said as she returned. 'If he's heard it he won't be long.'

Ali smiled again. 'Just one more thing. When he comes, is there somewhere private we could speak?'

The girl waved towards a door to the left of the desk. 'That's a visitors' room; you can use that. You go in, I'll tell him you're there.'

To suggest that the management was not very welcoming to their visitors would have been an understatement. The room was sparsely fur-nished with three easy chairs that had seen better

363

days and a low table on which were spread magazines months out of date and a vase of artificial flowers whose petals were covered in a layer of dust. Ali flicked through a couple of the magazines while he waited. Eventually Barry Penistone sauntered in, hands in his pockets, a half-smoked cigarette hanging between his lips.

Ali rose from his chair.

From the expression on his face, it was obvious that Penistone was less than pleased to see him. 'What do you want?'

'A moment of your time.'

Penistone removed the cigarette from his mouth, dropped it onto the pockmarked lino tiled floor and stubbed it out under his heel. Others had obviously done the same thing before him.

He glared at the sergeant. 'You lot 'ave had more than enough of my time. Say what it is you want then go and let me get on with me work.'

Ali sat down again and stretched over to pull the nearest chair closer to him. He beckoned to Penistone to sit down.

'Who's behind the raves?' There was no point messing around. This wasn't the information he wanted, but it was the quickest way in.

'You think I'm going to tell you?' Barry Penistone curled his lip.

'I hope so.'

'Why are you interested anyway? I thought you were supposed to be finding out who killed the Paki woman.'

'I am, but we're flexible, we detectives, we often take on two cases at once.'

'So what about that poncy inspector who nicked me? What's he doing?'

Barry Penistone wasn't the fool Ali had taken him for. He did know one copper from another.

He ignored the question. 'The girl who alleged indecent assault against you, did you know her?'

'She comes to some of the raves.'

'Have you talked with her at all, become friendly?'

'I'm there to be friendly.'

Ali leaned forward so that his mouth was close against Barry Penistone's ear. 'Taken it any further with her, have you? Been more than friendly?'

The big man turned, his face so intimidatingly close to Ali's that the detective could smell his tobacco-laden breath. Penistone prodded at him with his finger, bulldozing each word into the sergeant's sternum. 'Mind your own fucking business.'

Ali moved the finger away carefully with the back of his hand and sat back in his chair. 'Perhaps anabolic steroids are more my business.'

At the unexpectedness of the comment, Penistone's former arrogance slid away and he seemed to fold into the chair. The smirk on his lips was swallowed as his mouth tightened, and his eyes which had held nothing but contempt took on an air of stupefaction, laced with dismay. But he was a master in his dealings with the police and Ali marvelled at the speed with which he recovered his poise.

'If you say so.'

Acrid loathing tightened between them; it penetrated Ali's nostrils with the same pungency he had encountered in the urine-soaked doorways around the snooker halls. Penistone would be difficult to break; he had the knack of snatching control in a situation, sometimes by force, sometimes by more subtle methods, and Ali could feel his mental grip loosening. His fingernails dug into his palms. *He* had to manipulate the interview, not the thug opposite.

'You're working for Faysal Hussain. He supplies steroids, and any other drugs he can get his hands on. He organises the raves and you work for him. So what do you do up there, Penistone — apart from indecently assaulting young girls, I mean? Sell steroids, ecstasy, amphetamines, LSD?' He watched his adversary's eyes cloud with anger and hoped to God that he wouldn't jump him. There was no alarm system in here.

Ali waited for the anger to explode as it had at the hospital, as it had with John Handford and as it had with Karen Penistone. But Penistone, it seemed, had it under control.

'They found nothing on me when they nicked me. Nothing. So how about you going back to finding out who killed that Paki bitch and leaving me alone.'

It was warm in the room, but Ali suddenly felt chilled. He pulled himself from the chair and walked over to the radiator. Probably installed when the bakery was built, it was old, low to the ground and wide enough to perch on. He sat down, amazed at its efficiency as he felt the warmth penetrate his coat.

'How do you get to work, Barry?'

'What do yer want to know that for?'

Ali suddenly became tired of the prevarication. His eyes narrowed. 'Tell me, do your employers know about your record? Because if you don't answer my questions, a whisper in the right ear . . . ' He could see that Barry Penistone had understood.

'Are you threatening me?'

'Yes, Mr Penistone, I think you can say that.' He paused for a moment to let the point penetrate. 'Now, it's an easy enough question. How do you get to work?'

Barry conceded. 'By bus. There's one that stops just outside my house and brings me all the way here.'

'What break do you get at dinner time?'

'An hour. There has to be someone in the warehouse all the time, so we take turns between twelve and two. I go half twelve to half one.'

'Where do you go?'

'Well, not very far. There isn't time. There's a pub up the road, sometimes I go there, other times I bring sandwiches and eat them 'ere or I go out and get fish and chips.'

'So you don't go back home or anywhere away from the bakery?'

'Look, I'm fed up with this. I've just said, there isn't time.'

Ali was disappointed. He would check, but he had to admit that it was increasingly unlikely that Barry Penistone would be able to get to the nursing home, kill Rukhsana and be back at the

367

bakery within the hour.

'And you were at work last Tuesday.'

Penistone stood up and moved towards Ali. 'Of course I was at work last Tuesday. I'm always at bloody work. The only time I ever miss work is when you lot feel like having a go at me. And then I'm at the nick.'

'How did you get to work on Tuesday?'

Penistone's anger was showing through. 'I've told you. By bus.'

'On Tuesday?'

Suddenly Penistone's expression became more wary. 'Tuesday?'

'Yes.'

'That was the day of the bus strike.'

'Yes.'

'I walked.'

'All the way from home? That must have taken you some time. Couldn't you get a lift from someone?'

'No, I couldn't. Look, I walked, all right? They don't care about bus strikes here, you know. If I don't work, I don't get paid. I walked. And I got here on time. Check my clock card if you don't believe me,' he added triumphantly.

'Oh, I will, Mr Penistone, I will.' But Ali knew that it would be a waste of time. The clock card would show he had been at work.

'You don't have a car, then?'

Penistone hesitated for a second, but whether it was through disbelief at such a question or a need to get his answer right, Ali wasn't sure.

'A car? Me? How do you think I can afford a car on four pound ten an hour? It takes me all

368

me time to afford the bloody bus fare.'

Ali persisted. 'But you can drive?'

'So?'

'So, you could have borrowed a car, used one to get here on Tuesday.'

Penistone's anger was becoming less controlled. 'What's all this with Tuesday and cars? I haven't got a car; I didn't get a lift in a car and I didn't borrow a car. I walked here in the morning and I walked home after me shift. Ask anyone if you don't believe me. They'll tell you they saw me walking through the bakery gates. In fact, I met a couple of me mates just outside. Ask 'em.'

Ali sighed. There was no more to be gained by continuing. Without a car, the man just couldn't have made it to the nursing home in the time. He had been wrong about Barry Penistone and the DI had been right. The nearest thing to evidence Ali had was that the man was strong enough to have picked up a coping stone and smashed it on Rukhsana's skull, and the only motive he could come up with was that Penistone hated Asians, that he may have fathered Karen's son and that Rukhsana may have been aware of this. Ifs, buts and maybes. Circumstantial at best and, if he was honest, not even a very good best. Certainly there was not enough for a charge of murder.

He wrote down the names of the men who had come in through the gates with him, but he knew they would back up Penistone's story.

'All right, Penistone, that's all.'

He would have liked to question him about

Danny, but this wasn't the place; that needed doing at the station, and anyway he'd have to confirm Karen's story first.

Barry Penistone stood up. 'You know, Paki, you could 've saved yourself the trouble.' His lip curled. 'Why don't you just go back where you came from and give us all a break.'

Ali's fingers itched to wipe the smirk from the man's face. 'I'll tell you what, Penistone. Just so that my journey was not altogether wasted, how about you telling Hussain that we've got the measure of him? And while you're about it, remind yourself that as far as dealing is concerned, we've got the measure of you too.' He smiled. 'Selling drugs as well as indecent assault. They'll throw the book at you.'

He pushed past Penistone, casting a final glance at the man's expression, enmity clouded with apprehension. They'd probably not even lift the book, let alone throw it. Still, Penistone couldn't be sure, not yet.

★ ★ ★

Barry Penistone wasn't sure, not about anything. He leaned against the wall outside the visitors' room, and watched as Ali went through the doors into the yard. He wasn't sure how much the coppers knew or how much they were guessing; he wasn't sure if they were trying to trick him or set him up. And if they were, he wasn't sure why. That Paki sergeant, with his brown eyes set in that brown face, didn't give anything away; you couldn't tell what he was thinking, so you didn't know what he knew. One thing he did seem sure about, though, was the steroids, but that could have been a good guess. Barry frowned. No, that wasn't likely, not with steroids. With any other drug it could have been a guess, but not with steroids. Under normal circumstances the cops wouldn't give them a second thought, they weren't interested; that's why Hussain dealt in them. As far as steroids were concerned, he had the run of the city and beyond; they brought him and his dealers a good return, the punters weren't in any risk of being nicked, the Drug Squad didn't want to know and the big dealers couldn't give a shit, provided Hussain didn't stray onto their patch or into their merchandise.

His frown deepened. Assuming they knew about Hussain and the steroids, what else did they know? Ali had been more than interested in Tuesday and how he got to work. Tuesday was the day the Paki woman was killed. Did they think he had something to do with it? Well, they'd got nothing at all on him; they couldn't even fit him up.

He turned to walk along the corridor. The Paki woman. If anyone thought he would shed any tears over her, they were wrong. Served her right, the nosy bitch, digging into Karen's life, and into his. A cold sweat filtered through onto his brow, chilling his skin. He took his cap off and wiped it across his forehead. Had she said anything to anyone? Did the cops know about Danny and him? Well, even if they did, what did that prove? Karen would never let them charge him with anything. He was family. And she needed him to help bring up Danny. And he loved Danny; he never wanted to be parted from him.

Panic rose, swelling in him, tightening in a band across his chest so that he could hardly breathe. Pictures formed in his brain: a beer glass smashing against a man's face, his hand striking Karen's cheek, his fist colliding with the policeman's arm . . . He closed his eyes to shut out the images, turbulent in their desire to achieve prime position. Saturday night and the rave. Danny and the Paki. Karen and her Paki. The hospital waiting room and the Paki. Newspaper photographs of a white tent in the woods. Police, coppers, pigs. He leaned against the wall, covering his eyes with his hand; he couldn't bear any more. But as he shut out the images, voices took their place, words vying to be heard.

'They'll throw the book at you, Penistone.'

'He had 'is mucky 'ands up me blouse and in me knickers.'

'You knocked me out.'

'Were you at work last Tuesday?'

He stared at the gloss white wall of the corridor, stretching away into the distance. Did it lead to Heaven or Hell? Danny and the Paki. Karen and Mahmood. Hussain and the steroids. The rave and the white bitch. Wednesday night and Karen. The hospital and the Paki. Murder. Words and pictures inextricably linked, but jumbled, losing themselves in their confusion. One question stood proud.

'Were you at work last Tuesday?'

Tuesday. His brain cleared, the words, the pictures faded as if by magic. What was the matter with him? He could sort everything out, Hussain, Danny, Karen and Mahmood. As for Tuesday, it was nothing to do with him. He was at work on Tuesday, and they couldn't prove any different.

18

Faysal Hussain lowered the mobile phone from his ear, his thumb on the end-of-call key. The information Penistone had just passed on didn't trouble him particularly. The police had apparently visited the bakery and questioned Penistone about dealing for him. They hadn't arrested Penistone, so they couldn't have concrete evidence. And as Hussain knew, knowing was one thing, proving it was another and nowadays the cops had to have evidence. What troubled him more was that Penistone had been the one to tell him. He'd even sounded triumphant on the phone. Letting him know that the police knew had probably been the highlight of his sad little life. The question was, had it happened as he had said, or had he grassed on him?

Faysal made his way into the kitchen, taking pleasure, as he always did, in its smooth lines and gleaming work surfaces, maintained, like the rest of his house, by his daily, Mrs Agar, who gained as much delight from its cleanliness as he did. 'I always likes doing for you, Mr Hussain, proper picture book, your house is.'

He couldn't disagree with her. His home was the type of place the whites resented Pakistanis owning, a typical English middle-class address, expensive, detached, double garage, gardens back and front. Not that his neighbours had

374

anything against Pakistanis of course, but everyone knew that one living amongst them was the beginning of the end for the district; property values would inevitably begin to slide and friends move out. But because they'd nothing against Pakistanis, the residents were pleasant enough to his face, although they drew the line at welcoming him into their homes and when he'd extended an invitation to them, they'd turned him down, offering prior appointments as their excuse. Such busy people, with so many prior engagements. Sometimes, he'd ask them round just to see the expression on their faces as they declined — a mixture of embarrassment and sorrow. He smiled at the thought, but the smile didn't reach his eyes. Hidden in their depths was a tangle of emotions which only those who had experienced racial rejection would understand. And if they treated him like this when they knew him only as a respectable businessman, what would their reaction be, he wondered, if they found out how he had really earned the money to buy this place?

At one time the notion would have given him a certain amount of satisfaction, but not this time. He'd done everything he could to keep out of the eye of the police, but that was over now. However they had found out, they knew, and although at this moment they might be able to do very little, there would come a time when they would, when he'd get up their nose so much that they'd make him their priority — and not because he was supplying steroids and organising raves, but because he was a Pakistani making

375

money. And he knew that the person to hasten that day was the person who had given him the warning — Barry Penistone.

There were things that worried him about that man. He could just about cope with his racism and his temper. But what he found difficult to understand was, why, although he made good money from dealing, he never seemed to spend any. All his other dealers couldn't wait to hand theirs over, either to another dealer or to some flash car or clothes salesman, but not Penistone. As far as Hussain could tell, he didn't have a habit, at least not one he injected into veins or snorted up his nose, and he didn't seem to have made any attempt to change his lifestyle. He looked and acted like a poorly paid warehouse-man. By now he should have had decent clothes and a car of his own, instead of sharing that clapped-out Volkswagen with his friend. It may be that he was concerned that the police would wonder about the extravagant lifestyle of an ex-convict, but he doubted it. In his experience, Penistone cared very little about what the police thought.

So what was he doing with his money? Stashing it away for a rainy day? The idea stirred. Perhaps that was just what he was doing and under the cover of a police raid had taken the opportunity to inform on his supplier. Then, while he, Hussain was sharing a cell with some no-hoper, Penistone could, with little or no opposition, take over his business — and he didn't mean the restaurants.

Hussain grimaced as he took a sip of the now

cold coffee. Penistone may work on the principle that it was best to use your fists first, think afterwards, but he was cunning, sly even; according to him, the cops had found nothing on him from the rave, and as for the indecent assault, they only had the girl's word for that. The accusation wouldn't go anywhere; the police must know this so why had Ali, of all people, gone out of his way to visit the bakery on a case that wasn't his, to question Barry Penistone about something so minor? It had to have been an excuse to find out about the steroids, but even that was outside Ali's brief. It didn't make sense. Unless . . . unless they thought Penistone had something to do with Rukhsana's death. Surely not. No, he couldn't have. Why should he? He'd have no reason. Or . . . the thought cut through Hussain, or the police thought he, Hussain had killed her and a drugs charge would stop him from disappearing back to Pakistan.

Hussain shrugged. He poured what was left of the murky grey liquid into the sink and turned on the hot tap. As he rinsed out his mug, he watched the coffee dregs mix with the running water and lose their colour. As easy as that, he thought, to flush away the tainted. And since she had been tainted, it didn't matter much one way or the other to him who had flushed away Amajit's wife. Ali's hidden agenda when he visited Penistone wasn't important either; the police had absolutely no reason to suspect Faysal Hussain of the murder; his alibi saw to that. He certainly wasn't about to jump on a plane to anywhere; he had far too many business deals here to do that. But he did need to get the spotlight off him.

It was Penistone he had to warn off. He was the one who was most likely to go shouting off his mouth. And Hussain knew the best way to do it: get at Karen Penistone, his sister. Penistone was very possessive of his sister; hurt the sister and you hurt him. And the bonus was that it would also pass a message on to Amajit to leave the girl well alone. It would kill two birds with one stone; three, in fact, because the police would be so busy finding someone to arrest for what essentially would be — what did they call it, arson with the intent to endanger life? — that a few steroids would come way down their list.

He picked up his mobile and thumbed in a number.

'I think we've waited long enough,' he said when his call was answered. 'Do it tonight.'

★   ★   ★

Handford picked up the emailed statement and photograph from the Met. and leaned back in his chair.

My name is Bethany Cantrell and I am 24 years old. I work as a researcher for the BBC.

I have known Dr Ian Berridge for nine years. He treated me in the hospital in Belfast when I was fifteen for endometriosis, a condition of the womb. I was in his care for some two years. He wasn't like the other doctors I had known. He treated me as a

378

person not as a case. He explained everything and never talked down to me. Some of the time, while I was having treatment or being examined, we would discuss things we were interested in. My love is classical music; I play the piano and the flute. He said that was his love too. He made me feel special; as though I was his only patient.

One day, towards the end of my treatment, he rang my home and said he had managed to get two tickets for a concert in Belfast. His wife couldn't go but if my parents were happy he would like to take me instead. Since I was studying music at A-level they thought it would be a good opportunity for me. Concerts like that were something they couldn't afford.

Afterwards he suggested coffee back at his house. We talked, drank coffee, then brandy. He kissed me, apologised for doing so and kissed me again. I didn't stop him. We ended up in bed together. It was the first time I had done anything like that, but I was flattered and when he said he loved me and wanted to carry on seeing me, I couldn't think of anything I wanted more. He suggested that we keep our meetings a secret because in his job any relationship with a patient was frowned on. I couldn't believe my luck. I adored him, would do anything for him. And did.

We met when he was able, sometimes at his home, sometimes we'd drive out to a hotel. When I had my interview for London University, he made the excuse that there was a conference in London he particularly wanted to attend. It was the most wonderful three days. He talked about getting a job in London so that it could always be like this; he said he would leave his wife.

Four weeks after we got back I realised I was pregnant. I was devastated, although looking back I can't think why. Neither of us had taken precautions and I suppose I thought that since we'd been sleeping together for so long I'd been affected by the endometriosis and wouldn't be able to have children.

Anyway, it didn't matter because he'd said he wanted to be with me and I assumed he would stick with me. I could put off my place at university for a year, he could get a job in London and eventually we could get married.

When I told him he was furious, blamed me, called me a stupid bitch for not taking precautions, said I would have to have an abortion. No one must know, he said, the only thing to do was to terminate. He would book me into a clinic in London, pay for the abortion, no one need ever know. He never asked me what I wanted or how I felt. All he was interested in were his feelings, his career, his pride. He said he would ring me when he had made the arrangements.

It was about a week later before I heard from him and I'd had a lot of time to think. I'd decided I couldn't have an abortion, it was wrong and I couldn't do it. I felt sure he'd understand. We met in the park near my home. It was late February and there was no one around. I wasn't nervous about telling him because I thought he would understand. But he went mad; I'd never seen him like that before. He said that I was a selfish cow, that his career would be ruined if I went ahead. I tried to explain that abortion was like murder to me. He pulled me to him, held me, said he understood, but that the foetus was not a living human being, I wouldn't be committing murder. But I would be ruining his life and that of his wife and children and he was sure I wouldn't want that.

It was in that moment that I knew that he had no love for me; I was a conquest, another notch, probably one in a long line. I told him that I would not have an abortion and he couldn't make me. He pushed me from him and began to walk away. He hadn't gone more than a few paces when he turned to face me. I can't describe the expression on his face; it was almost like that of a child who had been refused a toy he wanted, a mixture of petulance, hatred and anger. He paced backwards and forwards, calling me names each time he faced me, demanding that I had an abortion. Then suddenly he walked towards me again, but this time he stopped and asked me for the last time, he said, would I have a termination? I said no and he lifted his hand and struck me hard across the face, so hard that I overbalanced on the stone edging of a flowerbed and fell. It didn't stop him, in fact it seemed to add impetus to his anger. He wouldn't let me get up, just kicked out at me, in the stomach, around my head. I couldn't believe this was the man I had loved for so long. Then suddenly it stopped and when I moved my arms from my head he was walking away. I could see him slapping at his thighs as he disappeared. He never looked back. He just left me there.

Eventually I managed to get up and struggle my way out of the park, but once out on the road I collapsed and the next thing I knew I was waking up in hospital. They said I'd lost the baby. My parents were furious and demanded to know who the father was, but I wouldn't tell them. I don't think it ever occurred to them it could be my doctor and if I'd told them they wouldn't have believed me. Ian never contacted me again. He didn't visit me in hospital, didn't ask my parents how I was, didn't apologise. When the police interviewed me, I said I'd been mugged.

Eventually I went off to university and decided that that part of my life had to be over, but that he wasn't going to get away with it entirely. I wrote to him to tell him that if I ever heard of him being mixed up with anything remotely like what he had done to me I would go back to the police and tell them. That's what I did when I heard about the other girl and why I'm giving this statement now.

The statement, given freely, was an account of four years of her life. Stark, bare words which didn't begin to describe the emotions that lay beneath them. Handford studied the photo sent through with it. Such a pretty girl; slim, even in a chunky sweater, sculptured features framed by copper-blonde hair, and the greenest eyes Handford had ever seen. He could understand why Berridge had fallen for her, just like he had fallen for Rukhsana. He could pull the beauties, so why not? Handford almost felt jealous.

He re-read the end portion of the statement. 'They said I'd lost the baby. My parents wanted to know who the father was, but I wouldn't tell them. I don't think it ever occurred to them it could be my doctor and if I'd told them they wouldn't have believed me. Ian never contacted me again. He didn't visit me in hospital, didn't ask my parents how I was, didn't apologise.'

How lonely she must have been. The baby gone, a lover who wanted nothing more to do with her, parents who would blame her and in whom she couldn't confide. Handford closed his eyes, images of his own daughters forming in his mind. Nicola was fourteen, only three years younger than Bethany when she had first slept with Berridge. How would he feel if it was her? Would he believe her? Would he know the identity of the father of any child she conceived? Did she have a serious boyfriend? He realised he had no idea. He loved his daughters, but he didn't know anything about them. He supposed they were working towards their futures, getting on at school, preparing for exams, but he didn't know, and what was worse, he didn't think that after all this time he could ask them. What did you say? How did you broach such a subject?

'Are you having sex? Are you taking precautions?' All these years in the job he had relied on Gill to bring them up, teach them right from wrong, keep them safe, and he had assumed she had done just that. He had been there at holiday times, the fun times; but as for the rest . . .

He sat up and pulled himself back to the present. He was going to have Berridge in and question him formally, under caution. He wouldn't arrest him, not yet, but he was fairly sure that would come eventually.

They had more suspects for Rukhsana's murder than they knew what to do with: her husband, any member of his family, Berridge, Barry Penistone and now, according to Warrender, Faysal Hussain.

'The sergeant asked me to check his statement, boss. He thinks Rukhsana might have known that he was dealing, threatened him with the law and so he got rid of her.'

Handford doubted it; he'd taken Hussain's statement himself and unless everyone was covering for him, architects, planning officers and builders, his alibi was watertight. No, his money was on Berridge. He had been seen with Rukhsana just before her death; he wanted her to have an abortion in case the baby was his; by his own admission he was angry and frustrated at her prevarication, and he admitted to hitting her when they were in the car park. The likelihood was that she walked or ran down to the woods to get away from him, he followed her, tried again to persuade her to terminate and when she wouldn't he got angry and picked up the nearest thing to hand and hit her with it. And he'd done something similar before. Seven years ago he had been lucky he hadn't killed Bethany Cantrell; last week with Rukhsana Mahmood, Handford believed, the man's luck had run out.

But he needed more information if he was going to nail him. The nursing home's security was sadly lacking; nothing much in the way of cameras, either in the car park or on the driveway, and those there were tended not to have tapes in them. Nathan Teale was their best bet since he had been around clearing leaves at the relevant times.

Handford walked through to the CID room and looked round.

'Warrender, has Graham asked you to interview Teale?'

'Yes, boss, but he's not back from the long weekend. He should have been at work today, but the nursing home manager took pity on him and gave him an extra day's holiday with pay,' Warrender said, his exasperation close to the surface. 'I'll go up first thing. Anything specific you want?'

'It seems Teale is the nearest thing we've got to security, so I want to know who and what he saw before Rukhsana was killed. Specifically, I need to know what time Dr Berridge arrived and more specifically what time he left. As soon as you have anything, let me know.'

'Sir.'

As Handford was leaving the room, he stopped. 'Is Sergeant Ali in the building, do you know?'

'No, guv, haven't seen him since this morning,' Clarke said. 'He was going to see Barry Penistone, he said, so he's probably following up on that.'

'Well, if he's back before I leave, ask him to come and see me. If I've gone and he has anything that's urgent, he can get me on my mobile, but if not I'll talk to him in the morning. It's parents' evening at my daughters' school and my wife will kill me if I'm not there.'

★ ★ ★

It was twenty past midnight when the Mahmood brothers crept up the path to Karen Penistone's house and poured petrol through the letter box. The flaming torch that Kamal thrust in fell into the dark pool of liquid, igniting it instantaneously. With a whoosh, the fingers of fire gathered momentum, lengthening, stretching outwards and upwards, engulfing everything in their path. Outside, the flames caught on the rivulets of fuel which had run down the door, creating a tributary of fire which swept downwards, bubbling a pathway through the paintwork.

Three minutes later, at twenty-three minutes past midnight, Karen's next-door neighbour made his nightly round of the two houses and saw flames licking against the small pane of frosted glass in the top of the door. At first he wasn't sure what he was seeing, but smoke began to seep out through the gap at the bottom, looking for space to spread and disperse. He thought also that he heard the screech of car tyres but he couldn't be certain and he didn't see a vehicle. Suddenly his reflexes caught up with his thoughts. Shouting to his wife to ring the fire brigade, he ran over the lawn and banged on the downstairs window to alert Karen, then dashed back to his house for a ladder. If he could make the bedroom window before the flames and the smoke reached the second storey, he could get her and the child out.

At the same time as the neighbour pounded on the window, Karen was roused by the sound of crashing glass as a photograph of her and Danny on the wall halfway up the staircase fell, its string melted by the flame which frolicked around it. Simultaneously she heard the screech of the smoke alarms and a loud banging which seemed to be coming from downstairs. Still drowsy, she slid out of bed and tiptoed towards the door, trying not to disturb Danny who roused in his cot, then coughed.

She opened the door and her body met a wall of heat. Bright flame and black smoke lunged towards her. Acrid fumes settled in her throat, and as she began to choke, she heard Danny's strangled crying mingle with a bout of coughing. Fear coiled round her like a python, squeezing her nerve endings so that her whole body tingled. Instinctively she slammed the door, imprisoning the two of them in the small bedroom. But it wasn't enough; whorls of smoke corkscrewed under the door, swirling upwards to envelop the ceiling in a thick grey mist.

Danny screamed. Sounds of her son in distress

cleared Karen's mind enough for her to act. She ripped the duvet off the bed and packed it firmly against the bottom of the door, then dashed to the window and threw it open. The cold air stung her arms and face. Panic overtook her and she heard herself scream out.

'It's all right, Karen. We'll soon have you out,' a man's voice shouted up. 'I've got a ladder. Where's Danny?'

Karen turned and rushed over to the cot. The smoke continued to slither under the door, finding pathways through the barrier of duvet and billowing upwards. From the other side she could hear the flames, crackling, chattering, lasering their way through the wooden panels. Grabbing at Danny, she wrapped him roughly in his blankets and dashed back to the window. Concerned features greeted her and the man to whom they belonged stretched out his arms.

'Pass him to me, and then follow me down the ladder yourself.'

Sirens blared as she handed the bundle over, then hauled herself onto the windowsill. She placed her bare feet gingerly on the top rung and cautiously turned herself round. She clutched at the ladder and let each foot in turn grope for the rungs. She could feel the heat from below as the fire raged through the sitting room.

'Come on, lass, quickly.' It was a strong voice, as strong as the arms that held on to her. She felt the firmness of the ground and the iciness of the frosted grass below her feet as she stepped off the final rung.

'We've got you. Come and sit over here.' A

blanket enveloped her. Her throat stung and the passageway to her lungs felt like an old exhaust. She coughed to clear it and gasped for air.

'Put this over your mouth and nose, it'll help you with your breathing.' Holding the blanket round her with one hand, she clutched at the oxygen mask with the other.

Men in uniform rushed past her, but it was a blur. Amidst the noise she was cocooned in silence. She let the mask fall. 'Danny?' she said. 'Where's Danny?'

'He's all right, just inhaled a bit of smoke, like you. We've got him over at the appliance. The ambulance is on its way, then we'll get you both comfortable.'

A shadow appeared close by. 'Is she all right?' The man from next door sounded concerned.

'She'll be as right as rain as soon as we get her into hospital. Just a bit of smoke. Good job you were there.'

'Me, oh I always do the rounds at about midnight. A lass on her own, you can't be too careful. Poor thing, she's had her fill just lately.'

Karen felt his breath at her ear. 'Do you want me to get your mam or your brother for you?'

She was silent for a moment, trying to clear her muddled mind. Did she want her mother? Did she want Barry? She wasn't sure she could cope with either of them, the one fussing and the other storming around threatening all and sundry with a good kicking — the council, the electricity board, anyone he thought he could hold responsible for the fire.

'No, we're all right. Let them know in the morning.' She hesitated. She knew who she did want. 'You could tell Amajit Mahmood though,' she said, faltering over the words. 'I'll give you his telephone number.'

19

Handford turned his head to look at the clock, squinting as he did so at the vivid red digital numbers. Ten past three. He groaned. What had happened for someone to call him at ten past three?

Gill stirred, turned over and snuggled down under the covers. He glanced at her. Over the years she had acquired the knack of completely ignoring the telephone if it rang in the middle of the night. Should one of the girls move, she was awake immediately, but if it was the telephone's shrill ring, which was no more than four feet away from her, she remained completely comatose.

He felt for the receiver and pulled it to his ear. 'Handford.'

'Sorry to bother you, John, it's Bob Milsom.' Bob was night duty inspector. 'But I thought you'd like to know there's been a fire.'

Handford was wide awake now, but grumpy. 'A fire? Why should I want to know about a fire?'

'Well, ordinarily you wouldn't. But I thought you'd want to know about this one. It's Barry Penistone's sister's house, went up in flames round about midnight and it looks like it's deliberate.'

★ ★ ★

Handford dragged himself into Central Police Station at eight o'clock the next morning,

391

wishing he could switch off the world for a few hours. Being woken in the night never rested easily on him and until he'd had a decent dose of caffeine, he pitied anyone who got in his way. Last night, he had snapped at Bob Milsom that Sergeant Ali was far more interested in the Penistone family than he was, and to wake *him* up. Then he had tried to settle, but it was after four when he finally succumbed to sleep, and even then it had been fitful. Berridge's treatment of Bethany Cantrell had got to him and although he tried to put it out of his mind, it insisted on filtering back each time he drifted off. Ian Berridge was everything Handford abhorred — unscrupulous, amoral, self-seeking, self-indulgent . . . He could have gone on, but tried instead to close his mind on the doctor, angry with himself. He was allowing his feelings for Berridge to swamp him, making it personal, and that was dangerous.

When he got to the office, there was a message saying that Russell had been called to a meeting in Wakefield and would see him for an update when he returned. Thankful though he was that he wasn't starting the day with a session with the DCI, a cup of his coffee would have been welcome. He felt let down, he'd been looking forward to it on the drive in; now he'd have to make do with instant.

He picked up a coffee from the machine and made his way to his office. Half an hour later, he sent for Ali.

'You look as though you've been up half the night,' Handford said with a grin when the sergeant came into the room.

'As if you didn't know,' retorted Ali.

Indicating that he should make himself comfortable, Handford smiled. 'A necessary part of the job, Sergeant,' he said, 'getting up in the middle of the night.'

Ali pulled up the chair and sat down, while Handford filled him in on Bethany Cantrell's statement.

'Sounds familiar, guv,' Ali remarked, 'but — '

'Don't say it, Sergeant. DC Clarke's already warned me that it's not evidence.' He sat back in his chair, his hands behind his head. 'So, what happened with Penistone. Did he kill Rukhsana Mahmood?'

Ali sighed. 'I don't see how he could have done, boss. Motive and means, but not the opportunity. There is no way he could have got from work to the nursing home and back again in the time, unless he had transport, and he hasn't. He has a licence, but no car is registered to him. I thought he might have use of one, if only to pick up his drugs from the flat, but according to Peter Redmayne, he uses a taxi, supplied by Hussain. He travels to work by bus every day. On Tuesday he insisted that he walked. I've checked just about every taxi firm, but no one dropped anyone off at the bakery at any time during the day and I can't find anyone who gave him a lift. Yet he was at work. He clocked on at eight thirty, off again at twelve thirty, back on again at a quarter to two or thereabouts, and then off again at five thirty. I suppose one of his workmates could have clocked him in and out, but it's a sackable offence if they're caught, so they're not going to own up to it. I even spoke to two men who he said he met at the gates as he arrived and they verify his story. He didn't have transport.'

'And the fire at his sister's. Did he have anything to do with that?'

'I've no idea, but I can't see why he should. In his own way he loves Karen and the boy.' He paused. 'He *is* Danny's father, by the way. It appears that on the night it happened he'd been out on a drinking session, drowning his sorrows. Apparently his girlfriend had gone to live with someone else while he was in prison; he tried to get her back but she made it quite clear she didn't want him. He got drunk and ended up raping his sister. She must have been about fifteen at the time.'

'Why on earth didn't she go to the police?'

Ali sighed. 'Frightened of Barry, and anyway she's a Penistone, who would have believed her?'

'You know, Ali, you hear and see some things in this job, and there are times when you think it can't get any worse. Then up comes something like this. Raping your own sister, it beggars belief. He wants locking up.'

'I agree. I went through similar emotions when I was told, but even if we used DNA, all it would tell us is that he is the father, it wouldn't prove rape.'

'No, more's the pity. So how did you find out?'

'She told Amajit, Saturday morning, I think. He passed it on to me; thought I ought to know.'

Handford didn't hide his surprise. 'Really?

They must be close, if she confided something as personal as that to him.'

'Yes, that's more or less what I hinted, but Amajit wasn't saying, just looked embarrassed.'

'Where is she now?'

'Still in hospital, I think. Incidentally, when I got there last night, Mahmood was with her. It seems she asked the next-door neighbour to phone him and he went straight down.'

'How did Penistone take that?'

'He wasn't there. She'd said she didn't want him or her mother, told the neighbour to wait until today to tell them. I just hope for his sake that Amajit Mahmood isn't still on the ward when they arrive.'

Silence lingered for a moment, then Handford said, 'I still think Berridge is our man. I agree Penistone might have been worried about what Rukhsana knew, but he's been involved with the police often enough to know that whatever she said, Karen would have to make the complaint. She hasn't done so yet, so why now? No, Ali, Berridge is a much better bet, we know for a fact he was up there. At the moment we can't put Penistone anywhere near.'

'I know,' Ali said. 'Yet Dr Haigh said that Rukhsana had her suspicions about him. If Penistone knew what she was thinking, he would have wanted rid of her; and he probably did know because he'd tried to get Karen removed from her list. After all, he's looking at one hell of an allegation. Rape carries life, and with his previous, he'd likely get the maximum. He wouldn't take the risk of Rukhsana shopping

395

him. I can't help feeling I'm missing something, sir. Can I carry on?'

Handford's voice took on a warning tone. 'Providing you don't make your theory fit the facts; it's got to be the other way round. If you do, you'll come unstuck. Now, the fire. Did he have a reason to set fire to his sister's house?'

'No, I can't see it, boss. He didn't like Rukhsana's interference, and he was probably worried about what she knew, but she's dead now, her influence has gone.'

'But her husband's hasn't. Penistone would have no way of knowing what either Karen or Rukhsana had told him, if anything. It wouldn't have been a problem if Karen's relationship with Rukhsana had been one of health visitor and patient but it wasn't, they were friends. And now, the minute his wife is dead, Amajit has Karen staying at his house and they're probably having an affair. What would you do, as a confirmed racist?'

'I'd set fire to Amajit's house, not Karen's. The *child* was there, John. Penistone wouldn't put Danny in that kind of danger.'

'He thinks nothing of slapping his sister around, knocking her out,' Handford persisted, 'and he doesn't care that the boy is there.'

'Yes, I know, but that's usually in temper; he blows and can't stop himself. Setting fire to a house is premeditated. Everything we know about Penistone tells us that he acts long before he thinks. I'm sure he didn't do it.'

'You're probably right.' Handford took a deep breath. 'So, he didn't set fire to Karen's house and unless we get more evidence, it's unlikely he killed Rukhsana.'

Ali's eyes clouded over. 'Not with his alibi.'

He looked tired, but more worrying to Handford, Ali was suffering from thinking he was wrong about Penistone. He had been so sure, had worked hard on proving his hypothesis but had been let down because he couldn't get him from the bakery to the nursing home and back in the time. Handford scrutinised Ali's features. They were colourless. The sergeant's adrenaline needed to flow again. Perhaps Ali wasn't mistaken, and it was as he said, he was just missing something. Handford knew from experience that in this job being wrong had to be absolute, you had to be one hundred percent wrong before you gave up, and as far as Penistone was concerned, perhaps they still had a few percent to go.

Handford leaned forward over the desk. 'Alibis can be broken, Khalid. You've said all along that Rukhsana's death was a result of a rage attack, and Berridge isn't the only one with a fiery temper. Stick with Penistone for the moment. He has motive and means, dig deeper into opportunity. Bring him in; question him more about the day of the murder. You say he would need a car, so did he borrow one? Steal one even? Check on stolen cars.'

As he talked, Ali's expression brightened.

'Get hold of the clothes he was wearing last Tuesday; if he did kill her, there'll still be traces of her blood.' Handford prodded at his enthusiasm. 'And have a go at his workmates;

lean on them, find out if they did clock him on and off. And check out what cigarettes he smokes — someone burnt that hole in her coat. We have the butts from the scene. Find out if forensics have been able to match DNA from any of them yet. Penistone's is bound to be in the data base, he's been arrested often enough, and while you're about it, find out from uniform who's dealing with the fire, then get someone from our team to liaise. I don't think it's coincidence that Karen Penistone had her house torched.' He paused. Ali was still busy writing. When he looked up, Handford said, 'While you're doing that, I'll stick with Berridge. Clarke's with me, you take Graham. Right, is there anything else?'

Nervously, Ali filled him in on his visit to Mohammed Aziz. 'I should have told you yesterday, but you were busy. I didn't want to disturb you last night. Anyway, that's the reason for your riot last year. Hussain wasn't worried about Aziz, just didn't want his dealings to come to light.'

'Then he's got more reason than ever this time to want us out of family business,' Handford murmured.

'But no reason to cause a diversion unless he killed Rukhsana because she knew of his dealings and threatened to tell the police. I asked Warrender to check out his alibi again, and I've got to say it's as sound as you'll get, what with the number of worthy citizens who can vouch for him. I'm sure he can't be lining all their pockets. I wouldn't like to take it in front of a jury.'

'Even so, I could do without it.' Handford's stomach clenched and the coffee squirmed around his gut. *I need psychological stroking as well,* he thought. But it wasn't forthcoming, so instead he swallowed a mouthful of the machine coffee. Its lukewarm bitterness swamped his taste buds. He shuddered. 'God, this stuff's awful,' he said and threw the cup in the bin.

'There's another thing, guv.' Ali shifted awkwardly.

Handford settled back in his chair and waited.

'Barry Penistone was arrested on Saturday night at the rave. A girl alleged indecent assault. Nothing to do with us, but the inspector said they had found a boot print up there near where it was supposed to have taken place.'

Handford gave Ali a hard stare. 'Why do I get the impression that I don't want to know the rest?'

'Probably because I asked the duty SOCO to compare the print with that found up at the murder scene.' He glanced at Handford. 'I know I should have asked you first, but you weren't there and — '

'Never heard of a mobile?' Handford interrupted.

Ali dropped his eyes, but ignored the question. 'And if Penistone had had something to do with the murder . . . ' his words tumbled out, nought to sixty in ten seconds ' . . . we would have lost the chance of comparing and lost a reason to check his boots, and uniform weren't going to spend money on it, not for an indecent assault.' Ali's voice trailed off.

Handford gave in. 'And have we got a result?' He moved from his chair to perch on the edge of his desk.

'No, sir, not yet.'

'Let me know when we have.' Handford rubbed his face with his hand, giving himself time to decide whether to chide Ali for making a decision that was not his to make, or to congratulate him on his initiative. He thought both were appropriate.

'Given that Penistone is a possible suspect, perhaps it's as well you did bring SOCO out. It may or may not be his print, but either way, we would have missed the opportunity of finding out.' He fell silent for a moment, then he leaned towards Ali. His words were uncompromising, although the tone of voice remained conversational. 'But please don't spend money again without my say-so.' He held the sergeant's gaze for a few seconds; then with a curt nod, which emphasised his displeasure and the need for Ali to take heed, he withdrew his attention and returned to his chair behind the desk.

He picked up a handwritten statement. 'I want a briefing tonight, half five. Make sure everyone knows, will you?'

Ali stood and made for the door.

'Ali.'

He turned.

'Wasn't Warrender on duty at the weekend?'

'Yes, sir.'

'Everything all right with him?'

'Fine.'

'You'd let me know if it wasn't.'

'Yes, sir. But there isn't a problem.'

Handford caught other words, murmured rather than spoken. They sounded like 'Not now'. But he let them pass; Ali obviously had things under control.

★　★　★

Amajit stared at the house. The front door had put up little defence against the heat of the fire, and the flames licking at the rendering around the windows had left deep cracks in the cement. Soot had fanned across the walls, to point at the blood-red graffiti: WHITE WHORE. OUT. OUT. OUT. It was raining and a cold wind was catching at the curtains, teasing them out into the open air, then with cruel abandon buffeting them, until eventually they caught on the cement of the walls and were held, exhausted, quivering like the wings of a dying bird.

Amajit pulled up the collar of his coat. He shouldn't have come; he'd only done so because Karen had asked him to, to see if there was anything left, anything she should salvage. He was exhausted and would have preferred to have gone home.

Following the phone call, he'd rushed down to the hospital and stayed there for the rest of the night. Karen and Danny were together in a side ward, and he'd tried to relax in the easy chair next to the bed, nodding off only occasionally. Both of them had coughed a lot and nurses had been in and out to make them more comfortable and to check their temperature and blood pressure. They had been kind to him, bringing cups of tea, even suggesting that he go home and rest, since there was nothing he could do here, but Karen had begged him, between bouts of coughing, to stay. She was frightened, someone had tried to kill her; they might try again. She didn't know why; couldn't understand any of it. What had she done? Why her? Why Danny? She had cried and he had comforted her as best he could. He had said he wished he could give her an answer, but he couldn't explain it any more than she could.

That's what he'd said, but it wasn't true. The graffiti, the fire, it had more to do with him than it had with Karen, of that he was certain. She had become caught up in his family feud; he was the cause, and the target, not her.

He cast his eyes over the besmirched council house. If only he could believe that Barry Penistone was the one who had poured petrol through the letter box. But he knew he wasn't. Whatever her brother was, he would never endanger his own son's life. He should not have raped Karen, but in his own inept way Barry Penistone loved Danny. Too much to risk having him burn to death.

Amajit's own family, on the other hand, would do it. It would be meant to scare, not to kill, but they would do it. They would call it a punishment, and he had given them a lot to punish him for: first his marriage to Rukhsana and now his friendship with Karen. He had brought and was still bringing shame on them. They would blame Karen, just as they had blamed his wife, but in the end he was the one to be punished, because he was the one causing the shame. He could attempt an explanation, but they wouldn't understand, wouldn't even try to. No more than the nurses in the hospital understood why he, an Asian man, was sitting up all night with a white girl and her white child. Oh, they were kindness itself, but he could tell by their glances and their whispers what they were thinking.

The police, too, hadn't understood. 'Why are you here, sir? What exactly is your relationship with Miss Penistone?'

Late though it was, the two uniformed officers had turned up at the hospital to ask questions, but gone away with few answers. Karen couldn't tell them anything, and he wouldn't. Because they knew the girl's family, their questions suggested that either it was one of the many petty criminals Barry had double-crossed, getting back at him through his sister, or it was Barry Penistone himself after some insurance money. Karen had tried to argue, but they hadn't really listened to her — she *was* a Penistone, after all.

When Sergeant Ali had turned up, he had been much more perceptive. Stopping short of suggesting that Amajit and Karen were having a relationship, he had asked if his family knew that she had stayed with him. Amajit had feigned anger and said there was nothing to know, but the sergeant hadn't believed him, as his next questions indicated. Did Faysal Hussain know that Karen had visited and that he had let her stay in his house for a few days? Had Faysal made any threats? Had any other family member made threats? Was he sure that Jahangier and Kamal were in Pakistan?

No, Sergeant, Faysal doesn't know and no, no one has made threats, and yes, I am sure Jahangier and Kamal are in Pakistan.

What more could he say?

Eventually, Sergeant Ali had gone, probably still as convinced that someone in Amajit's family had set alight to Karen's house as the uniformed officers were that it was Barry or one of his associates.

Amajit shuddered as the cold cut through his thoughts. He needed to pick up Karen's things and then go home.

'Can I go in?' he asked of one of the firemen. 'Miss Penistone wants me to see if there are any clothes of any use.'

'Yes, if you want, mate, but be careful. Those stairs are dangerous. CID are in there seeing what they can find, so don't get in their way.'

Amajit made his way gingerly into the house. He reiterated what he wanted to one of the detectives, who waved him up the stairs. 'Keep to the sides and you'll be OK.'

There was little light inside except for what shone in from the equipment still set up outside. The fire had done less damage in the bedrooms, but they reeked of smoke. He searched through the drawers and wardrobe, finding very little there in the way of clothes, either for Karen or Danny. He'd never thought about how she managed financially before, but the scant

404

furniture and sparseness of garments told their own story. Not knowing exactly what they would need, he emptied the contents of the drawers and wardrobe onto the bed. Cursing that he hadn't brought any bags to put them in, he made his way into the bathroom to pick up her toiletries. He was unused to this. What did women and children need? Back in the bedroom, he saw an unopened pack of nappies next to the cot. He put it with the rest.

The aftermath of the fire invaded his senses. The place stank of the malice that had forced its way into Karen's life, first with the graffiti and then with the petrol which had flowed onto the threadbare carpet. He didn't want to have to come back again so checked the rooms for anything he might have missed. Clothes, toiletries, what else? Prodding at his tired mind, he recalled the first time Karen had visited him. She seemed to have all she wanted, but Danny had had to play with tins from the cupboard, so he would need his toys. Those downstairs would probably have been destroyed, and anyway the police were busy down there and wouldn't want him disturbing the scene. Perhaps there were some up here. His gaze wandered the room until he spied a few at the bottom of the cot; they would do for the moment. Later, when Karen and the little boy were well enough, he would take them out and buy a few more. Reaching over the side to gather up the toys, his eyes caught the crumpled sheet. He stared at it, visualising Karen grabbing at her son and wondered just how close to death the child had been.

Why didn't you tell me, Mr Mahmood, that your wife was twelve weeks' pregnant?

The words flowed like a stream into his brain. He hoped, prayed, that the child Rukhsana had been carrying had been his. He would cling to that hope, because without it there was nothing.

The day before, the inquest into his wife's death had been opened and adjourned, and the coroner had released her body to the next of kin. Rukhsana was a Sikh; she had to end her days according to the Sikh religion. He couldn't do it. She had to be returned to her family. He had gone to see them. At first they had wanted nothing to do with him, but when they realised that he was prepared to give her back, they had told him that she would be cremated and her ashes taken out to sea and scattered on the waters. In the Sikh tradition, there would be no monument to her, they said, and Amajit must say his goodbyes before they received her body. They didn't want him at the funeral. He had agreed. He had spent an hour with her at the mortuary, held her ice-cold hand, told her how much he loved her and how much he always would. Then he had prayed for her and for himself.

Now he had nothing.

Sinking to his knees, he cushioned himself against the bed and smothered his face with Karen's clothes, letting his tears flow. Even in the smoke-laden air, they smelled of the girl to whom they belonged; but as he wept, her perfume dispersed and he pictured only his wife

406

and the child they might have had.

He sensed another presence in the room and flinched as a hand feathered across his shoulder.

'Come on sir,' a voice said, 'things are never as bad as they seem. It'll soon be as good as new again.'

20

As Handford walked into the interview room, Berridge made the first move, advancing towards him, hand outstretched. He attempted a smile but he was tense and his usual sparkle was absent. His hand, when Handford clasped it, was cold and clammy.

Handford marvelled at Berridge's resolve to try to use his charm even in these circumstances. At the best of times, shaking hands with a suspect seemed unnatural; usually, on the few occasions it happened, he followed the rules of courtesy and let the action pass over him, but periodically someone would come along and attempt to reverse the roles, vary the rules and hijack the interview, then he had to distance himself from his response. This was one of those times.

'Thank you for coming in, gentlemen,' he said, his tone formal.

The other man in the room stepped forward. His smooth, silver-grey hair was impeccably groomed, his dark pin-striped suit perfectly pressed. When he extended his hand, Handford noted the well-manicured fingernails.

'James Waterhouse from the Medical Defence Union, Inspector,' he said, his cultured tones silky and finely pitched. 'I'm here to represent Dr Berridge.'

Handford shook his hand. 'Thank you for

coming, sir. I'm Detective Inspector John Handford and this is Detective Constable Clarke,' he said, conscious of his Yorkshire accent.

Waterhouse took the initiative. 'You asked us here for two thirty, Inspector. It's now almost three o'clock. My client is a busy man; he's already cancelled his visits and would prefer not to have to cancel his surgery. The first appointment is at five,' he added pointedly.

Handford was unmoved. 'Yes, sir, I'm busy too. Whether Dr Berridge takes his surgery this evening depends on how quickly we get to the truth and what the truth is. I'm afraid I can't promise he will make it.' He pulled off his jacket and slowly hung it over the back of his chair, smoothing out the creases with quiet deliberation. His eyes remained fixed on Ian Berridge.

At first the doctor leaned back, adopting an air of disinterest, but as he noticed Handford studying him, he inclined forward, resting his arms on the table, allowing the fingers of one hand to play with those of the other, picking at some imaginary substance but not removing it. His earlier show of easy familiarity was gone. Good, thought Handford as he settled himself in his seat. He nodded to Clarke to unwrap the cassette tapes, slip them in the recorder and switch it on.

'This is a taped interview with Dr Ian Berridge timed at fourteen fifty-six hours, Tuesday, the sixteenth of November,' Handford said. 'Present are Detective Inspector John Handford, Detective Constable Andrew Clarke,

Dr Ian Berridge and Mr James Waterhouse from the Medical Defence Union. Before we begin, Dr Berridge, I must remind you that you are not under arrest and that you are free to leave at any time. I must also caution you that you do not have to say anything. But it may harm your defence if you do not mention when questioned something which you later rely on in court. Anything you do say may be given in evidence. Do you understand?'

Berridge nodded.

'Please answer for the tape, sir.'

The doctor's tongue flicked over his lips. 'Yes, I understand.'

'I've invited you here to help us with our inquiries into the murder of Rukhsana Mahmood in the grounds of the Moss Carr Nursing Home last Tuesday afternoon. You knew her, I believe.'

'Yes, she was a health visitor for the practice where I work.'

'Did you have any other relationship with her apart from that of colleague?'

Berridge prevaricated. 'I was her GP until Dr Copeman joined the practice, when Rukhsana transferred to her list.'

'Can you tell me why she decided to do that?'

'She said she preferred a woman doctor, and,' Berridge paused momentarily, 'she was pregnant.'

'She told you of her condition before she transferred?'

'Yes.'

'The last time we spoke, Dr Berridge, you

410

admitted that you had been having an affair with Rukhsana Mahmood. Do you still admit to that?'

Berridge glanced at his solicitor who nodded. 'Yes.'

'Did your affair with her have anything to do with her decision to change doctors?'

'You do not have to answer that, Dr Berridge,' the solicitor broke in.

Handford considered. He needed a response to the question, but wasn't going to get it without redirecting. He began again. 'Did you and Rukhsana discuss her changing doctors *before* she told you she was pregnant?'

Berridge glanced again at James Waterhouse. It was a fair question and there was no help to be had from the solicitor.

'No, we didn't.'

'So how long after she told you about the pregnancy did she transfer from your list?'

'Almost immediately.'

Handford placed an A4 plastic folder containing a typewritten sheet on the table. 'I am showing Dr Berridge a copy of his records on Rukhsana Mahmood, exhibit JH1. Do you recognise this, doctor?'

Berridge nodded, then before he could be reminded said, 'Yes. It's a copy of Rukhsana's medical records.'

'According to them she left you on the eighteenth of September. Dr Copeman joined the practice on the first of September. If Rukhsana was so keen to have a woman doctor, why didn't she transfer as soon as Dr Copeman arrived?'

'She was rarely ill and I suppose she wasn't aware that she was pregnant.' His voice was flat but his expression was wary; he knew very well that this was leading inexorably to the information he had been advised not to give.

'The postmortem report indicates that she was twelve weeks' pregnant when she died. She must, therefore, have conceived about mid-August. Surely she would have had her suspicions by the beginning of September?'

Berridge offered no response.

Handford insisted. 'Dr Berridge, did Rukhsana Mahmood discuss the pregnancy with you at this early stage?'

'Yes.' The reply was barely audible.

'Can you speak up for the tape please, doctor.'

Berridge cleared his throat. 'Yes, she . . . we discussed what she should do.'

'What she should do? What do you mean, what she should do? She was pregnant, why should she *do* anything?'

Berridge hesitated. 'I mean who should treat her.'

'And what conclusion did you both come to?'

'That it would be better for her to be cared for by Dr Copeman.'

'Why better?'

Berridge fragmented in front of Handford. The fingers pulled harder at the imaginary substance glued to his other hand. His gaze strayed towards the recording machine and he stared at it. Handford leaned back, watching. They both knew that the use of the word 'better' was the doctor's mistake.

The silence had gone on too long and Handford was not prepared to give him more time. He wanted him talking; when he was talking he was not thinking.

'Dr Berridge.' Their eyes met. 'You mean "better" because you were responsible for the pregnancy, and it would be "better" for you perhaps if it was confirmed by another doctor, one who didn't know either of you very well?'

Berridge sank deeper into himself. 'Perhaps,' he said, his tone ashen.

'What was your reaction when she told you?'

The question dragged him to the edge of his abyss. He glared at Handford. 'How do you think I felt? I was angry with her. She should have been more careful.'

Clarke took over. 'What's your religion, doctor?'

Berridge's gaze shifted to settle on the new questioner. 'I'm Catholic.'

'So when you had sexual relations with Rukhsana Mahmood, you didn't take any precautions yourself?'

'No.'

'And presumably Rukhsana didn't either.'

'Presumably not; I never asked her.'

'Why not? Surely you would have wanted her to avoid conceiving?'

'I assumed she was on the pill.'

'You assumed? Are you saying you didn't know?'

'It was her business, not mine.' Petulance swathed his words.

Clarke forced the issue. 'But you were her

413

doctor, you would know, wouldn't you, whether or not she was taking the contraceptive pill? Even if you didn't prescribe it for her, that kind of information is passed on to you.'

In desperation, Ian Berridge turned to his solicitor for help.

'I think this line of questioning has gone far enough.' James Waterhouse's cultured tones flowed between them. 'You've established that the child could be the doctor's. I can't see that trying to lay the whole blame at his door will further your inquiries.'

But Handford wasn't finished.

'Very well, doctor,' he said. 'You were aware that Rukhsana wasn't using a prescribed contraceptive. And you, as a Catholic, didn't use any form of contraceptive yourself.'

'No.'

'What were your views on termination then?'

Berridge's eyes darted from the inspector to his solicitor. He was trapped and he knew it. 'It's against the Church's teachings,' he said, trying to dodge a straight answer.

'So you follow the Catholic line on this?' Handford asked.

'Yes.'

'You wouldn't offer a termination to one of your patients, for example.'

'I would prefer not to.'

'Unless of course the patient is a woman with whom you've been having an affair,' Handford said grimly. 'Then, doctor, according to your previous statement, not only would you arrange a termination, you would also pay for it.'

414

'I think we need a ten-minute break, Inspector,' James Waterhouse said quickly. 'Dr Berridge is clearly becoming distressed.'

★ ★ ★

Barry Penistone wasn't having any better a time of it than Ian Berridge. In his opinion he'd been dragged down to the Central Police Station unnecessarily by the Paki detective. What had that man got against him? Was it just because he was white? Racist, that was what the Paki was, a racist, and at the earliest opportunity he was going to make a complaint against him. Give him a taste of his own medicine.

This was the third time he'd been in this bloody place within the past week. 'Why don't you just give me a key?' he'd remonstrated. 'Then I can visit any time I've got a mind.' It was also the second time in two days that Ali had been to the bakery but this time he'd questioned his workmates. That was worrying, as much because the cop wouldn't tell him why as the fact that he'd done it at all. But whatever it was he wanted he hadn't got it; his frustration was clear for all to see. That was why he'd brought him in, to take his frustration out on him.

'How long are you going to keep me here?'

'Until Sergeant Ali's finished with you,' Graham said shortly.

'He thinks I killed that Paki woman, doesn't he?'

Graham offered no reply.

'So what's he taken me clothes for — and me

boots?' He looked down at the disposable suit they had given him. 'I feel a right ponce in this. When can I have me clothes back?'

'You've already been told that they've gone to the forensic laboratory, and the reason why has been explained to you. Someone's gone to get something for you to wear from your mother. They shouldn't be long.' Graham threw him a wide smile. 'I can't see what your problem is, Penistone. I'd have thought you'd be used to wearing those. It can't be the first time, with your record.'

Barry glared at him. 'Just piss off, you pig, just piss off.'

★ ★ ★

'Now that you are more composed, I'd like to ask you about your movements last Tuesday, Dr Berridge.'

Berridge stared at the tea in his Styrofoam cup.

'You do not deny being in the nursing home car park at one o'clock?'

Berridge shook his head then, remembering, said, 'No.'

'Who were you with?'

'With Rukhsana Mahmood.'

'Had you gone there specifically to meet her?'

'It wasn't an arranged meeting, but I knew that's where she'd be.'

'How?'

'Because she was in Asian dress; the only time she ever wore Asian dress was when she visited

416

her aunt who is a patient up there.'

'Could you look at this for me.' Handford placed a second plastic wallet containing a colour photograph on the table. 'I am now showing Dr Berridge Exhibit JH6, a photograph of two people standing next to a car. Is that you with Rukhsana Mahmood?'

'Yes.'

'This photo is one of many taken for a new brochure for the nursing home. Can you tell me what you are wearing in it?'

Berridge seemed puzzled by the question. 'My suit and an overcoat.'

'And on your feet?'

'Boots.'

'You're a man with a good dress sense, Dr Berridge. Boots seem an odd type of footwear for a suit. Do you often wear boots?'

'Occasionally. I have patients who live up muddy back lanes; I take boots with me in bad weather.'

'So you'd visited patients before meeting up with Rukhsana?'

'No, but I sometimes wear them up at the nursing home, it can be muddy there.'

'In the car park?' Clarke's tone was sceptical.

'I thought Rukhsana and I could walk in the woods where we wouldn't be seen. It's always muddy there.'

'And did you walk in the woods?'

'No.'

'I think it's only fair to tell you, Dr Berridge, that we found the print from a boot close to where Rukhsana's body was discovered.'

Whatever colour was left on Berridge's face drained away. 'Well, it's not mine. I left her in the car park, I didn't follow her to the woods and I didn't kill her.'

'Are you saying that the print matches my client's boot, Inspector?'

'No, sir, I'm not saying that; we haven't got the results back from forensics yet.'

'Then until you have, there's little point discussing it.'

Handford conceded. His gaze shifted from the solicitor back to Berridge. 'Let's return to your decision to follow Rukhsana to the nursing home.'

'I didn't follow her, Inspector.' Berridge's tone showed some impatience. 'As I've already said, I knew she'd be there and so I went up. We needed to come to a decision as to what she was going to do about the pregnancy.'

'You mean whether she was prepared to terminate?'

Berridge sighed. 'Yes, whether she was prepared to terminate.' He threw a look of loathing at Handford. 'So I'm a bad Catholic; I'll make confession the next time I'm in the vicinity of the church.' He was becoming cocky, as if he didn't care any more. 'The fact was, I wasn't prepared to see my career destroyed because *she* couldn't make up her mind whose baby it was and what she was going to do about it.' His tone was ugly, contemptuous.

Handford smiled to himself. This was the real Berridge, the one he wanted out in the open, the one whose arrogance would finally break him.

418

He glanced at Waterhouse as a ripple of concern bruised the elegant features. This time the solicitor couldn't ask for a break.

'You blamed her for the pregnancy?'

'I could hardly do that, could I?' Berridge sounded sulky. 'But she should have taken precautions.'

'Because you wouldn't?'

Waterhouse stirred. 'Once again, Inspector, I fail to see why you must badger my client over the issue of contraception.'

Handford's manner remained calm, his voice smooth. 'Very well. Tell us what happened at the nursing home.'

'I met her and we talked.'

Clarke took over. 'Talked, doctor?' he asked.

'All right then, argued.'

'Because she wouldn't agree to an abortion?'

'She wouldn't agree to anything — termination or accepting it as her husband's and having it. It wasn't as though it would have resembled me, even if it had been mine; her colour gene would have been dominant. I told her that but she said that even if it wasn't white it could still resemble me facially, and then to top it all, she said she couldn't lie to her husband. My God, what did she think we'd been doing for the past nine or ten months?' His voice had risen and his anger flooded the room.

'Did you come to any conclusion?' Handford asked.

The mildness of his tone irritated the doctor even more. 'No, we didn't come to any conclusion. I couldn't get her to make a decision. We were running out of time and she just couldn't see the urgency.'

'So what did you do?'

'I shouted at her. 'For God's sake, woman, do you want to ruin me?' And do you know what she did? She began to cry. To cry, for God's sake.'

Berridge was no longer making any effort to present himself as the doctor with charm. The hand that James Waterhouse placed on his arm in an attempt both to calm him and warn him was brushed aside.

'Here she was, on the point of ruining my career and all she could do was cry. She just couldn't see sense.'

'Did you manage to make her see sense?'

'Have you ever tried to make a woman who is crying see sense? I walked away from her, but she called me back.' He stopped for a moment, then almost to himself he said, 'She shouldn't have called me back.'

'What do you mean, Dr Berridge, she shouldn't have called you back?'

'Then I wouldn't have hit her.' The doctor gasped out his anger, his breath laboured. He grabbed the Styrofoam cup and gulped at the tea.

When he had regained his self-control, he looked Handford in the eye and said, 'I hit her hard, Inspector, and she fell to the ground, but I didn't kill her. She was still in the car park when I left. On the tarmac, but alive.'

'Are you absolutely sure about that?'

'Yes, I'm sure. Find the man who was sitting

in his car, watching.'

'There was a man watching you?' Handford couldn't keep the astonishment out of his voice. 'Why didn't you mention him before?'

'Because I've only just remembered. Isn't that what your questioning is supposed to do, Inspector, help with recall?' Berridge's confidence was suddenly back.

Handford sighed. 'Tell me about this man.' His tone suggested disbelief. A man suddenly appearing, a man whom no one else had mentioned.

'I wouldn't have noticed him had he not made some comment about giving the bitches what they deserved. I was too angry with her to answer him.'

'Can you describe him?'

'A roundish face, well-built, wearing a donkey jacket. I was too taken up with my own problems to really notice.'

'And what about the car? Did you notice that?'

'Not until I drove away.' He pondered for a moment. 'It was a green Volkswagen Beetle'

★ ★ ★

Barry Penistone breathed in the cold air as he stood on the steps outside Central Police Station. The iciness of winter nipped at him, frisking his body as it penetrated the clothes his mother had sent. It had stopped raining, but the roads were still wet, glistening orange under the street lights, the colour diluted from time to time by the headlamps of the occasional bus which

421

passed by. For some months, the area had seen only public transport and pedestrians; all cars, except police vehicles, had to follow a one-way system which met up with the neighbouring dual carriageway. According to the planners, this central square was now almost completely environmentally friendly. Barry wished he could have said the same about the inhabitants of the building he had been kept in for the last six hours.

He'd been interviewed on and off since half past ten this morning, answering their questions, repeating the same points over and over, playing their games to their rules. Not that he'd admitted to anything. And nor would he; he wasn't going to make their lives easy by saying he'd murdered that woman. Eighteen months for GBH was one thing, but murder, that meant life. He wasn't serving life for anybody.

'We just want to get at the truth, Barry.'

The truth. They wouldn't recognise the truth if it sat next to them in a pub, because it was their truth they wanted, not anyone else's. They'd tried to get him to admit to their truth, but even after six hours, they hadn't managed to break his alibi and place him at the nursing home at the time of the murder. On Tuesday, he'd insisted, he'd walked to work and had stayed there all day, and if they thought he hadn't, then they'd have to prove it.

He was quite proud of his performance inside the police station, but now that he was outside, nervous tension sparked through his body like forked lightning. His hands shook as he patted the pockets of his coat, eventually locating the cigarettes his mother had sent him. He pulled one out of the packet, then felt for matches or a lighter. Nothing. The silly cow had forgotten them. While he was bemoaning the stupidity of women, the police station door was pushed open and an acned youth of about seventeen or eighteen joined him on the step.

'Got a light, mate?' Barry asked.

The lad groped around in his anorak pocket and took out a box. With thick fingers he withdrew a match and struck it. Barry cupped his hands round the flame until the tobacco glowed red.

'Been in there long?' the youth asked.

'Too bloody long.' Barry inhaled slowly, savouring the heat and the bitterness.

'Didn't get you, though?'

'No, and they never will.'

The young man inspected Barry, compassion on his spotty features. 'Here you are,' he said, throwing the box of matches at him. 'Keep 'em. You look as though you need 'em more than I do.'

Barry's gaze followed him as he went down the steps and disappeared into the gloom. He stood for a while, smoking. The cigarette calmed him. But as his nerves settled, fear began to seep through, filling the gap.

It wasn't just the questions of his whereabouts on Tuesday that unnerved him, it was the other things they knew about him. That he peddled steroids for Faysal Hussain, for one.

'Prove it,' he'd said to Ali. 'No one's ever

423

found anything on me, no gear, no money; so just prove it.'

And they probably would. If Hussain was going down, he wouldn't think twice about dragging everyone else with him.

But what was worse, much worse, was that they knew about Danny.

'You're Danny's father.' Just like that; not a question, a flat statement. He could have answered a question, but there was nothing there to answer. So he'd said, 'Don't be bloody stupid. I'm her brother. Karen got herself pregnant by some kid at school as like as not.'

'She didn't tell you who then?'

'No, she wouldn't. She knew if she did I'd have to cut his balls off.'

Then the Paki detective had said, 'We can do a DNA test, Barry. Prove once and for all that Danny's your son. We've already got your DNA from the last time you were arrested. We only need Danny's.'

Could they do that? Just take Danny's DNA, without so much as a by-your-leave. He didn't know, not for sure, but when he got out he'd make bloody sure Karen wouldn't let them.

But would she do as he told her? He couldn't even be certain about her any more. No one else could have told the cops; it could only have come from her. But, somehow he couldn't see her walking into a police station and describing what had happened. Particularly now, after three years. So she must have told someone else and they'd passed it on.

The more he thought about it, the more sure

he became who that someone else was and how it had got out. Pillow talk with Amajit Mahmood. It had to be. It made him go cold, thinking of the two of them in bed together — doing it. Him with his big black dick inside her. He shuddered.

How could she prefer him to family? She'd proved that she did by asking for him after the fire. According to the nurses, he'd been with her most of the night. They'd been quite impressed with him. Well, Barry wasn't impressed and if the coppers hadn't dragged him down to the station and spent half the morning and most of the afternoon questioning him, he'd have been at the hospital to bring them home when they were discharged. Instead, Amajit Mahmood probably took them back to his house.

And now because of that interfering Paki bastard he could be arrested and more than likely banged up. Although he wasn't sure for what. For having sex with his sister? Or for raping her as the police had suggested?

Did you force her to have sex with you? How many times had you done it before? Did you rape her, Barry?

No, he bloody didn't. At any rate he wasn't going to admit to it. If she said he did and they proved Danny was his, then he'd say it was all her fault, she'd made him do it.

How long did you get for sleeping with your sister? He didn't know. But he did know it could be life for rape. He wasn't going down for life, not for rape, nor for murder, not for anything.

Angrily he pulled at the cigarette and the hot

425

smoke curled round his mouth and stung the back of his throat. From the shelter of the canopy which straddled the main door of the police station, he watched the people go about their business. No one stopping them, questioning them, telling them what to do. No. Their business was their business, and his was his. Not the cops', not Mahmood's. His. And he would show all of them, particularly that Paki bastard, that it was against their best interests to butt into his life. Just as he'd shown that interfering slag of a health visitor last Tuesday.

He took a final drag on his cigarette, then flicked the stub hard in front of him. It fell into a puddle which had gathered where one of the concrete flags was broken.

He and Karen and Danny were getting out. Now. He'd pick up Billy Price's car, then go to his mother's and get his clothes and the three thousand pounds he'd saved from dealing, and then he'd get his sister and son from Mahmood.

And, just for the Asian, he'd make sure he was tooled up. The knife was good and sharp. He smirked. A swift swipe straight down his face — he wouldn't know what had hit him. It would be his parting gift to the Paki.

★ ★ ★

Handford had almost finished with Dr Berridge.

Warrender was back and had brought news that Handford would have preferred not to have. Teale had seen Berridge arrive at the nursing home at about half past twelve. Apparently he'd

426

thought how stupid it was for a doctor to come to see the old folks at dinner time. But he didn't see him leave. What he did see, however, was a car that very nearly knocked him down as it sped down the drive. He didn't know who it belonged to, but it was a green Volkswagon Beetle.

Damn. If the driver of this car could be found, and there was little doubt now that he existed, then Berridge would be off the hook for murder.

'Find the car and find the driver, Warrender; there can't be that many green Volkswagen Beetles around, they stopped making them in about nineteen seventy-eight.'

He might not be able to charge Berridge with Rukhsana's murder, but Handford was damn sure he wasn't going to walk out of the station with his reputation intact.

He smiled at him. 'I've put someone on to search for this car, Dr Berridge. If it exists then I can assure you we'll find it. In the meantime, I have just a couple more questions.'

Berridge looked bored.

'Do you have a temper, Dr Berridge?'

'No more than the next person.' It was amazing how such an intelligent man could be so stupid. After admitting to hitting Rukhsana, after the exhibition of temper he had subjected them to earlier in the interview, he ought to have been examining his words carefully before he uttered them. But he was sure of himself again and the certainty brought with it arrogance.

'You think the next person, as you call them, would hit a woman, do you?'

'No. Hitting Rukhsana was a one-off; it's not

427

something I do normally. I — I was scared. It had happened before I realised what I was doing.' He paused. 'And when I did realise, I stopped, controlled it, walked away. My anger did not go so far as picking up a coping stone and beating her around the head with it. I did not kill her.

'Would you say you were capable of killing?'

'Inspector, really.' James Waterhouse's voice was tinged with distaste.

Handford ignored him. 'Has your temper ever got the better of you so much that you wanted to kill?'

'Inspector, I must protest at this line of questioning. Dr Berridge has said many times that he did not kill Rukhsana Mahmood. You are being aggressive in the extreme. If you continue with this I shall have no alternative but to ask you to stop the interview and let my client leave.'

'Your client can leave any time he wants, Mr Waterhouse, as you well know. But before he does I would like to put one more question to him.' Handford's smile was conciliatory. He turned back to Berridge. 'Do you know Bethany Cantrell, doctor?'

It was beautiful. The words had been spoken without a hint of aggression; but the result they produced was heart-warming. James Waterhouse's expression was one of puzzlement; Ian Berridge's one of abject horror.

'Who is Bethany Cantrell?' Waterhouse demanded. 'And what has she to do with the murder of Rukhsana Mahmood?'

Handford's smile widened, smug in the

knowledge of what would happen next. 'Ask Detective Sergeant Jowett to come in, would you, Andy?'

Clarke left the room, to return a moment later with another man.

'Let me introduce you to Detective Sergeant Jowett, Dr Berridge. He flew in from Belfast this morning. He wants to ask you some questions regarding the assault on Bethany Cantrell some five years ago.'

'I really must protest, Inspector.' James Waterhouse was now standing. 'I demand to be allowed to talk with my client.'

Berridge had stayed where he was, all arrogance and confidence gone. His face was ashen, his features gaunt.

'You may talk with your client, Mr Waterhouse. I think he needs you more than ever now. But before you do, DC Clarke and DS Jowett will accompany him to custody so that he can be formally arrested.'

21

Barry drew the Volkswagen Beetle sharp up against the pavement a few doors away from Amajit Mahmood's and pulled on the hand-brake. There was someone in, he could see lights in the front room. His hackles rose. What were they up to? Pretending they were a family, playing with Danny, giving him his tea, getting him ready for bed, then watching television, screwing. Adrenaline flowed and impulses charged his muscles, urging him to force his way into the house.

No. Not yet, Barry; not yet.

If he was to do this and get away, then the time had to be right. The street was too open, too busy, not private enough. Breathing deep and hard, he clenched the steering wheel. Emotions cascaded into a pool of hostility and jealousy and he closed his eyes. In the darkness, pictures picked at the surface of his memory, to be released and cast like a film onto the membrane of his eyelids.

Images cavorted in front of him. Of a man pawing Donna, of a beer glass, of Donna pushing him, Barry, away and of Karen screaming at him to get off her. Then, finally, of Rukhsana Mahmood, disgust twisting her features as she warned him of what she knew and of what she was going to do. He saw the disgust turn to fear as the coping stone smashed down onto her skull, crushing the bones, and felt again the shock waves shudder through his body as he delivered each blow.

Then — nothing.

Barry sat motionless, his hands still clutching the wheel. Perspiration ran down his nose and his cheeks, his clothes were sticky against his body. But he was cold, trembling.

The police suspected him, of that he was certain, and it would only be a matter of time before suspicion became fact. They were missing one small detail, so trivial, so insignificant, but so important. Billy Price's car. He'd used it last Tuesday morning, parked it a few streets away from the bakery and walked to work. That's what he always did when he used the car. No point letting everyone know he had wheels; they'd all want a lift. And anyway he'd something to do. At lunchtime he'd driven to Karen's house. Karen had said that the Paki woman was coming to see her, and she always made her and Danny her last call before dinner. He'd intended to have it out with her, warn her to leave them alone. But as he'd arrived, she'd been leaving and he'd had to follow her to the nursing home. He remembered he'd made a remark to the man she was arguing with. That had been a mistake. Eventually the man would realise and go to the police. It wouldn't take that long to match the car to Billy Price and then to him. Then they'd come looking for him. He wasn't going to wait for that to happen. He was getting out to hide himself where he wouldn't be found. Ireland perhaps. But not alone, not without Karen and Danny.

Adjusting his mirror, he looked up and down the road. It was the end of the working day and it was busy. Night clung like a blanket, the darkness broken only by the phosphorescent pools from the street lamps and the fleeting illumination of the passing traffic. In silent waves, rays of light swept through the car as vehicles cruised towards and past him. Brightness, then for a moment darkness, until in front of him tail lights spooled out trails of colour as they disappeared into the distance.

People walked along the pavements, huddled against the wintry weather, anticipating, no doubt, a warm meal, a few cans of beer and an evening of television. There was a match on tonight; Barry had been looking forward to sprawling on the sofa and watching his home team beat the hell out of their rivals. Two men passed by, caught up in animated conversation. Lucky devils. They'd be talking about the match, anticipating the score. Two nil to us, Barry thought.

He flexed his muscles, feeling his own strength, and pondered on the packets of steroids in his holdall. There were plenty of ampoules to last him until he could set up in business on his own. His own boss. Away from Hussain. For a few moments he contemplated his future as it stretched in front of him. It would be good, very good.

The musings reinforced his impatience. It was a pity it was so busy. They needed to get off. But if he had trouble making Karen see sense, he would rather there was no one around to interfere. It could be that he would have to drag her into the car — she could be stubborn if she was of a mind.

He adjusted his mirror again and peered into it. The street stretched behind him. Most of the houses had their curtains drawn, the windows blushing rectangles of coloured light. He checked out the parked cars. As far as he could see they were all empty, no one sitting talking, no one waiting for a girl or boy friend. He moved the mirror again and inspected the other side. The same. He took his cigarettes from his pocket, lit one and inhaled. Better to leave it a little while longer; sit and wait. He glanced at his watch. Another half-hour and the televisions would be on. Once people were settled, they'd not want to move, no matter what was happening outside.

He closed his eyes and tried to snooze, but the Beetle was not meant for relaxing in, not with his bulk. As soon as he could afford to he'd dump it and get himself a decent car. He was shuffling to make himself more comfortable when a car's headlights seared into the mirror, blinding him for a moment.

For Christ's sake, dim those bloody lights!

Colours and shapes bounced at the back of his eyes. He rubbed at them, then refocused. The car was still there, stopped some way behind him, headlights still full on. He was about to jump out of the Beetle to remonstrate when he saw the other light, the blue one, slowly rotating.

In spite of himself, his stomach lurched. Coppers. Why had they stopped behind him?

Were they looking for him? Had they followed him?

He squinted beyond the headlights and into the darkness. He could just make out the form of a policeman walking round the front of the Panda. Then he turned away from Barry and wandered towards a car parked on the other side of the road. After what seemed an age, he pulled open the driver's door. The second copper duplicated his action at the passenger door.

Barry relaxed, watching while they eased two Asian youths out of their vehicle. He couldn't hear what was being said, but the Asians were arguing vehemently with the two cops, their arms flailing, pushing and being pushed. Eventually they were thrust into the patrol car, still shouting.

A moment later a second Panda drew up; the policemen conferred for a while, then one of them climbed into the youths' car and drove it away.

Barry pulled his head back into the Beetle, smiling. He wound up the window. It was good to see the Pakis getting what they deserved, even if the cops were probably fitting them up for it.

★ ★ ★

Handford looked up as Sergeant Hewitt knocked on the open door.

'We're ready for you, guv.'

'Thanks.'

'Oh, and there's been a message from the CID fire investigators. They've had an anonymous call saying that Jahangier and Kamal Mahmood were responsible for the fire at Karen Penistone's house and that they are in a red Ford Escort parked in Grange Road. The caller even gave the vehicle's registration number.'

'Grange Road? That's where Amajit Mahmood lives.'

'That's right. A patrol car has been sent to pick them up.'

'I knew those two weren't in Pakistan. We ought to have tried harder to find them.'

'Probably,' Hewitt conceded, 'but we didn't get much help from the community.'

'That shouldn't make any difference.' Handford sounded dejected.

'Come on, guv, you know what it's like; don't beat yourself up over it.'

He smiled at her. 'Do they know anything about the caller?'

'Only that it was an Asian-sounding voice.'

'Does Sergeant Ali know?'

'Not yet, guv.'

'Tell him, will you?'

Handford picked up the list of actions completed that day and scanned it to refresh his memory and a moment later he walked into the incident room.

The usual buzz of conversations met him as he entered, but for the first time he sensed an air of weariness. They'd been on the case a week now and so far all leads had taken them to a dead end. The first forty-eight hours in a murder inquiry were crucial; after that, information became sparse, people's memories lagged. Out on the street the murder had turned into fish and chip paper news and now, after five days of nothing, most editors had assigned it to an inside page. But the well-ordered slog had to continue, boring, dogged detective work. And it was his job to make sure it did.

He stood in front of them and attempted to sound more encouraging than he felt.

'Right, everybody, let's get done and then we can go home.' Handford glanced at his notes. 'First of all, I don't think Berridge is our man. Immoral he may be, self-centred and arrogant, a doctor who preys on vulnerable women and who should be struck off, as hopefully he will be, but I don't think he's a murderer, not yet anyway.'

'What about forensics on his clothes?' Ali asked.

'Nothing back,' Hewitt answered.

'Well, I won't rule him out completely until we've heard from the lab but,' Handford shrugged, 'let's forget him for the moment and concentrate on other suspects. Who are they?'

'Amajit Mahmood.'

'Barry Penistone.'

'The Mahmood brothers.'

'Faysal Hussain.'

Handford held up his hands. 'OK, let's look at them one at a time. The husband first. Any sightings of his car in the lay-by?'

Clarke picked up a sheaf of paper. 'Plenty, guv. The trouble is that not one of the witnesses can agree on the make, the colour or even that it was Tuesday that they saw it. The best fit we have is a Mr Collingwood who passed the lay-by at about the right time and saw a car there. He noticed it particularly because the driver was resting back against the seat and he thought he might be ill. Decided in the end that he was probably taking a break from driving. But he thought the car was blue, not green. We've nothing concrete to back up Mahmood's alibi.'

Warrender turned to his neighbour. 'If it's not Mahmood, then it's Hussain or the brothers or all three,' he whispered. 'It's always family. If the DI wasn't such a wimp we'd have concentrated on them in the first place.'

Handford glared at him. 'You got something useful to say, Warrender? Because if you have, say it out loud so that we can all reap the benefit.'

Warrender reddened. 'I just think it's more likely to be family, guv. That's what they do.'

Handford made his hostility clear. This time he wasn't going to let it pass; a short sharp comment now, then a session later in his office. 'Is that a general observation on families, Warrender, or is it specific to the Mahmood family?'

Warrender had dug his own hole and he knew it. 'I just think it could be a punishment killing, sir,' he said. His tone was sullen.

'I think we're a bit short on evidence to come to that conclusion, Constable,' Handford said with a touch of asperity. 'Perhaps Sergeant Ali can give us his views.'

Warrender glared at Ali who countered with a wide grin. 'Certainly, sir. Firstly,' he said, holding up one finger, 'if it had happened two years ago, I would have agreed with you, Warrender. But so long after the event? No, I can't see it. Even in our culture punishment tends to be immediate rather than delayed.' He held up another finger. 'Secondly, a revenge killing is premeditated, organised, planned. We're nothing if not thorough.'

Warrender squirmed.

'The weapon,' continued Ali, 'would be gun, a car, a knife. I've never seen one where a coping stone has been used. That, DC Warrender, is more like a rage attack. Pick it up and hit her with it and carry on hitting her until she's dead. Anger, rage, frenzy.' He kept his eyes focused on the detective, raising his eyebrows as he questioned the man's premise and at the same time warned him not to argue. He allowed the silence to penetrate, then he unfurled a final finger. 'Thirdly, and probably more importantly, each and every member of the family has an alibi. And those alibis stand up. So the nearest we're going to come to 'one of them' doing it is her husband — and we've almost ruled him out.'

As Ali finished, the silence deepened. The sergeant had done well and everyone, including Warrender, knew it.

A telephone rang loudly, shattering the quiet. Hewitt answered it. She listened for a few moments, then lowered the receiver, covering the mouthpiece with her hand, and relayed the message. 'Forensics, guv. There's nothing of interest on Dr Berridge's clothes and the boot print is not his. But it does match the one found at the rave. Do you want them compared with the other boot which came in today?'

438

Handford smiled at Ali. 'Tell them yes. And can we have the answer yesterday?'

Hewitt put the receiver back to her ear, then she laughed. 'I'll tell him.' She looked at Handford. 'She said she heard that, and which yesterday do you mean, the one before today or the one after tomorrow?'

Handford smiled at her as she replaced the receiver. 'I think, people, I must amend my earlier statement. Dr Berridge is no longer on our list of suspects. Not one shred of evidence against him, more's the pity.'

'We've still got him for Bethany Cantrell,' Clarke interrupted, 'and James Waterhouse told me, in confidence, you understand, that Berridge's wife has left him. Taken the kids and gone back to Ireland.'

Handford didn't join in the observations of 'Shame!' that rippled round the room.

'Yes, well, I can see that we all feel very sorry for him, but we've still got to deal with him because now he's turned from a suspect into a witness. It looks like he saw the same car that nearly ran down Nathan Teale. Do we know anything about it yet, Warrender?'

'Yes, sir, I've found it. As you said, there aren't many of them, only one in Bradford, in fact. It's registered to a Billy Price. I've checked him out and he's unemployed, a bit of a petty crook, some thieving, some burglary, some TDA. Nothing too bad. Not into drugs. Known associates are Ritchie Barrett, Eddy Kennedy and Barry Penistone.'

At last a link between witness statements and a

suspect. Something to work on. The excitement was palpable. Things were moving again.

Warrender waited before continuing. 'I talked to Billy and apparently he and Penistone share the car. It's registered in Price's name, but Penistone pays the insurance and the road tax. They fork out for their own petrol, which means that Price hardly ever uses it. I asked him about Penistone and he said that he tends to use it mainly at weekends or in emergencies. He doesn't use it for work, unless he's going somewhere afterwards. Or if for any reason he can't get there by bus.'

'Did you ask him about Tuesday?'

'Well, Price didn't use it, he was on community service all day. They're picked up by a minibus and dropped off wherever they're doing their service. I checked it out and he was there. Ten to half past four. He doesn't know whether Barry Penistone used the car or not, but doesn't think so. Can't remember whether or not it was parked in its usual spot when he came home.'

Handford felt the despair return. 'We need to put Barry Penistone in that car on the day of the murder. If Rukhsana suspected Barry was Danny's father, then he had as good as motive for killing her as either Berridge or her husband. We've ruled out Berridge, we've almost ruled out Amajit; but we've got to be able to put Penistone in the right place at the right time. Unless he used Price's car on Tuesday, he couldn't possibly have got to the nursing home and back in the time. We've two witnesses who say someone was

440

up at the nursing home in that car, so someone must know who it was. Tomorrow we work on that, we pick up the car and get SOCO to go over it with a fine-tooth comb. Get hold of the woman with the photographs, I want every last one of them. And I want them examined with the biggest magnifying glass you can find. She might have caught the VW on film. I want to know who was in Billy Price's car.'

The adrenaline was flowing again. Handford knew everyone would be ready to pick up the pieces in the morning. They were that close.

He turned to Ali. 'Ring forensics back. I need to know if that boot print could be Penistone's.'

Ali picked up the phone. He spoke quietly to the person at the other end, then, 'You're as sure as you can be at this stage? Thanks.'

He replaced the receiver and looked up, a smile covering his face. 'Forensics say that without more time they can't be a hundred per cent sure, but providing you don't quote them, then from eyeballing the new boot and the print, they're pretty sure they are the same.'

Handford's grin matched Ali's.

'Then I think, Sergeant, that we've got him. Let's find him and bring him in.'

★ ★ ★

As Ali left the station in search of Barry Penistone, Handford returned to his office and sent for Warrender.

The man's expression implied that he knew what he was in for. He stood, hands behind his

441

back, silent, waiting.

'I don't know you very well, Warrender, but it seems to me that you're a good detective; too good not to be in the job. Unfortunately, it seems to me also that you're too opinionated and too much of a racist for the police service.'

Warrender stayed silent.

'I think you've got to make your mind up which it's to be. Are you going to continue to be opinionated and racist and find yourself out of the job, or be a good detective and stay in it? Because if it's the former, I will do everything in my power to get rid of you. I've no room for racists in my squad.'

Warrender cleared his throat. 'Sir.'

'You've been putting in for sergeant, I understand.'

'Yes.'

'And you haven't managed it yet?'

'No.'

'Well, perhaps you ought to consider the truth of why that is. It's not, as you may prefer to think, that the Khalid Alis on the force are taking the promotions away from you. It's because of you; of what you are and how you are.' Handford stood up and walked round the side of his desk. He turned on the detective. 'You'd be the worst kind of sergeant, a racist bully.' He took a step closer. 'Get rid of that chip, Warrender, and concentrate on what's important. Because if you don't I will make it my mission to have you off the force. Now get out and leave me in peace.'

As Warrender closed the office door, Handford's telephone rang.

It was the officer from fire investigation.

'We've got the Mahmood brothers in custody, sir. There's no doubt they're the ones who torched Karen Penistone's house. They've admitted as much and we found the can with some petrol in it still in the boot, as well as an anorak soaked in petrol and splashed with red spray paint, so it's likely they're responsible for the graffiti as well. Their reason for carrying the petrol was in case they ran out while driving. Would you believe, their car runs on diesel?' A deep chuckle flowed down the line.

'Any idea who it was who shopped them?'

'Yes, we know. When they heard the recording, they went ape. Called him every name they could think of in English and in Urdu. At least I imagine that was what the Urdu was. It didn't sound too complimentary.'

'So, who was it?'

'Their cousin, Faysal Hussain.'

Handford's stomach lurched. He tried to concentrate on what the officer was saying.

'God alone knows why he grassed on them. I'm not sure the brothers know either. They insist they were only following his orders. Warning off Karen Penistone.'

'Warning her off what?'

'Off Amajit Mahmood. Hussain didn't want him associating with a white girl. Said he'd brought enough shame on the family.'

It was like Amajit had said; the woman was always blamed, never the man. It was Rukhsana's and Karen's fault alone that shame was brought on the family, and their fault, too, that

443

Faysal Hussain was again finding himself in the spotlight. In the end, all he was doing was taking it off himself so that he could continue with his more dubious but lucrative work unhindered.

Life was cheap for some people.

22

The door bell rang authoritatively. The knocking was even more commanding. Then, the solid determination of ringing and rapping.

For a moment there was silence until the letter-box flap snapped open.

'Come on, Mahmood, I know you're in there.' Barry's voice rasped through the hallway and into the living room.

Amajit and Karen stood, their eyes questioning the other's as to what they should do. Karen's features had drained of colour and she grabbed at Danny as he played on the floor, trapping him in her arms.

'He's come for us,' she said, her voice quavering. 'I don't want to go with him, not back to my mother's.'

'Don't worry, I'll get rid of him. You stay here,' Amajit said, stroking her arm reassuringly. He walked out of the living room and into the hall, closing the door behind him. Remembering his two previous encounters with Barry Penistone, he wondered whether it wouldn't be a better move to call Handford. Get the police to move him on. But realistically he knew there was no time for that. If Penistone wanted in, then he would come in. It wouldn't be the first occasion he'd broken into the house, after all; the new unpainted frame in front of him bore witness to that. Nor would Karen agree to having the police involved; Barry was still family. No, best just tell him to come back tomorrow when she'd be feeling a little better. Surely, as her brother, he would understand that.

Amajit wished his nerves were as unruffled as his thoughts. Remain calm, he told himself. Calm and convincing. Calm and convincing.

Turning the Yale knob, he opened the door the distance of the chain that held it and peered into the face of Barry Penistone.

'Where is she, Mahmood?'

'Leave her tonight, Barry,' he said in as friendly a tone as he could muster. 'She needs rest and peace. She's all right here with me.'

Barry's anger exploded. 'She's not staying with a bloody Paki, not ever. They're coming with me. So you let me in, you black bastard.'

Amajit's reflexes weren't fast enough. Barry's foot smashed through the opening before he could close the door, the chain's fixings flew from the frame in a shower of splinters, and the door powered into Amajit like a train hitting the buffers. He stumbled backwards against the small telephone table which crashed to the ground, the telephone shattering as it fell.

Winded, Amajit felt the movement of air as Barry launched himself towards him. He tried to roll himself into a ball to cushion the impact, but was grabbed and thrust into the living room then dropped like a redundant piece of sacking. Scrabbling backwards, he found himself checked by the settee.

Karen had scrunched herself into the corner by the window, still clinging tight to Danny.

446

'Go away, Barry. Leave us alone,' she said, her voice hoarse from the effects of the fire.

Striding over to her, Barry made a grab for her arm. 'You're coming with me. Get your things.' His voice had mellowed a little, but his tone brooked no argument.

She snatched her arm away. 'No, I'm not. I'm staying here. We're not coming home.'

'We're not going home, you silly bitch.' His tone softened even more. 'If that's all you're worried about, we're not going home. I've got the car outside and we'll go anywhere you want to go. You, me and Danny. Just get your things.'

Karen pulled away. 'I'm not going anywhere with you, Barry Penistone. Nowhere. Amajit says I can stay here until they've repaired my house or given me somewhere else to live, and that's what I'm going to do.' She buried her head in Danny's hair. 'You go where you want, the further the better, but we're not coming.'

Barry was quivering now. Once again, the air congealed with his anger. He would fracture at any minute. He gripped her arm tightly.

'Leave her.' Amajit's voice came out as a half-strangled cry.

Barry spun round, still maintaining his hold. 'Mind your own fucking business, Paki. This is between me and her.' And he turned back to Karen.

The strength Amajit had used on Berridge a few days previously fountained back into his body, and he sprang towards Barry, only to meet his fist head on as it whipped round faster than he could see it. Amajit crashed down onto the

447

floor, dazed and disorientated. Then he felt more hammer blows pummelling at his head and chest.

From a distance, he could hear screaming and a child's cries. His head reeling, he dragged himself to his feet. Barry had gone back to Karen and was hauling her across the room. As she resisted, the two of them played tug-of-war, her feet slipping and sliding on the thick pile of the carpet.

Suddenly, Barry let her go, and as she fell backwards he grabbed Danny. Karen screamed, 'Let him go, let him go.'

Her brother sneered at her. 'You stay here with that Paki if you want, but Danny comes with me.'

Jumping up, she snatched at his arm, but he pushed her away. She tried again, pulling him back, screaming, 'No, Barry. No!'

Amajit catapulted himself towards the child and made a grab for him, but with the fluidity of a ballet dancer Barry transferred Danny to his other arm. Amajit snatched at him again, jerking like a child plucking at a present just out of his reach. Barry turned and twisted, laughing at his frantic buffoonery.

He didn't know how, but suddenly Amajit made contact with the child who slid from Barry's arms and into his own. He thrust Danny towards his mother.

'Run, Karen, run,' he yelled. But before either of them could move, Barry was barring their way.

'No one's going anywhere,' he snarled and lunged forward.

Amajit never saw the knife, but he felt it sear through his upper abdomen like a scalpel. The next thing he knew, Barry was standing over him, the knife in his hand, blood smearing the blade. Amajit clutched at his left side, blood seeped through his fingers; then he felt the pain, the burning inside him. And he heard Karen's screaming. The ear-splitting sound resonated through his body, tearing at every organ, until mercifully he sank into darkness.

★   ★   ★

'What on earth was that?' Mrs Clough lifted her head from the matinee jacket she was knitting for her first grandchild, due in a few weeks.

Mr Clough was absorbed in the football. 'What was what?' he said vaguely.

She put down her knitting. 'That. That noise.' She moved over to the wall dividing their house from Amajit Mahmood's and put her ear to it. 'Turn that telly down,' she instructed. 'Come on, turn it down.'

As the cheers of the football crowd diminished, the piercing screams took their place. Husband and wife looked at each other.

'It's coming from next door,' Mrs Clough said. 'It sounds like there's a real fight going on. Go round and see.'

'I'm not going round,' Mr Clough remonstrated. 'Ring the police, woman. That's their job.'

★   ★   ★

Sergeant Ali heard it first over the radio. A patrol officer demanding back-up. He let the request drift around the vehicle, until the officer gave out the address, when in a reflex movement he swung the car round, screeching on all tyres. Graham clung on to the door's armrest as Ali, ignoring the speed limit, manoeuvred through the traffic and drove, his foot hard on the accelerator, from the western edge of the city where Billy Price had said he might find Barry Penistone to Grange Road in the east, arriving some twenty minutes later.

He found it blocked off by police vehicles, but once their identities had been verified, the two detectives were flagged into a parking space and asked to walk to the location. Tapes cordoned off the immediate area. A couple of ambulances were waiting a distance away and three or four other police vehicles, blue lamps still rotating, were slewed across either end of the road, preventing access to all but official traffic. An ARV was also parked up, but as far as Ali could see the armed men had not yet been deployed.

The duty inspector filled him in. The patrol car had arrived at the request of the neighbour to find the owner of the house, Amajit Mahmood, being held against his will by one Barry Penistone. The officers had tried to talk to him through the letter box but had been warned off in no uncertain terms. There was also a girl and a young child in there; the girl, they believed, was Penistone's sister. Whilst they were attempting to talk to Penistone, the girl had screamed out that Mahmood had been stabbed. As far as

450

the inspector knew, there were no other weapons, but the residents had been evacuated just in case. A negotiator had been requested and they were currently setting up communication in the house to the right of Mahmood's: Mr and Mrs Clough's.

Ali, filling the inspector in on his involvement with the people in the house, asked if he and Graham could stay and said that he would ring DI Handford to get him over here as well. The inspector could see no reason why not.

★   ★   ★

The DCI, however, could.

'There's plenty for you to do here, Handford, tying up loose ends. And anyway, you know the rules, we leave this kind of thing to the negotiator.'

Handford protested. 'I need to be there. Barry Penistone almost certainly killed Rukhsana Mahmood, and it now looks as though he might be on the verge of doing the same to her husband. Perhaps I can talk to him.'

'You can do nothing, John.' Russell was adamant. 'Leave it to the negotiator. Ali's there, he will keep us in touch with what's going on.'

'But, sir — '

'But nothing, Inspector. In this mood, you'll get in the way. You stay here and that's a direct order.'

Handford left Russell and returned to his office. He closed the door and leaned against it. He had never felt so useless. He needed to be at

451

Mahmood's house, yet thanks to the DCI he was
having to stay here and do — do what? Tie up
loose ends. Write reports. He ought to be up
with Amajit, doing his job. It ought to be him,
not Ali up there. Wonderful Ali, the pride of the
force. He closed his eyes. He was thinking like
Warrender.

He sat down and covered his face with his
hands. He couldn't stay here, holed up in this
building. Perhaps he ought to go over Russell's
head and see the chief super. That would be fine
if he agreed to let him go, not so fine if he
upheld the DCI, which he would be much more
likely to do because the rules did say leave it to
the negotiator, that's what they were there for.
No, going upstairs wasn't an option. If he went
ahead and did what every bone in his body was
suggesting he should do, it would be one thing
disobeying Russell, quite another disobeying a
chief superintendent.

He worked out his strategy.

He picked up the phone and tapped in Ali's
mobile number. Now was the time to see how
wonderful the sergeant was; just whose side he
was on. He hoped Ali hadn't turned his mobile
off; if he had, he'd remember the carpeting of
last week as a minor skirmish.

Ali answered almost immediately.

'Khalid. I've filled the DCI in on what's
happening and he's told me to stay here and
leave it to the negotiator.'

'Do you want me to keep you in touch?' Ali
asked.

'No, Ali, I want you to come and fetch me. I

452

daren't use my car. At least if it's parked up here, they'll think I'm somewhere in the building. I'll come out via the underground car park and meet you across the road at the theatre. I can mingle with the crowds there. I'll even buy a programme if I have to.'

'Are you sure, sir? You could get in a lot of trouble.'

Handford appreciated the concern in Ali's voice. 'And so will you if you go along with what I've asked. It was a direct order he gave me. You can say no if you want.'

'I'll be with you in ten minutes, sir,' Ali said before he cut the connection.

23

As they drove, Ali told Handford that the negotiator hadn't arrived when he'd left and no one, as yet, had attempted to talk to Penistone.

Officers had been posted at the back and the front of the house. The back was particularly vulnerable since the land led up to the woods adjoining the nursing home, the woods where Rukhsana Mahmood had been murdered, and if Penistone escaped by that route, they'd have the devil's own job finding him again. It was a good mile away and once up there he could go in any direction.

Handford took in everything that Ali was telling him. He was worried that they were waiting for the negotiator and that no one was attempting to make contact with the house. Somewhere in one of the box files back in his office there was an 'interesting at the time' handout, in big black type, mostly capitals, he seemed to remember, headed something like GUIDELINES FOR UNTRAINED NEGO-TIATORS.

Desperately trying to recall the information, Handford wished he'd taken more notice of it. One thing he was sure of, though, was that, with an injured hostage, someone should be trying to talk to Penistone.

It had taken Ali ten minutes to drive to the station; he did the return journey in seven. He pulled up in the area designated for police cars and Handford had the door open almost before the car stopped. Waving his warrant card at the policeman at the end of the street, Handford ducked under the blue and white tape and ran towards the incident commander who was handing out orders to a group of uniformed officers.

'What's happening?' he asked urgently.

'Nothing at the moment. It's fairly quiet. We're waiting for the negotiator, but he's to come from Wakefield.'

'Who is it?'

'Don't know, some DCI, I think.'

'Have you got communication with Penistone?'

'Everything's set up and ready. There's a telephone link and we've checked the house in case we have to go in. They're old houses and the communicating cellar walls have some kind of escape route from one house to the other — in case of fire, I think. If we have to we'll be able to get into Mahmood's house that way.'

'But no one's actually talking to Penistone?'

'No, not yet.'

'Well, someone should be. Come on, you're incident commander. I know him, let me have a try.'

The inspector was dubious. 'All right, if you think so, but when the negotiator arrives, you're out. And no argument.'

In spite of the police activity, there was an eerie silence about the street. Police lights illuminated Amajit's house and the one next

455

door, but waned into a shadowy gloom a few metres back, adding to the unnatural atmosphere. The interior of Amajit's house was in darkness, except for the downstairs window, where a light was on but the curtains were drawn. At the moment, there was no means of knowing what was going on in there. That so much horror could overtake one man in so short a time appalled Handford. Only a week ago Amajit had been one of the majority; not without his problems, but with as much pleasure in life as most people have the right to expect.

The incident commander accompanied Handford to the Cloughs', introducing him to the two DCs in the room.

Handford shook hands.

'Have you had any communication with Penistone?' he asked.

'He answered the phone, but I can't say we've had serious dialogue. The only words he seems to know are 'piss' and 'off', so we don't really know what's going on in there.'

'I'd like to try.'

The man shrugged. 'Why not? If nothing else, the hostages will know we're around. Lift the receiver and press the recall button.'

The phone rang five times before it was picked up.

'Barry, this is John Handford. We met a few days ago, do you remember?' Handford rubbed at his arm; he still had the bruises.

'I'll tell you what I told the other copper, just piss off.'

Handford had expected the receiver to be

456

slammed down immediately, but the line remained open.

'I can't do that, Barry. You've got a child in there with you. I've got to know he's all right.'

'You think I'd hurt Danny?'

'No, but he's only a child, he may be frightened at what's happening.'

'If he's frightened, it's you lot who's frightening him, not me.'

Handford changed the subject. 'What about Amajit Mahmood? We understand he's been injured. We need to know how badly.'

There was silence and the line went dead.

'Damn.' He'd jumped in too quickly; they did need to know how badly Amajit was hurt, but it was unlikely Penistone would tell them.

'Leave it a few moments, sir,' one of the DCs said. 'Then try again. At least you got him talking, which was more than any of us managed to do. Go and get some fresh air.'

Handford wandered out into the night. Blinking through the lights, he spied Ali coming towards him.

'Any luck, sir? The paramedics were wondering about Amajit Mahmood's injuries.'

Handford sighed. 'I tried, but I made a complete balls-up of it. When I mentioned Amajit, he put the phone down on me.' He peered into the gloom. 'Where's that bloody negotiator?'

'He's stuck in traffic, John, so I'm afraid for the moment it's up to you.'

Handford wished he didn't feel so inadequate. They couldn't leave the hostages in that house

457

without any outside contact, but it worried him that his attempt at contact might make things worse.

Back in the house, he gave the DCs a bleached smile. 'Time to try again?' he asked, hoping they would say no, wait for the negotiator. But they didn't.

Handford pressed the recall button. This time it was as if Penistone had been waiting for him, for he picked up the phone almost immediately.

'Mahmood's not coming out, but you can send us some bandages in.' Barry's request was curt.

'Bandages, yes, we can do that for you.' He glanced questioningly at the officer beside him, who nodded.

'How long will you be?'

'Only a few moments, there's a paramedic ambulance at the end of the road. They'll have some. We could send a paramedic in as well.' One of the officers shook his head vigorously. Another blunder.

'Yeah, I know,' Barry sneered. 'It would be a copper dressed to look like a paramedic. You must think I'm an idiot.'

Not you, Barry. Me.

'Right, we'll get the bandages. I'll let you know when they're here.' He replaced the receiver. 'Sorry, I didn't think.'

'No, sir, you're doing well. It's just that if we send in a paramedic we give him another hostage. We can't risk that.' He put his hand up to his earpiece, listening to what was being said to him. 'Right, we've got the bandages. There's an officer at the door now. How does he want them delivered?'

Handford re-established contact with Barry. He relayed the instructions. 'He won't open the door, so you'll have to post them through the letter box, one by one.' He turned back to the phone. 'Barry, we have the bandages, they're about to be put through the letter box. Tell me when you've got them.'

A moment's pause.

'Right, I've got them.'

'Is there anything else you want?'

'No, except you to get lost.'

A girl's voice screamed out. 'You've got to let Amajit go! Please, Barry. He's bleeding again. He'll die.'

The line went dead.

Handford pressed the recall button.

'What?'

'Barry, let me talk to Karen. We need to know how badly injured Amajit is.'

'What, so that you can come in and get him? Get lost.'

'Barry.' Handford couldn't keep the urgency out of his voice. 'Barry, don't put the phone down. Let me talk to Karen. She needs to know what to do.'

The silence stretched.

'No funny stuff then. Just tell her what to do.'

Karen sounded strained. 'Please help him. He's going to die. He's very pale and he's shivering. He wants to go to sleep, but I'm not letting him. He'll die if he goes to sleep.' Suddenly she screamed. 'Barry, please let him go.'

459

Handford spoke softly. 'Karen, try to keep calm and do just what I tell you. Barry only wants me to give you instructions for helping Amajit; but I need to know a bit more. So I'm going to ask you some questions and if the answer is yes, I want you to say yes, so that Barry thinks you're understanding my instructions. If the answer is no, then say nothing. You understand?'

'Yes.'

'Right. Has he been stabbed in the stomach?'

Silence.

'Higher?'

'Yes.'

'A lot higher?'

Silence.

'Beneath the ribs?'

'Yes.'

'Left-hand side?'

'Yes.'

'Good girl. You're doing really well. Now put some pressure on those bandages, try to stem the bleeding, and I'll get some help to you as soon as I can. All right?'

'Yes.' He could hear her voice breaking. 'Now put the phone down,' he said to her. 'I'll be in touch in a bit.'

Handford turned to the paramedic who'd brought the bandages. 'The knife went into his upper abdomen somewhere on the left-hand side around the bottom ribs. She says he's pale and shivering and he's tired and wants to go to sleep.'

'Sounds like the spleen.'

'And that's serious?'

'Could be. It is a very bloody organ, the spleen. He'll be bleeding internally as well as externally. It sounds to me as though he's already going into shock. His heart will be racing and his blood pressure will be low and he'll be in desperate need of fluids. You need to get him out of there.'

'How long?'

'Difficult to say. The worst scenario could be one, two hours before he's lost too much blood for us to be able to do anything for him. On the other hand, if I'm wrong, he could have hours, days.'

'Thanks.' Handford pressed the recall button.

Barry answered almost immediately. 'What yer doing?'

Handford ignored the question. 'Barry, if you don't let Amajit go, he's going to die. Now, I'm not going to mess around with you. We already know that you killed Rukhsana.'

'I was at work.'

'No, you weren't. We have forensic evidence to prove you were there. We also know about Billy Price's car. It's standing outside the house now.'

Barry said nothing, but the line stayed open.

'There's nothing I can do about Rukhsana's murder,' Handford went on, 'but you'll make things a lot worse if you let Amajit die.'

Barry laughed. 'Life for one, life for two; what's the difference?'

'The difference is that you might well not serve the whole sentence for one murder; for two you surely will. Then there's taking hostages, as well as a possible charge of incest against your sister.'

461

'You can't threaten me, copper. So don't even try. If I come out of here, I want me, Karen and Danny to get in that car and leave. Otherwise it's no deal.' And the phone went dead.

⋆ ⋆ ⋆

Karen looked up at Barry, horror in her eyes. 'You killed Rukhsana?

'Don't be daft, you stupid bitch.'

She stood up and hit out at him. 'You did, you bastard. I heard the copper say so.'

Barry swatted her aside. 'Then you heard wrong.'

She hadn't heard wrong, she was sure she hadn't. 'Well, what did you mean by 'life for one, life for two' then?'

He took a step towards her. 'You 'eard nothing! Nothing.'

Without taking her eyes off Barry, she returned to Amajit. Her brother had killed Rukhsana. Why? What had she ever done to their family but be kind?

'Why, Barry?'

'Why not? Good riddance, I say; she was an interfering bitch.'

'No, she wasn't. She helped with Danny, which is more than you've ever done.'

Barry slumped on one of the dining room chairs. 'But she knew,' he yelled. 'She knew I was Danny's father.'

'No, she didn't. How could she?'

'Because of his bloody feet. Genetic, she said they were. When she left you I followed her up to

462

the nursing home. She met another man there and they had a real barney. Then when he'd left she went down to the woods. I only wanted to warn her off, Karen; nothing more. But she got me mad.'

'And you hit her with that coping stone?' She wanted to say more, to shout at him, to hit out at him, but all her strength had gone into the struggle to rationalise what he had told her.

He ran his tongue over his lips and nodded towards Amajit. 'How is he?'

'He needs to go to hospital.'

'Well, he won't, not until they let me, you and Danny go.'

'That's not going to happen. They want you for murder. You're going nowhere but prison.'

'Then neither is he. And if they don't want him dead, then they'd better let me walk out of here. If he dies then they're the ones what's killed him, not me.' Barry strode over to Amajit and looked down on him. 'Even the police don't care about you, Paki. If they did they'd let me go.'

Amajit's eyes rolled upwards and he moaned.

Barry turned back to Karen. 'Look at him. Not so important now, is he? Can't screw you any more, can he? He can't, can he?' he shouted. He kicked out at Amajit's lifeless form. 'You can't, can you, you fucking Paki?'

Karen grabbed at Barry's arm, desperate to pull him away from Amajit. In one movement Barry wrenched it free, brought it back over his chest, then whipped it across her face.

She fell backwards onto the cushions, and as

she struggled to get back up, she saw the chair descending towards her. Lifting her arms to protect herself, she screamed, then yelled at her brother, 'Do it then, Barry. Make it three.'

For a split second Barry hesitated and Karen scrambled onto the arm of the settee. Tears rolled down her cheeks. 'Go on, you murdering bastard, make it three if you dare.'

Suddenly the phone rang and Karen clawed her way over to it. 'He's killing us,' she screamed down it. 'Do something.'

★　★　★

'We're going in. Now.' Handford dashed to the door. 'Get in there,' he shouted. 'And I'm coming with you.'

It took only minutes.

They went in as had already been agreed, through the cellar. The former escape hole had been filled with a weak mixture of cement and sand instead of bricks, so that all the officers had to do was kick at it and they were through into the next house. From there they climbed the steps into the kitchen. Handford was amazed at the stealth with which these men worked. Hardly a sound. Orders were passed by gestures and in no time they were either side of the door leading into the living room, Handford to the side of them and away from any danger.

He could hear Danny crying, but no other sound. What had Barry done to them? He dreaded the sight that would greet them.

At his commander's signal an officer kicked at

464

the door, his boot slamming into it. It offered no resistance and the men crowded through, guns at the ready, shouting at those inside to get down on the floor.

Karen was next to Amajit who was slumped against the settee, his shirt covered in blood, his features waxen, his eyes rolling into the back of his head. Her sweatshirt, too, was red with his blood, as were her hands which she was pressing against the bandages round his chest, to stem the flow. Tears were streaming down her face. Handford wanted to go straight to them but had to let the men do their job, so he stood back. Nor could he comfort Danny who was now screaming. A dining room chair was lying on the floor close to the settee. Barry made to pick it up, but the armed officers were too quick for him.

They pointed their guns at him. 'Face down on the floor,' one of them barked, 'arms stretched above your head.'

At first, Handford thought from his wild expression, Barry intended to use his strength to force his way through, but the men stood their ground. Snarling obscenities, he knelt down, then fell forward on to the floor.

One officer kicked Barry's legs further apart as the other jerked his arms behind his back and strapped them together by the wrists. Barry screeched that they were hurting him. The policemen ignored him. They hauled him upright and pushed him towards Handford.

'Yours, I think, sir,' the sergeant said.

Handford grabbed him by the coat collar and

pushed him out of the door. Keeping a tight hold on him, he signalled to the paramedics to go in. Ali was waiting with them.

'Charge him then put him in the van,' Handford told his sergeant.

Barry screamed for his sister. 'Karen. Don't leave me. Bring Danny.'

Karen ignored him. She stood outside the house, Danny in her arms, a blanket from the ambulance protecting them from the icy air. Handford walked over to her.

'Are you all right?' he asked gently.

She nodded.

'He did it, didn't he?' she said in a hoarse whisper.

Handford knew exactly what she meant, but he wanted to fend off the moment when he had to confirm her fears.

'Who did what, Karen?'

'Barry. He killed Rukhsana, didn't he?'

Handford placed his arm round her and the boy. 'Yes, I'm sorry, but I'm afraid he did.'

'I heard you on the phone. You could hear quite a lot of what was said. He would have let Amajit die as well. And he came for me and Danny. He could have killed us all.' She was quiet for a moment. 'He was very frightened, you know.'

Handford offered no response. He felt desperately sorry for the girl, and there was nothing he could do to alleviate her suffering. Only time would be able to do that — maybe.

'Come on,' he said gently. 'Let's get you and Danny down to the hospital.' He signalled to a

WPC who took her from him.

Karen turned, 'Can't I wait for Amajit?' she asked.

'They could be working with him for a while, Karen. Best leave it until he's at the hospital; they'll let you see him then.'

Obediently Karen allowed herself to be led to the waiting ambulance. 'I'll go with her, sir,' the WPC said. 'Don't worry about her.'

It was a good twenty minutes later before Amajit was brought out on a stretcher.

Handford walked with it. 'Will he make it?' he asked one of the paramedics.

The man shrugged. 'He's not dead yet, so we'll get him down to the hospital and you pray.'

Handford held the ambulance door. 'Go with him,' he said to one of the constables.

The ambulance drove away, lights flashing, sirens warning.

The incident commander was busy issuing orders. He would bring a SOCO team in and Amajit Mahmood's house would become just another scene of crime. In an hour or two they would let the people back into their own houses, and everything would return to normal.

'You did a good job, sir,' Ali said.

'Did I?' Handford wasn't convinced.

'Yes, you did. You got them out.'

'But probably not soon enough for Amajit Mahmood. I don't call that a good job.'

Ali placed his hand on Handford's arm. 'You didn't stick the knife in or refuse to let an injured man out for treatment, that was Penistone. If anyone's killed Mahmood, it's him.'

Handford looked at the sergeant, who spoke with such compassion, and wondered how he could ever have doubted him.

'Let's get back to the station,' he said. 'There's nothing more we can do here and we need to process Penistone. If we can get his solicitor out we can start questioning him, if you feel up to it. And I suppose I'd better go and grovel at the DCI's feet as well.'

They walked towards the car.

'You don't need to.'

'Oh, but I do. I shouldn't be here, unless you've forgotten.'

Ali bent down to put his key in the car lock. 'No, I haven't forgotten. But while you were with Karen Penistone, Russell rang me. Said he was going home and will see you in the morning for a debrief. He said well done.'

'He said what?'

'He said, well done. Apparently the duty inspector filled him in. Russell probably knows he should have let you come in the first place, it was your case; but since 'sorry' isn't at the top of his vocabulary list, 'well done' is the nearest thing you'll get to an apology. Enjoy it and forget him. And I know it's not normal for me, but how about stopping off at the nearest pub? You could probably do with a stiff drink and I can always have an orange juice.'

Handford looked sceptical; they ought to get back.

Ali grinned at him. 'I'm buying,' he said.

'Oh well, in that case, why are we waiting?'

24

John Handford stood at the foot of the bed, silently watching mother and baby. So preoccupied was she with the child that she hadn't noticed his arrival. He wondered not for the first time since he had left the florist, whether it had been a good idea to come at all. It was a long time since he had been in the maternity ward, and he felt a bit out of his depth. But he'd deemed it necessary, for although the flowers could have been delivered, the other parcel he needed to dispatch could not.

Barry Penistone's trial was into its fifth day and on the fourth, only a few days after the birth of her baby, Karen had been called to give evidence for the prosecution. He had noticed her in the waiting area, first sitting, then wandering, obviously nervous, and would have liked to talk to her, reassure her, but any encounter would have been seen as interfering with a witness. Eventually a volunteer from the support service took pity on her and led her to a private room, and afterwards she must have been whisked back to the hospital because he didn't see her again.

Now, with the ordeal behind her, she was absorbed in her baby, seemingly unaware of him or her surroundings. He glanced at the other beds. Unlike hers, they radiated colour, the congratulatory flowers and cards for mother and baby packed onto the small lockers or garlanded along the bed head. Karen's was bare. No colour, no flowers, no cards to conceal the solitary water jug and glass.

Feeling self-conscious, he was just about to tiptoe away and leave the flowers with the sister, when Karen raised her head and saw him. Her eyes lit up, first with astonishment, then with pleasure until finally they clouded over. It didn't come as any surprise to him that mistrust had elbowed its way through.

'I hope you don't mind my popping in,' he said quickly in the hope of thrusting her concern aside. 'I've brought these for you. From the detectives on the team.' He laid the flowers on the bed beside her. 'We didn't realise you'd had the baby or they'd have been delivered earlier,' he added unnecessarily. He was burbling and he knew it. 'Oh, and there are a couple of little presents . . . ' Slipping two brightly coloured parcels from under his. arm, he placed them next to the flowers. 'For the baby and for Danny.'

She slid from the hospital bed and placed the child in the crib, pulling the blanket over her.

'No Sergeant Ali?' she said.

'He's back in Broughton.' Handford bent towards her. 'Between you and me,' he said confidentially, 'I don't think he's quite cut out for visiting young girls who've just had babies, do you?'

She laughed. 'Probably not.'

'Actually, he's transferring back to Central at the end of the month. One of my sergeants has made inspector and Ali is taking his place. I'm

470

sure he'll be happy to meet you again. Pop in if you're passing.'

'We'll see,' she said and turned from the cot to pick up the flowers. She held them close, savouring both their colour and their fragrance. 'They're lovely,' she said. 'I've never had flowers like this before, properly wrapped at the shop, with a card.' Her eyes twinkled. 'No one'll ever believe I got them from a bunch of coppers. Thank you, Mr Handford.'

He smiled. 'It's our pleasure,' he said and tiptoed to the cot to bend over the sleeping baby. He gazed at her for a moment, then lifting his head whispered, 'She's lovely.'

Karen beamed. 'Yes, she is, isn't she?'

The baby's skin was fair, but there was no mistaking whose daughter she was with her black hair and fine features. The image of her father. Handford wondered if Rukhsana's baby would have resembled him too, for the child was his. He pictured Amajit as he had known him, grief-stricken, relying on a young girl for his strength.

'I'm glad you've come,' she said. 'I wanted to see you, but they told me I couldn't until I'd given evidence. I wanted to thank you for what you did for Amajit. Without you he would have died.'

Handford continued to look at the baby. 'I think he's got you to thank for that, not me. You were the one in there; the one who did the right things and kept him alive. All I did was talk to Barry and calm him down, in the hope that he would see sense and give himself up.' He glanced

471

up at her. 'To be honest,' he said, 'I hadn't the vaguest idea what I was doing. Negotiating is harder than you think.'

'I don't believe you, Mr Handford. Amajit was close to death, a few more minutes without help and he would have died. It was you who gave him those few minutes.'

Handford stroked the baby's cheek with his forefinger. She stirred, spreading her arms above her head, stretching out her tiny fingers then curling them again as she settled. He looked up at the young mother. Sadness clouded her features.

He smiled at her. 'How are you feeling after yesterday?'

'Tired,' she said shortly. 'I'm glad the doctor suggested I stay here another day.'

'Yes, it can't have been easy for you giving evidence so soon after the baby.'

She placed the flowers back on the bed. 'It was awful, if you really want to know. My stitches hurt and my back ached and that man defending Barry was a smarmy bastard, smiling at me while he talked as though everything that had happened was my fault.'

'I can imagine, but you mustn't take it personally; he was only doing his job.'

'By making out I'm a slag who sleeps with anyone I happen to meet? By suggesting that I'm a liar, that I egged Barry on the night he raped me and that by giving evidence against him I'm trying to get my own back.'

'I know,' Handford said gently, wishing he could touch her, put his arms round her as he

472

would have his own daughter. Instead he settled himself in the visitor's chair at the side of the bed. 'Honestly, he was only doing what he's paid to do. He gave me a hard time too.'

'Yes, well,' she smiled, her anger retreating behind her words, 'you hadn't just had a baby.'

He smiled back at her. 'True,' he said.

She picked up the larger of the two parcels and began to open it. His eyes followed her fingers as they pulled off the sticky tape and she unfolded the small coat and dress. 'Oh, it's lovely,' she cried. 'It'll be just right for when the weather gets colder. Say thank you to everyone, won't you?' Her eyes shone as she looked at him. 'I'll let Danny open his himself, if you don't mind.'

'No, it's a good idea.'

Her eyes met the detective's. 'How is he?'

Handford knew it was Amajit she was asking after.

'Not bad. I expect the Saudi sun is doing him good. He's been there for seven months now.'

'I didn't know.' She paused for a moment. 'I haven't seen him since he went in the ambulance. His cousin said I mustn't go anywhere near him. If it hadn't have been for you and Sergeant Ali letting me know that he would recover, I would never have known whether he had lived or died.'

'Apparently his family agreed to welcome him back, provided he reaffirmed his faith in Islam. He made a pilgrimage to Mecca for a couple of months after he'd recovered, then found a job in Saudi and stayed there.'

'Faysal could have let me see him before he went.'

'I think he thought that you would change Amajit's mind for him, particularly once he knew about the baby. Faysal likes everyone where he can keep an eye on them, and prison and Saudi Arabia are as good places as any.'

Faysal Hussain had a lot to answer for. Except for Peter Redmayne's damning feature in the local press on the dangers of using anabolic steroids, and Hussain's part in supplying them, he'd got off lightly. He admitted supplying the class C drug but because it was a first offence, he avoided a custodial sentence and was fined five hundred pounds and costs.

He denied playing any part in the arson attempt on Karen's house. He agreed he had given the car to Kamal and Jahangier, but only as a present, he said. The jury had believed him. Kamal and Jahangier on the other hand had been given custodial sentences and had been dragged from the court swearing vengeance on Faysal.

Suddenly Karen pulled her hand away from the wrapping paper and looked at him.

'What is it?' he asked.

She hesitated as though afraid of the question or possibly of the answer. 'Barry will be found guilty, won't he?'

'I would say so,' said Handford, mentally crossing his fingers. 'Beyond reasonable doubt' hung over any case like the sword of Damocles. 'There's plenty of forensics to link him with Rukhsana when she died, and no one can deny that he had a hand in the attack on Amajit, or that he held both you and him hostage. Why? Are you worried about it?'

'No, not really. I just wondered which prison he would be in if he's found guilty.'

'Difficult to say. Why?'

Karen scrutinised her fingers. 'Do you think it will be one near enough for visiting.'

Handford was unable to hide his astonishment. 'You don't intend to visit him surely, after all that has happened? I would have thought that would be the last thing you'd want to do.'

She shrugged. 'He's my brother, Mr Handford, and he's Danny's father. I don't think we can desert him. And anyway, my mother will want to see him.' She pulled a face. 'He's her favourite, always has been. I'm not sure how she'll cope without him.'

'You're not going to live with her then? Now you've got the two children.'

Karen pulled a face. 'Would you live with your mother?'

He laughed. 'Perish the thought.'

'No, and neither will I. I'll be around for her, but that's all. She'll not like it, but with Barry gone, I'm all she's got left and she's just going to have to come to terms with that.'

'I'm sure you and her two grandchildren will make sure she does.'

Karen's eyes widened. 'With Amajit's daughter and Barry's son? I don't think so.'

'Oh, I don't know,' Handford said. 'Children have an uncanny knack of bringing people together.' He stood up and walked back to the cot. The baby was sleeping peacefully. 'Have you given her a name yet?'

'No. I wanted to call her Rukhsana, but that's not fair on Danny, because sometime I'm going to have to explain to both of them what happened, before they hear it from a stranger. And if his sister's called after the person his father murdered, he'll never be allowed to forget, will he?'

Handford had no answer for her, except the obvious. Her shabby candlewick dressing gown hung from her shoulders, framing the T-shirt which moulded itself over her belly, still enlarged from carrying a child. One hand caressed the flowers, the other played with a corner of the paper which had wrapped the present. What was she? Eighteen? Nineteen? At that age he'd been enjoying the fruits of youth. He might have been the luckier of the two of them, but he wondered if he was the stronger. In spite of his years, he thought not. At that moment, he hoped he'd done a better job with his own daughters than he'd managed to do with himself. Thinking back on the mistrust he had fostered throughout the investigation and his initial suspicion of Ali, he couldn't help feeling that Karen was probably the better role model.

'Why don't you let Amajit help you choose a name? He's back for the trial.'

She looked at him, tears beginning to build in her eyes. 'Because Faysal will never let him come here to see me. I'm the white girl his cousin screwed. But according to him, I'm not the mother of Amajit's child and never will be.'

'Do you want to see Amajit?'

'I want him to see his daughter, and I want him to be allowed to know her.'

'But do you want to see him?'

'Yes.' Her voice dropped to a whisper. 'Yes, I want to see him.'

'So, would you like me to arrange it?'

'Don't do this to me, Mr Handford. Faysal will never allow it, I think he'd kill me first.'

'Faysal Hussain won't bother you, I'll make sure of that.'

'Well, if you can arrange it, but I'm leaving here tomorrow, so it will have to be soon.'

'How about now?'

Her eyes lit up. 'You mean he's here?'

Handford smiled. 'In the waiting room. Do you want me to fetch him?'

She nodded her agreement as tears flooded her eyes.

Handford walked over to the door of the ward. A nurse was passing. He touched her arm.

'Miss Penistone is ready for her visitor now, nurse,' he said. 'Could you ask him to pop along?'

We do hope that you have enjoyed reading this large print book.

Did you know that all of our titles are available for purchase?

We publish a wide range of high quality large print books including:
Romances, Mysteries, Classics
General Fiction
Non Fiction and Westerns

Special interest titles available in large print are:
The Little Oxford Dictionary
Music Book
Song Book
Hymn Book
Service Book

Also available from us courtesy of Oxford University Press:
Young Readers' Dictionary
(large print edition)
Young Readers' Thesaurus
(large print edition)

For further information or a free brochure, please contact us at:
Ulverscroft Large Print Books Ltd.,
The Green, Bradgate Road, Anstey,
Leicester, LE7 7FU, England.
Tel: (00 44) 0116 236 4325
Fax: (00 44) 0116 234 0205